WHEN THE STARS FALL TO EARTH

NOVEL $\mathcal{A}$ $\mathcal{f}$ AFRICA

Rebecca Tinsley

LANDMARC
P R E S S

For general information on our other products and services or technical support, please contact LandMarc Press at (936) 544-5137, fax (936) 544-2270, or on the web at www.LandMarcPress.com.

ISBN 978-0-9845129-5-9

Printed in the United States of America.

10 9 8 7 6 5 4 3 2 1

For my husband, Henry Tinsley,
a life-long fighter against appeasement.

ACKNOWLEDGMENTS

This novel would not have been possible without Carol Kline, Nancy, Jim and Matthew Land, Gill Lusk, and Rosemary Monreau. Thank you for your help and guidance.

Thanks to David Alton, Asha Abdillahi, Christa Bennett, Benedetta Cassinelli. Caroline Cox, Christina Lohrisch, Sophie McCann, Louise Roland-Gosselin, and Olivia Warham.

My work in Africa would not be possible without the kind support of David and Vanda Bliss, Diane Giles, Mary Harvey, Anne Miller, Rob van Mesdag, Lorraine Sheinberg, Judy Writer and the team at INSPIRE!africa, Jubilee Action in the UK, and Jubilee Campaign in the United States.

Sincere thanks to my friends in California: All Saints By The Sea in Santa Barbara, Midi Berry, Betsy and David Kain, Stacey Lydon, Melissa Musgrove, and Karen Pick.

Finally, thanks to the heroic Linda Melvern, Eric Reeves, and the late Alison des Forges for their tireless work in exposing the reality of what genocide means, and the complicity of those who should know better.

CAST OF CHARACTERS

Zara: Granddaughter of Sheikh Muhammed

Martin Bennett: An American teacher in Darfur, father of Rachael Bennett

Muhammad: Student in El Geneina who grows up to be Sheikh Muhammad

Uthman: Student in El Geneina who grows up to be Sheikh Uthman

Ahmed: Soccer player in Sheikh Adam's village

Khalil: Arab shopkeeper and Ahmed's friend

Hawa: Daughter of Sheikh Adam

Rashid: Sheikh Uthman's grandson, engaged to Hawa

Janjaweed: Arab militia paid and armed by the Sudanese government

Snowbeard: Friend of Sheikh Muhammad

Makka: Snowbeard's daughter

Abdelatif: Brother of Zara

Cloudy: Brother of Zara and Abdelatif

Alia: Zara's cousin, engaged to Abdelatif

Karen Freeman: Human rights researcher from New York

Mama Mounah: Village woman who shelters Hawa

Rachael Bennett: Daughter of Martin Bennett; Sudan activist from New Jersey

Safia: Zara's "cousin"

Sumah: Zara's mother

Mary: Nurse from southern Sudan

Abdallah: Warlord leading a Darfur rebel faction

Field Marshall Bashir: President of Sudan

Mrs. Edwards: Zara's neighbor in Doncaster, England

Ismael: Darfuri refugee in Leeds, England

Halima: Ismael's wife

Yusuf: Zara's little brother

T-Bone: Darfuri rebel officer

Jibril: Darfuri rebel officer

Sandrine Truscott: Human rights campaigner, London, England

Bill: Police officer from New York

Ursula: Human rights campaigner, London, England

PREFACE

If you want a weighty academic book about what's happening in Darfur, then please look elsewhere. This is not an account of politicians making historic decisions, or the exploits of daring war reporters in battle zones. The story just happens to be set in Sudan, in the heart of Africa and in a war zone.

Instead, this is a novel about people who find themselves in the middle of a conflict, and how they survive. Their choices affect their families, the people they love, and the course of their lives. Their stories start before the events in Sudan touch them, following them through challenges and triumphs, as they rebuild their lives. What they have in common with the rest of us is that their journeys are about finding out what kind of people they are; Should they try to draw strength from their anger or should they let it go? Is it better to stick with what you know, or find the courage to change?

I do have an ulterior motive, however. I hope that by the time you finish the story you care about Sudan. When I first visited in 2004, the survivors I met urged me to take their stories to the outside world, to be their voice. I was astonished by their request because I make such an imperfect voice: I'm from North America, and my life has been easy. "But you're here and you've listened to our stories," my new friends pointed out.

I have done my share of interviewing African war-lords, monitoring elections in jungles, attending human rights trials, and working with survivors of genocide and civil war, from Bosnia and Turkey to Rwanda, Liberia, Mozambique and Uganda.

But I'm also aware that most of us run a mile from depressing documentaries about Africa. So this novel is a work of imagination about people who are fundamentally like us, not a catalogue of horrors about dusty refugee camps. This story is about how we survive challenges while keeping a sense of ourselves, with our humanity intact. It is also about how we rebuild our lives with dignity so we can call ourselves survivors rather than victims.

Sudan effects us all because this remote region of Africa is the front line in a struggle for one of the most fundamental human values: tolerance, or "live and let live." The military dictatorship that runs Sudan from the capital, Khartoum, is ruthlessly imposing its joyless, medieval version of Islam on Darfur. The regime's philosophy, "Islamism," is what guides Osama Bin Laden and the Taliban. Islamism demands that everyone obeys its extreme and intolerant version of Islam, imposed by force if necessary.

The people of Darfur practice a peaceful version of Islam. They want free speech and elections, and they yearn for modern schools and hospitals. And because Darfuris resist Islamism, they are being ethnically cleansed by the Khartoum regime, forced off their land and killed. There is a global civil war within the Muslim faith. We should not turn our backs on Sudan, because a victory for Islamism in Africa diminishes human civilization everywhere.

If, at the end of the novel, you are interested in helping the people of Sudan, you will find a section at the back of the book outlining a number of clear and concrete steps you can take to make a real difference. Sudan is not an insoluble problem: There are simple things we can do to stop the violence without sending our own soldiers there. It just needs enough of us to care.

—Rebecca Tinsley, Januray 2011

CHAPTER ONE

Zara flattened her back against the sheer rock face, hoping the over-hang above would make her invisible.

Not that long ago the most challenging part of her days had been helping her mother with the domestic chores.

Now, at the age of fourteen, she was alone in the world, running for her life, trying to avoid the helicopter gunship hovering above her. The steep, narrow canyon walls around her amplified the thwacking pulse of its blades. It prowled along the dry riverbed, low enough to spot signs of life, but just high enough not to stir up swirling clouds of sand. Even so, Zara's long skirt flapped in the helicopter updraft. She pulled the skirt, once bright yellow and green, but now filthy from her journey, tight against her slender frame to keep it from revealing her hiding place.

Lowering her gaze to scan her surroundings, her eyes widened in alarm as she spotted one of her flip-flops lying in the sun about ten yards away. It was bright pink and glowed like a beacon against the sandy ground, drawing attention to itself. She wondered if its lurid color was visible to her pursuers. She had been running so fast to escape them that she hadn't noticed when it had come off. Now it taunted her, daring her to dash forward to fetch it.

Paralyzed by indecision, Zara closed her eyes against the glare of the afternoon sun, her heart pounding in her ears. Her broad, dark brown forehead, so like her mother's, was smeared with dirt, and her

1

black cornrow braids were dusty and coming undone. Like her father and grandfather, she had hazel eyes, unusual among her people, the Fur, for whom the region of Darfur was named.

She was so thirsty that she felt herself wilting. The dry air caught in her throat like prickling needles. For a week she had done nothing except walk across the hard, parched earth, feeling no bigger than an ant on the vast plain. She grabbed a few hours of shallow sleep whenever she could find a suitable hiding spot. And when she wasn't walking, there were terrifying intervals when she ran to find cover from the Sudanese armed forces who were hunting any survivors from her village. During the moments when she could think, she couldn't help wondering why the soldiers wanted to kill everyone in her village. It seemed so unfair to be hunted like an animal but this hunt had no purpose except destruction.

The noise of the helicopter engine surged, and Zara feared her eardrums would explode as it passed overhead, shaking the air around her. The sound flattened out as the helicopter moved on, along the twisting route of the stony riverbed. She muttered a prayer, willing the Sudanese military to disappear and leave her alone.

Still she pressed back into the wall, knowing from experience that the killing machine could wheel around and loom above her once more within seconds. Only when the deafening sound of the rotating blades had disappeared completely did she dare to open her eyes, and then sink to the dusty ground, her knees trembling.

She hugged her long, aching legs, trying to decide which of the conflicting messages in her agitated brain she should listen to.

Rest here for a few minutes and then keep walking because they might come back.

It's okay to stay put; you're safe now because they won't return to this place today.

What was she supposed to do, she wondered, a lump rising in her throat. She blinked away tears of frustration, wishing her grandfather would appear, offering his reliably wise advice. For a moment Zara forgot her fear, furious that at her age she was expected to know how to cope in an alien place, under such monstrous circumstances. Her father had taught her about African history, not about surviving in the wild.

Her mother had taught her how to sew and cook, but not how to escape from Sudanese soldiers or aircraft.

When her breathing returned to normal, she realized once more that her stomach was throbbing. Before she could stop herself, Zara imagined finding a handful of spicy peanuts in the pocket of her skirt, overlooked in the previous seven days. Then she thought about sinking her teeth into roasted corn on the cob, washed down with the cool water from the well at home in her village.

How pathetic—fantasizing about eating a meager handful of peanuts! she thought. Then Zara recalled the other people in her village, and she felt ashamed. At least she was still alive, even if she was alone and terrified.

As she rested in the shade, mulling over her options, she recalled the first time she had seen a Sudanese military helicopter, just the month before. She had spotted it on the horizon, mistaking it for a bird of prey. Then it had fired a flaming rocket that tore into the ground with a thunderous growl.

Zara had run to her grandfather, telling him that she had seen what looked like a star falling to earth.

Sheikh Muhammad had gently set her straight, reluctantly confirming that the frightening rumors she had been hearing were true; civilians in villages like theirs were being targeted and killed by 'Khartoum,' as people in Darfur referred to the regime holding power in the Sudanese capital. The war had arrived at their doorstep.

"Why are they doing this to us?" Zara had asked, on the verge of tears.

"The rulers in Khartoum want everyone in Sudan to live according to their extreme variety of Islam. They make the rules, they tell us what we can say and where we can go, and they decide who gets to work and who starves. And they say anyone who disagrees with them is a bad Muslim and must be killed."

Zara had frowned. "But the Koran says Muslims shouldn't kill Muslims."

Sheikh Muhammad had nodded sadly, "You're right, but they only pick the parts of the Koran that suit them. I'm ashamed how they've twisted our faith like this." He hesitated. "And they think the people in

Darfur are inferior because they say we're black Africans while they are Arabs."

Zara was quiet for a moment as she tried to understand this. "So, the men in Khartoum are going to send more helicopters to kill us?" she had asked, hoping he would tell her she was overreacting, that her question was childish, and that everything would be all right. Her heart sank when he nodded, his face lined with worry.

Now, as Zara huddled near the rock face, fearful that her pursuers might reappear, she thought back to her grandfather's sorrow at what had happened to their remote western region of Sudan. The sheikh was not normally a gloomy man, so his pessimism had unsettled her. It had been like a warning to Zara; their lives were changing, and events were beyond their control, even in their village.

Zara leaned back against the hard surface of the rock. The rational, realistic part of her knew it was very unlikely her family had survived the recent attack on their village. But her optimistic side still believed some of them might have reached the refugee camps across the Sudanese border in Chad. *They could even be waiting for me,* she thought, feeling the strength return to her legs.

Zara, and the people in her world, had plenty of experience using the sun and stars to navigate. She resolved to start walking once the sky was clear of helicopters. She would find somewhere to hide when it grew dark, and when the sun rose the following morning, she would start walking again. *That way,* she told herself sensibly, *she would reach Chad eventually.*

"I'm going to make it," she said out loud, comforted by the sound of a human voice, even though it was her own. "Grandfather would expect me to be strong."

Then she rested, closing her eyes, distracting herself with a happy memory of sitting by her grandfather beneath a shady tree as he taught her about the world beyond their village.

※　※　※

"And here's your favorite," her grandfather said, passing her a dog-eared postcard of the Chrysler Building in a city called New York.

It didn't matter to Zara how often her grandfather showed her his collection of American postcards; she was never bored. In her world there were few books or magazines, and fewer photographs or paintings, so the postcards of famous American landmarks had an enormous impact on her imagination.

Nor did she tire of listening to Sheikh Muhammad translate the messages that accompanied the exotic and colorful images from his friends so far away in the States.

The men of the village respected her grandfather, and sheikhs from elsewhere often came to consult him. That made it doubly important to Zara that this revered man thought her worthy of his time, insisting she go to school and fulfill his dream that she become a doctor.

Each day when she came home from classes, her grandfather would fetch one of the battered old schoolbooks from his hut—"the books my American friend Martin gave me," he called them—reading to her in slow, simple English, making sure she understood. They sat in the shade of his preferred tree in the family's compound, studying together for an hour or more, discussing what they were reading. Using a stick, he would write the new words they encountered in the dirt. She lost track of time, and her heart sank when her mother called, reminding her to go for firewood, thus breaking the spell.

Sheikh Muhammad had explained to Zara that in order to study medicine she must know English. Like everyone else in their region, they spoke the Fur language at home, while elementary school lessons were in Arabic, the language of their rulers in Khartoum.

"I like learning English," she had assured him. "It's easier than Arabic."

"All well and good, but don't forget that you only really appreciate the Koran when you read it in Arabic."

Zara had nodded obediently, not fully understanding what he meant, but never doubting the wisdom of his advice.

Every week or so, as a reward at the end of their lessons, her grandfather would fetch his postcard collection and leaf through them, watching her eyes grow wide in amazement. The pictures were mostly of famous buildings in America, sent by a man the entire family knew as "Martin in New Jersey."

To Zara the most astonishing card of the bunch was the Chrysler Building in New York City. She had never seen a house or a building more than two storys tall, and to gaze at the Chrysler Building was to experience a miracle. She loved the smooth lines and strange decorative metal birds and the millions of windows glinting in the sun like a mosaic. Her pulse quickened as she imagined a city filled with such structures, like perfect angular stalks of corn, crowded together and stretching up to the sky.

Most people in Zara's world lived in mud huts with conical straw roofs. The only other buildings were in the towns, and they were ugly, squat cement cubes, dilapidated, unpainted and crumbling. By contrast, New York looked like a perfect, shiny paradise created by the all-powerful masters of the universe. *I want to go there one day,* she thought.

ⵣ ⵣ ⵣ

Zara opened her eyes once more, glancing up at the cloudless sky, the memory of her grandfather still vivid. She could hear no helicopters or military vehicles. *Still,* she thought, *I'll wait until the sun moves toward the west.*

She scuttled forward, retrieving her pink flip-flop. Then she settled the back of her head against the rock face, and closed her eyes, willing her grandfather's comforting voice to return.

CHAPTER TWO

Muhammad was waiting when the bus pulled into El Geneina, creaking and wheezing as it came to a shuddering halt. All morning the schoolboy had been practicing his words of welcome in English. Now, watching the passengers climbing down the steps, he felt elated when he spotted the one white face among them. Mr. Bennett, the teacher from America, emerged blinking into the sunlight, and Muhammad sensed he was about to begin the most important chapter in his young life.

Martin Bennett was relieved to escape the ancient, reeking bus. The twenty-one-year-old heaved his backpack into place, and surveyed his new home: El Geneina, the western-most city in Sudan, in the remote region of Darfur, right up against the border with neighboring Chad.

The streets were unpaved and rutted by the wheels of donkey-drawn carts. Men in long cream-colored robes and turbans sat on their haunches in the shade, many staring at Martin in open astonishment, gaping at the sight of the tall young man with unfamiliar white skin and shoulder-length hair who had just stepped off the bus.

It's the Wild West, he thought. *I've stepped back in time, but instead of cowboys and saloons there are black Africans and donkeys and mosques.*

He wearily stumbled to the shade of a stunted tree, his head pounding from lack of sleep and dehydration. He had been traveling across

Sudan for the previous five days. *Why did I think this was a good idea?* he wondered and then he recalled the rush of inspiration he had felt six years earlier, watching President Kennedy's inauguration, hearing the call to serve. Like thousands of other young Americans, Martin had left the certainty and safety of home to teach overseas.

"Good afternoon, Sir," said a voice in heavily-accented English.

Martin turned abruptly, finding a tall, slender young black man standing to one side, like a statue, perfectly still. It was hard to work out his age. His very dark skin was smooth and unlined, like a child's, yet, his manner seemed too formal and mature for an adolescent. The young man's long robe fluttered around his delicate ankles. Martin noticed he wore flimsy, scuffed, plastic sandals.

"My name is Muhammad, and I welcome you to Darfur," he continued in English. The young man had sparkling, hazel eyes, a broad smile, and a set of beautiful white teeth in a crowded jaw. He looked relieved at having delivered his English greeting successfully.

Martin smiled, mopping the perspiration from his brow with a handkerchief now grey and stained from the journey, during which it never got cooler than 96 degrees.

"Do you speak Arabic?" the young man continued, abandoning English.

"Not very well," Martin admitted. The version of the language of the Prophet that Martin had learned was a pure, elegant Arabic, taught by a Syrian academic back in the States. So far the local variation sounded like someone clearing his nasal passages.

"I bring respectful greetings to you from my school," Muhammad continued in English. "I'm here to take you to your room."

Pleased to have delivered his speech and been understood, the young man bobbed down and picked up the backpack as if it weighed no more than a pound or two. Slender but strong, he smiled again and asked Martin to walk with him. The American struggled to keep up with Muhammad on the rutted, stony path, in spite of his sturdy American desert boots. As Martin looked around, he saw no vehicles, no stores, no garages, no hotels or restaurants. There weren't even any sidewalks or streetlights—just high walls and battered metal gates, shutting the world out of private compounds.

"We're very happy to have you at our school," Muhammad told him with another dazzling smile.

"Are you a teacher?" Martin asked.

Muhammad grinned, "I'm a student, and I got the top mark in English classes, which is why I have the honor of meeting you from the bus."

"Thank you. How old are you?"

"Thirteen years old, Sir," he replied in English, flashing another toothy smile.

Martin tried to hide his astonishment. He had been warned that childhood was relatively short in Africa because the harshness of life meant that young people matured quickly, but he was still taken aback by the young man's poise.

"Where do you live?"

"I live with my uncle and his family, here in El Geneina," Muhammad explained, reverting to Arabic. "My parents are in a village twenty-five miles away. They sent me to stay with my uncle in his compound while I get an education. We live with our extended families, many cousins and relatives, all together inside walled compounds like these," he explained, nodding toward the high plaster walls along the street. He hesitated as they negotiated their way around a donkey and cart pulling sacks of dried beans. "I think it is different in America but here we have many half brothers and sisters because if your father has money he also has several wives. So, I'm very fortunate that my father has allowed me to go to school."

Martin nodded, not sure he had understood all the information that Muhammad had offered in the unfamiliar Arabic, but he couldn't help reflecting on the free education that he and his friends in the States had taken for granted.

"I'm the only boy in my village who's at high school level," Muhammad continued earnestly. "My father believes that in the new Sudan we must embrace learning and the modern world. Here in Darfur, we've had fewer opportunities for development. We're far from the capital, as you know, and we don't have the hospitals and schools and roads that they have in Khartoum."

"The new Sudan?" Martin asked.

"We gained our independence in 1956, and we're building a modern country after our years as a colony. We've been ruled for centuries by outsiders, like the Egyptians and the English, and now it's our turn to make our nation an advanced African country."

Martin nodded, assuming he had just been given the upbeat speech required of all citizens. He had been told that those lucky enough to go to school in Africa were given a thorough grounding on the sins of the "colonialists" and "imperialists" that had preceded the wave of liberation across the continent in the previous decade. The American anticipated platitudes about brotherhood and unity, the new frontier and progress, but the boy lapsed into silence, coming to a halt.

"Here we are," he said as they reached a pair of tall wooden gates.

Martin followed him into a courtyard in which an old man rested beneath one of several trees. Children played and two women squatted by large bowls, shelling what looked like beans. Several goats chewed at tufts of tough-looking grass in the center of the area.

The man beneath the tree got to his feet quickly, smiling as he walked toward them. There was a rapid conversation in the local Fur language that Martin did not understand, and a hand was extended for a firm shake.

"My uncle," said Muhammad. "You will stay with us." He hesitated, registering Martin's confusion. "This is your home now."

"The school said it would provide me with somewhere to live for the next eighteen months," Martin began warily.

"It was a terrible room. This will be better."

"And what will I have to pay you?"

Muhammad looked as if Martin had tried to poke him in the eyes. "We are honored to have you. It's our tradition here."

Registering Martin's disbelief, Muhammad continued, "I'd like to practice my English." He gave a shy smile and reverted to Arabic. "It will be like living with a private teacher always available." He paused and looked embarrassed. "My friends tell me I am always asking questions about the world."

Arriving at work the following morning, Martin was surprised by the silence in the school yard. "Have we got the right day?" he asked

Muhammad. "I hope they're not staying away to protest the arrival of a foreign teacher."

Muhammad looked confused by Martin's comment, but led him into a grim, dark little classroom. It was only when Martin's eyes became accustomed to the gloom that he saw fifty-five boys sitting quietly on benches, eyes bright with anticipation.

He began their conversational English class asking each boy to introduce himself. As the day unfolded, Martin learned that some boys walked two or three miles to school each morning, their stomachs empty. They walked home again still hungry, knowing an afternoon of farm chores awaited them.

Over the weeks and months that followed, Martin realized that most of the boys did their homework by the light of a lantern, telling him they were grateful to be among the few lucky ones who were allowed to learn. They were never noisy or rude, but they fought over whose turn it was to invite the teacher back to meet their family.

Martin's life developed into a pattern. After school each day Muhammad would lead him around the town, quizzing him about every aspect of American life as they walked. Martin also had his share of questions. He asked about everything he saw: the market where people laid out their produce on blankets on the ground; the livestock tethered together; the conical piles of spices, and heaps of unfamiliar leafy vegetables. They also discussed the differences between their respective societies, and the lowly status of the local women whom Martin had little contact with because they were always doing domestic or farm work, and they ate separately from the men in the family.

The American was astonished by Muhammad's maturity and wisdom, and once he felt he knew the boy well enough, he asked him if he would be going to university in the Sudanese capital, Khartoum.

"Probably not," the boy replied, his usually cheerful demeanor vanishing abruptly.

"Is it a question of money?" Martin asked cautiously. He was aware that Muhammad's family owned many fields and dozens of head of cattle, a status symbol in Darfur.

Muhammad averted his eyes. "No, but I'm the eldest son of a sheikh, and when my father dies, I take over his role."

"What does that involve?"

"The sheikh has to settle all types of disputes, he allocates how land is used, he keeps the peace among his fellow villagers, and he acts as a leader for the people of his community," the boy said as they walked. "They expect the best behavior from their sheikh, and he must be a worthy role model."

"Yes," Martin replied, still not understanding why it should keep Muhammad from attending university in Khartoum.

The boy hesitated, his eyes sliding away to one side. "There are two problems," he continued, lowering his voice. "First, my father may not live much longer."

Martin nodded. Listening to the daily conversation of Muhammad's family, he was astonished by how simple illnesses, easily treatable in America, decimated communities here. Many children died before they reached ten years of age, and women died in childbirth at a rate not seen in the West for hundreds of years. Many girls died after the traditional female genital mutilation ceremony at the age of six, and there were few medical facilities or doctors to save them.

Muhammad explained that the uneducated rural people put their faith in God, assuming it was a matter of fate if so many of their babies died in infancy. If your child was born disabled, that was the way of the world, and some people might even suspect it was God's judgment on some past evil act by the parents. Disease came not from dirty water or unwashed hands, but from divine will. "We have so much to learn from America, you see," Muhammed explained, embarrassed.

Martin had also experienced the nutritionally limited Darfuri diet. At mealtime the men and boys, taking the majority of the food, shared dishes, using their right hands to scoop up a tasteless bread-like starch from a communal bowl. Apart from beans, there wasn't much protein, and meat was a luxury.

"It's also hard for boys from here to get into university," Muhammad continued as they walked, his voice barely above a whisper. "Sometimes we're looked down on by our rulers in Khartoum. Few of the benefits of development reach here, as you've seen for yourself."

Martin thought back to his brief stay in the capital. The city had struck him as a poor, ugly, dirty, charmless sprawl, with open sewers along the main street. Now, comparing it with the town in Darfur, he could see that it was much wealthier. Given a choice, he preferred it here in El Geneina, with its polite citizens and gentler lifestyle, its fields of maize stretching to the horizon and its innocent isolation. But if he were a Darfuri, he might wonder why his children had to die for the want of simple medicines that were more readily available in the capital.

"A few Arabs, not many of course," the boy added quickly, "point to the passages in the Koran that justify taking black people as slaves, and they say that God created the black Africans to serve the Arabs. Very few think like this, I hope, but it's not pleasant when they call you 'slave' to your face, or treat you like a backward child."

Martin tried not to look astonished. To him the Arab people in Khartoum looked every bit as black and African as the Darfuris.

Muhammad saw Martin's baffled expression. "For centuries the Egyptians ruled our country, and they called this land Sudan, which is a corruption of their word for black. In other words, the Egyptians thought the Arabs here looked just as black as the non-Arab tribes, and ever since then, the Sudanese Arabs have had an inferiority complex about their skin color. Hence the dislike of those of us with more African than Arab blood in our veins."

The boy's eyes flashed with pain. It wasn't hard for Martin, who was a Jew, to imagine the countless indignities the Darfuris suffered. He recalled his father's fury when, driving through Maine on a family vacation, they had been unable to stop at motels because they displayed signs reading, "Restricted Clientele."

"I don't wish to give you the impression that all Arabs regard Africans as racially inferior," Muhammad continued. "We're all Sudanese and there's been a lot of intermarriage, but what matters is how you think of yourself and your identity, not the precise composition of your blood."

Martin nodded. "And you share the land here, the Arabs and the Africans?"

"We've lived together here for centuries, yes, but as a rule, the Africans tend to be the farmers, and the Arab tribes are nomads, moving their animals to where there is the best grazing. It gives rise to disagreements, but over the centuries we've solved them through negotiation and compromise."

It sounds like the disputes between the farmers and the ranchers in the Old West, thought Martin. "And in Khartoum?" he prompted, intrigued.

"Let's just say that the less-educated Arabs have been known to show hostility toward people from Darfur," the boy continued, as if weighing each word. "And toward people from the south of Sudan. Of course in the south they are Christians or animists, whereas here we're all Muslims."

"Christians, in southern Sudan?" Martin asked, surprised.

"The colonialists left us with borders that put several different ethnic and religious groups in the same country together. Let's hope this will be a source of strength for us in the future."

"Let's hope so," Martin echoed doubtfully.

Suddenly Muhammad stopped and met his eyes, his mood still uncharacteristically somber. "I have something to show you this weekend, if you will come with me."

"Of course," Martin replied, who was loving every minute of his life-altering experience as it unfolded.

CHAPTER THREE

On Friday, after school finished, Muhammad and Martin began their hike into the countryside, leaving the battered cement and stone buildings of El Geneina behind them. Carrying only their sleeping mats, they passed women and girls bent over in the fields, hoeing the earth with short, inadequate homemade implements. Their labor looked back-breaking and inefficient to Martin, especially in the intense heat. When they weren't working the soil, they were pumping water to irrigate the perpetually thirsty earth.

The hikers passed a steady stream of barefoot women and girls on the unpaved path, baskets balanced on their heads, posture perfect, slender and erect, never breaking their elegant stride. Their multi-colored robes and scarves glowed vividly against their dun-colored surroundings. Even in the middle of nowhere, they passed people on their way from somewhere miles behind them, heading to somewhere miles ahead.

"They don't look the least bit despairing or resentful," Martin commented. "I mean, they all smile and greet us."

"What good would it do them to complain?" asked Muhammad simply. "In Darfur we accept, and we improvise and cope. That's how we survive." He paused. "This is what I wanted you to see: the real Africa."

15

They spent Friday night with some of Muhammad's cousins in a village composed of a few dozen compounds, gathered around a water source. The compounds were fenced by shoulder-height woven reed walls, containing mud huts with conical grass roofs. If a man was wealthy, Muhammad explained, he had several huts housing each of his wives and her offspring. The less affluent kept their animals in the compound with them, fenced into a corner at night.

Apart from a little mosque, standard in every village, there were no public buildings—no shops or restaurants or gas stations, or indeed any indication that they were not still living in the year 900, when Islam arrived in Darfur courtesy of caravans of Arab traders. Martin knew there were as many varieties of Islam as there were Christianity or Judaism. The faith practiced in Darfur seemed as peaceful and tolerant as he could imagine. People were interested that he was Jewish, but no one was hostile.

Eating dinner that night with Muhammad's cousins, Martin was especially impressed by how people made so much time for each other. They managed with so little and found contentment and satisfaction in leisurely conversation.

The next day, he noticed women braiding each other's hair in the shade during the heat of the midday sun; he saw how the men cared for their older male relatives, tenderly helping them, making time to listen respectfully to their favorite reminiscences, asking their advice.

"We function as family units," Muhammad had explained at Martin's prompting. "We come to collective decisions, and we try to act for the benefit of the group. Many people in the countryside will never see money or goods that they haven't made themselves, but at least they know they'll be supported when they need help."

Martin took a deep breath, savoring the aroma of the plowed fields on either side. "You know, I came to Darfur to teach you, but there's a lot people here are teaching me. You mustn't believe that the Western way is always the best way. No single society has all the answers. I wish everyone could experience what I am experiencing. It's enlightening."

"Enlightening?" asked the boy as they walked toward the mountains on the horizon.

"I mean coming to see that the world would be a better place if we respected each other," Martin explained.

Muhammad smiled. "I think you're enjoying your time in Darfur."

Martin laughed. "You know, it's like each day counts. I'm like a toddler again, discovering exotic new things."

Because Muhammad had no knowledge of television, Martin could not explain how he felt that he was in the middle of one of the National Geographic specials he had watched in his youth: the vast savannah; the primitive villages; men riding camels and donkeys; colorful, pungent, noisy spice markets; the sound of African drumming; the smell of the sunbaked earth. But it was so much more than those television shows portrayed.

"I just hope I never lose this sense of wonder." He glanced at Muhammad. "And it's your job to make sure I put this experience to some use when I go home. Don't let me forget it."

Muhammad grinned. "I won't. I think you'll get sick of getting letters from me."

When Martin denied it, the young man became serious. "We must never lose touch. So even if it's just a postcard with a few words on it, please write to me. I'd like my children and grandchildren to know your children and grandchildren."

They shook hands, and continued their walk.

That night they camped in the mountains, and the following morning, Muhammad woke his teacher at dawn. "This is what I wanted you to see," he explained, leading him to the edge of a cliff overlooking a savannah stretching to the horizon. They watched the sun rise on a scene that appeared untouched since the beginning of time. Muhammad gestured, his arms stretching wide, "This is the Africa I want you to remember." No people or buildings or power lines or roads or vapor trails in the sky or distant glow of city lights. *How many guys from New Jersey have ever seen anything like this?* Martin wondered.

That night they lay on their backs examining the stars. Martin was astonished by their steady brightness, thrilled by how many were visible when there was no electric light for hundreds of miles around. Until he came to Darfur he had no idea how many shooting stars streaked across the heavens each night. From where he lay, it looked as if they were falling to earth, coming toward him, close enough to make him blink.

The next day, they returned to El Geneina. Martin began to leave his shutters open at night so he did not miss dawn, the best time of the African day—the unfamiliar bird calls, the sound of people singing as the sun came up, the muffled bleating of the goats, roosters greeting the new day in a neighboring compound, the squeak of donkey cart wheels in the road beyond their gates.

At school Muhammad was always at the top of his class. He showed off shamelessly, wanting the stage to himself, confident he could sparkle, charm, and impress. Martin was tempted to tell the boy to stay quiet for his own good occasionally; to listen, and to judge when to be less obviously clever. But the American feared he might inadvertently extinguish Muhammad's ambition and energy, so his reservations remained unspoken. It was impossible not to love the boy like a younger brother, despite the grandstanding.

There was another boy in the same class who was Muhammad's intellectual equal, even though he had little enthusiasm for learning. Uthman was twelve years old and as sharp as a knife. Yet what perplexed the American was Uthman's lack of independent thought or ambition. Martin found it dispiriting to watch the self-interested calculation behind Uthman's perpetually sulky eyes, knowing he was bright enough to search for a more enlightened path, but had chosen not to.

Occasionally he talked to Uthman in the shade of the tree beside the school. The contrast between the boys was stark: while Muhammad, fizzing with energy, wanted to walk for miles during their discussions, his face animated, keen to see Martin's reactions, Uthman slouched against a tree trunk, his broad, flat face apparently vacant, his features blank and unreadable.

The boy was short and plump, unlike most of his classmates. It was clear he was from a wealthy family because only rich Africans carried so much weight, the American had soon learned. Chatting with him, Martin realized that although the boy's eyes were empty of expression, he had a mind like a calculator, generally, he was several steps ahead of the others in the class.

During their talks, Martin tried to instill some sense of purpose in Uthman, but he met with resistance. He too was destined to be a sheikh when his father died, but he had little interest in expanding his awareness through books.

"My father says the Koran is the only book men need," he declared with a truculent set to his jaw.

"So why is he sending you to school?"

"To learn mathematics so I'll be a good businessman, like the traders in El Geneina who are always trying to cheat my father."

"Really?"

"They think because we're country people we must be gullible," Uthman continued, "My father says you can never trust a stranger."

"Yet the people here are generous to strangers like me," Martin responded.

"That's our duty," was the boy's sullen reply.

"I'm sorry you don't enjoy discovering new things during our lessons. What do you like doing?" he asked.

Uthman's eyes narrowed, as if he suspected he was being asked a trick question.

"What do you do with your friends, for fun?"

"Friends? My father says all a man needs is his family. They're the only ones you can depend on."

"And do you have fun with your family? Do you like music, or riding horses, or dancing at celebrations?"

Uthman stared at Martin as if the American was half-witted, making no attempt to answer. *I've never seen you smile,* Martin wanted to say, but did not dare. He could only imagine what a dour killjoy Uthman's father was. *How could the same relatively privileged social position and environment produce a live wire like Muhammad on one hand and the miserable Uthman on the other,* he wondered. Then he realized the same thing occurred in America, where two boys from different families often had quite different temperaments and ambitions. In fact, even brothers from the same family often had different ambitions.

"You're smart enough to become a doctor, you know, Uthman. Then you could help your people."

Uthman turned his glassy, dark eyes on the American. "I'm going to be the sheikh of our village. I'm not supposed to be a doctor," he said matter-of-factly.

Martin guessed that asking Uthman if he wanted to be the sheikh was a waste of time. His father had determined what his eldest son would do, and that was the end of the matter in such a traditional family. Yet, he sensed anger burning within the boy, manifesting itself as adolescent sourness. Perhaps he was not so resigned to his fate as he let on.

One conversation in particular stuck in Martin's memory. Much to Muhammad's irritation, Martin coaxed Uthman into joining them for their regular afternoon trek. Although they were from the same social strata, Muhammad avoided Uthman, and Martin suspected Uthman disliked Muhammad, the classroom paragon. However, the American hoped to get the boys talking, to challenge Uthman's sense of resignation. Secretly, he hoped Uthman would see that he was every bit as clever and capable as Muhammad.

In an attempt to get the boys debating each other, Martin was deliberately provocative.

"You know, Africa would develop faster if you let the girls go to school. Then you'd have twice the brainpower at your disposal. Your economy's going to be stuck in the Stone Age if you keep the women farming like this."

"That's the way we've always done it," said Uthman.

"And that's why you're so far behind the rest of the world."

"In your eyes we're behind, but to us you are morally primitive," the boy snapped.

"How do you explain why people in the West are so much richer?" asked Martin. "Is that fate? Why does your God allow my people, who you see as morally primitive, to be rich and healthy, while his own people endure poverty and disease?"

Uthman ignored the question, trudging along the road, his expression stony. "Anyway," the boy resumed abruptly, "women are inferior, and you can't trust them. They're ruled by passion, not logic. Men are logical."

"Don't you think men are ruled by their sexual desires?" Martin challenged. "I know lots of men who've made big mistakes because they followed their physical urges rather than their brains."

"No," said Uthman. "It's the women in your society who lead men into temptation. Your women are like prostitutes. But ours aren't because we cut them so sex is painful for them."

"Are you saying all Western women are like prostitutes?" Martin asked. "Including my mother?"

Uthman glared straight ahead, once again refusing to be drawn into argument. "We cut them because it's the only way to keep them from being unfaithful. A girl is her father's property until she gets married and then she belongs to her husband. We must prevent them from bringing dishonor to our families."

"So when you get married to a girl you love, are you saying you won't care that she finds making love with you painful?"

"It'll be her duty to serve me and stay faithful."

Martin noticed that Muhammad was listening carefully, but he decided not to bring the young man into their conversation, hoping Uthman would continue talking.

"If you were nice to your wife, perhaps she wouldn't be unfaithful to you."

Uthman ground his teeth. "Her duty is to give me lots of sons. And when I have enough money I'll have several wives, and everyone will see how strong I am because I'll have lots of sons."

Martin sighed, "I suppose I can see why the men here want the women to be mutilated, but why does each generation of women do it to the next? So much pointless suffering."

"Every mother wants her daughter to get a husband," he retorted angrily. "This is impossible if they're impure."

"But so many girls die after the ceremony," Martin persisted. "They get infections, they bleed to death, and then they have complications during childbirth. Just on the grounds of health alone, it seems completely irrational."

Martin saw Uthman smarting at his use of the word "irrational."

"This is how it is here," the boy explained, his voice rising. "It's always been this way, and to change it would be going against God's will."

"But there's nothing about mutilating girls in the Koran, is there?"

Uthman's eyes flashed with fury. "It's not our way to challenge the ways of our elders," he exclaimed.

"Then how do you ever make progress, if you always accept what you're told, and if you never examine new ideas? That's illogical," added Martin.

"That's not our way," Uthman retorted, spittle flying from his lips. "We must submit. We are in the hands of God." He paused, his chest heaving. "It's fate."

"And when you're a sheikh, you'll allow no debate?"

"You don't understand the position a sheikh has within our communities. This stuff about asking questions leads to no good at all."

Martin was silent, sensing Muhammad was anxious to join in. Finally he turned to the tall boy, who was almost twitching with eagerness. "What do you think?" he asked his young friend.

"We are the masters of our own destiny," Muhammad countered. "God gave us brains so we could decide our own path. We should be guided by God, and by what is written in the Koran, of course. Islam is our source of strength and inspiration, and from the Koran we get our eternal values. But it mustn't be the cause of enslavement."

Uthman was suddenly silent. Martin wondered if the boy was a little afraid of where they were daring to tread. Why else was he almost shaking with anger? Even years later, Martin would remember Uthman's dismal expression that afternoon, although it was the memory of Muhammad's toothy grin that would never fail to cheer him.

On the day Martin left Darfur, Muhammad escorted him back to the same bus stop where they had first met. The two young men renewed their vow to keep in touch, although there was no false hope that they would meet again. Both wept as they parted, aware that each had opened up unimagined opportunities for the other. And Martin had left Muhammad his most valuable possessions—his books, including the dozens he had been sent by friends and family during his stay in Darfur. He had a feeling they would be treasured for decades to come, displayed like military medals, read many times by many people.

Not long after arriving home from Africa, Martin began a career at the UN development agency in New York, trying to deliver effective aid to people who were already making an effort to help themselves.

True to his word, over the next two and a half decades Martin sent Muhammad postcards of America and photographs of his family and their house in New Jersey. He mailed him a studio portrait of the woman to whom he became engaged, explaining that Nancy was a pediatrician he'd met through the UN. He also posted him a photo of their wedding day, and a snapshot taken of his daughter Rachael when she was two hours old. And he sent him crates of books.

Muhammad responded with letters written on shiny, thin airmail paper, recounting his own news: the death of his father and the assumption of the title of sheikh when he was nineteen. There followed the announcements of his wedding and the birth of his children; his second and third weddings, and the births of more children. He also told of his sadness when his beloved second wife died in childbirth, and when two of his younger brothers died of malaria and dysentery, respectively.

Martin often wrote to Muhammad about his work, asking his friend's opinion about the best way to operate within the traditional structures, rather than against the grain of African culture. Muhammad would question Martin about world events, trying to understand the American perspective on this subject or another. Both men felt that as distant as they were from each other, somehow they were family.

At the turn of the century, Muhammad wrote to Martin about his granddaughter, Zara. Though she was still very young, Muhammad saw an intelligence in her that was unique. Though he would never admit it to anyone in his immediate family, she was his favorite. "It's as if this child looks right into my soul," he confided in a letter to Martin.

Then one day, a letter came from New Jersey that wasn't from Martin. Muhammad opened it with shaking hands, fearing the worst, praying that he was wrong. Rachael, now a young woman, wrote telling Muhammad that Martin was dead. He had died at his desk at the UN from a coronary. He'd been only fifty-one years of age. Muhammad wept openly for his friend, bewildered to have lost the man he respected most in the world.

But the link between Martin's family and Muhammad's family did not wither. Rachael continued where her father left off, sending post-cards of famous American buildings and national parks and holiday cards down the years. Rachael sent him her graduation portrait from Harvard Medical School, and her wedding photos arrived at the post office at El Geneina where Muhammad made a monthly trip with his sons, on his way to market.

Muhammad boasted to Martin's daughter that he was the first in his village to send a female child to school. His granddaughter was a brilliant scholar, exceptionally mature for her age, and she would be the first young woman from their area to go to university in Khartoum.

"Zara will be a doctor, like you and your mother," he promised Rachael. "We have a new century, and I hope we can build a new Sudan. The future is full of great possibilities," he assured her.

CHAPTER FOUR

It was dawn in the place known as Sheikh Adam's village, named after the hereditary leader whose family owned many of the fields in the district.

Each morning one of its poor young inhabitants, a lanky fifteen-year-old called Ahmed, rose just before the sun came up, when the air was still relatively cool. He put on his shorts, vest, and his most prized possession—his pair of running shoes—and headed for the dirt track leading south, across the fields from his village to the nearest market town. The moment the young man with the high forehead and almond eyes was clear of his family's modest compound, he began trotting. By the time he had reached the outskirts of the village, he was sprinting.

I'm like a streak of lightning, he told himself. *I'm like the wind. My muscles are so finely tuned, there's not an ounce of fat on me. Perhaps I'm a little arrogant about my athletic reflexes and my finely sculptured legs and arms,* he conceded as he ran. *Certainly, I'm proud. Maybe a bit vain. But it isn't luck that keeps me running to this standard, it's hard work.*

As he ran, he counted to one hundred out loud and in English because it was more difficult and therefore took longer than using his native Fur language. At the number one hundred, he slowed to a gentler trot, starting to count to two hundred. The slower segment was followed

25

by another spurt of speed for one hundred counts, his thigh muscles burning, his chest heaving, and then a slower, less exacting two hundred. Ahmed kept up the pattern and rhythm all the way to the market town, three miles away, and then back again.

There was no motor traffic on the track because almost no one had a private vehicle. Occasionally he had to move over to allow a truck to lumber past, but otherwise it was human traffic he dodged: hundreds of people rose at dawn, walking to their fields before the heat of the day sapped their energy. There were very few buses, and the fare was too expensive for most farmers, so they walked for hours, patiently, philosophically, and steadily. They usually wore old plastic sandals or flip-flops, carrying their agricultural implements over their shoulders or balanced on their heads.

Stretching to the horizon in every direction the land was flat, painstakingly irrigated by hand with well water. In the fields were fruit trees or crops of millet, beans, and vegetables, all of which had to be tended conscientiously if they were to survive the hostile environment.

The pedestrians were used to seeing Ahmed speed past, talking in a foreign language. He was a local phenomenon, famous for his athletic prowess, and a source of pride to the villages in the region. Almost everyone liked soccer, and almost everyone had seen Ahmed play.

He had learned his limited English listening to soccer commentary on the radio. He also taught himself how to train for physical endurance and speed by reading secondhand soccer magazines, most of which were in Arabic. Ahmed found the dog-eared copies that Sudanese soldiers and police serving in Darfur had discarded. Local businessmen returning from a trip to Khartoum, would often bring back the latest publications for Ahmed.

One such friend was Khalil, an Arab shopkeeper in the market town to which Ahmed ran each morning. Before he retraced his steps home, Ahmed would call on Khalil, who was usually opening up his store by the time Ahmed appeared. Khalil gave the runner a bottle of water and continued stacking his displays of grapefruit and guava until Ahmed's breathing had returned to normal. Then the friends would discuss the previous day's soccer results for ten minutes or so, before the boy embarked on the return half of his run.

The local passion for soccer had arrived in Darfur relatively recently, with the advent of affordable radios. Consequently Ahmed and Khalil followed the North African and Arab teams closely, although Ahmed was more interested in the European and West African clubs. Thanks to the radio, they both knew about Argentine, Brazilian, and Mexican players, too, and they shared an encyclopaedic knowledge of the leagues in the United Kingdom.

Ahmed was especially keen to follow the careers of African players who had been hired by overseas teams, and he occasionally allowed himself to fantasize about one day playing for his beloved Manchester United.

This morning Khalil was in the mood to tease Ahmed, speculating about how the boy's lifestyle might change, "once he made it to an important team." It was one of Khalil's favorite themes, and he returned to it often. Ahmed had wondered if it was the shopkeeper's way of encouraging him, in which case, he misunderstood the athlete's motivation.

"You'll be rich, my brother," Khalil gushed. "You'll be able to build a house like a palace, buy a fast car, and drive around with your super-model girlfriends. They'll be throwing themselves at your feet, I bet," he grinned, revealing tombstone-like buckteeth.

Ahmed shook his head, prompting the cream-robed Arab to hastily add, "I mean, after you've built a stadium for the village."

Seeing the boy's cool reaction, Khalil turned away, hoisting a crate of fruit to the front of his store. "And handed out the sports scholarships," he hurried on.

Ahmed sipped at his water, working the muscles in his neck. "We need elementary schools and high schools in each village, you know, more than we need a stadium."

Khalil shifted their conversation to tonight's sporting events. The shopkeeper was uneasy talking about schooling, but not because he did not agree with Ahmed; he did. Rather, he was embarrassed because of the boy's personal circumstances. When Ahmed was twelve years old, his father had died from a burst appendix. The eldest son was needed to help on the family's small farm, tending the animals, taking produce to market, supporting his younger siblings. Consequently, Ahmed had stopped attending school.

Khalil guessed from what Ahmed had revealed over the years that if his father had lived, it was likely the farmer would have insisted that his bright, handsome boy stay in school, no matter the cost to their family. But life had not worked out that way, and the shopkeeper felt bad about it, although he was powerless to help Ahmed, except in small ways. He gave Ahmed soccer magazines and bottles of water, and for his fifteenth birthday, he had ordered from Khartoum the pair of running shoes Ahmed wore each morning and for every game.

They swapped predictions about tonight's match, a game both of them would listen to at home, on their respective radios. It was impossible to listen together because there was no lighting on the three-mile path between their houses, and only the wealthy owned flashlights in a place where batteries were so expensive. But they knew they would dissect the game tomorrow morning at the same time, God willing.

After catching his breath and finishing the water, the runner began the journey back to his village. When he reached home, he washed standing behind a reed screen, using a bucket of cold water and a bar of gritty soap. His body was still tingling as he took his place on a reed mat beside his siblings at the communal porridge bowl.

His mother, only twenty-nine years old and already as bent over as a fifty-year-old, avoided making eye contact as she passed her son his bread. Stick-thin and sharp-featured, she was usually never short of shrewd observations or spirited commentary on the state of the world, meaning their village and its one hundred and seventy inhabitants. Her uncharacteristic silence this morning was louder to Ahmed than a referee's whistle.

"What's up, Mother?" he asked, helping his little brother to a sip of milky sweet tea.

Her bloodshot eyes shifted away then rapidly back to his. She blinked and, like all her gestures, did it at twice the speed of anyone else.

"I heard something at the well," she began, fiddling with the bright blue scarf around her head. "It's about Hawa. They say Sheikh Adam has found her a husband," she added.

His younger brothers and sisters, who had been squabbling over their share of mango slices, fell silent, sensing their mother's unhappiness. The children thought highly of Hawa, the powerful local sheikh's daughter, a tall, beautiful fifteen-year-old with kind eyes and a slightly upturned nose; someone who smiled and greeted them with a friendly wave when she saw them playing and running around the village.

However, the siblings were too young to understand that although they were of the same Fur ethnic group, Hawa's father, Sheikh Adam, was the head of a grand family, while they were poor farmers. Their relative social positions made links between them unlikely, but not impossible.

Ahmed focused on his porridge, deliberately avoiding his mother's strained expression. "What did you hear?" he asked, his voice flat and tense.

"Apparently they had a visit yesterday from Sheikh Uthman, you know, that fat trader."

Uthman, who lived ten miles away, was an associate of Sheikh Adam, who was himself a trader, and therefore much wealthier than families such as Ahmed's who survived by subsistence farming. Everyone in the village had seen Uthman come and go over the years, doing his deals with their Sheikh.

Ahmed, who had a feeling he knew what was coming, kept his eyes down, mechanically eating his breakfast, but tasting nothing. "I know Uthman, but Mom, it was Hawa's older sister I was interested in. And she's married now, if you recall. And she's had a baby," he added.

She pretended not to hear his comment, distracted by her younger children who were watching her with unblinking eyes. She clapped her hands. "You lot should go and get ready for school instead of sitting around, watching the grass grow. Come on!"

Reluctantly the children pulled themselves upright, sorry to miss out on the family drama. When they had gone, she selected a mango from the basket and sliced it expertly into bite-sized pieces.

"So, it seems one of Uthman's grandsons will marry Hawa. I forget his name." She paused, dabbing her tears away with the corner of her scarf. "The wedding will be in two weeks' time."

She had long believed Hawa and Ahmed were an obvious match, even if Ahmed protested that he wasn't keen on the girl. And even if

Sheikh Adam was too traditional to allow his daughter any say in her choice of husband. Adam, a wiry man whose severe features seemed to have been squeezed together, was respected but unloved by his people. And Hawa was a chattel to be bargained away for material advantage, although the sheikh believed he was doing it for the benefit of the whole family.

"It's a wonder that girl's as nice as she is, given the home she comes from," his mother commented. "That hatchet-faced snob of a mother."

Ahmed remained silent.

Never one to allow a quiet interlude when chatter could fill the vacuum, she charged on. "She's never been known to smile, that woman, and they say she cursed God for sending her only daughters."

Ahmed was familiar with the gossip. After Hawa's mother had produced Hawa, her third daughter in a row, Sheikh Adam had promptly rejected her and found a second wife, who dutifully presented him with a son within nine months of their wedding night.

Ahmed shrugged, his eyes rooted on the remaining streaks of porridge drying along the sloping sides of the bowl.

"Hawa's never had a chance with that mother," his mother continued.

Ahmed slid a mango slice into his mouth. "She's a bit aloof, Hawa is," he offered.

"She's just shy. That girl's never been allowed to express an opinion," she chided. "The first daughter was the same, God rest her soul, until that infection took her, poor little thing. Really, she's better off in paradise. And as for Hawa, years ago, someone overheard her mother stopping little Hawa from playing with the other children."

Ahmed nodded, at a loss for words.

"Her mother said Hawa had to help her with the chores, and she'd made a mistake allowing her first two girls to play like little boys. She actually said it's never a good idea to allow girls to develop an imagination because it makes it more difficult to find them husbands." She hesitated, dabbing her eyes once more. "What a way to treat a child, like a little household slave," she continued. "That woman, she attracts the dark things in life."

"Maybe she's just a bad person," Ahmed replied, annoyed by his mother's philosophical theme.

"I don't believe in bad people and good people," his mother retorted. "We're all of us a mix of good and bad. It's a question of what you allow to run loose in your heart."

Ahmed looked away, unable to find the words to match his mother's humanity.

Five hundred yards across the village, within Sheikh Adam's larger and more elaborate compound, Hawa was scarcely more cheerful. Her mother, a sharp-chinned woman with hooded eyelids, was making her forthcoming wedding sound like a brutal business transaction: her good name and her virginity in exchange for Uthman's money.

Hawa had been raised to be a good worker, quiet, obedient, and no trouble to her superiors: in other words, to be attractive to men. She knew to keep her opinions to herself and her eyes downcast.

She had a female cousin who had gone to America to study medicine several years ago and had stayed. Now the cousin was a doctor, but Hawa's mother had insisted she was a pathetic and sad creature, an embarrassment to their family because she had never had a baby.

Nevertheless Hawa was puzzled by the photographs that had arrived, showing the cousin and her husband, standing by their swimming pool in California, looking so happy. Why was their cousin not ashamed? Why was this man willing to be photographed with a barren woman? Did he have another wife who bore him children? It was a mystery to Hawa, but she never mentioned it because to do so would be seen as an open challenge to her mother and their strict, traditional version of Islam.

Under Islamic Sharia law, Hawa's duty was to submit wholly to the man who possessed her, be it her father or the man her father chose to be her husband. She had to ask permission to go anywhere beyond their compound, accepting any amount of punishment if she caused displeasure. If, God forbid, she produced no children, then she would be considered hardly human at all. Her husband would be able to throw her out of the village like garbage, letting her starve, simply saying, "I divorce you," three times. As a woman she had no right even to the custody of her children, if she managed to fullfill her purpose on earth by producing some.

Hawa had been brought up to understand that her honor was all she had. Any man was free to visit a prostitute as often as he liked because Sharia allowed men to have "temporary marriages," but if Hawa so much as glanced at a man, her family could murder her with impunity to save their honor. In all legal aspects, she was worth only half what a man was. Such was the joyless, extreme version of Islam under which Hawa had been raised by her family.

She had seen Sheikh Uthman's grandson, Rashid, the young man she was supposed to marry, when he accompanied his grandfather to Sheikh Adam's compound, but Hawa had never spoken to him. The role of women and girls in their family was to serve men food and refreshments, and to otherwise keep out of the way.

"What's wrong with you, Hawa?" her mother demanded that morning. "Uthman'll provide well for you, so long as you serve Rashid properly. Just make him happy when you submit to him and make sure you satisfy him."

Hawa burst into tears, horrified at the prospect.

"You'll just have to get used to it because you're going to have your husband crawling on top of you every night until the day he dies," her mother commented. "Just shut up and don't complain about the pain. It's over in a few seconds, I promise you, and then they roll off again. It doesn't matter who you lie with, believe me. It'll be painful and unpleasant. Hopefully you'll be pregnant so often you won't have to do it too much. But never refuse, whatever he wants, or he'll get another wife."

Hawa looked terrified at the prospect. "Will it always hurt?" she asked.

Her mother frowned. "You should be proud you were circumcised, unlike the filthy women who live in the big cities. Not only are you pure and honorable, but your husband will get extra pleasure because you are so small and tight. That's what men care about. Don't you understand?"

Hawa blinked her tears away, more distressed by the moment.

"Your place on this earth is to serve your husband," her mother had concluded. "And to provide lots of sons."

Hawa buried her head in her hands, begging God to give her strength to withstand what lay ahead and not shame her parents.

🦴 🦴 🦴

It soon became clear to Sheikh Adam that the timing of Hawa's wedding was unfortunate. Everyone in the area had family members living in nearby villages that had been attacked by the Sudanese government. The air raids were getting closer each day, and the villagers watched as caravans of people passed by on the main road, their possessions loaded on donkeys, heading west to the refugee camp near El Geneina. They gave the wretched travelers water from their well and fruit from their orchards, listening as they recounted their terrifying tales, all the while praying the war would not spread to their village.

However, Hawa's father shut his ears to the refugees' stories, unwilling to confront the unthinkable. He had a business to run and a wedding to plan. But, with the recent escalation in violence in mind, he dispensed with the usual weeks of preparation before Hawa's ceremony, and sought Uthman's agreement to hold the wedding in five days' time. An elaborate celebration was an expression of his position in the community, an important part of the many customs that made the Fur people special, in his view. Whatever else the regime might be doing to his fellow Darfuris, they weren't going to take this tradition away from them. Not without a fight, he vowed.

But what Sheikh Adam had not counted on was that the war was already bearing down on him, and a postponed wedding would soon be the least of his problems.

CHAPTER FIVE

SHEIKH MUHAMMAD'S VILLAGE, WESTERN DARFUR, NOVEMBER 2004

The woman was about eighteen years old and heavily pregnant. She was riding sidesaddle on a donkey led by a young man of about the same age. They looked tired and bewildered, their robes dusty and their eyes narrow from squinting in the sunlight.

As the strangers entered Sheikh Muhammad's village, everyone stopped what they were doing. Several abandoned their work and went toward the newcomers to offer help. It was unusual to see a woman out so late in her pregnancy: the locals assumed only the most extreme circumstances would force the young couple to leave their home on a journey.

An older village man known as Snowbeard because of the striking whiteness of his facial hair reached the young man first, greeting him warmly. After a brief conversation, Snowbeard led the couple to his compound, calling his daughter to help their unexpected visitors. She led the young woman gently to a hut where she could rest out of the sun, and then she brought her something to eat and drink.

Meanwhile Snowbeard fetched the exhausted young man a pitcher of water and a mug, and sat him down in the shade of a tree, urging him to satisfy his thirst before he told his story.

"A merchant came through our village yesterday morning," the young man began, his voice shaking. "He told us the Janjaweed were gathering a mile away," he said, using a local expression meaning "thieves on horseback."

Since the start of the war, Janjaweed was how everyone referred to the poor local Arab nomads who had once lived peacefully among Darfur's African ethnic groups. Now the Janjaweed were being armed and paid by the Sudanese regime to force the black African farmers out of Darfur. Often the Sudanese air force bombed the villages first to scare the local farmers away, and the Janjaweed followed in their wake, killing those unwise enough to stay.

"I told the rest of my family," the young man resumed, "but they thought I was overreacting, especially with my wife in her condition." His words trailed off and he hung his head, overwhelmed for a moment.

"Do you know what happened after you left?" asked Snowbeard.

The young man glanced up, his eyes wide and startled. "Oh, we could see it, even from miles away. We could feel the earth shake when the bombs fell. And sure enough, after the air force finished, the Janjaweed came, a vast column of them, maybe two hundred men across and three deep."

Snowbeard nodded, knowing better than to ask the young man if he knew what had become of the family he left behind. He passed him some fresh bread and bean stew, brought to them by his solicitous daughter. "Stay here until the baby's born and your wife has recovered. We've got plenty of room."

The young man gazed into his eyes and then turned away, overcome by tears. "Thank you so much," he sniffed. "But what if the Janjaweed come here next?" He paused, looking bewildered. "I don't understand it. We've been their neighbors for centuries, and yet suddenly they think of themselves as Arabs, and they see us as black Africans."

"It didn't used to be like this, all these labels dividing people," Snowbeard nodded. "The Janjaweed are used by the regime to do their dirty work for them, but once they've cleared us off our land, those dogs in Khartoum will abandon them."

Snowbeard could see the young man was not comforted by his prophesy. "Look, you must eat and get some rest," he continued with a kindly squeeze of his shoulder. "I'm going to tell Muhammad, our sheikh."

In the many years since Muhammad had been Martin's pupil in El Geneina, only a few more pounds had accumulated on his tall, spare frame. His forehead was now lined with a criss-crossing of wrinkles, like the dried up tributaries of an ancient river. He kept his beard short, and it was flecked with grey, but he stood as straight as he had when Martin had known him.

When Snowbeard arrived, Muhammad was sitting in the shade of his favorite tree, having a business meeting with his old schoolboy acquaintance, Sheikh Uthman, from a village two hour's ride away. They were discussing the sale of some of Uthman's livestock to Muhammad, to meet the expenses of the upcoming wedding of Hawa to Uthman's grandson, Rashid.

Sheikh Uthman had never been Muhammad's friend—it was said the businessman had no interest in friendship and relied solely on his family—but as someone of considerable wealth and influence, Muhammad came across him from time to time.

When Snowbeard arrived, Muhammad's granddaughter, Zara, was lurking in the background, hoping no one would notice her. The villagers, most of whom were less modern in their outlook than Muhammad, would have found it unthinkable that any female, young or old, would participate in a business meeting.

A dozen local men and boys, all dressed in long, loose white cotton robes and turbans, sat on the ground in a circle around their sheikh and his visitor. Most attended Zara's grandfather's court regularly. Others were there because Sheikh Uthman's arrival was an event of some interest, and they had nothing better to occupy their time right now. Their women took care of the agricultural and domestic work, fetching the water and firewood, leaving them free to participate in Muhammad's famously lively discussions.

Snowbeard, out of breath and flustered, acknowledged Uthman respectfully, but he was too preoccupied to sit down. All eyes on him, he told the group about the arrival of the young couple escaping the Janjaweed attack.

"It's typical of Arabs," one frail old man offered, prodding the earth with the tip of his walking stick. "They're too lazy to work in the fields and grow crops, so they steal our land, once we've done all the hard work, and then they slaughter us," he growled, bubbles of spit forming on his lower lip.

"If you say all Arabs are thieves and murderers, then you're as bad as the people who are stealing from us," suggested Sheikh Muhammad. "I know many Arabs who are appalled by what's being done in their name. And remember, the regime in Khartoum is quick to lock up any Arabs who object to their master plan for Sudan."

"Fate has been very unkind to our tribes," said their visitor, Sheikh Uthman, as if he was conceding a self-evident truth.

"Fate has nothing to do with it," snapped Sheikh Muhammad.

Zara looked at her grandfather, surprised by his tone. He shrugged apologetically.

"Forgive me, Sheikh Uthman, but just look at the corrupt thugs who run Sudan!"

Uthman spread his fingers as if he were trying to smooth out fabric. "Instead of blaming our brother Muslims, you should perhaps look at the actions of the foreigners, raping this continent for centuries."

"Really?" Snowbeard snorted. "And why does the ruler of Uganda have a bigger private jet than the leader of Japan? Did the foreigners make him buy it?"

Sheikh Uthman raised a hand in warning, his eyes settling on Muhammad. "You should perhaps be more cautious with your words, Sheikh Muhammad. Talk of overthrowing our friends in Khartoum will get us all in great trouble."

"I said nothing of overthrowing anyone, but we do deserve a share in this country's wealth. And I resent having their version of our faith rammed down my throat," he added. "No one gave them the right to rule in the name of God."

"Ah, you are too clever for me, I'm afraid. You and your books! But what good will books do us? Take my grandson here;" Uthman continued, pointing at fifteen-year-old Rashid, who sat quietly, slightly behind his grandfather.

"He's happy minding the goats and cows, aren't you?" Uthman asked, directing his words at the other men, rather than Rashid. "You don't want to go and sit in a dark classroom, do you?"

Zara noticed a cloud pass across Rashid's broad face and wondered how happy he was after all. *Had Sheikh Uthman ever asked the boy what he wanted to do?* she wondered. From the slope of his shoulders and the quiet pain in his eyes, she could imagine how he felt about being categorized so glibly by his grandfather.

"And he doesn't want to marry some woman who's got ideas from books," Uthman went on. "If she won't obey him, he'll have to beat her all the time."

Sheikh Muhammad shook his head. "But why does an intelligent man want to marry an ignorant woman? It'll be boring for him if his wife is a simpleton."

Uthman groaned, "God help any man who's so lonely he has to talk to his wife!"

The others laughed, and Uthman continued, "Hawa understands her place, and she'll serve him well, won't she?" he prompted his grandson.

Rashid shrugged, not even bothering to look up.

Zara watched as Sheikh Uthman studied his silent teenaged grandson for a moment, clearly dissatisfied by Rashid's lack of enthusiasm. "Anyway," he continued with a thin smile, "this is all very interesting, Sheikh Muhammad. I always learn so much when we have these talks, but I'm just a simple man, as you know, and with your kind permission, I'd like to discuss goats."

"I'm sorry for getting carried away," Sheikh Muhammad said, his tone contrite. "We face such serious times."

Sheik Uthman acknowledged this with a nod, saying, "We'll be fine here. We have a good relationship with the local authorities. They'll protect us from the Janjaweed raids."

"But the police, the intelligence services, the army: they're all working for the regime in Khartoum," Muhammad said. "They can't arm our tormentors with one hand and protect us with the other hand, my friend."

"I bow to your superior knowledge, of course." Uthman's smile sent a shiver down Zara's spine. The man's eyes revealed nothing, whereas her grandfather's were the window to his soul, alive with emotion.

They arranged that Rashid would deliver the livestock the following day, and Uthman got slowly to his feet, slapping the dust off his robe. "I'm overjoyed," he commented, shaking Muhammad's hand and backing away with shuffling steps.

Zara studied the man's face, but the smile on his lips did not match the cold look in his eyes. She glanced back at her grandfather, wondering if he had noticed this, but the sheikh was already listening to a long-winded question from a local man regarding his cow, who had a persistent running sore on her knee.

The following day, Rashid appeared with the goats, as promised. Zara was helping her mother with the cooking at the time, so she wasn't able to slip away and watch the transaction, as she would have liked.

"Where do you want them?" Rashid asked Sheikh Muhammad. "In your field over there?" he said, pointing his head to the north.

"That's very kind of you, but my grandson, Cloudy, will put them in a field away from the village, just to be safe." Cloudy got his nickname because he was so tall that people in the village teased him that his head reached the clouds.

Rashid duly accompanied Cloudy to the fields well beyond the village. Zara, still lurking by the door of the kitchen hut, watched Rashid's labored steps. His eyes frightened Zara, as if they were dead and yet angry. She wondered what was making him so unhappy, and why his grandfather hadn't noticed it or had chosen not to notice. Perhaps Rashid would have liked to be given the option of going to school. Uthman was rich, so it should not have been a problem for them, but her grandfather had told her they were also very old-fashioned and mean with their money. Uthman seemed to have decided the boy's future for him, without considering his feelings.

For Zara, the opposite was true. She and her grandfather had a standing joke about reading each other's thoughts, so quick were they to pick up each other's mood.

"That's because we're so similar," Sheikh Muhammad had told her often. "Even when you were a tiny baby, I could tell from your eyes that you could see right through me, so I made a decision to always tell you the truth," he had laughed. She couldn't imagine Sheikh Uthman having such a conversation with his smoldering grandson, and she felt sorry for Rashid. *He's like a neglected plant,* she thought.

Later, when she served the family men their dinner, she heard her grandfather ask Cloudy if the goats were healthy. When he was told that they were, her grandfather seemed relieved.

"But I think it's best I stay with them, Grandfather," Cloudy continued. "Several of the other families are moving their goats farther away, just in case we're attacked."

"Make sure you take enough blankets to keep warm," his grandfather warned. Then he gazed out over the village, "He's a strange one, Uthman, and I don't understand why he isn't more worried about the Janjaweed."

"Perhaps because he's such good friends with the authorities," suggested Zara's father sarcastically. "You heard him."

"That's what worries me. God help the poor man, if he thinks they're going to protect him."

CHAPTER SIX

At five forty the following morning Zara awoke with a jolt, gripping her blanket tightly with both hands. She sat up, awake and alert, even though the grey dawn light was only just seeping into her hut. Her two half-sisters, with whom she shared the hut, were also emerging from sleep, startled and asking what was going on. Then, at the same moment, each girl realized what had woken them—the deep drumming of horses' hooves. They scrambled from their beds, heading for the door, pulling their blankets around their shoulders like robes.

The air in their compound was already filled with dust, stirred up by the horses, as if a sandstorm had swept across the valley, engulfing their village. Through the dirty, swirling cloud came guttural, rasping, Arabic shouts: "Get up, you lazy slaves! Get out of here!"

There was a whooshing noise frighteningly close to her right ear, and something landed on the roof with a thump. Zara's knees went weak, and she thought she was about to faint from fear. But instead she ran faster than she knew possible, followed by her half-sisters, all of them too terrified to look back.

Zara's father appeared at the door of his hut, scanning the compound, confused. Seeing the flaming torch on the roof of his daughters' hut, he rushed to the girls, hugging them. An instant later her mother and her grandfather were there too, comforting them, stroking their hair.

"They're brave girls," her father commented, blinking tears from his hazel eyes. "And quick too, thank God."

They stood watching trails of smoke rising from the thatch roof of Zara's hut. Hundreds of insects that made their home in the densely-packed dried grass stirred, emerging like a hazy layer that hovered uncertainly above. Then suddenly the flames crept across it in a smooth blue and yellow wave. No one rushed to fetch buckets of water because they knew it was too late. Within three minutes the thatch had been consumed by a roaring, snapping fire. Ten minutes after the torch was thrown, the hut was a sizzling, blackened shell.

"What about Cloudy?" asked Zara, recalling that her half-brother had spent the night minding the recently purchased livestock in their field beyond the village. She felt her heart lurch as she wondered how well concealed he had been.

Zara's older brother, Abdelatif, turned to their grandfather. "I'm going to check on Cloudy. We should warn him what's going on."

Zara's pulse began to race at the prospect of her tall, skinny brother confronting the Janjaweed. Although she had never told him, she thought of Abdelatif as an egret, a long-limbed, graceful bird with a small head, thin neck and angular features, not as a fighter or a tough guy. *Was her father really going to allow eighteen-year-old Abdelatif to put himself in danger?* She wished everything would slow down for a moment. Most of all, she wanted to rewind time and stop the creeping fear flooding her veins. She squeezed her eyes closed and hung on to her father.

"Is it safe to leave the village yet?" Zara asked.

"It's over," remarked Sheikh Muhammad. "They've delivered their message, loud and clear."

Zara noticed her grandfather's voice sounded strained, as she had never heard it before. She was even more alarmed when her beloved Abdelatif walked out of the compound, his head held high. She prayed her grandfather would have second thoughts and stop him, but the sheikh was already talking to the villagers who had gathered at the gate.

"God is merciful, and thankfully no one was hurt," Muhammad told the local men, his voice suddenly calm and reassuring once more. "The Janjaweed won't come back today. Go home and be with your families."

A moment ago, Zara thought, her grandfather had been shaking with fury, but he now had himself under control. Even if he was doubtful and afraid, she knew he would be strong in the presence of the others. Slowly the crowd shook itself out of its collective shock and people wandered off to get on with their day.

Her hands were still quivering as she ate her breakfast of porridge from the communal bowl. She felt a further tremor of dread as she realized that everyone in their village had been living in a happy bubble in which Janjaweed attacks happened to other Darfuris, but not to them.

We're all blind fools, she thought. *We'll have to leave our village, just like millions of others across Darfur; just like the caravans of people we've seen passing by our village, on their way to the refugee camps. This is it,* she realized, terrified and yet too stunned to cry or express her fears. The time had come to be strong like her grandfather. She carried the porridge bowl to the kitchen hut, resolving to wash it, and do all her other tasks and errands, before her mother asked her to.

𝍐 𝍐 𝍐

Cloudy was already awake and eating breakfast when the Janjaweed appeared. He had slept badly, unaccustomed to bedding down with just a blanket, outdoors. Nevertheless he was in a cheerful mood, humming an Egyptian pop song he had heard on the radio the previous day.

He was planning to return home to the village as soon as one of his brothers came out to take over goat-minding duties. When he heard the crack of branches behind him he assumed one of his family had arrived. He turned, a smile on his lips, only to find a horse before him. A teenaged boy was in the saddle, a rifle resting awkwardly at his hip. Although the rider wore a scarf pulled up over his nose, Cloudy recognized his eyes. He was an Arab boy from the next village. Cloudy couldn't recall his name but they had played on opposite sides in several soccer games recently. They greeted each other but the rider's friendliness was rapidly replaced by a fearful expression. He raised his hand, as if motioning Cloudy away, but at that moment three more men on horseback crashed through the brush, coming to a halt at the Arab boy's side. Then suddenly the air around them was filled with the noise of shouting, snapping branches, and horses hooves.

"What are you waiting for?" demanded one of the older riders who had drawn up at one side of the young horseman.

"I know him," the young rider replied quietly. "He's my friend."

The older rider spat on the ground in disgust. "Don't be so feeble," he grumbled, raising his rifle in one smooth, practiced motion and shooting Cloudy without a moment's hesitation. "Don't let me see you do that again," he warned the young man. "Now help us get these goats together, boy!"

ㄐ ㄐ ㄐ

An hour and a half later, Abdelatif returned to his grandfather's compound, his long white robe filthy.

"What took you so long? Are the animals okay?" Muhammad asked. "What happened? Speak!"

"They're gone," Abdelatif explained, avoiding the sheikh's eyes. "The Janjaweed stole them all."

Sheikh Muhammad turned away, shaking his head. His fists gripped by his sides, he started to walk away in anger.

"Grandfather," Abdelatif called after him.

"There's more?"

"It's Cloudy."

The sheikh's eyes widened. "What?"

"He's dead. They killed him." Abdelatif shook his head, glancing away, his eyes filling.

"Oh no," Sheikh Muhammad wailed, his hands covering his face. After a moment he glanced toward the hut of his third wife, Cloudy's mother, bracing himself for the heartbreaking task ahead of him.

Zara felt a slight push in the small of her back. She looked around and her father gave her a single nod of encouragement. She stepped forward and into her grandfather's arms, grasping him tightly, her eyes closed, her head against his chest, listening to him mutter his prayers to God. She joined in, praying for her half-brother Cloudy. And she prayed for her grandfather and his third wife, who must now endure such pain. *I'm so scared*, she thought. *Please God, help me to be brave.*

Zara's mother turned to her husband. She was a short woman, whose arched eyebrows and high forehead gave her the appearance of being permanently surprised. This morning, Zara noticed, she looked ten years older. "How did they know to look there for the goats? I thought they were hidden."

"Only our people knew where they were." He indicated the village around them with a nod. "And Uthman's family," he added.

Sheikh Muhammad patted Zara's shoulders and pulled away. "Look what they've done to our family," he said, his lower lip trembling. Then he studied the smoking remains of Zara's hut. "We're citizens of Sudan, and the authorities should be protecting us," he announced, his voice suddenly clear.

Zara's father snorted with astonishment. "We'd do better joining the rebels and killing these dogs, just like they kill us."

"I shall go and see these rulers of ours and demand they intervene."

Zara stared at her grandfather in disbelief. The vast majority of Sudanese, be they Arab or African, nomad or farmer, town dweller or villager, young or old, avoided armed representatives of the Khartoum regime at all costs. In each district there were much-feared agents of the National Security and Intelligence Services, either in uniform or mingling with the locals, reporting back conversations and activities that were interpreted as unhelpful to the paranoid and suspicious military dictatorship. When people spoke of "the security" they meant the National Security and Intelligence Services' armed officers and their spies, supported by the army and the police: they all worked together, the long arm of the ever-present Khartoum regime.

"Right after the burial ceremony we'll go talk to them," the sheikh continued.

Abdelatif cleared his throat. "Grandfather, I've already buried him, to stop the vultures," he added. Seeing Sheikh Muhammad's astonished expression he continued, "And it's not safe out there anymore."

"But this is our land," the sheikh thundered, his hands gripped in tight fists. "And we bury people with dignity, just as we have for centuries."

Zara felt as if the earth was shifting beneath her feet: the man she relied on for wisdom, above all others, had abruptly lost his sure touch. Even she, a fourteen-year-old, had grasped that the war was about to alter everything. Customs such as burial ceremonies would be sacrificed on the altar of self-preservation. And going to see the very security services waging war against them was not a wise move.

The sheikh shook his head, slowly retreating to the home of Cloudy's mother. A moment later Zara's blood ran cold as she heard a wail of disbelief from within the hut. She busied herself, helping her mother shell some beans, but the sound of anguished sobbing filled her mind.

Fifteen minutes later, Muhammad emerged, his eyes sunken and bloodshot, his demeanor suddenly that of an old man. Zara watched as he glanced around the compound, and then pulled himself upright once more, willing himself into his role as their leader.

"Are you coming with me?" he asked Zara's father.

"They'll laugh at us."

"It's my duty to demand that our security forces protect us. It'll be a matter of record that we asked for help. I'll warn them that if they don't protect us we'll have no choice but to take up arms and kill the Janjaweed when they return."

"But the Janjaweed, the Sudanese army and police, the security services—they're one and the same. You said so yourself."

"Then let them tell me that to my face."

Zara saw her father's eyes go glassy, a sure sign he disagreed, but accepted that it was not his place to argue further.

Zara stood at her mother's side, watching her grandfather and father ride off on their donkeys, heading toward the district headquarters of the Sudanese army.

"Bye," she called out after them. Inside she was shaking with fear and uncertainty.

Zara's mother made no comment on the expedition, but, as usual, she disguised her concern by tackling domestic chores. "Let's make your father his favorite dish," she began in a cheerful tone that was so strained, Zara thought her mother might scream at any moment. "You go and get some lentils."

Zara did as she was told, praying frantically that her father and grandfather would return in time to enjoy the evening meal.

CHAPTER SEVEN

"This is fortuitous," began the commanding officer, taking a seat opposite Sheikh Muhammad. The man, sporting a bushy mustache beneath a hooked Arabic nose, rested his fingertips on the edge of the wooden table, perching on his chair. He wore his peaked hat at a jaunty angle, and he seemed to be suppressing a laugh. "We were about to come and see you, so you've saved us the trouble."

Sheikh Muhammad narrowed his eyes, waiting for the man to continue. However, the officer grinned and drummed his fingertips lightly on the table. *What are we waiting for?* the sheikh wondered. Muhammad could sense his son, sitting alongside him, growing ever tenser by the moment.

As the door opened the officer said, "Good," his eyes following the sergeant who had joined them. The sergeant stood between father and son, just behind them.

"So," the officer resumed, "you've been going around encouraging people to overthrow the government."

Sheikh Muhammad's forehead creased, "That's nonsense."

"We have witnesses who've heard you spreading lies and stirring up the simple people of your village."

Muhammad leaned forward, fixing his steady gaze on the officer, determined not to be intimidated. "My 'simple people,' as you call them,

51

are citizens of this country. Yet, we're being attacked by Janjaweed, and it's your responsibility to protect us."

"You're spreading sedition and encouraging revolt," the officer interrupted, "and that's against the law."

"Nonsense," Muhammad frowned, his features grim.

The officer nodded slightly to his sergeant, and a second later a truncheon swung down on Muhammad's head. As he collapsed, the chair rattled across the cement floor.

His son instinctively reached out to him, and the truncheon sliced through the air, catching his wrists. A jolt of fire-like pain shot up his arms, and he hunched over, almost breathless with surprise. A second blow from the truncheon caught the top of his spine, and he plunged forward onto the floor. The sergeant planted his feet on either side of his prone body, delivering a third blow to the side of his head, after which he lost consciousness.

"Leave my son alone," Muhammad gasped, pulling himself upright. "It's me who's to blame for whatever you think I've been saying."

"So you admit you're plotting to bring down the government?" the officer commented, clearly amused.

"Why are you doing this to our country?" Muhammad asked, blinking the blood out of his eyes.

The officer smirked, and sat back in his chair. "It's not your country, and you don't belong here," he said, his voice turning into a snarl of contempt. "You slaves have to be cleared out so this land can be for the Arab people. We gave you the chance to live as proper Muslims, but you want to have it your own way."

"It's called democracy," Muhammad retorted wearily, trying to pull himself upright. "And it's perfectly possible to have democracy and Islam."

"Not in Sudan, it isn't," the officer grinned, watching the older man struggle to his feet.

"You seem so certain that you're right and everyone else is wrong," the sheikh continued, trying to stand upright. "But no one gave you the right to kill people in the name of God. You're more of a slave than I am; you're dancing to the tune of a gang of corrupt murderers in Khartoum, and you'll pay the price before God one day. Then maybe you won't be so sure of yourself."

The officer's eyes narrowed as he considered Muhammad's words. For a moment the sheikh thought he saw the doubt register; the man ground his teeth, preoccupied. Then he nodded to the sergeant, and sat back once more, a look of distaste quickly replacing the uncertainty.

卄 卄 卄

It was just before dusk that evening when Zara heard the high whine of a vehicle approach. Mother and daughter were squatting, side by side at the fire's edge, stirring a cauldron of spicy lentil stew, making flat bread on the inner sides of a pot-like earthen oven.

Zara was immediately wary. Cars and trucks were not a daily sight in their village, and the appearance of a military jeep brought everyone from their huts. Zara went to the gate of their compound, her heart in her throat, hardly able to breathe. She could see from the faces of her neighbors that she wasn't the only one who was petrified. As they stood side by side, the bright fabrics of the women's robes and headscarves looked like a glowing mosaic of color in the dying rays of the sun. The kaleidoscope of peach, rose, turquoise, emerald, and yellow was in sharp contrast to the crowd's wary mood.

The jeep stopped at the narrow entrance to the sheikh's compound, and two soldiers leapt down from the back, machine guns strapped across their chests. They let down the tailgate, struggling with a large sack. Meanwhile the driver and the officer climbed down from their seats.

The villagers took several steps back, silently watching the soldiers lifting their load out of the jeep. There was a gasp as a bare foot flopped out of the sack, and the crowd withdrew further. Zara almost cried out, but she was too frightened to make a sound. A moment later she felt her mother by her side, her breath shallow and rapid on the back of Zara's neck.

The soldiers dragged the sack behind them, pulling it into the center of the family compound. At the officer's instructions they upended it, and the broken and lifeless body of Zara's grandfather slid awkwardly onto the ground. His face was a raw mash of flesh and bone, while his long white robe was torn and smeared with blood.

Zara stared, unblinking, at the sheikh, her soulmate and inspiration, too appalled to even move.

The officer surveyed the crowd of villagers, flashing them a smile. "It seems your sheikh suffered from a weak heart," he announced.

The villagers gaped at him, hardly daring to breathe.

"He had a heart attack in our offices, and we've brought him back to you, with our condolences."

The crowd reacted with a subdued muttering, too intimidated to challenge the soldiers or to show disrespect. Then Zara heard a wail of grief as Sheikh Muhammad's youngest wife, the mother of Cloudy, stepped forward, her fists beating her chest.

"My husband!" she shrieked. "Look at what this cowardly dog has done to my brave husband!"

An arm reached out from the crowd, pulling her back, but she shrugged it off and surged forward, screaming abuse at the officer.

"Have you no heart?" she rasped. "First my son, and now my husband? What kind of dogs are you?"

She stepped forward, shaking both fists at the officer, her screams echoing around the compound. The officer scowled, reaching for the pistol on his hip. He pulled it from its holster, leveled it at her, and fired two bullets into her abdomen.

"One less stupid black bitch," he snarled, replacing his pistol. As she lay moaning, he gazed down at the spreading puddle of blood. "That's what you get if you attack an officer of the Sudanese security."

The crowd, frozen with shock, hung back as the dying woman whispered her prayers. Blood seeped through her yellow robe as she curled into a fetal position, her breath coming in panicky gulps. Zara heard her begging for mercy, in the name of God. Then the woman groaned as the officer nudged her head with the toe of his boot. Zara looked away, shaking and weeping, clinging to her mother, and bracing herself for the inevitable kick. When it came, several villagers screamed and two people fainted. Zara heard the officer kick the woman once more, and finally, Sheikh Muhammad's youngest wife lay still, her agony at an end.

The officer looked around at the stunned crowd. "Please tell your next sheikh that we'll be delighted to address his concerns if he graces us with his presence at our headquarters." He climbed in beside the driver and they pulled away, in no particular hurry.

After a moment, Zara found her voice. "Where's Father?" she asked her mother, her eyes wide with fear.

Her mother held her close, unable to answer. Over the girl's shoulder she said quietly to her eldest son, Abdelatif, "They need to hear from you." She nodded toward the crowd. "Tell them what they must do."

The eighteen-year-old understood his duty, and without missing a beat he headed for the group standing at the gate of their compound. Zara heard him graciously accepting expressions of sympathy from those who could find a voice. He listened as villagers poured out their fears and anger, and then he asked everyone to help him dig graves and perform the burial ceremony immediately.

"Your brother's a good boy," her mother murmured, holding onto Zara.

But where's my father? Zara screamed silently.

꒰ ꒱ ꒰

The village's new sheikh returned the following morning. He limped when he dismounted from his donkey, but soon sank to the ground. Abdelatif helped him to his hut while Zara, her hands trembling, brought him several mugs of water. When her mother had washed his face, he began to talk, through bleeding, cracked lips.

"I kept blacking out, but the one thing they kept saying to Father was that he was trying to overthrow the government of Sudan. They said they knew he was plotting against the regime."

Sitting beside Abdelatif, too petrified to take a deep breath, too stunned to move, Zara listened to her father's halting story in silence.

Later, as she and her half-sisters lay in the hut that had belonged to Cloudy's mother, Zara was bombarded by waves of grief and anger. For hours, sleep eluded her, as she recalled the sight of her grandfather's broken body and that of his wife at the officer's feet. It was as if she were being jabbed by a sharp knife again and again; the shock got no better with familiarity.

Then Zara recalled the way that Sheikh Uthman had twisted her grandfather's words, deliberately making him sound as if he were plotting against the regime in Khartoum. But their visitor was a Fur, like them, and the idea that he would betray his own people to the security was unthinkable. Still, she wondered, was she the only one who had been present who was now reflecting on Uthman's words? She would choose the right moment to ask her father, she decided.

The next day she felt ashamed for her uncharitable thoughts, when news reached the village that Uthman and his family had their own problems. Uthman's brother in El Geneina was gravely ill, at death's door, and the wedding of the sheikh's gloomy grandson, Rashid, had been cancelled at the last minute. Apparently Uthman's whole family had left their village at great speed, keen to reach El Geneina as fast as possible.

The following day a neighbor told Abdelatif he had seen their stolen goats being sold by a trader in a livestock market twenty miles away. The trader freely admitted he had bought the animals from a friend in the Janjaweed. Then the rumors about Uthman's connections to the district authorities started, tentatively at first, and then gathering force, until another trader told Abdelatif that the Janjaweed were boasting that a sheikh had tipped them off. Zara knew better than to pester her father and brother with questions. Uppermost on their minds was when the Janjaweed would return.

CHAPTER EIGHT

It was eleven o'clock, and Ahmed was packing up the unsold tomatoes he had carried from his village to the market, hoping someone would buy them. His mother would be unhappy when he returned with the vegetables, but she would not be surprised. There were no longer enough customers around their district to take all their produce. Gradually the countryside was emptying as people left to stay with relatives in Chad. Those without family connections were reluctantly coming to the conclusion that if the worst happened, they must head for the big refugee camp in El Geneina.

Ahmed's path home, the same one he ran each morning at dawn, took him past Khalil's store, and as usual they exchanged a few words. "What have you got there?" asked the shopkeeper, indicating the covered reed basket at Ahmed's feet.

When Ahmed bent over and pulled off the cloth protecting the produce, Khalil made appreciative noises. "The wife was just saying she needed some for tonight's dinner," he lied unconvincingly. "Here," he said, stuffing some notes in Ahmed's hand. "Give me the whole bunch."

Ahmed, just as unconvincingly, pretended he didn't need Khalil's charity, but the matter was soon settled. With feelings of mutual relief, the two friends parted, and Ahmed continued his journey.

Ten minutes out of the town, though, he was surprised when two Sudanese army trucks rumbled past, heading toward his village. It was unusual to see the army on the road because the market town was largely inhabited by Arabs, whom they left alone for the most part. His pulse quickened as he wondered why they were heading for his village, populated entirely by people from the Fur tribe.

Then suddenly the trucks veered off a hundred yards ahead, turning down a track. The only building along their route was a boarding school, frequented by the female offspring of the more affluent Fur families in the region. It was famous for its strictness and the fervor with which its students studied the Koran, but Ahmed knew no one who attended the school.

Nevertheless, he was concerned. He cut across a field and joined the track taken by the trucks. Ten minutes later, he caught up with them. They had parked within the school compound, and when Ahmed reached the buildings, he found the trucks were empty.

Alarmed, Ahmed kept to the shadows, hugging the walls of the main structure, and crept up to an open window, straining his ears. At first he heard girls whispering, accompanied by the thump of boots against cement. Ahmed realized he was listening to girls being herded along a corridor. He stooped, ran to the next window, and listened. It sounded as if the girls and their teachers were being assembled in one place. The teachers were encouraging the girls to keep calm and quiet, but Ahmed detected terror in their voices.

He crouched by the window and slowly edged around the sill, looking inside. The girls, perhaps one hundred and fifty of them, were standing at one end of the hall, all dressed in bright blue uniforms and head scarves. Before them were a dozen or so women, most of whom wore glasses and looked like teachers. It seemed to Ahmed they were trying to form a protective barrier between the girls and the soldiers, who stood at the other end of the hall, their rifles trained on the students. Ahmed looked from one girl's face to the next, his heart fluttering in his chest. Mostly they stared at the soldiers with wide, unblinking eyes, but several girls were crying quietly, arms around each other.

Oh, no, he thought, seeing the excitement in the soldiers' eyes. *Just leave them alone and get back in your trucks and go away.*

Ahmed wasn't close enough to hear what was said but one of the teachers appeared to be talking to the commanding officer, holding her hands out, imploring him, her head on one side. Without warning the uniformed man stepped forward and swung his truncheon at the woman with such force that she lost her balance and fell to the floor. The teachers on either side rushed to her aid, holding handkerchiefs to her bleeding nose, but the officer and two soldiers closed in on them, beating them off her.

I have to stop this! Ahmed thought as the officer motioned to his soldiers. *But what can I do?*

The soldiers kneeled on either side of the teacher, pinning her down, while their commander ripped her clothing away. The girls fell back further in panic, hands held over their mouths, their whimpers like a chorus of startled lambs.

The officer was soon on top of the teacher, ramming himself into her as she screamed in pain. Ahmed noticed the expressions of the soldier on each side of the teacher, their faces sweaty and their mouths hanging open in excitement. A murmur of approval came from the other soldiers as they stood watching their commander get to his feet and zip himself up. He turned to acknowledge their grins and then motioned toward the pack of girls at the far end of the hall.

What can I do to stop this? Ahmed asked himself again. He ducked back down beneath the windowsill. A moment later he heard a schoolgirl's scream piercing the stagnant midday air, heavy with heat and insects.

He didn't have to look to know what was happening. Then more screams spilled from the room. Horrified and flushed with fury, his first instinct was to rush into the hall, hoping to grab a gun and start shooting the soldiers. But he doubted he could kill more than a couple of men before he was gunned down. Instead, he knew he must find help from the international monitors who had been stationed in Darfur by the African Union, the regional version of the United Nations. Only they had the authority and the power to stop what was happening in the school.

Ahmed crept away, making sure no one could see him if they happened to look out of the windows. When he was beyond the school compound walls, he slipped off his plastic sandals and started running.

He moved as he never had before, like the wind; like a wild cat, despite the heat and his bare feet; like lightning across a sky bristling with electricity. When he reached the main dirt track he turned toward the market town once more, heading for the camp on the outskirts where the African Union monitors stayed when they were rotating through the region. If he were lucky, the monitors would be there at the moment. If he were less lucky, he would find someone with a phone to summon the monitors. Khalil could point him in the right direction, he reasoned. Ahmed didn't consider the other alternatives, he simply ran.

There was only one African Union jeep in the monitor's camp, its hood up, and a Nigerian soldier tinkering with the engine. When Ahmed addressed him in Arabic, the Nigerian shrugged, warily taking in the tall, athletic young man before him, sweating and gasping air into his lungs. Ahmed noticed the Nigerian flag on the soldier's shoulder. If a nation had a soccer team, then Ahmed recognized their flag.

"English?" he asked, and the Nigerian smiled.

"My English not good," Ahmed continued, still panting and perspiring. "Problem. Danger. Army," he pointed. "School, girls, big trouble. Please help. Call monitors, please."

At first mystified, the Nigerian started nodding. "I understand," he responded, and then the animation drained from his face. "There's no diesel," he explained, pointing at the jeep's gas tank. "And the battery's dead," he added.

"No," Ahmed roared. "Help now, please!"

The Nigerian held out his greasy hands, inviting Ahmed to look around. There were no soldiers with whom he could go and investigate what was happening at the school. "They left me to fix the jeep, but it's no good without a battery, and the Sudanese authorities have stopped our shipments, so the batteries are still at the port."

"Phone?" Ahmed shouted. "Phone help?"

"I haven't got a phone, either," the Nigerian explained. "Someone's supposed to pick me up once they've got some diesel and a battery. Tonight. Maybe tomorrow."

"No!" cried Ahmed, tears welling up in his eyes.

"I'm sorry," the lone Nigerian monitor explained, his eyes flashing with anger. "I hate this, you know? They won't let us have any weapons, and we don't have the authority to stop them, even if we had guns."

Ahmed left the frustrated Nigerian and ran to Khalil's shop. His friend's jaw hung open, taking in the stark terror on Ahmed's face. His chest heaving, the young man explained what he had seen happening at the school.

"The hospital has a phone," Khalil offered, summoning his eldest son to mind the shop in his absence.

Although he struggled to keep up with Ahmed as they crossed the town, once they reached the hospital, Khalil took charge, telling every bureaucrat he encountered that he must see the administrator immediately. Within seconds the startled but obliging Arab who ran the hospital was on the phone to the district governor's office in El Geneina.

Ahmed paced up and down, unable to stop imagining what was happening in the school. While the administrator waited to be put through to the right person, Khalil discussed the feasibility of alerting the police or another branch of the security services, but just as quickly dismissed it, knowing they would not help the girls. It was out of the question to expect them to intervene against the army. The police were a powerful wing of the regime whose tentacles reached out from Khartoum; they were not there to protect civilians or solve crimes. Arab citizens like Khalil and the hospital administrator were just as wary of the security apparatus as everyone else.

"There must be something we can do to get the African Union guys here," Ahmed pleaded, his tone frantic. "I mean, they've got helicopters, haven't they?"

The administrator looked embarrassed, admitting "I don't know."

Eventually, he was given another number, for the Africa Union barracks on the outskirts of El Geneina, more than thirty miles away. As they waited for someone to answer, Ahmed was almost jumping in place with nerves, remembering the screams of the girls being attacked, furious with himself for being unable to help them. Then he listened as the administrator asked if the African Union could send a helicopter, but Ahmed noticed his voice did not register any relief or optimism as he expressed his thanks, ending the call.

"No helicopter, but they'll dispatch a jeep immediately." He chewed at his lower lip for a moment. "Our hospital will be ready, whenever the girls arrive here." He looked away, his eyes hidden behind his glasses. "We have no ambulance to send. I'm sorry."

"Is that it, then?" Ahmed asked, the veins in his neck bulging. "One jeep? How many guys? Will they be armed?" he spluttered.

"Ahmed," said Khalil quietly. "Please, let's go."

"It'll take hours to reach them," the young man persisted. "And what are they going to do when they get here? Are they armed?"

Khalil took him gently by the elbow, leading him out of the administrator's office. "He can't get involved in Sudanese army business."

"But this is crazy," Ahmed shouted. "It's going to be too late."

"They'll do their best," Khalil said, trying to get Ahmed away from curious onlookers. "You've done *your* best. Now we need to get out of here before we draw attention to ourselves."

"We haven't done *anything* to stop them," Ahmed protested.

"Please be quiet," his friend urged him. "You're only making things worse."

"I'm going back to the school," the young man declared, his voice shaking.

"No, you're not," Khalil said, steering him out of the hospital and on to the street. "You're coming back to my shop now, until you've cooled off. You're going to get yourself killed, and that won't help anyone, will it? Who's going to support your family? Think clearly for a moment. Please. And for God's sake, lower your voice."

"I don't understand," Ahmed responded, suddenly sounding weak. "This can't be happening. If the monitors had helicopters, they could stop this."

Still gripping him by the upper arm, Khalil hurried him through the streets. He said nothing until they were back in his shop, and then he handed Ahmed a bottle of water without a second thought, out of habit. "Look, you're not going to help anyone by going out there. Do you understand? Promise me."

Finally, Ahmed met Khalil's eyes. He shrugged and then his shoulders sagged, as if he had accepted defeat. "Okay, I won't go out there. But I need to tell the African Union what I saw because the army will try to cover it up."

"Good thinking. Now listen, the African Union guys are bound to come through here, and I'll make sure they find you to get your testimony."

Ahmed rubbed his eyes. "This is a nightmare. I don't know what to do."

Khalil shook his head, also at a loss for words.

☬ ☬ ☬

Within a week, people all over the region were talking about what had happened at the girls' school. The Sudanese army had stayed there for almost two days, repeatedly raping the students and teachers. Several of the younger girls had been taken away with the soldiers when they finally left, and their families never saw them again. There was a rumor that they had been spotted at El Geneina airfield, being forced onto an air force Antonov heading for Khartoum. The older girls returned to their families, never again to be allowed to study away from home. Before they left the school, the soldiers took all the teachers out back and shot them.

The Africa Union monitors had eventually sent one jeep with three Rwandan soldiers and a translator. They had arrived a full 24 hours after receiving the report from the hospital administrator because they had insufficient diesel to make the journey. Though the Rwandans risked their lives by trying to question the soldiers, they were too late to stop the violence. The soldiers wouldn't even let them enter the school.

The Rwandans also came to see Ahmed, carefully writing down his statement and assuring him they would keep their source anonymous. They explained to him that the African Union had given them no authority to do anything but compile a report, which they did. Ahmed was raging with anger that it had taken so long for the monitors to arrive, but he knew the Rwandan officers had put themselves in considerable danger, just being there and asking questions.

A week later, Khalil told Ahmed that the incident at the school had been mentioned on the radio news. Evidently a copy of the Rwandan monitors' report had found its way into the hands of a U.S. senator. The senator had asked the U.S. State Department and the United Nations how long episodes like the girls' school would continue before the world acted. Why didn't the international community support the African Union monitors with the proper resources, rather than expecting them to do the job with their hands tied behind their backs? he had asked.

For several days Ahmed and Khalil listened to each radio bulletin, hoping to learn how the world's diplomats would respond. However, the Rwandans' report was quickly forgotten, buried in the avalanche of dispatches about famine, civil war, terrorist attacks, kidnappings, natural disasters, and tyranny from around the globe.

CHAPTER NINE

The following morning Zara's father convened a meeting of elders beneath her late grandfather's favorite tree. Zara took in their nervous faces and downcast eyes as he spoke. She had expected anger, but she realized they were as frightened as she was.

"The time has come to abandon the village and go to Chad," her father concluded, his voice emphatic. "I know many of you have relatives there, and you can try to make a new life. So," he said, like a general issuing an order, "tomorrow morning, we'll get an early start. Tell your women and children and the elderly that they must prepare for the trip now."

The new sheikh's announcement was met with silence. Finally one of their neighbors spoke up. "Everything we have is here."

"Not for much longer. Next time they'll kill us all."

"Not if we don't provoke them," another man said, his face drawn. "All due respect to Sheikh Muhammad, may God rest his soul, but he wouldn't work with the Sudanese authorities. He pulled their tails, and they had to make an example of him."

Zara saw a spark of irritation in her father's hazel eyes. "The point of their political ideology, this 'Islamism,' is they want to wipe us off the face of the earth!" he exclaimed, banging his fist on his knee.

A one-eyed farmer with only three teeth in his head spluttered in disbelief. "We're warriors! We can't just run away."

Zara stared at him, wondering if he was going to openly accuse her father of being too cowardly for the job of sheikh. There were grumbles of agreement, but no one gave voice to an outright challenge to their new sheikh's authority.

"Don't you realize that every tribe believes they're the bravest on earth?" Zara's father snapped. "They tell their little boys the same stories that we do. We are brave but the army's taken all our weapons away so we have no way to protect our families, our village."

This statement of the obvious stunned his audience into a momentary silence. "The first group leaves tomorrow morning," their sheikh announced. "I'll stay here with those who want to fight." Then he rose, ignoring their bleak expressions, and limped toward his hut.

"Father!" Zara called, running after him. "When will you join us in Chad?"

"Later on," he said. "But I must lead by example. You know that, Zara. Don't ever forget our position and what it means."

She glared at her feet, ashamed and tearful.

"Listen," he continued. "You have your grandfather's big brain, so you must be a leader too. Make sure the other kids behave, okay?"

She nodded, watching him hobble away, still in pain, but forcing himself to stand upright, looking just like her grandfather. Then she went directly to her mother, offering to help with the packing. But all the while she was screaming inside at the prospect of her father, armed only with some old rifles, remaining to fight the Janjaweed.

For the rest of the day Zara helped her mother with the preparations, but that night sleep was impossible. The following morning she was startled to find that only four other families had gathered at the sheikh's compound. Suddenly, far too quickly, it was time to leave, and Zara's mother was blinking away uncharacteristic tears.

"Listen to me," her father said. "They'll change their minds about being heroes when they see the helicopter gunships." Then his tone became more affectionate. "I'll join you in Chad soon, so make sure you have a bowl of my favorite spicy mutton stew ready for me. Okay?" he smiled.

Zara watched as her mother forced a smile and dried her tears. When it was Zara's turn, she hugged her father fiercely, while a good portion of her mind refused to believe they were saying goodbye, unsure if they would meet again. She knew he would be disappointed if she cried because she was supposed to be strong before the other children, but inside she was quaking with fear, terrified of losing him.

A moment later their little caravan of donkeys left the village. Zara, her half-sisters, and her mother were at the front, hoping to force the others to keep up a good pace, with Abdelatif and their cousin Alia bringing up the rear, encouraging the stragglers.

Over the next few days whenever they stopped to sleep, they did their best not to grumble about how tired they were. Snowbeard's daughter, Makka, famous for her comedic impersonations, made a valiant attempt to entertain the children by pulling faces, her meaty shoulders shaking when she laughed. The group endured and carried on as best they could, singing and joking and gently teasing each other to keep their spirits up as they walked.

Zara watched as her mother offered the same forced, brave smile, day after day. She gave only sympathy to the other women, acutely aware of her role as the sheikh's wife. When no one else saw them, Zara made a point of giving her a hug, realizing, for the first time, that her mother was small and delicate. Her fine features were drawn with exhaustion and her broad forehead was lined. All her life Zara had taken her mother for granted, as her source of comfort and courage, always there to solve her problems and dry her tears. Suddenly Zara saw that her mother was a frail but determined person, putting on a brave face, probably just as frightened and unprepared for the trip as Zara was. *Maybe it means I'm growing up,* Zara thought. *Maybe everyone else is just pretending they know what they're doing.*

Three days into their journey, a gang of thirty or so Janjaweed men riding horses and camels attacked their caravan. They appeared from behind a rock and headed straight for the column of donkeys, swinging up their guns. Shots rang out like firecrackers, and the families in the caravan scattered in every direction, like startled birds.

Zara felt her mother's hands on her back, pushing her and shouting, "Run!"

Zara dropped the bag she was carrying, heading for the thick, thorny bushes about two hundred yards away. She knew only a fool would stop and turn around to look back, so she kept on running until she reached the bushes and plunged into the spiky foliage, ignoring the scratches and the pain. Behind her she heard gunshots, screams, and the braying of terrified donkeys. Finally, in the heart of the thick brush, she stopped, catching her breath. It was clear the Janjaweed had not followed her, but neither had her family or neighbors. *Where were they?*

Trembling with fear, she crept back to the edge of the brush and peered through the foliage. Her blood ran cold as she saw the Janjaweed walking in among the bodies, clubbing those who were still moving, going through their pockets and bags. One Janjaweed lowered himself on top of someone, while three militiamen stood around watching and laughing. They waited their turn and then got on top of the body for a few moments. Then, when they had finished, one of them took out a knife and swung it down on the body in a huge arc. Zara watched in disbelief as they stabbed the woman three times and then walked away. *Was that my mother they killed?* she wondered.

The Janjaweed roped together the donkeys, still loaded with the villagers' supplies and possessions, leading them away. Soon the vultures appeared, wheeling in circles overhead. When it seemed the Janjaweed had gone she emerged slowly and cautiously, walking back to what was left of their column. She was desperate to find her family, but at the same time she was terrified of discovering them among the dead bodies on the ground.

As she drew near it seemed that a huge collection of rags had been left in a pile. Then she noticed the flies and the blood. She recognized several of the neighbors' young boys among the dead bodies. They had large holes in their chests and backs where they had been shot.

Then she found her cousin Alia. Her clothes had been cut away, exposing her naked, battered body. There was a bloody mess between her legs. Zara pulled the robe back across her, hiding her face.

She wandered among the other bodies, searching for her family, her heart pounding, her stomach turning. She found both her half-sisters. Each woman in the caravan had the same wounds, including three girls younger than Zara. *This could have been me,* she kept telling herself.

Suddenly a hand grabbed her ankle. She screamed and jumped, sprinting away. She halted as her name was called and a hand waved from the heap of rags. Before her lay Snowbeard's daughter, Makka, half dressed, her body smeared with blood. "Zara, help me please," she moaned.

Zara crouched down, taking Makka's outstretched hand. Her face was bruised, but the main problem was the blood oozing from between her legs. With shaking hands, Zara ripped strips of cloth from a nearby robe, and together she and Makka eventually succeeded in stopping the bleeding.

"Just lie there while I find you some water and something to wear," Zara explained, still desperate to find her family.

Twenty yards away she found a water container beneath a body, and she struggled to pull it free. She allowed herself a long swig of water, knowing she must keep herself going too, and then took it to Makka. *Where's my mother? Where's my brother?* she kept asking herself. *Are they among these bodies?*

As she handed Makka the bottle, the woman's eyes suddenly narrowed, focusing on the horizon. Zara turned abruptly, following her line of sight.

Two bedraggled figures had emerged from behind a cluster of bushes. One was wearing a blue and yellow robe that Zara recognized. She had washed that same robe so many times in the big plastic bucket outside the kitchen hut. She had hung that robe up to dry on the thorny bush at the edge of their compound, and on countless occasions she had folded it carefully for her mother.

Zara started running, forgetting all about her tired legs. She dashed across the hard earth, tears stinging her eyes. The next thing she knew she was wrapping her arms around her mother, praying that she wasn't dreaming. Then she felt her brother's arms around her too, hugging her tightly and kissing her hair.

Zara pulled away abruptly and met Abdelatif's eyes. "You mustn't go near the bodies," she began, but was unable to continue without weeping. Her brother had been particularly fond of his cousin Alia, and it had been taken for granted that they would marry in due course. Zara held his hand tightly. "Don't," she whispered.

He closed his eyes and exhaled shakily. "Oh, no."

"Only Makka survived," she added, her voice thin.

Abdelatif paced away from them quickly, hiding his tears, staring at the savannah, while the women returned to Makka's side.

When Abdelatif joined them once more, they began to walk westward. Over the following days, they walked every moment they were awake, never allowing themselves the luxury of rest, always alert to the possibility of ambush. Two days later, they reached another Fur village. Abdelatif explained their predicament to the local sheikh who allowed them to stay in his compound. That evening, over a shared meal of vegetable stew and bread, Abdelatif warned the local Fur elders that the air force or the Janjaweed, or both, could strike them at any moment. The elders thanked him for his advice, but he saw the same denial in their eyes that his father had encountered back in their own village.

Zara's group slept badly, and they were already up, preparing to resume their journey when the attack began. It gave them an advantage over the locals because as soon as they saw the air force Antonovs, they started running toward the hills. The planes flew low over the village, dropping their bombs packed with scrap metal and explosives. The earth shook; animals screamed and broke loose from their pens; vast craters opened up in the ground, sending earth flying into the air like a dirty curtain in the sky. White hot metal ripped into thatched roofs, and within seconds, large houses became carbonized skeletons. Everyone scattered, stunned and sleepy-headed, running for safety in the hills half a mile beyond the edge of the village. Only the elderly, the infirm, and the very young were left. And the dead.

Makka, still in pain, limped behind, but Zara went back for her and dragged her along by the arm. A moment later Makka stumbled and fell, and Zara heard her cry out as several people tripped over her, screaming as they too were trampled. Zara was swept forward in the crush of fleeing villagers, and when she disentangled herself she tried to get back to where she had last seen Makka. Suddenly the air vibrated as an Antonov made another low pass over the village, its engines roaring, louder than anything Zara had ever heard. The plane disgorged a large spherical metal object from its belly, and the bomb wobbled gracelessly as it plummeted to earth.

Zara was thrown onto her side, and a veil of dirt broke over her like a wave. Stunned, she struggled to her feet and looked around, finding a crater where Makka had been. She hesitated for a moment, searching the crowd for her family, until a passing villager pulled her away roughly.

"The plane's coming back," he cried. "You've got to run."

She followed the man and his family, knowing that the local people would head for a smart place to hide, hoping her family was up ahead of her. Like an animal driven by the instinct to save itself, she focused all her strength on getting away from danger as fast as she could.

Ten minutes later they reached a parched riverbed in a narrow valley. The survivors sat in absolute silence, eyes upturned, straining their ears for the hum of aircraft engines or helicopters. It seemed that even the smallest children knew, for once, to be quiet, and not to pester their parents. The villagers crouched tentatively, anticipating they would have to leap up again abruptly.

When they guessed that the Sudanese air force had gone for good, the villagers started moving around, shaking the cramps out of their muscles. Zara, too numb to even speak, listened as the elders conferred, asking the same questions she had heard in her own village recently. Eventually the elders decided they would walk to the refugee camp across the border in Chad. Those who had listened regularly to the radio knew the United Nations was helping people there. Surely the Sudanese regime would not dare to attack the UN, they assured each other.

As the villagers assembled for their long march, Zara wandered through the crowd, once more searching for her family. She wondered if she should stay in the hills, hoping they might arrive. *Or should she return to the bombed-out village and search for their bodies or follow the locals who seemed to know where they were going?* She wept openly, confused, uncertain what to do, and still hoping she would suddenly catch sight of her mother in the crowd.

As she replayed the attack on the village in her mind, Zara knew the bombs had most likely killed her family. Yet, at the same time she tried to convince herself that they had reached safety elsewhere. Perhaps they were waiting for her to join them in another gorge in the hills, she thought hopefully. Then she felt a fresh wave of tears welling up as she confronted reality once more.

As the villagers started off, she ran to the edge of the gorge, looking back at the village from which they had escaped. Even from a distance she saw vultures diving into the ruins of the huts, no doubt picking their way through the charred bodies. At that moment, Zara knew it was pointless to stay. She walked at the end of the villagers' column, keeping to herself, hardly able to talk.

As she walked, hour after hour, day after day, it seemed as if she thought about her mother and Abdelatif each minute. Whenever her mind began to wander toward other, less miserable subjects, it soon jerked back to the horrible realization that the people she loved most in the world were probably dead. And what of her father and the rest of the family, back in their village?

On the fourth day, as they were setting off in the dawn light after a brief and chilly night's sleep, the villagers' column was attacked. Numb with terror, scarcely able to believe it was happening again, Zara ran and ran. She ran until she reached a dried-up river in a rocky pass in the mountains. A helicopter flew over, forcing her to stop and rest. She leaned against the rock wall, glaring at her pink flip-flop lying out in the open, hoping it didn't alert her pursuers. *I'm going to survive this,* she assured herself.

CHAPTER TEN

All over Darfur families like Zara's were fleeing their villages and heading for the refugee camps that had sprung up along the western border with Chad. In one of those camps, just outside the market town of El Geneina, a human rights worker named Karen Freeman sat in the shade of a tree, a notebook on her knees, her pen poised for action. The sand had defeated her tape recorder within days of arriving in Darfur, so she was back to traditional methods of testimony collection.

Beside her, perched on the rough wooden bench, was her UN translator. Before them sat twenty-seven Darfuri women, chosen by staff at the camp clinic because they came from different villages and had suffered a variety of experiences during the conflict. The women crowded around Karen, their babies on their laps, other children clustered like orbiting moons. They stared at her unfamiliar Western clothes, blonde hair, and white skin, intrigued. They were unaccustomed to meeting outsiders, so they did not realize that her perfectly manicured nails and pressed khaki trousers were at odds with the caricature of the rumpled war reporter or human rights worker.

The Khartoum authorities did an excellent job keeping the media out of the killing fields, and consequently few Westerners visited Darfur. It was easier for the aid organizations to work across the border in Chad, where government officials did not deliberately harass and intimidate them on a daily basis. Karen Freeman was in El Geneina due to a mixture of persistence and being economical with the truth whenever she ran into Sudanese officials.

Karen, an attractive, petite New Yorker, began by explaining through an interpreter why she was visiting the camp. "I'm gathering evidence about what's happening in the villages. One day, with the help of your testimony, we'll hold the men in Khartoum responsible for their actions. The regime denies the genocide has anything to do with them, but we know they're sending planes and helicopters to bomb you and that they are arming the Janjaweed."

The women nodded.

"We need to know what happened to you and when. What did you experience? Who came to your village to attack your families, and when did it happen? How many militiamen or soldiers were there, and what were they wearing? Did they have horses or camels or vehicles? When we have the facts, we can prove they're lying when we finally get them into a court of law. With your permission I'd like to interview you separately, in private, so you can tell me whatever you wish. And although I'll write down your name and personal details, I'll make sure your real name is never known by Khartoum."

There was a moment's silence as the women absorbed Karen's message. A few of them nodded, but before she could begin the individual interviews, an old woman with a slack jaw and few teeth spoke.

"There must be justice," she said through cracked lips, her eyes yellow. "They should admit what they did to us is wrong. The world must see this." She paused and worked her jaw, as if she was chewing over her thoughts. "You must be our voice because we're powerless. Nobody hears us but maybe they'll listen to you. So please take our story, and be our voice; we have no other voice at the moment. To the world, we do not exist."

The younger women waited to be sure that the old woman had finished before they added their comments. They spoke uncertainly at first, politely, and one at a time. Gradually they became bolder as they relived the horrors they had endured.

"It's nice of your country to send the food, but this is Africa, and we're used to being hungry," offered one woman with a deep scar still healing on her cheek. "What we ask is that you take the guns away from the men who are killing us."

"They must admit what they did to us is evil, so yes, I'll tell you about what the Janjaweed did to me," another said.

Karen asked for their patience as she interviewed each woman, but they looked uncomprehendingly at her; There was nothing else to do in the camp except domestic work and waiting. No one had appointments to rush off to. Indeed, waiting for their turn giving evidence to the white woman was vastly preferable to washing clothes or sweeping out their tents and huts.

Karen expected she might encounter reluctance to speak to her separately because her audience was used to thinking communally, reaching a consensus through gentle and respectful discussion. She feared the women might lack the confidence to tell their own stories without the support of their friends.

However, five minutes into her first interview, it was evident that talking individually was not going to be a problem. The biggest problem was that her subjects were being distracted by their children. Sensing Karen's frustration, one woman said, "You should ask the children what they saw. They're very troubled by it. I'm worried about what'll happen to them, after what they've witnessed."

Karen pulled a thick pad of paper and some colored pens from her bag, giving them to the children.

"Please ask them to draw me a picture of their strongest memories," she instructed the translator. "But only what they saw, not what they heard others talking about."

At the end of ten days, Karen had dozens of detailed accounts of attacks on villages, names of people who had been killed, descriptions of the vehicles and aircraft used in raids, and blow-by-blow accounts of the torture, rape, and sadism that characterized the daily attacks of the Janjaweed and the Sudanese armed forces.

Karen also had more than 500 children's drawings showing Antonov aircraft releasing bombs, helicopters strafing villages, huts burning, women being led off to slavery, men's heads being cut off, babies being thrown on fires, men being lined up in mass graves, and Janjaweed looting possessions, like medieval invaders using twenty-first century technology.

At night in her tent, by the light of her flashlight, Karen studied the drawings, aware she was in possession of something special. To her surprise the children drew themselves and their families with black skin, while they gave the Janjaweed Arabs and Sudanese army pink skin. To Karen's American eye, everyone in Sudan looked black. She knew that both Arabs and African tribes had shared the same land for centuries and that there had been intermarriage. To her, they were all black.

Yet, the drawings reflected the change in the way people now saw themselves, with devastating consequences. The people being targeted in Darfur now identified themselves as non-Arabs with black skin, and the children were growing up to view themselves as different from the Arabs in their communities.

The children had drawn the Sudanese armed forces weaponry in extraordinary detail; tanks rampaging through villages while flying the Sudanese flags, directly contradicting Khartoum's insistence that their armed forces weren't involved. *But since when did illiterate Arab nomads have tanks, helicopters, and Antonov bombers?* Karen mused.

The pictures also showed soldiers in Sudanese army uniforms hiding in trees, shooting fleeing children. These drawings would make it hard for Khartoum to deny that its forces were systematically working in concert with the Janjaweed.

The average Darfuri villager had no video recorder with which to capture the moment the bombs rained down on their huts, or how the Janjaweed stormed in on their camels and horses. No intrepid reporters had been given sufficient access to Darfur to risk their lives filming old people being roasted or girls being raped. In the absence of photographs or film, the children's drawings were the closest Karen had seen to visual images of the ongoing genocide sweeping across western Sudan.

Before leaving the camp, Karen sewed the drawings and the interview notes into the lining of her luggage. She hoped she would be able to leave Darfur, and cross the border into Chad, without being stopped and searched by the security forces. She suspected the regime would do everything in its power to stop the drawings from reaching the outside world, if they knew Karen was collecting them. She set out on her journey, excited by what she carried in her bag, but more than a little nervous.

☒ ☒ ☒

Rashid twisted the boy's arm behind his back, pushing his face into the dirt. "Take back what you said," he yelled.

The boy, several inches shorter, was at a physical disadvantage. However, to Rashid's surprise he didn't seem intimidated.

"Everyone here knows your family is friends with the Janjaweed," the boy said, spitting the sand from his mouth. "And the regime, too." The boy squirmed away from Rashid, and with one heave, he wriggled out of his grip and shot off, laughing.

Rashid knew he should follow the boy and beat him to a pulp, but his energy suddenly seeped away, like water running over bone-dry earth. He sat down in the shade of a tree, trying to calm his pounding heart.

Ever since Rashid's family had arrived at the refugee camp outside El Geneina, the place had been buzzing with gossip. People said his grandfather, Sheikh Uthman, had been given advance warning of the Janjaweed raid on their village, and that the entire family had left for El Geneina only hours before the murderers on horseback arrived.

Rashid knew the cheeky boy's taunts were true. Ten days ago the sheikh had suddenly informed his family that Rashid's wedding must be postponed. The village was told that Uthman's dearest brother was at death's door. Not a single local had the impertinence to point out that no one could recall the existence of a brother in El Geneina. It wasn't the place of a humble peasant to contradict the sheikh or his sons or grandsons.

There were also rumors going around the camp that Sheikh Uthman had tipped off the Janjaweed in advance that he was selling his goats to the notorious troublemaker, Sheikh Muhammad. The blabbermouths were also saying that his grandfather had told the Janjaweed where Sheikh Muhammad's goats were being hidden. Rashid had beaten a boy who repeated the story, breaking his nose. *That would stop such talk*, he thought. But it hadn't.

The day after Sheikh Uthman's family left for El Geneina, the village was burned to the ground in a Janjaweed attack. Shortly after

Uthman and his family arrived at the camp, the wretched survivors from their village began trailing in after their desperate journeys. They huddled in food lines or in the shade of trees, discussing the latest results of the Khartoum regime's brutality.

Uthman had sold their remaining livestock during the journey to the camp. Over the years, Rashid had heard the sheikh complain about how hard he worked to sustain his excellent network of connections throughout the region. Clearly, those contacts were not restricted to business and trade, for when they had arrived in the camp, Uthman's sizeable family was allocated several comfortable UN tents, fortuitously near the water standpipe.

Rashid had watched in awe as his grandfather chatted to the local African officials in charge, giving people tokens of his esteem. Later, the sheikh had explained to his sons that the bureaucrats, Sudanese hired by the UN, were grateful for his cooperation. Uthman was a community leader who could be counted on to pacify the camp inhabitants in times of trouble or strained relations.

The previous day Rashid had heard his grandfather laughing as he told his family that someone had just asked him who's side he was on in the conflict. "I'm on my side," he had boasted.

Rashid had watched each day as refugees from all over the region trailed into the camp, bloody, exhausted, and still shaking from their ordeals. Bewildered, they were shown a patch of earth and told to build their own shelter, lucky if they could beg a few scraps of UN plastic sheeting to keep out the seasonal sandstorms and rains. Their women were forced to venture back out to the bush to collect branches, reeds, and long grass with which to make a hut, knowing they risked attack by the same people who had chased them from their villages. Those who had hoped the El Geneina camp might offer safety were alarmed to find that the nearest Janjaweed camp was less than three miles away.

The female survivors wove the branches and reeds to form flimsy walls and made the leaves and grass into thatching. Meanwhile, their men registered with the UN refugee agency where they were given identification numbers. Then the women spent their days standing in lines for rations from the World Food Program, or making the hazardous journey out into the bush to collect firewood for cooking.

When Rashid asked why the men didn't accompany the women on the trips out of the camp, his father had laughed, making no effort to hide his contempt. "Collecting firewood is *women's* work."

Rashid had nodded, feeling stupid that he had not understood that the traditional rules did not change just because there was a war.

His father had added, "Anyway, they'd kill us if we went out there. As it is, they just attack the women. But that's better than murdering us."

"Why don't the rebels protect the women?" asked Rashid. "Or the African Union peacekeepers?"

"Don't make me laugh," his father snorted. "Anyway, they're not peacekeepers, Rashid, they're monitors. They write reports so the white men can say they're monitoring what's going on in Darfur."

"But what about . . ." Rashid resumed.

His father grimaced, "Don't you have something to do?"

In truth, Rashid had nothing at all to do. His grandfather had thirteen grandsons apart from Rashid, and there wasn't enough work for the males even before the war. Rashid no longer had any livestock to watch, and when he asked if he could attend the camp school run by a humanitarian group, Uthman declared they were foreigners with suspect ideas. No grandson of his would be going there.

Anyway, Rashid was too old to learn anything from books, his father added. When the war was over, they would return home and pick up where they left off. Grandfather would buy more animals; Rashid would marry Sheikh Adam's daughter, Hawa, and have many sons. End of story, his father said firmly, leaving no room for discussion.

Sheikh Uthman regularly rode into the large town of El Geneina where he loaded his donkeys with provisions, although he was careful not to flaunt it in front of others in the camp. Having food was the just reward for a lifetime's hard work, his grandfather had told his family, reminding them they were not like the feckless fools from their village.

Each day Rashid watched as the women and girls in the camp cleaned their little huts, washed their clothes, stood in long lines in the sun, and took care of their babies and their elderly and ailing relatives. Some women cultivated the tiny patches of hard, dry earth beside their huts, trying to grow tomatoes or corn. Many of the women were living alone with their children because their men had been killed during

the attacks on their villages. Some of them were now pregnant with
Janjaweed babies. Rashid's grandfather had told him that women only
got pregnant if they'd enjoyed having sex, so, gripped by fury, Rashid
stomped on their tomato plants when they weren't looking. The less
he had to do, the more he found himself consumed by anger at others,
whether they were whining refugees or impure women. The power of
his emotions frightened him, but he didn't know what to do about it.

In the evenings, the UN people and the humanitarian staff working in the camp returned to El Geneina, exhausted by the heat and the
bureaucratic obstacles routinely put in their paths by the Sudanese authorities. The foreigners were relatively safe in their gated compounds,
guarded by men with guns, whereas the refugees back at the camp had
no one to protect them; the Janjaweed could ride straight in whenever
they wanted food and medicine.

Despite the constant threat of attack, from Rashid's perspective,
the camp became much more interesting at dusk. As soon as the foreigners and humanitarian workers had pulled away in their trucks and
four-wheel drive vehicles, the various local rebel groups appeared, like
shadows in the growing gloom of the evening. The rebels brought with
them news from the front lines, and people crowded around them, eager
for any word from their villages.

When the war had started, eighteen months previously, there had
been two rebel groups, both committed to securing a fair deal for Darfur
from the dictatorship in Khartoum. But soon a dozen or more so-called
rebel militias sprang up, all claiming they had pure political motives,
and that they were protecting the Darfuri people from the regime. However, many people who had encountered them believed the newer militia
gangs were nothing more than bandits, cashing in on the chaos of war
and displacement.

Like most boys in Darfur, Rashid had been raised on stories about
his courageous ancestors, valiant men who faced down invading tribes
and wild animals to defend their people. The Fur men were of warrior
stock, able to endure hunger and sandstorms, unfailingly brave when
attacked by outsiders, armed only with their swords and sabers. They
were the greatest horsemen in the world, the toughest fighters, and the
most daring heroes.

For as long as he could recall, Rashid had wanted to be a soldier, to uphold the honor, traditions, and glory of his people; to ride out at dawn, facing death, never wavering in his commitment to defend his clan, his village, and his tribe. As he had minded the livestock back in their village, he had daydreamed about this more worthy calling, but his father and grandfather had told him, repeatedly, that his role was to follow the goats around, not to enlist in the army.

When the war began, Rashid's first thought was to join the rebels, to defend Darfur. Uthman was a generous donor to one of the rebel factions, and as a result, they were respectful to him. They asked his help in encouraging the men and boys to join their forces and to fight the Khartoum dictatorship. Rashid had heard his grandfather's speeches about the sacrifice that all Darfuri families must make to win a free Darfur, saying he had lost almost everything in the war, but he was happy to donate what little he had left for the cause.

Knowing of Uthman's support for the rebels, Rashid had been surprised when his grandfather forbade him to join them. After summoning up the considerable courage necessary to confront his grandfather, Rashid had pointed out that Uthman had urged others to sacrifice their offspring and was handing the rebel leader wads of currency. In response the old man had responded, "Business is business, boy. It's best to have a foot in each camp."

Despite Uthman's financial support, Rashid was tormented daily by disrespectful gossip, such as the taunts from the stupid little boy he had just beaten up. Rashid had asked his father why people dared to say such things about a sheikh, but instead of answering, his father wanted to know exactly which boys were repeating such slander. He demanded that Rashid give him names because, he explained, the boys were only repeating what they had heard at their father's knee. He told Rashid that he and Rashid's uncles would go and "set the story straight."

Rashid never disobeyed his father, so he told him which boys had been saying that Uthman was working with their oppressors in the Sudanese district authorities. His father went off after dark, accompanied by his uncles and older brothers, armed with clubs, to pay a visit to the families of the boys who had taunted Rashid. Their intervention had not put an end to the gossip, but all conversation ceased when any relative of Sheikh Uthman appeared.

"They respect us," his father explained. "Be proud that you're the sheikh's grandson, and for goodness sake, grow up."

Rashid burned with shame, aware that he had nothing to do apart from attending the mosque regularly. He made sure the other boys in the camp were afraid of him, but he worried that it wasn't exactly the same as being respected. It jarred with the heroic image he had of the traditional Fur warrior, defined by his brave actions on the field of battle—honorable and fair-minded, honest and strong, admired and trusted.

"Anyway, we won't be here long," his father added. "This war will end soon and we'll be in a position of great influence in the new government of Darfur. Your grandfather's taking care of that."

Rashid accepted his father's judgment, and whenever awkward questions surfaced in his mind, he forced them away. He recalled Uthman reminding his family that Sheikh Muhammad had spent his life questioning the order of things and reading books, and it hadn't done him any good. In fact, Uthman had commented just the previous day, no one had heard of Muhammad's family since the attack on their village. He said he expected them, or what remained of them, to arrive in the camp any day now, a pathetic sight, reduced to dirty peasants, like the rest of the refugees huddling in their improvised homes around the camp. "A fat lot of good their precious books will have done them," he had gloated.

Each day, to pass the time, Rashid walked through the camp, making a mental note of the new arrivals, hovering around the groups who gathered to hear their stories. Then he would return home feeling important, able to tell his grandfather which families had appeared and what had become of their villages. However, Uthman never thanked him, or remembered his name. "I have so many grandsons," he often laughed.

Hearing this, Rashid's cheeks would burn and his heart would thump as he struggled to hide how hurt he was by the old man's indifference. If his grandfather valued him so little, *why wouldn't he let him join the rebels?*

Rashid turned his practiced impassive and empty expression on the world. Yet, he felt a festering hatred within, sapping his energy and shaming him because he knew he was always supposed to honor his male elders. The battle raged behind the boy's silent, glassy eyes; the duty to obey and accept his place was in conflict with a strong desire to reject the narrow role he had been so callously allotted. Although it was too painful to dwell on, he knew that despite all the evidence to the contrary, he still held out hope that one day his grandfather Sheikh Uthman would recognize that he was a young man worthy of his attention and esteem.

For want of anything better to do, Rashid took his daily walks through the camp, keeping an eye out for Hawa and her family. It would be a gigantic headache if Uthman had to renegotiate Rashid's marriage with another suitable family. So, he was keen to be able to report to his grandfather that Hawa's family had arrived safely.

As he patrolled the alleys and lanes, it struck Rashid as peculiar that Hawa's people weren't already there. The day before the attack on their village, Uthman had sent Rashid to visit Hawa's father, Sheikh Adam, to explain that the wedding had to be postponed, and then quietly, to warn him about the imminent attack. But instead of being grateful, his future father-in-law had narrowed his eyes. Then he had become quite brusque, failing to offer Rashid a glass of tea, as would have been polite under the circumstances.

Clearly Sheikh Adam had not acted on the warning. Why would the man choose not to save himself and his family? Perhaps they had headed for another camp, or like many others, had decided to go to Chad, Rashid reasoned.

On Rashid's daily journey through the camp, he was careful to make a thorough search of each pathway, looking for Hawa. Yet no one from Sheikh Adam's area had arrived, and no one knew what had become of their village, except that the Janjaweed had attacked it, just as Rashid had warned.

In the wake of the Sudanese regime's recent bombing offensive, the camp had grown to 25,000 huts, all arranged in rows a few feet apart. He heard one peasant complaining that it was hard for a farmer to live so close to his neighbors. "I'm used to living one hundred yards away, not one yard."

Rashid sympathized. He was also adrift, a goat herder without a herd, and a young man who yearned to be a soldier but who was forbidden to join the rebels. "This won't last long," his father had assured him. "We'll be heading home soon. End of story."

Ψ Ψ Ψ

Rashid was strolling aimlessly through the camp when, out of the corner of his eye, he thought he recognized Hawa's yellow and red embroidered shawl wrapped around the hunched-over form of a tramp. He had given the shawl to Hawa to mark their engagement.

Rashid peered at the wretched bag of bones sitting on the ground before a tiny makeshift hut, her knees pulled up, hugging her long legs. Her head was resting on her equally long arms, but she had turned away from the path so her face was not visible.

Rashid wondered if perhaps this vagabond had stolen the shawl from Hawa in another camp. Then something about the long limbs and the delicate slope of the tramp's shoulders made him hesitate.

"Hawa?" he said. "Hawa?" he raised his voice, and the body stirred. She looked up at him with red-rimmed eyes. Her cheeks were sunken, the whites of her once sparkling eyes appeared to have gone yellow, her lips were blistered, and she had lost a vast amount of weight. She blinked in the glare of the daylight, as if she had been living underground.

"It's me, Rashid," he said, feeling foolish. "Don't you recognize me?"

"I know who you are," she said at length.

"What's wrong with you?" He sounded angry rather than concerned, and she turned away, putting her head back on her knees, closing her eyes, as if she was overwhelmed by the effort of conversing.

"Where's your family?" he demanded.

She did not react.

"Hawa, you must tell me where I should go to greet your father."

She groaned and then lifted her head a fraction. "Everyone is dead," she said, letting her forehead rest on her knees once more.

Rashid froze, feeling a lump of panic rise in his throat. "I warned you to leave that place," he rasped, and then lowered his voice to a hiss, "Why didn't you go?"

Hawa glanced up and curled her lip in disgust. "My father stayed and fought for his people. He died as a man should die. Maybe you've forgotten, but that's our tradition," she added.

Rashid's cheeks burned. "Why do you speak to me with so little respect? I won't tolerate this when we are married."

"We aren't getting married," she mumbled through swollen lips. "Not after what they did to me." She watched her words register, and then she turned away. "Now, leave me alone."

Rashid stood before her, so shocked he could hardly move. Janjaweed attacks happened to other people, to the lower classes, and certainly not to the lofty family into which he was marrying. *What had Hawa done to put herself in a position where she was raped?* he wondered. He could guess how his grandfather would explain it—she had clearly offered herself to the militiamen, rather than doing the honorable thing and fighting them until they killed her. Hawa, who was to have been his property, had been shamed, defiled, and ruined.

Rashid's first instinct was to slap her until her pretty, superior face was just a bruised, rotting piece of fruit. He wanted her to beg for forgiveness, pleading to him for compassion and mercy. Instead she ignored him, just like his elders did.

"You filthy piece of garbage," he fumed. He expected her to flinch, but his words seemed to have no effect at all. "I will not marry you," he roared, spraying her with spittle.

She shifted around turning her back to him. Rashid trembled with fury, struggling to keep from hitting her. Evidently she thought no more of him than his grandfather. He had hoped that when he got married he would possess at least one person who would respect him and think him an important man. He had assumed Hawa would fear him and serve him dutifully, like a good Darfuri wife, working day and night to keep him in a good mood, as was her duty. So much for his plans for life with a pure and honorable woman.

He glared at her, his eyes stinging, his heart thumping in his chest. Finally, as he mastered the desire to hurt her, the anger was replaced by worry. If he told his grandfather what had become of Hawa, somehow, he knew, it would reflect badly on him. It always worked like that, he found. His words would be twisted, and he would look either foolish or incompetent. Rashid would be punished for the inconvenience of having to find another match. Yet, if he failed to mention that Hawa had arrived in the camp they were bound to find out eventually what had happened to Sheikh Adam. Then they would think even less of him for not passing on the important information. Dismayed by these unappealing choices, he turned away, heading slowly for home, his legs as heavy as if he had run for miles.

Hawa kept her head buried in her arms, resting on her knees, until she was sure Rashid had gone. Then she edged into her hut and lay down on her mat. She moved slowly and cautiously, as if she were made of glass. She was still suffering great discomfort from her ordeal, eight days ago. The bleeding had finally stopped, but there was a throbbing pain inside her, and she felt feverish and sick.

She had been told there was a clinic in the camp, run by kind people from overseas, but she saw no point in asking them for help. It was only right that she should die now, since she had failed in her sole mission. This morning her little nephew, born of her beloved older sister, had died. She had pulled him out of the fire in which the Sudanese army soldier had thrown him; she had carried the poor little fellow for seven days, walking through the heat of the savannah, keeping him warm through the cold nights while sleeping rough.

Yet this morning, after their first night in the camp, her little nephew had died. Her one link to her sister, her best friend in the world, was gone. Hawa could only justify her survival if she saved the last remaining male in her family. Even if one whole side of his body had been burned in the fire, at least he could have eventually fathered his own son. He could have fulfilled his role, as she would now never be able to.

Hawa shivered despite the heat, pulling the shawl tight around her, draping it over her head, giving her the privacy to cry alone. Her shoulders shuddered as she wept, and she felt as if she was convulsing, repeatedly tormented by images of the army men, forcing themselves into her.

CHAPTER ELEVEN

The officer went first because it was his privilege to have the virgins. When he finished, they held Hawa down and branded her. She felt the red-hot metal against her breast, and heard the soldiers laughing as she howled in pain and writhed on the ground.

"Look how black her skin is," the officer commented in disgust. "She's almost blue. But now you are a proper slave," the officer laughed, "And you'll have an Arab baby when we've finished with you." "We'll dilute your filthy black blood, and your race will be wiped out forever," the soldiers chanted as they circled her naked body, fingering their trouser zippers, impatient for their turn on top of her. She smelled her skin burn as they pinned her to the ground, branding her on her other breast.

She lost consciousness for a moment, and the next thing Hawa knew the soldiers had moved on to another girl, outside her compound. *Is it over? Am I alive?* she wondered, pulling herself onto her hands and knees. *I must get out of the way in case they come back.*

She crawled, naked and bleeding, to the far side of her mother's hut, out of sight, hoping she could hide. She pulled herself into a ball, trying to block out the deafening bursts of machine gun fire and the shrieks of pain as the bullets ripped into the flesh of her neighbors. She passed out once more—for how long, she didn't know—and when she regained her senses, she heard soldiers shouting nearby. *They've come back for me,* she thought. *Please, God, don't let them look behind this hut and find me. Please save me.*

She could smell the burning of thatch very close. She pulled herself onto her knees and shuffled forward, peering around the edge of the hut, trying not to reveal her presence.

She saw fires sweeping across her village, leaping like the devil from one roof to the next on every gasp of breeze. Her stomach contracted as she saw the bodies of her family scattered around the compound like broken dolls abandoned by a child having a temper tantrum.

Today was to have been Hawa's marriage to Rashid, and her extended family, including the sister to whom she was so close, had arrived yesterday in time for the celebration. However, last night Uthman had sent Rashid with a coded warning. Her father had been appalled by the assumption that he would abandon his people and had asked Rashid to leave immediately, saying he had to stop the wedding preparations.

Crouching behind her mother's hut, hoping no one would return to her part of the compound, Hawa realized that if it had not been for her impending marriage, her adored older sister would still be alive. The person she cared most about in the world was lying dead, only twenty yards away, and it was partly Hawa's fault.

From her hiding place behind the hut, Hawa saw one remaining officer moving from one hut to another, emerging with a radio and cooking pot, clothes and sacks of grain. As the commanding officer, he had the pick of the village sheikh's possessions. The other soldiers had moved on, fanning out across the village. Suddenly Hawa heard her little nephew cry out. She looked around but couldn't see him. *Be quite!* she wanted to scream at him. *Stop crying, I beg you, little one.* How had he survived, while his mother, Hawa's beloved sister, had been murdered, she wondered? Hawa peered about the compound as his wailing continued. *Stop crying!* she urged him silently.

At that moment, the officer emerged with a rug in his arms. He stopped in his tracks, eyes darting around as the crying grew louder. *Keep walking, you dog,* Hawa begged him silently. *Just keep going, away from here, away from the baby. Haven't you done enough to my family?*

The officer dropped the rug and in two strides he reached the lifeless body of Hawa's sister. *No, no!* Hawa prayed. *Just leave him on the ground and go away.* He scooped up the baby, tossing him onto the fire, as if he were a sack of garbage. Then he picked up his loot and sauntered out of the compound.

Hawa crouched behind the hut until the moment the soldier had turned his back. Then she darted forward, pulling the infant from the flames. She grabbed a robe from the pile on the ground and wrapped him in it. Then she rushed back to her hiding place.

He was still breathing but otherwise he did not move. "Don't stop fighting, little one," she whispered. "Just don't make another sound."

She examined his body, her hands trembling, and saw that the skin on one side had been burned away. Wrapping him up again, she prayed he would stay silent until the troops had gone. Beyond that, she had no idea how to save him. He was completely still, and she wondered if he was about to die.

She heard the army roaming around the village, finishing off those they had shot, and raping girls and women. She peered around the edge of the hut and saw them carrying piles of loot to their military vehicles. Then, when they had evidently taken everything that interested them, they assembled just outside Hawa's family compound. They had herded together twenty women and girls, all naked, bloody, battered, and clearly terrified of what was about to befall them. At their officer's command, the soldiers made the naked women and girls stand in a line while they tied their hands behind their backs. Then they roped them together by their throats.

It was no great mystery what would become of the women and girls. Hawa knew they would be presented to Sudanese officers as gifts, slaves in all but name, whom they could rape at will. The women would sleep on the floor of the kitchen in their master's home, be given just enough food to survive, and they would work twenty hours a day, expected to do all the domestic duties. They were also available as a source of entertainment for the family children who would be free to torment or humiliate them.

If the women lived long enough, they would inevitably get pregnant. Their offspring would be taken from them as soon as they could walk, and would be given to other families to be trained as servants to their individual requirements. The children were known to make excellent wedding presents. The captured women would often be savagely beaten by the officer's wife, who would be jealous that her husband became so aroused at the prospect of raping the young girl weeping in terror on their kitchen floor.

Hawa surreptitiously watched the girls and women, whom she had known all her life, as they were led off into the savannah at gunpoint, knowing she could so easily have been with them. Once the troops were gone, she turned her attention to the baby. His breathing was shallow and irregular, but his eyelids fluttered like the wings of a butterfly. "Hang on, my little man, and I'll get you to safety. I'll get you a doctor," she told him quietly.

She found some clothing to make herself decent, tied him onto her back, and then looked around for water. She discovered that the village well was clogged with corpses, so she went from hut to hut, frantically searching for any water containers that might have been overlooked. Finally, she found some bottles of Fanta orange, and she coaxed the baby to drink the sticky liquid. She also drank a bottle without stopping for breath, putting the remainder in a makeshift sack around her shoulders. Then, her hands still trembling and her mind numb with shock, she started walking toward El Geneina, the largest town in the area, and the place where Sheikh Uthman's family had advised them to go for safety.

"Don't give up, litle man," she begged her nephew. "I promise you we're going to be okay. Just hang on."

As Hawa trudged across the flat, arid landscape with the baby on her back, she talked to him constantly, urging him to keep fighting, telling him about the life he had ahead of him, as the leader of their family, as the sheikh of their village. *Except the village is gone and the family is dead,* she thought.

On the first day of her trek, the locals chased Hawa away from their village, clearly suspicious of a woman traveling alone. Later she stopped in an Arab community, untouched by the Sudanese government or the Janjaweed, and a local Arab family took pity on her, giving her food, water, and a place to sleep for the night. On the second day, after hours of walking in the baking sun, Hawa came to a Fur village. She had fed the last of the Fanta orange to the baby, and she knew he needed more liquid to keep his little heart beating.

Hawa approached a short, skinny, elderly woman in a faded yellow robe, working in her little garden on the edge of town. Hawa hovered by the gate, waiting for the woman to notice her. She braced herself for a cascade of abuse, but instead of censure she saw shock and then compassion in the woman's eyes. The wiry little woman put her hands to her heart and cried out.

"You poor thing," she uttered. "Where have you come from? What did they do to you?"

She gestured for Hawa to come into her hut, untying the baby from her back. Without a word of explanation from Hawa, the old woman seemed to understand what had happened.

"How can these Janjaweed men do this to us? Don't they know we're Muslims? Why do Muslims do this to other Muslims? I don't understand it," she said.

The woman, who introduced herself as Mama Mounah, told Hawa to lie down and rest while she examined the infant. She bathed the baby tenderly, singing to him as she did so. Then she applied a mixture of traditional herbs, blended into a paste with sesame seed oil, directly onto his blistered skin. Satisfied she had reduced the pain, she went off to find a mother in the village who was lactating, and when the woman joined them, half an hour later, she fed the baby. Neither the mother nor Mama Mounah asked Hawa the questions she had been bracing herself for: *Where is your husband? Why are you traveling alone? Why have you come to our village?*

As Hawa lay there, stunned and exhausted, she reflected that her own mother would have turned away these humble people had they arrived at her gate. Or she would have made a great show of helping the "poor little people" in the village, hoping that everyone would witness her kindness.

When her infant nephew was sleeping, the women turned their attention to Hawa, bathing her with the same gentle touch, dressing her burn marks, and applying ointment to her wounds. They gave her lamb to eat, a luxury even for the wealthiest family, and insisted that she sleep in the hut until she felt better.

The next thing Hawa knew, it was morning. Every step she took sent a sharp pain through her abdomen, but she felt stronger. She noticed her nephew was sleeping peacefully, his breathing normal.

When Mama Mounah returned, they sat together in the shade, sipping sweet, milky tea. At length, Mounah asked her to tell her what had happened to her village. Hawa did so haltingly, concerned that at any moment she would say something that would earn Mounah's displeasure. However, the old woman patted her hand and clicked her tongue in outrage at what Hawa and her people had endured.

Hawa completed her story with a warning, "It's only a matter of time until they do the same thing here. You must leave and go to the camp outside El Geneina."

Mama Mounah nodded, apparently unimpressed. "So they say. That's why I'm eating all my lamb. I'll be damned if some Janjaweed is going to steal my livestock. I'm going to have a real feast for a few weeks, and then they can come and kill me, if they like."

"But you can save yourself," Hawa said, surprised by her own uncharacteristic passion. She wanted to rescue this stranger who had in turn rescued her. "Come with me," she urged.

"I've been here all my life, Hawa, and I'm not shifting an inch so some filthy Janjaweed thief can take my grandmother's land."

Hawa gaped at her, impressed by her cool defiance.

"We go back generations here, we do," Mounah continued, "and we put everything we had into these fields. Before the rains stopped, this used to be a wonderful place to live," she paused, grinning. "We never had a famine, ever. Some of the Arabs used to curse us because we worked hard and grew fantastic crops. We had full bellies and strong families," she added. "We had the best wedding feasts and the most elaborate festivals with terrific displays of horsemanship. I remember the races we would have. Magnificent horses. And the singing and dancing! It went on for days, and people came from miles around to join in," she laughed, the light dancing in her bleary old eyes.

"That's our heritage you're describing, Mama," Hawa commented, moved by her passion. "We need your wisdom and your memories to pass down to my nephew and his generation. That's why you must save yourself."

The old woman shrugged, "My time's come a little earlier than it might have otherwise, but I've had a good life, dear. Anyway, it's up to you to save our tribe."

"My nephew's the last of our family line and I have to get him to safety."

"Hawa, you're also part of the family line. That's who I meant."

Hawa shook her head, looking away, "Not after what happened to me, I'm afraid."

The old woman waved her hand as if she were swatting a fly. "We're in a war, for goodness sake. Any man with a heart will understand. He'll know you had to save yourself for the sake of the baby and for the sake of our tribe. You've got enough to worry about without all that stuff about honor, dear."

Hawa raised her eyebrows in surprise.

"Oh, I've shocked you, have I?" Mama Mounah said, a crooked smile on her lips. "I'm too old to be judging people. It's the women who carry on the lifeblood of our tribe. They make the sacrifices, they work until they drop. The blood of Darfur's women has nourished this soil for a million years. This is my land just as much as it belongs to the men."

Hawa had never heard such forthright, heretical opinions. "But men have always owned everything," she ventured.

"Well, they won't own anything at this rate," Mounah commented. "Not if we don't get the white countries to help us."

"Whites?"

"Shocked again?" Mama Mounah asked, clearly amused by the effect she was having on the timid girl. "Do you care who hands you the pail of water when your house is on fire?"

Hawa shrugged. Her mother had never uttered opinions on anything beyond the domestic sphere, except to criticize others for being insufficiently pious. Hawa was startled to hear a woman talking with such confidence. "You know so much," she ventured timidly.

"I just listen to the radio, dear. And I know we need the white boys from the United Nations. If they come here, they'll find it so hot and unpleasant they'll get the job done properly and quickly, so they can go home to their snow and ice, where they're happy."

Hawa was incredulous.

"Look," Mounah continued. "They're so amazingly rich, these white boys, that our money's nothing to them. They won't take bribes to look the other way while civilians get slaughtered and women get raped. The moment they turn up, the regime's soldiers will run all the way back to Khartoum, peeing their pants like the cowards they are."

Hawa was so caught up in the old lady's fighting talk that she found herself laughing. Mama Mounah laughed too, punching the air with her fist. They laughed until the tears trickled down their cheeks.

Later, as she walked out of the village with the baby on her back once more, Hawa realized she could not recall the last time she had laughed. Her mother, so joyless compared with the other women in their village, had disapproved, saying it was unbecoming in a woman. "When your man says something he thinks is funny, you must smile. But don't laugh or he'll think you are some common old hag," she had instructed her daughters.

Her dead daughters, thought Hawa as she trudged down the road toward El Geneina. *I'm the only one left, the only survivor out of all my grandfather's daughters, too. And the baby is the only surviving son and grandson. He matters because he's a boy. And whatever Mama Mounah may say, I only matter because my job is to carry him, like a donkey transporting sacks of grain.*

Then she looked at the fields stretching flat and broad to the horizon, and she thought of Mama Mounah's stirring declaration. The blood of women had nourished the soil of Darfur. Startled by the old woman's unconventional opinions, she was also thrilled and energized by the courage it took to defy the rules, to be different. *I'm not strong enough to do that,* thought Hawa, *but I wish I was.* She kept walking toward El Geneina.

☿ ☿ ☿

Karen Freeman was a great believer in the power of prayer. As she approached the dusty border post between Sudan and Chad, she offered as many prayers heavenward as she could manage, muttering under her breath, hoping her Creator was keeping a watch over her at this moment. "Thank you, Lord," she said out loud as she set foot on Chadian soil half an hour later, her secret cargo undiscovered in her suitcase.

Her journey home was overland across Chad, and then by air from N'jamena to Paris. She planned to spend a few days in London before completing the final leg of the long journey back to New York. As soon as she reached Heathrow, she phoned Gillian Lusk, the well-respected Sudan specialist who wrote for the authoritative British newsletter, *Africa Confidential.*

"You don't know me," Karen began, "but I've just come back from the Darfuri camps, and I have something you might want to look at."

Sitting in a coffee shop, the children's drawings on her lap, Gillian's eyes grew wide. A short, middle-aged woman with salt-and-pepper hair, the journalist leafed through the pictures, taking in the startling detail, in sharp contrast to the naïve and awkward depiction of the houses and animals. Gillian reached for her phone, calling the director of a human rights group.

"Sandrine? It's Gillian. There's something here you ought to see."

米 米 米

Over the next few months Karen was amazed as the drawings were published in newspapers around the world, from Lithuania to South Africa. Children in classrooms in Italy, and in Sunday schools in California, drew pictures and sent messages addressed to Karen's Darfuri child artists. Human rights activists in Mexico sewed a quilt made up of messages of support and solidarity. Karen planned to return as soon as possible to Darfur, as soon as she could raise the money, taking the quilt and drawings with her to show the child artists that people across the world wanted them to know they were in their thoughts, and that their artistic messages had been received, loud and clear.

The International Criminal Court in The Hague also spotted the children's drawings in the press. In due course, they accepted them as evidence of genocide, providing the context for the events in Darfur. The Office of the Chief Prosecutor confirmed to Karen that the drawings would be used in an audiovisual presentation during the opening arguments in the trial of Field Marshal Omar Bashir, president of Sudan.

It was widely understood that Bashir was no more than the figurehead of the regime, a named individual in a ruthless one-party system that had stealthily placed its supporters in positions of power in each village across the country. The party controlled every aspect of national and local life, closing down media, running commercial operations, hoarding the oil revenues, arresting and silencing independent voices. But Bashir would be the one indicted for war crimes and crimes against humanity, the face the party had chosen to present to the world.

Nevertheless, even as the children's drawings appeared on television screens as far away as the Czech Republic and Hong Kong, Bashir remained in place, and Karen's young artists lived in daily fear of being attacked and murdered by the same men who had killed their fathers and brothers, their uncles and cousins.

I've got to get back to Darfur to show them what their drawings have achieved, Karen thought. *They need to know about the role they're playing in alerting the world to what is being done to their homeland. If anything can empower them and make the wait for justice more bearable, that will.*

In the meantime, Karen became an active member of the New York area branch of Save Darfur, a citizens' action group. The local founder and chair was a doctor named Rachael Bennett, whose father had, coincidentally, once taught in a little school in El Geneina.

Martin Bennett had instilled in his daughter a love and respect for the Darfuri people whom she had never met, but with whom she felt a bond. Rachael told Karen that her recent letters to her friend, Muhammad, had been unanswered, but still she wrote regularly, hoping he was receiving them, praying that he and his family were safe. And as Rachael searched the Internet for reports on the fighting in Darfur, she felt an icy hand closing around her heart whenever she read of attacks near El Geneina.

"I have to help Muhammad and his family," Rachael told her own family when they complained that she was going to yet another

Save Darfur meeting, attending yet another rally, spending yet another evening writing letters to her elected representatives or the local newspapers. "I owe them," she explained.

"What do you owe them?" countered her husband.

"They made my father the human being that he was," she said simply.

CHAPTER TWELVE

It had been two days since Zara had hidden in the canyon to avoid the helicopter gunship. Now she was walking west, hoping she would find the road leading to the border with Chad.

As she walked Zara prayed to God for strength, and for her family. She had not eaten for two days, and she had finished the last of her water several hours before. It took an enormous effort of will to think of anything except water, or how alone she was, or how scared she felt.

She trudged on, across the burning earth, her pink flip-flops on the point of disintegration, her feet aching, her head pounding. Then suddenly she recalled that she was not quite as alone in the world as she imagined. If she could make it to Chad, she would contact Rachael, her grandfather's friend in New Jersey. Perhaps she would emigrate to America, as many Sudanese had over the years, seeking an education and better prospects. The more she thought about it, the more Zara liked the plan, impossible as it sounded and unlikely as it seemed. She knew she was still a long way from safety and the regime's helicopters might easily reappear without warning.

The next moment, however, Zara nearly jumped out of her skin. A shape appeared out of the corner of her eye, and she jerked around to find a woman drawing up to her side.

The woman, who appeared to be a couple of years older than Zara, smiled and wished her peace with traditional good manners, as if they were meeting at a party, rather than on a forced march across the savannah. Zara was struck by her perfect rosebud lips and the light of intelligence dancing in her eyes. She was shorter than Zara, and more voluptuous, as far as it was possible to tell beneath her robes. Although the fabric was dirty, it was of a quality unusual in rural areas: Zara suspected her clothes were from Khartoum.

"Are you going to Chad?" the woman asked Zara conversationally in Fur.

The stranger's manner struck Zara as odd under the circumstances, but she went along with it. "I hope so."

"Can I walk with you?"

Zara smiled and introduced herself.

"I'm Safia," the woman said. "Would you like some water?" She held out a plastic bottle.

Overwhelmed that her prayers had been answered, Zara started to cry.

"Please," insisted Safia. "You need to drink this."

"I'm sorry," Zara said, after a long drink of water. "I've been alone for a while."

"Well, you're not alone now." Safia flashed her a dazzling smile and pulled her tattered red and blue scarf around her head. "Shall we go?"

Zara nodded, still unsure what to think about the confident young woman walking at her side, but relieved to be alone no longer. On they walked, chatting aimlessly but enjoyably. After talking to her sophisticated new friend for a couple of hours, Zara realized Safia had been properly educated, probably at a private boarding school in Khartoum, she guessed, which meant she was from an important family. Yet at no point did Safia mention what had happened to her, or the life she had left behind, or absent relatives, or her fears about the future.

Then, without warning, Safia reached across and grabbed Zara's hand for a moment. She squeezed it quickly, saying, "I'm glad I'm not alone anymore. We'll stick together, won't we?"

"Of course," Zara responded without missing a beat. *She's as scared as I am.*

Over the next five days, the two girls talked endlessly, discussing the African history that had so interested Zara's grandfather and father;

talking about how the global warming they heard so much about on the radio was making the Sahara spread south into what had once been good farming land, while creating floods elsewhere in Africa; and even swapping notes on the best way to add flavor to tough mutton.

They devised increasingly incredible stories to explain their presence on the Sudan-Chad border, including Safia's favorite tale about how she was escaping from a vicious and psychopathic future mother-in-law. They talked constantly, mulling over the challenges ahead. Would they be denied entry into Chad because their identity documents had been lost during their escape from the Janjaweed? How would they persuade the border guards to let them out of Sudan? These officials were representatives of the same government that was systematically killing their people, after all.

They begged for water in each village they passed through, although their route took them by many communities that had already been scorched by the Janjaweed. The stink of decomposing flesh was so powerful that even the birds avoided the area. By some unspoken agreement, neither girl mentioned the odor, nor what had happened in each village, knowing they could do nothing about it.

They're emptying our land, Zara thought. Even as they hunted through the remains of empty villages for food and water, they swapped funny stories, always pointedly avoiding the reality around them. Zara was grateful for the diverting conversation because it distracted her from the constant worry about her family.

As they scavenged, they invented a shared family history to be offered verbatim to the authorities, in case someone tried to split them up. Henceforth, they were cousins, and they would refuse to be separated. If anyone had the misfortune to ask, the girls would treat him to a long-winded account of exactly how they were related. It was a fact of life in Darfur that even illiterate people could recite complicated family trees, stretching back a dozen generations.

However when they got to the border, there was no problem crossing. The border guards were UN refugee officials rather than Sudanese officers. It seemed half of Darfur had beaten them to it. They mingled among the largest crowd Zara had ever seen, all of them dusty and just as tired as she and Safia were. Some people had salvaged a few possessions during their exodus, but most arrived at the border in the clothes they were standing in.

They waited their turn to cross the border beside a man who was weeping over his donkey. He said it had carried him for two weeks across the savannah, never complaining or being stubborn. And yet the moment they had reached the border, the poor donkey had collapsed and died, its mission complete.

Another family standing nearby had lost the ability to speak. When their turn came to give their details to the UN refugee official, none of them could say a word. Their eyes were wide and bloodshot, and the father's hands shook as if he were an old man. His wife gulped constantly, as if she was trying to swallow something stuck in her throat.

When it came to Zara's turn, she gave her full name and date of birth, and her grandfather Sheikh Muhammad's name, and the name of their village and the nearest town. The official seemed surprised that a girl so young could volunteer so many details, but the man could not know how seriously the late sheikh had taken her education.

"Some of these people have forgotten everything," he commented, shaking his head sadly. "And I'm afraid I have bad news for you. This village you come from? It was attacked earlier this week. It was on the radio," he added.

Zara stared at his lips, hoping she had misheard him. Finally she asked, "Have any of the survivors arrived here yet? My mother is called Sumah and my brother is Abdelatif. Maybe you have their names?"

"No one from that village has registered with me. I'm sorry. Perhaps they spoke to another official," he offered with an unconvincing smile.

He gave Zara a registration number and food ration cards, and assigned her to share a tent with "her cousin Safia" in Farchana camp.

Together they picked their way through the mass of people, everyone milling around, looking startled and alarmed, as if they had just been jolted awake from a bad dream. There were lines everywhere, and it took an hour and a half to fill their water container, but finally they found their way to the correct path and their allotted tent.

"We're going to be very happy here, God willing," announced Safia, as they sank to the ground on either side of the tent pole. "Luxury."

"A palace!" remarked Zara, trying not to think about the fate of her village so many miles away.

"Thank God for the United Nations," Safia yawned. Her eyelids drooped, and she eased herself onto the mat like an old woman. "I'm about to shock you, Zara, but I'm too tired to keep talking."

"Try to get some rest," Zara said.

"You need it, too," Safia mumbled. "Lie down, okay?"

"Good thinking," Zara agreed, although she doubted sleep was possible when all she could think of was the news about her village. She curled up on her mat, her heart heavy. She thanked God for bringing Safia into her life at just the right moment, but before she could ask God to look after her family, wherever they might be, she slipped blissfully into a dreamless void.

When she woke the following morning, Zara realized she had not slept so well since the torch had been thrown on her roof. Though it seemed like years ago, it had been less than two weeks.

When her companion awoke, Zara volunteered to join the water line, while Safia went to find some food. When Zara returned, she found a UN official loitering outside the tent, and her first thought was that her lie had been discovered and that she and Safia would be separated.

"You better come with me," he said. "Come quickly."

She trotted to keep up with him, terrified of what lay ahead, but as they entered the UN tent, Zara's heart stood still, and then she thanked God rapidly. Her brother, Abdelatif, was standing to one side, dressed in Western trousers and a long-sleeved shirt, with a cell phone pressed to his ear, and a look of deep concentration on his face. The moment he saw Zara, he rushed to her side, sweeping her up in his arms. As he squeezed her, the phone never left his ear, and she understood she must say nothing to interrupt his important call.

"Yes," he said in Arabic, as he set her back down on the ground, "the United Kingdom would be perfect. That's where our cousin Hasan lives, in Doncaster. Thank you, thank you!"

Then he passed the phone back to a UN official, a perspiring, balding white man who picked up the phone conversation in a language that was neither Arabic nor their tribal language. Zara realized it was English but he spoke too rapidly for her to understand.

"We've been looking everywhere for you!"

"Where did you hide?" asked Zara, suddenly feeling very young again. "Where's Mother?"

"She's in our tent, and she's fine. Anyway, where did *you* hide? We searched and searched, and then we realized you must have gone on ahead with the others."

"What others?" she asked dimly, still reeling from the shock of finding her family alive.

"The people from the village. The ones we were walking with," he reminded her gently. Then he saw her look away, upset, and he cleared his throat. "I guess they didn't make it. Sorry."

"Is Makka here?" she asked, wondering if Snowbeard's daughter had survived.

Abdelatif closed his eyes for a moment. "No."

"What happened at home?" Zara asked. "What about Father?"

Her brother avoided her eyes, "We've heard from someone who passed through the village, afterwards—after the attack." He took a deep breath. Then he shook his head and glared at the ground between his feet, covering his eyes with one hand.

It was enough to confirm Zara's worst fears. Everyone else in her family had been killed. Part of her had realized this from the start, but another part had kept hope alive, refusing to accept the likely outcome. Now she felt as if a ton of rocks had been poured into her stomach. She was hit by a wave of dizziness and staggered slightly. She steadied herself against Abdelatif, and he squeezed her hand. She silently said a prayer for the family she would not meet again on earth. They stood together in silence, each offering their own prayers.

"So," Abdelatif began after a moment, trying to sound more cheerful. "It turns out that having a cousin living in Britain is going to be a big advantage."

When Zara's eyes narrowed in confusion, he added, "Hasan."

"Have I met Hasan?" Zara asked, glancing warily toward the white man who was just finishing his phone call.

"He left years ago, but the rule is that if you have family already living in Britain, it means you have a better chance of going there, until the war's over," he added quickly.

"Have you ever met Hasan?" she asked.

Abdelatif gave her a look. "Of course not, but don't tell them that. Look, Mother and I have been here long enough to work out that this camp isn't a great place to stay. The Janjaweed come on raids across the border, and there's no one to protect us. . . ." He halted, and Zara saw the sadness in his eyes. "Well, who knows how long this is going to carry on?" he continued. "If we've got an opportunity to get out, we should take it. The Chadian government doesn't like having all these uninvited guests, and the locals are already grumbling about us taking their firewood and water. They say they're as hungry as we are, and they ask why the UN is favoring us."

At that moment, the white man summoned Abdelatif, and they were joined by a third man, a Chadian, who translated the white man's words into Arabic. Her brother wrote several notes on a pad of paper, nodding vigorously, and thanked the white man several times. After shaking hands all round, Abdelatif started for the door, putting his arm around Zara, guiding her out of the tent. "We're going to England," he announced, sounding giddy, like a little boy with a new soccer ball. "Good thing Grandfather taught you English," he added, smiling.

"He only taught me a little," Zara warned. She didn't like the sound of Hasan or England. She wanted to go to New Jersey.

Abdelatif stopped in his tracks, turning back toward the UN office. "Come on," he said quickly. He approached the translator, looking apologetic and said something quietly. The man laughed and raised his finger, as if urging patience. Then the translator retreated to the back of the tent, rummaging through a pile of cardboard boxes.

"Why aren't we going to New Jersey?" asked Zara while they waited.

"New Jersey?"

"Where Rachael lives," she said. "Martin's daughter."

Abdelatif, who had never been bewitched by their grandfather's postcard collection, shrugged. "I told you, we've got Hasan living in England already. Anyway, England's closer, for when we come back, after the war ends."

"But we have friends in New Jersey," she persisted.

"We'll see about New Jersey later, once we're all safe."

Suddenly Zara recalled Safia, feeling a stab of shame. "But we have a cousin here," she piped up, "and she *must* come with us."

"What? Who?"

Zara felt the eyes of the UN officials on her. "You remember, Uncle Daoud's fifth daughter, Safia? I will *not* go to England unless Safia's with us. We can't leave her here. All the rest of her family were killed, and we're all she has in the whole world," she added, tears springing to her eyes.

Alarmed, Abdelatif searched Zara's face. Then she saw a light flash in his pupils. "Oh, *that* Safia. I thought you meant Suleiman's Safia, the one who looks like a camel. So, she survived? God be praised. This is a day for wonderful news."

When the translator returned, carrying several English language instruction books, Abdelatif looked up and cleared his throat. "Actually, my sister tells me that one of our cousins has survived, and she has no one else in the world, so can she also come with us, please?"

The white man frowned as the words were translated into his language. Then he shifted his weight with a grunt, removed a handkerchief from his pocket and mopped his brow. He sighed, taking a swig of water from the bottle on his desk. Then he muttered something and looked back at the papers before him.

The translator smiled. "He says he's too tired to argue. Just bring him her details by this afternoon. And I'm told you want these," he added, handing Zara the books. "Your brother says you're the clever one, so you better start learning now so you can greet the Queen of England properly when you meet her."

CHAPTER THIRTEEN

Hawa felt arms around her as she was lifted. Yet, when she opened her eyes, she saw only red. There were strong arms, holding her firmly, confidently, hoisting her out of her hut as if she weighed no more than a bag of sawdust. She closed her eyes, too tired and confused to make sense of what was happening. When she opened them again, she realized the red was a man's shirt. Before her eyes was the crest of the Manchester United Football Club, a symbol recognizable across Africa.

"Ahmed?" she asked.

"Hello, Hawa," he answered, matter-of-factly. "How are you feeling?"

"Am I dead?"

"I don't think so," he said quietly.

"Are you carrying me to paradise?"

"Welcome to El Geneina."

She groaned and her head lolled on his chest once more. "Where are you taking me?"

"To the clinic. Your neighbor tells me you've been lying in that hut of yours for days."

"Ahmed?" she began, but she did not know what to say next. "Are you all right?" she asked after a moment.

He paused. "You remember what a good runner I am? How fast I am?"

"You win all the races, and one day you'll play soccer for a European team," she added.

"Well, my running was useful," he said, his voice flat.

Hawa thought about what his words implied. "What about your family?" she asked warily.

He did not answer, and she listened to his even deep breathing as he carried her along the path. Finally he said, "They couldn't run as fast."

"I'm sorry, Ahmed."

He hesitated. "And you, are you here alone?"

She knew what he was asking, and she could think of no gentle way of telling him that her older sister, whom she knew he had loved, was dead. "I'm all alone, yes."

After a moment he said, "Well, I'm glad you survived."

"Thank you," she said, resting her head against his chest. "It's a nice surprise to see you here."

They lapsed into an awkward silence, and Hawa realized it was the longest conversation they had ever had. Back in the village, Ahmed had only ever had eyes for her sister.

When they arrived at the tent with the big Red Crescent symbol on it, Ahmed set her down gently on a chair, squatting beside her to wait. "I'm going to try to translate," he told her.

"Why did you bring me here?" Hawa asked.

"You're ill and you need medical help."

"It's better for me to die," she said in a small, weak voice, avoiding his eyes.

"You survived for a reason, Hawa. God helped you, so you should make an effort to get better."

"I survived because I was supposed to save my little nephew," she sobbed, turning away to hide her tears. Then Hawa explained what had happened in her family's compound. "When we finally arrived here, the baby just gave up and died. I took him to the medical people but they said he'd gone too long without water. I gave him as much as I could find," she wept, "but it wasn't enough. And now my family's dead, and it's because of me."

"It's the fault of the officer who threw the baby on a fire," Ahmed corrected her. "And your family's alive just so long as you're alive, Hawa."

Her laugh was hollow, "You don't know what they did to me, Ahmed. No one will want to have a baby with me."

He lowered his voice. "Do you believe you're the only girl who's been attacked in that way by the regime's soldiers?"

"What do you mean?" she dried her tears on her shawl, meeting his eyes for the first time.

"Thousands of women and girls have suffered like this. It's one of our enemies' weapons of war. It's how they're trying to wipe out our race."

"Well, it's a good plan because no one will want any of us girls now."

"Not everyone feels like that, Hawa," he began, but at that moment a nurse in a white robe and headscarf came up to them. She was plump, her cheekbones were high and shapely, and she had the roundest, biggest bottom Hawa had ever seen.

When Ahmed spoke to her in Arabic, the nurse frowned.

"Do you speak Fur?" she asked Hawa abruptly. "Well then, let's try that. Excuse us," she said pointedly to Ahmed. "I'm going to examine her in private, so you should come back later."

Ahmed rose to his feet, looking startled. "Sorry, I assumed you were from the south."

The nurse's eyes seemed to bulge as she glared at him. "I *am*, but I've been in El Geneina since 2002 before the fighting started."

Ahmed stared at her, his mouth slightly open, "You've been working in this clinic since 2002?"

"And I'm a *Christian,* and this is a Western humanitarian aid agency," the nurse explained, with special emphasis on the word Christian. "Is that going to be a problem for you?" she snapped.

"May God bless you. It's very kind of you to come here to help us," Ahmed said. "And it shames us that people from the south travel all this way to help us, when our Muslim brothers are slaughtering us."

The nurse nodded, evidently satisfied, and then shooed him out of the way with a flick of her thick fingers. She turned to Hawa and began to pull up her robe. Hawa clutched at the garment, fear flashing in her eyes.

"I'm not going to eat you, girl. What's wrong?"

"It's better that I die," Hawa sobbed.

The nurse crossed her arms, not even trying to disguise her irritation. Hawa brought her legs up to her chest, despite the discomfort it caused. The nurse saw the pain register on her face.

"So you'd rather suffer than find the courage to survive?"

Hawa stared at her through bleary, bloodshot eyes.

"It's your choice, Princess," the nurse said.

Hawa frowned, "Why do you call me Princess?"

"Because even though you look like a tramp, with your filthy hair and your bloody face and your smelly body, you have your snooty little nose in the air like you're royalty. That's why," the bug-eyed nurse snapped. "You obviously have a very high opinion of yourself. I mean, you didn't even thank that boy for carrying you here."

Hawa felt tears of fury prickling her eyes. "You shouldn't talk to me like that," she fumed, looking away.

"Because I'm not as posh as you? Or is it because I'm from the south? You see the white UN workers in this camp? They think you and I are the same. That's what the regime thinks too. We're all black Africans to them, and they want us out of their country."

"What do you mean?" Hawa asked, twisting around to look at the nurse.

"Don't you know about the war in the south?"

Hawa shook her head. "I'm not educated," she explained, her face expressionless.

The nurse's eyebrows arched in surprise at the girl's bland admission. "This regime spent twenty years killing my people in the south of Sudan to get us off our land, telling us we were just slaves, and Sudan was only for their fanatical followers. They paid the local Arab nomads to sweep through our villages, looting and murdering."

"Just like here?" Hawa asked uncertainly.

The nurse nodded. "And they want to take our oil."

"That's terrible," Hawa remarked. "I didn't know that. I'm sorry."

"They've killed two million of us in the south, so far."

"Two million?!"

"It's as if every barrel of oil they take is half-filled with our blood. They've just signed a peace deal with the south, so everyone says the war's over for the time being. But that doesn't erase all the suffering."

Hawa took in the nurse's angry expression. "I'm sorry I didn't know about this, and I really don't think my tribe is superior to yours. But it's a waste of time for you to try to help me," she paused. "It's better that I die. My job was to save my nephew, but I failed in the one purpose I had on this earth, and it's God's will that I should die."

"Did He tell you so?"

Hawa's eyes narrowed suspiciously.

"I don't care what faith you are, Princess," the nurse continued. "None of us is in a position to say we know better than anyone else what God has in mind."

Startled by the nurse's words, Hawa surrendered her grip on the garment and lay back while the woman examined her wounds and burns. She was reminded of Mama Mounah and how she had touched her with such care. The nurse was also gentle, in fact gentler than her own mother had ever been. Hawa felt the tears welling up again.

"What's your name?" Hawa blurted out, to divert her thoughts from further misery.

"Mary."

"Where's your family? In the south?"

"Mostly they're dead," Mary said, putting disinfectant on Hawa's wounds.

"I'm very sorry."

The nurse concentrated on applying a cooling cream to the burns. After a moment, she resumed thoughtfully, "I know this regime well enough to tell you that when they finish the ethnic cleansing here, they'll go back to killing the people in the south." Seeing Hawa's incomprehension, she added, "You should start listening to the radio. Then you might begin to know what's going on."

"My father said the radio was for men."

Mary shook her head. "He must have been a frightened man, your father, if he needed to keep the women around him so ignorant."

"He was brave!" Hawa exclaimed.

Mary shrugged, unconvinced. "Can't you read or write?"

"My father said no one would want to marry me if I had too many ideas in my head."

The nurse snorted, "And what do you think about that now?"

Hawa was silent. Mary looked at her, adding, "Hasn't anyone ever asked you what you think?"

Hawa shook her head, tearfully, "My mother told me no one wants a girl who talks. We haven't got brains like men do."

"That's not going to get you very far in the twenty-first century, Princess."

"What do you mean?"

Mary scrutinized Hawa's burns as she talked. "We were like this in the south too, before the war. But how long do you think our tribes can carry on with no books or computers, set apart from the modern world?"

"But it's our tradition," Hawa protested.

"Just because it's a rural custom, doesn't make it a good thing."

Mary looked at Hawa's expression, finding incomprehension. "Haven't you ever asked why the men sit around chatting under the trees and the women and girls do all the work?"

"The men protect us and do the thinking and make the decisions."

"You really think so little of yourself, that you are so inferior?" asked Mary.

Hawa's eyes blazed, "Women should get married and have babies. Everything goes wrong when they get ideas in their heads. Things fall apart," she added, reciting her father's words.

"Who does it fall apart for?" Mary asked mildly. "Not for the women. Life begins when women learn to read and write, when they can pick up a book and find out that women down through the centuries have felt the same pain and joy and fear and have had the same dreams that they have."

"But we've got to have the babies and take care of the ill people and do the farm work—we can't read books, too. It's too much," Hawa whimpered, feeling panicky and frightened.

"Tell me," Mary asked. "How successful have the men been at protecting you?"

Hawa turned away, her eyes closed, weeping as she thought of her dead sister and nephew.

"Don't you see?" Mary persisted. "Our rules were made for another age when our men fought tribal battles against other men with spears and shields, not against helicopter gunships and computer-guided rockets."

Hawa shook her head saying, "You're getting me confused. Please stop it."

"You're not confused, Princess. You're waking up. Why don't you go to the literacy class in the camp? You'll pick it up fast as anything."

Hawa shook her head. "I'm stupid."

"No, you're not. And tell me, what else are you going to do here?" Mary asked, as she smoothed a large bandage over Hawa's burns. "You might as well find something useful to do, so you can read God's words for yourself."

Hawa was silent as Mary continued bandaging her. Suddenly she blurted out, "It's okay for you. You haven't been . . ." She searched for the right expression, since "rape" was an unacceptable word in her culture. "You weren't attacked, so you don't know what happened to me, or why I'm of no use to anyone."

Mary slowly opened the top two buttons of her nurse's uniform and exposed the burn mark on the swell of her left breast. "Four men raped me. They branded me like a slave and left me to die," she explained, her voice not much more than a whisper.

Hawa gaped at the burn mark, so like her own. "But you're a nurse," she sputtered in disbelief.

"And I have a university degree and a husband, in case you were wondering."

"A man married you, after what happened? What kind of man?"

Mary slipped a clean robe over Hawa's head, helping her fit her arms into the holes. "He's a doctor here, in El Geneina."

Hawa's mouth hung open, and Mary tried not to smile at the girl's astonishment. "It's quite possible to make a life for yourself, even after what was done to you, Princess."

Hawa shook her head, still tearful.

"Look," Mary persisted, "I can cure your infection, and we can treat the HIV if it turns out you've got it. And we can stop these burns getting infected, but you have to decide what you're going to do with your life now. Everything has changed."

"I haven't got the brains to change," Hawa protested, her voice a childish whine. "I'm just a girl."

Mary frowned. "Why are you such a coward?"

Hawa curled up into a ball, sobbing, "I didn't cry when they attacked me and killed my sister. So why are you calling me a coward, making me cry?"

"Because it's time you cried. And it's time you became a woman." Mary took her hand and squeezed it briefly. "A real woman is not a slave to any man, or a slave to some ancient rules that say women shouldn't have a thought between their ears."

Hawa sniffed, "But I want to be a good Muslim."

Mary handed her a pill and a mug of water. "There are lots of good Muslim women who also have brains and careers and intelligent thoughts, and who make decisions for themselves."

"Really?" Hawa asked, handing back the empty mug.

"All over the world, Muslim women are going to university, becoming doctors, lawyers, teachers, and running businesses."

"You must not say these things to me anymore. Please! You're confusing me."

Mary sighed, wiping her hands on a towel. "Women are the future of Africa, if only they realized it."

Hawa shook her head, tears seeping out of the corners of her eyes.

"Okay, Hawa, I'll leave you to sulk and feel sorry for yourself."

Hawa squeezed her eyes shut, and pulled the clean robe around her, praying that the pill would make her go to sleep.

"Let me know when you want to stop wasting oxygen and start helping the world." Mary walked away, and a moment later Hawa could hear her talking to another patient.

Please, God, let me die, thought Hawa, as she drifted into sleep.

CHAPTER FOURTEEN

Shortly after he had arrived in the refugee camp, Ahmed started to organize soccer games, knowing boys needed a way to blow off steam while they were confined in the squalid city of huts and tents. Each day just after the sun rose they played until the heat became too intense, by about eight thirty. The boys had a second match much later, when it cooled off before sunset.

Ahmed began with a team of survivors from his area, but their games attracted so much interest that before long he had an entire soccer league in the camp, villages competing against one another. After two months, he found he was doing more teaching and coaching than playing, but he was happy to stay occupied, hoping to take everyone's mind off the uncertainty and fear, as well as the monotony, that punctuated every day.

Rashid resented the way in which Ahmed assumed control of the entire league's organization. Who was he to tell the grandson of Sheikh Uthman what to do? However, he was comforted by the knowledge that when they all went home after the war, Ahmed would return to obscurity, his position in their society negligible and static. Everything would go back to normal, once they were away from the camp.

Some aspects of life remained the same, however. People from certain clusters of villages kept to themselves, speaking their own tribal languages. Their homes had been destroyed and their livestock stolen,

115

but the men were still meeting daily, discussing the news, listening to soccer games on the radio. The only change Rashid detected was that the boys were becoming less obedient than they had been, and they were questioning their parents' authority in a way that would have been unthinkable before the war.

As for the women, even though they could no longer work in their fields, their lives had a similar pattern in other ways. Each day they swept out their huts, washed clothes, went to the well for water, standing in line for hours chatting to their friends, then returning to their huts to prepare food. Babies and old people had to be cared for. And when necessary, they made the hazardous trip beyond the camp to collect firewood.

Everyone knew it was an illusion to believe the camp was safe because there were no peacekeepers guarding it; not even a fence. The Sudanese army and security services were in evidence, but that was hardly a comfort. Some survivors had been terrified to discover that the very same Janjaweed who had rampaged through their villages were now lying in wait at the perimeter of the camp.

It had become a morning ritual for the men to listen to the radio, in the shade of a tree. No one could afford coffee or cigarettes, so they sat quietly, conserving their strength, exerting no unnecessary energy in heat that reached at least 90 degrees by midmorning.

Rashid and Ahmed were regulars, listening to the news bulletins on the BBC's Arabic service. Most of the men understood some Arabic because it was the language of the Koran. To Rashid's surprise, Ahmed spoke Arabic well, having supplemented his meager schooling by listening to soccer commentaries on the radio. However, Rashid's grandfather had decreed that goat herders did not need to speak Arabic. Back in their village, when they went to sell their livestock in the nearest market town, his older brothers haggled over the price with the traders, while Rashid kept the beasts from wandering off. Furious that he had been summarily pigeonholed by his elders, Rashid had gone out of his way to pick up enough Arabic from the radio over the years to get the drift of the daily news bulletins in the camp.

Sheikh Uthman never joined the circle of men and boys beneath the tree. It was understood he was engaged in important discussions with the humanitarian agencies, and less publicly, with representatives of the rebel faction led by an influential, if feared, man from northern Darfur called Abdallah.

Rashid regularly went into his grandfather's tent, bringing him news and gossip picked up on his walks around the camp. The boy knew Uthman had his own radio, as well as a Thuraya satellite phone with which he managed his interests, including his investments in a bank in a nation unfamiliar to Rashid.

Rashid was also aware the sheikh made a habit of slipping quietly into El Geneina to manage his business interests, taking coffee in the office of the governor of the Sudanese civil authority. It was not a connection the family advertised, fearing the other camp residents might misinterpret Uthman's motives. Hence his generous and public support for Abdallah's rebels. Business was business, as the old man said.

One morning the previous week, Rashid had accompanied his grandfather into El Geneina, charged with loading two boxes onto the donkey and covering them with a blanket to obscure the UN logo. It was a symbol Rashid recognized instantly from the UN tents, grain sacks, and vehicles around the camp. He assumed the supplies were the result of his grandfather's connections.

Rashid's job that morning was to make sure the blanket remained draped over the boxes until they reached the governor's office. Once they were inside the compound and the gates had been closed, the sheikh had removed the blanket, instructing Rashid to follow him into the important man's office. Rashid had made two trips with the boxes, setting them down in a corner. There had been much hand shaking and exchanging of elaborately polite Arabic greetings between his grandfather and the governor. Rashid would have liked to stay for the meeting, to sit quietly and look around the room because it contained so many unfamiliar objects. However, his grandfather had given him a few bills and had told him to run along and buy a lamb shish kebab, and then to go home. Disappointed, Rashid obeyed, wishing his grandfather would not always dismiss him so easily.

¥ ¥ ¥

The radio news bulletin on the BBC's Arabic service contained a report about a "breakthrough in the Darfur peace process." Abdallah's rebel faction, Uthman's friends, had signed a peace agreement with the Khartoum regime. Those listening, including Rashid, sat up straighter, as if it might help them focus their attention. They listened as a British politician was interviewed.

"After my meeting today, we have a four-point plan to ensure the future security of Darfur, and we'll be holding the Sudanese government to its commitment," he concluded, sounding satisfied with his achievements.

There followed a clip of Sudan's president, Field Marshall Bashir, saying there was a Zionist conspiracy to re-colonize Sudan, to get its oil. Bashir declared himself a man of peace who had worked hard to bring stability to his country and to bring progress to the simple people of Darfur.

The men and boys listening to the broadcast were mystified when the bulletin moved swiftly to another subject.

"Bashir's always signing four-point plans," said one of the men. "They're idiots if they believe what Bashir tells them." "Why don't these foreigners stop selling weapons to the regime?" said another. "And create a no-fly zone over Darfur, to stop them bombing us."

Heads nodded, and their conversation gradually settled on the same unhappy central truth—no one was coming to help Darfur.

и и и

After dinner that evening, as Rashid was leaving his grandfather's tent where the men of the family ate, the sheikh called him back.

"Stop a moment, boy," he said, and then turned to Rashid's father. "Tell him not to go out tonight. Tell him to stay here."

Rashid tried not to smart as the sheikh yet again forgot his name. He also knew that his grandfather had no idea where he went each evening, nor did his father. Rashid had been intending to join Ahmed's soccer game. It was his favorite moment of the day, when he could forget he was stuck in a camp with thousands of other refugees. Disappointed, Rashid returned to his father's side and passed the evening listening to his conversation, although he was at no point included in it.

� � �

Ahmed's team usually had more players than were needed, so Rashid's absence was not noticed. The boys were using an African soccer ball — that is dozens of plastic bags, skillfully wound tightly like a ball of thread to make a light yet durable ball. They played barefoot because flip-flops were impractical. Although only a few of them had eaten properly during the day, they tore across the patch of barren land that served as their playing field. They were watched by a crowd of about three hundred or so enthusiastic boys, cheering and jumping up and down.

Ten minutes into their game their shouts were drowned out by the roar of engines. One by one the players stopped, looking around for the source of the noise. At this time in the evening, the humanitarian workers were long gone, back to their gated compounds in town, and no trucks or jeeps were seen in the camp.

Searchlights jerkily scanned across the huts as the vehicles rocked across the rutted ground. Brakes squealed and orders were shouted out in Arabic, followed by the drumming of boots on the metal tailgate of a military truck.

The soccer fans began running, and in the gathering dusk they tripped and fell in their panic. There were cries as bones broke and people were crushed. Ahmed headed toward Hawa's hut, his legs carrying him like a streak of lightning across the field and into the maze of alleys. He heard screams, and more Arabic shouts, then a sound like firecrackers, and more screams.

A massive bulldozer, its lights blazing, ground forward, crushing huts. Walls made of interwoven reeds and branches were no match for the mechanical monster. Behind it was a trail of chewed-up plastic sheeting, and a few meager possessions. In its wake were several jeeps and two military trucks. Fanning out from them were forty or so Sudanese army soldiers, swinging batons at survivors. The soldiers pressed forward, shooting above peoples' heads as they emerged from their huts. Women carrying babies, and the elderly, who did not move quickly enough, were thumped with batons. Many collapsed and were beaten, their screams drowned out by the roar of the bulldozer mowing down huts.

Ahmed changed direction, avoiding the soldiers and the flood of terrified survivors. He found Hawa standing by her doorway, hugging herself, her eyes wide.

"They're knocking down huts," he blurted. "Come on."

As he pulled her along she asked him, "Why are they doing this?"

"I guess they want to scare us, to remind us they're in charge."

"Are they going to wreck the whole camp?"

"Not so long as the UN people are here. It's the only thing that stops them slaughtering us, just having the UN here. Thank God."

Just then the sound of the bulldozer ceased abruptly, and the wailing of injured and terrified people welled up. A public speaker system crackled into life.

"You must gather around," said a voice in Arabic. "Come and listen. We will not hurt you."

At that moment several soldiers appeared, swinging their batons in a wide arc. "Move now, you slaves! Get going!" they shouted, advancing on the crowd, herding them toward the bulldozer. Ahmed pulled Hawa out of the soldiers' path, but they were carried along in the wave of bewildered refugees stumbling toward the amplified voice. Ahmed took Hawa's arm, peering to the left and right, seeking an escape route. "Be ready to run," he told her. Petrified, she stood as close to him as she could.

Several soldiers hoisted a Sudanese army officer onto the tailgate of a military truck. Two sergeants followed him, handed him a bullhorn, and stood respectfully one step behind him.

"It is time for you to go home," the officer began in Arabic. "The rebels have signed a peace deal and the war is over. You must return to your villages immediately." He hesitated, "This camp is being closed down."

His words were translated into Fur and then Masseleit and Zaghawa, the other main languages in the region. "You must be gone by noon tomorrow. This is your final warning."

The crowd stayed where it was, too astonished to move. They looked at each other in disbelief, hoping for clarification, assuming they had misunderstood. The vehicles roared into life, the soldiers piled in, and they crunched over the detritus, back toward El Geneina.

Hawa, stunned and frightened, felt Ahmed tugging at her arm. "Come on. Quickly," he hissed.

She followed close behind him as he dodged through the crowd toward the section where the bulldozer had rampaged. Several people lay on the ground, relatives hovering, offering comfort or trying to lift them without causing more pain. Five bodies had been covered with pieces of plastic sheeting.

Ahmed squatted beside a woman who seemed to be alone, a baby in her arms. "Have you got any family here?" he asked.

She shook her head.

"Do you think you can move?"

She covered her eyes with one trembling hand.

"Can I look at your injury?" Ahmed asked gently.

"Let me hold your baby," Hawa offered.

The woman passed the bundle to the girl. Then she pulled away her robe, exposing a mangled lower leg, white bone emerging from a mass of blood and flesh, her foot pointing in an unnatural direction.

A moment later Hawa was carrying the baby, following Ahmed through the crowd, the injured woman sagging in his arms. They found hundreds of people in various states of distress and injury on the ground outside the clinic tent. Many held rags to their wounds and others were unconscious, guarded by fretful relatives. Infants howled, and children looked on, their eyes wide with fear and incomprehension.

"Stay with her," said Ahmed, setting the woman down gently. "Keep her talking so she doesn't go into shock," he instructed.

Hawa watched him pick his way over the legs of the wounded into the tent. Then she sat back to back with the woman, allowing her to rest against her, but not to slump down.

"It's okay, I've got your child," she said, looking at the infant's face. "Tell me about your baby."

"What?" the woman asked faintly.

"Talk to me about your baby. Where are you from? Tell me your story," Hawa prompted.

Presently Ahmed returned with Mary, the nurse from the south. After one glance at the woman's wound, Mary indicated Ahmed should bring her into the tent. "Let's see what we can do."

Hawa followed, watching as Ahmed laid the woman on half of a narrow cot, shared head-to-toe with another woman, also with a leg injury. Hawa sat on the floor beside them, "I've got your little boy," she assured the woman. "He's doing fine."

"I'm going back," Ahmed told her. "Take care of them."

She watched him leave the tent, fearful and wishing he would stay with her, but knowing it would make no difference, even if she begged him to stay. It puzzled her that Ahmed visited her hut each day, asking how she was. Hawa enjoyed seeing him, but she wondered if she was his last link to her older sister whom he had loved.

The nurse glanced at Hawa. "Take her baby and find him some formula while I try to help this woman. Just tell one of my colleagues Mary sent you."

A moment later, Hawa was preparing formula for another twelve babies, all of whom had been brought in with injured mothers.

"Clean them up while you're at it. And make sure none of them have been hurt," a harassed nurse instructed, evidently assuming Hawa was one of the clinic's volunteers. Bewildered at first, Hawa shook herself into action, wondering when and if Ahmed would return.

Throughout the night Hawa took care of all thirteen infants, rocking the ones who cried, feeding, then cleaning and dressing the wounds on two of them. Ahmed returned with an old woman in his arms, and then he asked Mary how he could assist her. The clinic had run out of pills or injections to reduce pain, except for aspirin, so Ahmed dispensed the aspirin where needed, helping people sip water from a communal mug, getting patients as comfortable as possible. He kept an elderly man company while he died, praying with him, and then carried his body out to the Red Crescent truck that carted the bodies away whenever it had a full load.

At seven o'clock the following morning, a white doctor was scheduled to arrive, but the police prevented her from driving to the camp from El Geneina, saying she lacked a permit required by a new law that had not existed the day before. When a nurse arrived to take over from the night volunteers two hours later, Ahmed and Hawa stumbled out into the new day, their heads swimming.

"Look," he remarked, as they stood side by side, surveying the camp. "No one's leaving."

"Where are they supposed to go?" Hawa asked.

"Chad?" he suggested, knowing she would shake her head. "What if the army comes back at noon?"

Hawa glanced around at camp life going on as usual. "Darfur's where we belong."

"You're not going?"

"All I have is the land farmed by my great-grandfather and his great-grandfather." She paused, recalling Mama Mounah's words. "Actually, it was my great-grandmother who farmed it."

At that moment, Mary appeared at their side, blinking in the sunshine. "It looks like we're going to be short staffed tonight again, so I'll see you both back here. You," she pointed bossily at Hawa, "at seven, and you, after your soccer game." Retreating into her tent, she called over her shoulder, "Go and get some rest, or you'll be no use to me."

ӂ   ӂ   ӂ

By the end of the following shift, Hawa knew how to clean and dress wounds. Although it was strictly against the rules set down by the Dutch NGO that paid for the clinic, Mary explained that capable local volunteers found themselves performing medical procedures such as stitching up wounds in the absence of professional staff.

Mary showed Hawa their tiny collection of medicine, explaining each pill's use. "We're always short of drugs because the authorities hold up shipments at the ports, or they stop our convoys. And the Janjaweed steal the medicine that makes it this far," she explained. "We try to make our patients' death a bit easier with an aspirin," she added. "You'll soon learn to judge who's on the way out and who's going to hang on."

Hawa could not read the labels so she memorized the brand logos, colors, and shapes of the pills. "We must get you literate," Mary said.

Hawa hung her head. "It'll be too difficult for me," she murmured. "No it won't!" Mary countered, meeting the girl's fearful eyes. "You didn't think you could dress wounds, and already you're the best one here."

Hawa shrugged, her attention rooted on the medicine bottles, terrified she would make a mistake and be asked to leave the clinic. The prospect of going back to her solitary life in her hut was too much to bear. Yet, she still could not quite believe she could be of any use to anyone. Even Ahmed had praised her for her competent manner with the patients.

"You treat them with respect, and yet you also show them you care," he had observed earlier that day. *Once he realizes I'm so inferior to my sister, he'll lose interest,* she worried.

Later, when Mary, Hawa, Ahmed, and the other volunteers were sitting outside the tent, having a cup of tea, Ahmed asked if anyone knew what had become of the army's threats to empty the camp. The army had not appeared at noon, and no survivors had left.

"Political pressure," Mary said without missing a beat. "The Americans made a fuss, and President Bashir backed down, as he always does when someone stands up to him. It was on the news."

"Our camp was on the news? The BBC?" asked Hawa, astonished.

"Voice of America. That's what my husband listens to. Better basketball coverage," she explained. "My husband said one of the foreigners visiting the camp this week called an American journalist," Mary explained, cupping her hands around the mug. "He got a clip of the bulldozer on his cell phone. It's only a few seconds but it shows the army at work. The Americans broadcast it, and the American government called Bashir and told him to stop it. And he did."

Hawa was so astonished she didn't know where to begin. "We're so lucky there was a foreigner here. I haven't seen many around."

"That's because the regime keeps them out," Mary said between sips of the sweet tea. "They don't want them seeing what's going on here, and even when doctors get a visa, the soldiers are forever pulling over their vehicles and arguing with them about their permits and trying to stop them from bringing us medicine."

"I don't understand," Hawa confessed, feeling foolish. "If a phone call from the Americans can stop them from destroying our camp, why don't all the countries of the world phone Bashir?"

"It's politics, like so many things in Africa," Mary replied, smacking her lips as she drained her mug of tea.

Hawa frowned. "What do you mean?"

"The big men in Africa keep friendly with each other in case there's a business deal to be done; one day they may need support at the United Nations. They all understand the game."

Hawa's eyes flashed. "But it isn't a game like basketball or soccer."

Mary smiled, registering Hawa's anger, "That's exactly what it is for these splendid leaders of ours."

"They probably take their soccer more seriously," Ahmed grumbled.

"We have to make the international leaders phone Bashir all the time," Hawa said, her fists bouncing on her knees.

"Ha!" Mary laughed. "I met a journalist from Canada when I was in the south, during the war. She told me she kept sending her editor stories about the terrible things that were happening, and her editor said, 'Let us know when there's something new.' And she replied, 'Here's what's new. Another 500 kids have fled from their homes, and 2000 people were killed this week.' And the editor said, 'That's not new.' She was really unhappy about it, this Canadian girl, but she found quirky, amusing stories instead, and it turns out that's what her editor wanted."

"What do you mean 'quirky'?" asked Hawa.

"Stories that show Africans are quaint. For instance, old men reminiscing about the last time they stalked a lion with a spear, or what hippo tastes like. Or a man being forced to marry a goat."

"A goat?" Hawa's eyes widened.

"A court made a man marry a goat because he kept having sex with it."

Hawa shook her head. "It's shameful that the foreigners think we're like that."

"Or they like stories about one individual African and his courageous struggle against adversity. No one is interested in 500 children, but a good journalist can make them care about one pretty little kid, if you spin a nice, sentimental story about him."

Hawa looked confused. "Why?"

"Because they don't think we're quite as human as they are, but if you give one cute kid a face and a story, then there's a connection," Mary explained.

Hawa studied her mug of tea. Ahmed watched her carefully and then turned to Mary. "I'm going to be late tomorrow because there's a meeting."

"What kind of meeting?" Hawa looked up, curious.

"Ha!" Mary said. "I think I can guess."

"The rebels are coming to see us," he said quietly.

"Yes, but which rebels? The thieves, or the guys who say they're fighting for us?" Mary asked with a shake of her head. "We went through this in the south, and you don't want to get involved, Ahmed, believe me."

"It's because of the rebels that you eventually got a peace deal in the south," he said.

"After twenty years of bloodshed," Mary shot back. She handed Hawa her empty mug, the discussion terminated abruptly. "Once you've washed up, I need you to hold down that man over there while I try and find the bullet inside his arm." Hawa nodded. "And I want you to work out a rotation for all the volunteers so we always have enough people here to help."

"Me?" asked Hawa in disbelief. "I can't write a rotation?"

"Well, from now on, you're in charge of all the volunteers, so you better learn to write pretty fast, my girl."

Hawa's eye widened, and she watched Mary's enormous bottom as it retreated into the clinic tent.

I'm going to fail at the first test she's set me, Hawa reflected, walking back to her hut in a gloomy fog. *She'll tell me to go away and not return. There's no room for someone like me at the clinic.* She felt profoundly sad as she reached her little home, fearing she was destined to spend her days alone in her hut.

I really want to work at the clinic each day. Then she considered her options as she settled down on her mat. *I'll ask Ahmed for help, and maybe he'll take pity on me. Or maybe he won't. I just don't want to disappoint Mary,* she thought as she plunged into an exhausted sleep.

꙳ ꙳ ꙳

The following day, Ahmed started out for the meeting as soon as his soccer game ended. Rashid caught up with him, as he threaded his way along the narrow pathways in between huts.

"Are you still working at the clinic every night?" Rashid asked.

"They need help."

"What are they paying you?"

"I'm a volunteer," Ahmed retorted, increasing his pace, trying to shake off Rashid.

"You're joking! Are you crazy? You should make them pay you."

Ahmed clicked his tongue. "They don't have enough money for bandages, so how can they pay someone like me, with no skills?"

Rashid laughed contemptuously. "They've got enough money to buy land cruisers and pay those doctors a fortune."

"By the standards they're used to in the countries they come from, they're earning very little here, Rashid."

"Oh? So why are they here?"

"Some of them are driven by their religious faith to help other human beings, and others just think it's the right thing to do. They risk their lives to do what they believe is morally right."

Rashid was quiet for a moment, panting as he struggled to keep up with Ahmed. "You should ask them for money."

"I'm happy to have something useful to do. In case you hadn't noticed, it's boring in this place," snorted Ahmed. "Apart from when they're trying to kill us."

Rashid made a noncommittal noise, unable to think of a suitable response. Somehow, Ahmed always made him feel small and childish.

"I'm embarrassed by the teachers in this camp who refuse to give lessons because they want to be paid," Ahmed continued testily. "They'd rather sit around, complaining, while there're hundreds of kids here they could be teaching to read and write."

"My grandfather says it isn't the African way," Rashid added. "All this education."

"Then why do millions of African kids all over the continent get up at five in the morning and walk three or four miles to school?" Ahmed asked rhetorically. "They sit there learning all day, on an empty stomach, and walk back home again. And then they do the household chores, and they beg for the chance to go to those schools."

When there was no response from Rashid, he continued: "Your family is so rich, you don't think you need to improve yourself. Everything's been given to you."

"You can't talk to me like that!"

"Oh? Are you going to run back to your granddaddy and tattle like a little boy?" Ahmed taunted.

"What do you mean?"

"You betray people," Ahmed said without emotion. "That's why they hate you."

"They respect my family because we're powerful," Rashid sputtered.

Ahmed laughed. "I've survived the Janjaweed, which is more than you have, and I'm not afraid of you or your family."

When Rashid said nothing Ahmed added, "My parents would have given anything to send me to high school."

Rashid lapsed into silence but as they approached the crowd, Ahmed leaned toward him and whispered, "Hawa isn't too proud to volunteer at the clinic."

Rashid grabbed his arm and spun him around. "She's lower than a dog!"

"She faced down the soldiers while you ran away, hiding beneath your granddaddy's robe." Ahmed said, crushing Rashid's fingers in his large hand. "I guess you're here to spy on the rebels, eh?"

"My grandfather supports the rebels," Rashid spat after Ahmed's retreating back. "He's very generous."

Ahmed swung around, his eyes blazing. "Yeah, he's generous with the medicine and food that's meant to go to the refugees here, not to Abdallah's traitors."

"No!" Rashid shouted.

"Abdallah sold out his own people for a bag of gold. He's been made vice president of the regime."

"You're telling lies!" Rashid screamed at him.

Ahmed stalked off to sit near the front of the gathering.

To Rashid's embarrassment, the rebel commander opened the meeting by denouncing Abdallah's now infamous deal. The audience was instantly on its feet, punching the air and demanding that Abdallah and his band of traitors be hanged. The commander, dressed in military fatigues and an Arnold Schwarzenegger t-shirt, strutted back and forth, punctuating his words with sharp jabbing gestures.

"We cannot give up now," the commander continued. "We must strengthen our resolve. We need as many men as possible to join us. Now is the moment to come to the rescue of your people."

Having been boisterous and rowdy, the crowd abruptly became silent, sobered by the thought of making a personal sacrifice.

"We need money for weapons and ammunition, and we need brave men to help us protect our villages and stop the Janjaweed from killing our baby boys and attacking our women," the commander said. "Let me see some courageous men volunteer to come with us to defend Darfur," he asked, with a theatrical gesture.

"I'll volunteer," shouted a young man, raising his hand. When he stood, everyone applauded, relieved someone had done the decent thing. The rebel commander beckoned him to the front of the meeting. "This is a real man," he declared. "This is the lion who will build the new Darfur."

Another young man got to his feet and was brought to the front as the crowd cheered and applauded. And so it continued until seventeen young men were standing at the commander's side, basking in the admiration of the audience.

Rashid slipped away before the end of the meeting, wandering home across the garbage-strewn sector where hundreds of huts had been destroyed by the army's bulldozer.

I want to be a warrior, like those volunteers, he thought. *Maybe I can rescue our family's honor if I join up and fight.*

Yet, he quaked at the prospect of confronting his grandfather, Sheikh Uthman, and he hated himself for it. As he walked, he reflected that when he had finally mentioned to his grandfather that Hawa had arrived in the camp and was the only survivor of her family, his grandfather had been totally uninterested. With Sheikh Adam dead, there was no need for the connection, he said, and the question of Rashid's future had not been discussed, evidently a matter of little importance.

I'll make you change your mind, thought Rashid, nearing home. *One day you'll apologize for misjudging me. One day, I'll be a rebel hero.*

Ahmed also left early, going directly to the clinic. As they prepared bandages from bits of old rags, he gave Mary and Hawa edited highlights of the meeting he had attended.

"I pray to God you aren't going to do something crazy like join these rebels," Mary commented. "Apart from anything else, we need you here." She shared a look of dread with Hawa, who nodded.

"You must stay here, please, Ahmed," the girl added, not daring to meet his eyes. When he shrugged Hawa felt disappointed. *Perhaps his interest in me, or the memory of my sister at least, is entirely in my head after all.*

Ahmed busied himself washing out the pail that served as a bedpan, but Mary planted herself in front of him, unwilling to be dismissed so easily. "Look, Ahmed, you're doing more good here than you could ever achieve with those rebels."

Ahmed avoided her steady gaze. "Most of our rebels are doing a good job," he said. "Not all of them are scoundrels, but if I'm going to stay here, you better make sure you keep me busy."

During the night several patients who had been injured by the bulldozer died as Hawa sat beside them, tending to their wounds or just holding their hands.

By four o'clock in the morning, things were quiet enough for the staff and volunteers to take a tea break, sitting on low wooden benches outside the clinic. Hawa, exhausted and stunned, sat to one side, peering into her tea mug.

Terrified of disappointing Mary, Hawa had asked Ahmed to help her memorize how to write the name of each volunteer in Arabic. During the day, before their shift had begun, Ahmed had written out all the names, and the alphabet, for her. To her surprise, she had been able to complete a simple rotation. When Mary eased herself down onto the bench beside her, the girl wondered if the nurse would criticize her child-like effort.

"Thanks for the rotation list," she said at length. "It would be a big help if you could be in charge of all that from now on—scheduling the volunteers and the staff."

Hawa nodded, quietly thrilled, and they sat in a comfortable silence for a few minutes. Suddenly Hawa blurted out, "Where do you get so much strength?"

Mary laughed softly. "Oh, that's no mystery, Princess; my father."

"Please tell me about him."

Mary settled herself on the bench. "Well, he taught me that God created all of us as equals, and although we may grow up in different faiths and nations, we're really all the children of Abraham, so we shouldn't fight with each other. We should live and let live."

"What do you mean about Abraham?"

"Abraham's descendants went on to found three religions—Islam, Judaism, and Christianity. And all three faiths accept the Old Testament of the Bible as a holy book."

"I didn't know that."

Mary sighed. "People seem to have forgotten it. You know, a thousand years ago, when the Arabs had a great empire, they allowed the Christians and Jews they ruled to practice their own faith. They taxed them, but they tolerated them. My father told me all about it." She smiled to herself. "My brothers and sisters, we would gather around him at the end of the day, and he would explain what was happening in the war in the south, and why our people were dying. He said most Muslims wanted peace, but not the ones who were running Sudan. And my father, being the man he was, told everyone what he thought."

"What happened to him?"

"He was always being arrested and beaten by the security people because he was a Christian and a leader. The regime wanted everyone in the south to obey Sharia laws, even though we weren't Muslims, and my father refused to be ruled by a faith that wasn't his own. He wasn't against the Muslims, you understand, but he wanted the right to follow his own faith in peace. So, he paid the price." She paused and sipped her tea, looking out into the darkness. "They came for him one day, and we never saw him again."

"I'm very sorry," Hawa said, thinking about the sacrifice her own father had made defending his village. She admired him, but she couldn't honestly say she missed him. "I bet your father would be very proud of you," she ventured. "If he knew all the good things you'd done with your life."

Mary chuckled. "Oh, my father knows exactly what I've been doing. And so do my mother and my brothers and sisters."

Hawa peered at her, confused.

"I carry them around with me," Mary continued, her voice melodious and happy. "It's like having them sitting on my shoulder, these dead people, giving me their advice and support, encouraging me when I feel like giving up. They're always there when I need them."

"I wish my sister was with me."

"She is," Mary replied without missing a beat. "Just open your heart and you'll find she's been there all the time."

Hawa hung her head in her hands, finally allowing the tears to come. As she sobbed, Mary rubbed the girl's back until she was quiet. When Hawa pulled herself up straight once more, she took a deep breath. "My sister tells me it's time I got back to work," she said, offering Mary a small smile.

CHAPTER FIFTEEN

"Are you a Paki or what?" the scrawny young white woman demanded.

"Please repeat?" asked Zara. She and her family had been in Britain for six months, but she still struggled to understand the locals when they spoke quickly.

"Are you a bloody Paki?" The young woman's grey cheeks flushed pink, Zara noticed with alarm, and her nostrils were as red as the pustules on her forehead. She swung her long, lank blonde hair out of her eyes, but it flopped back again immediately, only increasing the girl's irritation. "Are you bloody deaf?"

Zara took a step back, frightened by the young woman's harsh tone and expression. "I come from Darfur. There is a war in my country."

She had been careful to learn that phrase, using it often since arriving in Britain in February. Although she was dressed in her school uniform with a matching navy blue headscarf, Zara guessed she still looked exotic to the locals. What puzzled her about the angry young woman's tirade was that people from Pakistan had light brown skin and Caucasian features, and could be easily distinguished from Africans. *How could the young woman mistake me for them?* she wondered.

"Well, you should piss off back to wherever you come from, and stop scrounging off us," the young woman spat, her arms rigid at her side. In one fist, Zara noticed, she gripped a white plastic shopping bag,

133

bulging with purchases, in the other a smoldering cigarette. "You and your terrorist friends, you should all be sent back," the young woman added with a furious toss of her hair. "Britain should be for the British!"

Before Zara could formulate a reply, the young woman stalked off. Shaken by the bewildering exchange, Zara hurried back to the apartment in the housing project, wondering what she had done to upset the white woman. She dissected their discordant encounter, word by word, searching for clues.

Zara wondered if the young woman had been in the supermarket, witnessing her make a mistake of some kind. Zara had smiled politely at the cashier, saying please and thank you repeatedly. But the cultural rituals of the English were still a mystery to her. Evidently Zara had inadvertently committed a social sin. Yet, the woman on the cash register had not been angry; nor had the old man standing in line behind her. In fact, he had made a friendly comment about the weather. "I expect you find this cold," he'd said to Zara with a sympathetic twinkle in his eyes. Not like the fierce young woman finishing her cigarette outside the betting shop.

Grey faces, grey sky, grey earth, and grey buildings. *So many unhappy people*, Zara thought, picking her way along the garbage-strewn path from the sidewalk to the apartment lobby. The skyline of Doncaster was like a hundred dirty, broken teeth—tall, ugly apartment blocks made of stained concrete, none of which looked like the Chrysler Building she had admired on her grandfather's postcards.

The lobby door hung off its hinges, and the floor was awash with empty cartons from the Chinese carry-out restaurant. Zara crossed the vestibule as quickly as possible; it smelt strongly of urine and vomit. The stairs weren't much better; greasy fast-food wrappers, hypodermic needles, empty cigarette packets, and used condoms. There was also evidence that people used the stairs as a bathroom. Zara found this puzzling in a country where everyone had a flushing toilet inside their homes.

The elevator was usually out of order, so Zara climbed the stairs, all ninety-two of them, as she did each day after school, bringing back food from the store. Her mother was afraid of going to the supermarket because a man had pointed at the pregnant swell beneath her mother's robe, commenting harshly. Zara did not know what his words meant, but the man had pushed past them aggressively. Another mysterious social exchange and another mistake by the recent arrivals from Sudan.

Her mother Sumah had announced she was pregnant soon after they had arrived in England, while they were at the hostel for asylum seekers. She told the girls she reckoned it had happened on the final night they spent in the village. Zara had worried that her mother's condition would make her miserable, reminding her constantly of her dead husband. But the opposite seemed to be the case—Sumah took joy from having a living part of her beloved husband within her. "God has sent this baby to comfort me," she told them, weeping bittersweet tears.

When Zara reached the fifth floor, a neighbor was emerging into the corridor from her apartment next door to Zara's home. She knew the woman's name was Mrs. Edwards because last week Zara had handed her some letters that had been pushed through Zara's family's door by mistake. Zara had knocked on her neighbor's door, holding out the mail. "Please, Mrs.," she had smiled.

The woman had looked terrified, snatching the letters from Zara's hand. "I suppose you'll be stealing anything that isn't bolted to the floor," she had remarked sourly, slamming the door.

The following day Safia had offered to carry Mrs. Edwards's grocery bags up the ninety-two steps, but their neighbor had called her a "bloody thief," refusing to walk up the stairs at the same time as Safia.

Now, Zara held the door from the corridor to the stairs open for Mrs. Edwards. The woman stopped in her tracks, looking Zara up and down as if she were a wild animal.

"Good afternoon," said Zara with a dazzling smile, hoping to assure the old woman she was not a terrorist or a thief.

Mrs. Edwards rushed past, scuttling down the stairs as if she feared Zara would chase her and rip out her throat.

Why were her eyes so unkind? Zara wondered, searching her pockets for the key. Mrs. Edwards' icy blue and green irises cut through her in a way the liquid brown eyes of Africa never did.

The girl had been puzzled that people in Doncaster walked about avoiding eye contact, passing each other in the street without a word of greeting, pretending to be alone on the planet, struggling along in miserable solitude. The only time people talked was when the bus was late, and then everyone grumbled. But as the bus heaved into view it was back to scowling. They were so rich, these people, and yet no one sang in the morning.

Even in the poorest African village, people began the day with a song. They swept out their huts and they sang. They walked to the well and they sang. And the old people had someone to talk to, someone's baby to keep an eye on, or a child to whom they could relate an ancient story or a favorite joke.

It made Zara wonder, yet again, how long they would be stuck in Doncaster, a cold, sad town in the northeast of England, rather than in New Jersey, land of sunshine and beautiful, smiling people.

But as Zara stepped into their apartment, her troubles vanished. Her older brother Abdelatif waved at her to join him on the sofa, beside Sumah and Safia.

"Quickly," he said, pointing at the television. On the screen was a black man in a business suit and tie. The nameplate before him said "United Nations Secretary General."

Zara let the shopping bags sink to the floor, easing herself onto the sofa beside Sumah. Straining her ears to catch the man on the television's exact words, she heard him mention genocide. Then, helpfully, a strip appeared at the bottom of the screen reading, "Breaking News: We will never let Rwandan genocide happen again — Annan."

Zara's pulse quickened, and she blinked tears from her eyes. The camera abruptly left the black man, returning to the television studio, where a woman newsreader had a picture of a refugee camp floating in the air over her left shoulder.

"Just to recap," she said, "the United Nations Secretary General, Kofi Annan, says under the new Responsibility to Protect doctrine approved by the UN today, nations will have a right and an obligation to intervene to stop genocide wherever it occurs."

"What did she say?" asked Sumah, turning to her daughter.

As Zara translated, Abdelatif, Sumah, and Safia began weeping.

"This is what we've been waiting for," said her brother through his tears. "Now America will save us. The dictatorship will collapse, and we'll have democracy, with free speech, just like in America!"

He reached for his cell phone and called Ismael, his new Darfuri friend in the nearby city of Leeds. As soon as they had arrived in Doncaster, their cousin Hasan, who had vouched for them with the British immigration authorities, had given Abdelatif a phone number to reach Ismael, a recent immigrant who was active in the Sudanese Diaspora in the north of England. Now they were all involved in the British Council of Darfuri Refugees, a fact that pleased Zara because it gave her brother something to do.

Zara could not recall her brother sounding so happy in months, and seeing his joy at the news from America felt like a weight being lifted off her shoulders. She too was excited by Kofi Annan's announcement, but she didn't claim to understand what his fine words might lead to. In fact, she was afraid of looking too far ahead, or being too optimistic. She survived by taking each day at a time, learning a few more words of English, and counting her blessings they had survived.

It had been an exhausting journey to Britain, over three days and via several places, followed by five hours waiting at the airport in London for an interview with the immigration official. Through the translator they had explained many times why they considered themselves to be refugees seeking asylum from political persecution. The official had a cold, and seemed more concerned with his dripping nose and the text messages coming through to his cell phone than with the death of Zara's family, and their connection to Hasan, who was now a British subject, living in Doncaster.

Finally, the family had been sent to a hostel for asylum seekers for seven weeks, during which Zara and Safia had kept their heads down, learning English together. Then came a month in a dispersal hostel, awaiting a place in a public housing project near their cousin in the north of England.

As soon as they were allocated their apartment in Doncaster, Zara and Safia started school, several years behind their local peers, but nevertheless incredibly proud of their uniforms. All summer the girls attended every free class they could find, polishing their English. Abdelatif, however, hung around like a limp garment drying on a bush. He was keen to work so that he would not have to accept benefits from the

British government, but it was forbidden for him to do so legally. He wanted to meet with the other Darfuris in the UK, apart from Hasan, but he didn't have the coach fare to London, hundreds of miles to the south.

The following day, while Safia did the shopping after school, Zara and Abdelatif went to the public library to read the newspapers, hoping to get more information about Kofi Annan's announcement. Abdelatif needed Zara's help with the language, so the library had become a regular stop for them.

After struggling through *The Independent,* the only British newspaper covering Darfur to their satisfaction, Zara conceded defeat. "Let's try the Internet, Abdelatif. It's free here, and we can look at the Arabic papers."

"Starting with *The Daily Star of Lebanon,*" Abdelatif agreed, naming the only Arab paper he trusted.

An hour later, he sat back, stunned. His lips trembling, he turned to Zara, "It says just because the UN has passed a resolution it doesn't mean they'll do anything in Darfur. They pass resolutions all the time. They're just words."

Zara leaned forward in her chair, dizzy all of a sudden. Then, as the bad news sank in, she felt foolish for believing anyone would help Darfur. It wasn't as if they were asking for the international community to send troops, she thought sadly. *Just stop selling the regime weapons. Is that so hard?*

"Let's go home to Mother," she said, tugging Abdelatif's sleeve. "But first let me forward that article to Ismael," she said, having become computer literate in only a few weeks.

Zara noticed with disappointment that when they returned home Abdelatif switched on the television and watched a game show, rather than networking with his Darfuri friends.

Zara studied in the bedroom she shared with Safia, each of them focusing fiercely on their schoolwork. At ten o'clock, when they switched off the light, they could hear the drone of the TV and the canned laughter filtering through the thin walls from their sitting room.

Out of nowhere Zara felt a surge of fear. Stifling a sob, she pushed her face into the pillow, overwhelmed by what was happening to her family and her people. She needed Abdelatif to be strong because if he wasn't then she would have to be doubly strong.

Then she heard a familiar inner voice, one that she imagined belonged to her grandfather, telling her that everything would be fine. *I hope so, Grandfather,* she responded silently. She felt her breathing return to normal and finally she drifted toward sleep, like a leaf riding the current of a river.

CHAPTER SIXTEEN

Karen Freeman was determined to return to Darfur as soon as possible, and with the help of Rachael Bennett and her friends at Save Darfur, she raised the money for the airfare. Since her first trip to Sudan, Karen had collected newspaper clippings about the children's drawings from around the globe, and printed out Internet reports, hoping they would give the refugee camp dwellers a flavor of the excitement their pictures had caused. Then she sewed them into the lining of her luggage and began the arduous journey back to El Geneina.

The first thing Karen noticed on arriving at the camp was that it had tripled in size since her previous visit, and there were many more humanitarian workers from overseas. Whereas once it had felt like a community, drawn together by its shared suffering and determination to survive, now she sensed an uneasy tension. Restless young men were openly questioning traditional tribal authority and disregarding the power structures that had endured for centuries; rebel groups were coming into the camp, recruiting child soldiers and demanding that the bewildered inhabitants subscribe to their particular political manifesto. Something important had been lost with the arrival of so many refugees, she observed.

On her first morning in the camp, Karen assembled the child artists and the mothers she had interviewed on her previous visit. Her audience was unfamiliar with television news reports or magazines, but, through her translator, Karen did her best to explain the impact the drawings had made on a world that knew little of what was happening in their remote corner of Africa.

As she spoke, she held up a map she had photocopied from an atlas, pointing out Darfur, in the middle of Africa. Then she indicated each country where the drawings had been featured in news reports.

As Karen passed around the clippings, she studied the mothers' expressions. At first there was confusion and a few blank faces. The children gazed at their own creations, plainly astonished, and some giggled, either surprised or confused. Eventually they began smiling.

One boy, aged thirteen, sat open-mouthed, gazing at the newspaper clipping of his own drawing. "You say this is from Italy?" he asked Karen.

She nodded.

"Italy, like AC Milan?" he queried, mentioning a famous Italian soccer team.

Karen nodded again.

"So the Italians know about what's happening here because of the picture I drew?"

"That's right," she answered, watching him glow with pride.

When they had digested the enormity of their achievement, Karen pointed to the Netherlands on her map. "This is where the United Nations has its court, the International Criminal Court," she explained. "They want to arrest the men who are killing your families. They're going to charge them with war crimes and crimes against humanity, to bring them to justice."

Blank faces. The notion that the all-powerful regime ruling Sudan could be stopped in its tracks by a court in a faraway country was too great a stretch.

"Your fathers and brothers and husbands may be dead," she continued, "but the court wants to make sure the masterminds behind the genocide are punished."

The mothers and their older children listened carefully.

"The officials at the court have been collecting evidence against the regime in Khartoum, and they want to use the children's drawings to prove what's been happening here. The court is going to present these pictures when they begin their court case. They'll announce to the world that Bashir and the rest of the regime are responsible for the suffering here."

"Do you mean they'll give our children's drawings to a judge?" someone asked, incredulous.

Karen nodded, explaining that the pictures were important because they documented on what dates specific villages had been attacked, they showed what the air force and the Janjaweed had done in each place, and which type of military equipment had been used.

"Your children drew the tanks and helicopters in such perfect detail that the regime cannot deny their forces were there," she added.

Heads began nodding.

"So you can see what an important role your children have played."

There was applause and then dozens of beaming smiles. However, one mother wiped the tears from the corners of her eyes. "My child is a hero," she told the others.

"You're all heroes," Karen responded.

꙼ ꙼ ꙼

In another part of the camp, each morning when Hawa awoke there was a brief moment when she assumed she was back in her previous life. In the muddled seconds between sleep and consciousness, she forgot she was in the refugee camp near El Geneina, or that a war was raging around her.

In the blurry mental no man's land of dawn she was back in her village at the beginning of another normal day. Before her lay the usual tasks: fetching water from the well, walking out into the bush to collect firewood, cooking beans and grains over a fire.

Then, with a jolt, Hawa's sleepy brain was bombarded by a summary of the attack on her village. Each morning it was like being thrown against a wall, bruised once more by the fear, shame, sorrow, and humiliation. She was relieved to pull herself upright, blinking furiously to clear the images from her mind. But they would linger for hours, springing back to life whenever she closed her eyes. *Did everyone else in the camp experience similar nightmares? Did Ahmed and Mary? Why did no one talk about them?* Then she ordered herself sternly to stop reflecting and probing.

It had been eight months since the Sudanese army bulldozed the camp and Hawa had returned to help at the clinic each day, relieved to keep busy. She never worked less than twelve hours a day, seven days a week, and the exertion usually guaranteed a sound night's sleep.

With Ahmed's help, she had learned the Arabic alphabet and was memorizing vocabulary and grammar. In quiet moments, she sat in a corner of the clinic, stumbling through children's readers donated to the camp. Sometimes she was frustrated by how slowly her brain functioned, as if it was wading through honey.

But on other days the words came easily, and she felt a charge of excitement. For the first time in her life, she noticed that writing was everywhere, and once she knew what it said, it was as if she had become a member of a select club—all manner of secrets were revealed, and at times she felt superior and powerful.

She also wanted to prove to Ahmed that she was capable of completing the tasks he set her, learning more words and phrases. She still suspected his interest in her was solely because she represented a last connection to her dead sister, but she accepted as much of his company as she could get, on whatever terms he was prepared to offer it.

She reveled in the affirmation she received from Mary, who pushed her to do more each day, never doubting Hawa could pick up her nursing skills or understand complicated medical problems or organize the clinic volunteers. Although Hawa was still scared she would fail and let the clinic down, she also felt a pressure from within to please Mary.

The first time she had stood before the clinic's two dozen volunteers, Hawa had thought she might faint from nerves. She also wondered if they would ignore her—especially the men. But once she had started talking, explaining the timetable she had drawn up, and how the volunteers were to be deployed, and who was to learn what particular skills at designated times, her fears evaporated. Everyone paid attention, respectfully, and asked her questions, as if she was the expert.

What was more, the volunteers and the newer staff members often approached her during their shift, asking for advice, and they deferred to her when she expressed opinions at meetings. And Mary seemed to notice, because she kept giving Hawa more responsibility, and teaching her more complicated nursing procedures.

The previous month Mary announced that the Dutch charity running the clinic wanted to employ Hawa and Ahmed as temporary staff, paying a small allowance. Hawa was astonished that they valued her services, and she felt a glow of pleasure that made her stand a bit taller.

Now, she felt as if she was in the process of becoming a different person. It scared her, but it was also thrilling, as if she was walking farther away from her base camp every day, exploring territory she had been afraid to visit. At the end of each exhausting session at the clinic, she knew more than when she had started the day.

And Ahmed encouraged her constantly, sitting with her while they studied together. He was another reason she volunteered at the clinic, although she couldn't admit it, even to herself. Mary started the day by giving her staff a warning they had received from the UN officials in the camp. They were to beware of any foreign volunteers who might turn up, offering to help.

"But if they've got skills we need . . ." Ahmed began, but Mary silenced him with a withering look. She eased herself down onto the edge of a cot.

"You know, some of the strangest folks tend to turn up in emergency situations. But the biggest problem is the child molesters who arrive at disasters, looking for orphans to steal."

Ahmed looked aghast. "That's disgusting."

"That's why they're issuing a warning. Apparently there's been a problem in one of the other camps."

Hawa gazed at her, profoundly shocked. "So many bad things."

"But also so many good things," Mary commented, scanning Hawa's list. "Think of the kind people in faraway countries who keep telling their leaders they must help Darfur."

Hawa nodded, recalling a radio report about a huge demonstration in the United States, where Jews and Christians and Muslims had marched together, black and white people, arm in arm, demanding that the international community take action about the war in Sudan.

"And think about the widows here who have nothing, yet they take in orphans," Mary continued. "Or the people who sacrifice themselves to slow down the Janjaweed, giving their families a chance to escape."

Hawa nodded and gazed at the floor, thinking of her father, guessing he had done exactly that, valuing his duty as a sheikh more than his life.

When the morning briefing was over, Mary came to sit beside Hawa. She studied the girl's serious expression and narrowed her eyes. "What is it, Hawa?"

"Aren't you ever afraid?" she blurted.

Mary's eyebrows arched. "All the time," she replied with an amused shake of her head. "I'm scared the security people will find an excuse to arrest me or my husband, and I'm terrified the army will come in here again and kill everyone, or that the air force will bomb us. And I'm also afraid the Janjaweed will attack us."

"But you seem so . . ." Hawa struggled for the right word, and then gave up.

"I wear a mask," said Mary, lowering her voice. "Lots of women do. They pretend to be confident and calm and professional, when really they're wondering how they can keep going with all the pressures they face."

"A mask," repeated Hawa. "Like a shield?"

"Exactly. Anyway, come on, Princess. Back to the grindstone," said Mary affectionately, handing her a bucket of blood-soaked bandages.

As Ahmed appeared at her side Mary added, "On the radio they said there were aerial bombardments yesterday, just twenty miles east. So we'll be getting more people, if they survive the journey."

"God help them," muttered Ahmed, pulling the bucket from Hawa's hands. "I'll get started with this. You're one of the bosses now, Hawa, so you shouldn't waste your time on this." He smiled at her, and she smiled back, shyly.

CHAPTER SEVENTEEN

bdelatif knocked on Zara and Safia's bedroom door. Both girls were working at the desk they shared. On the walls above them they had pinned several carefully trimmed pages from British newspapers, showing reproductions of the children's drawings that Karen Freeman had brought back from the camps. The girls' heads were bent over their books, pens in hand.

"What's the subject tonight?" he asked.

"History: World War II. We're studying what they did to the Jews," Zara told him earnestly, her hazel eyes sparkling with her grandfather's intelligence.

"What did they do?" he said, a half smile on his lips. "And who were 'they'?"

" 'They' were the Nazis in Germany, who were a bit like the Islamists in Khartoum, actually. They were absolutely certain everyone should live exactly how they decided. Anyway, they rounded up six million Jews and killed them systematically. Apparently that's how you can tell it's genocide." She glanced back at her notes. "It's systematic, and they pick on one religion or race or type of person," she continued when Abdelatif said nothing. "It was called the Holocaust, and first they herded the Jews into camps and ghettos, and they worked them to death, or they killed them." She spoke so rapidly she gulped her words. "The Nazis said the Jews were racially inferior."

147

Abdelatif's smile had long ago faded. "That sounds familiar." He crossed his arms and leaned against the doorjamb, shaking his head gravely. "So, Zara, you're coming with me to Leeds tomorrow, when you get home from school." What he failed to mention was that he still lacked the confidence to buy the tickets or find his way to the meeting of the British Council of Darfuri Refugees.

"Mom says it's okay?" she grinned. "Great!"

Abdelatif retreated to the sofa, smiling, and Zara heard him turn on the television. Ever since they had left the village, the direction of their lives had been beyond his control. In the camp and at the English detention center, bureaucrats had held their future in their hands. Zara knew enough about Sudanese men to understand her brother must be feeling ill at ease and powerless. He was at the mercy of the grudging generosity of the British taxpayer, unable to lead his family, unable even to buy a loaf of bread without it being a cultural and linguistic challenge.

Zara had heard Abdelatif on the phone to fellow refugees, discussing exactly what they would do when they got home, but increasingly she wondered when it would be safe to return. She knew they became elated each time Darfur was on the agenda at the UN Security Council, thinking finally there would be action. They would follow Internet reports about American students marching, expressing their solidarity with the people of Darfur. Hollywood celebrities would describe the human rights abuses, demanding that Darfur's nightmare must end.

Then President Bashir would call for African solutions to African problems, and his fellow dictators across the continent would stand by him, heaping abuse on the Americans for being neo-colonialists. The Arab nations would suggest there was a Zionist plot to revile yet another wretched Muslim country, always a popular refrain in the bazaars of the Arab world. Then, with a few honorable exceptions, the newspapers would swiftly turn to other disasters around the globe.

When Zara had finished her homework, she went quietly into the living room. Abdelatif was asleep on the sofa, the light of the television flickering across his fine, bird-like features. She picked up the remote control and turned off the television.

She disliked most of the programs except the news. For her, the British shows seemed vulgar, and even the colors in the TV studio were horribly bright. People's laughter was fake and noisy, and the women dressed indecently. All their emotions were on display for the world to see. It was puzzling to Zara because when she saw British people in the streets during the day, they were nothing like the loud creatures on TV.

She looked down at her brother, slumped on the sofa, the Methodist sofa, as she thought of it. Every piece of furniture in their apartment had been given to them by the local Methodist church. The first Saturday morning after the family had arrived in Doncaster a group of Methodists had brought them boxes of cooking utensils, plates, towels, and sheets, in addition to a sofa, a dining table, and the beds in which they slept.

Sumah had given them a cup of tea and some of the hard little cookies the English ate at every opportunity. The Methodist minister, who was a woman, had asked Zara to translate her questions, addressed to Sumah. (This was a snub to his masculinity but Abdelatif had tried to take it in stride.) The Methodist leader and her assistants had listened quietly while Zara told their story, and their eyes had brimmed with tears.

"I thought that after Rwanda this would never happen again," the minister said sadly, wiping her eyes. "The world's crazy, isn't it? I'm so sorry for what you've been through."

"Tell her we thank her, but things are going to get better now," instructed Sumah. "Make sure she understands how grateful we are for their help. They've been like sisters and brothers to us."

Zara translated, and the Methodists' eyes filled once more. Sumah was sorry to see them looking sad because they were clearly such kind people, so she asked Zara to change the subject. "If you're the minister in your church," the girl asked the minister, "do the men do what you order them to?"

The other Methodists had laughed, slapping their knees. "We're terrified of her," one of the men said, and there was another gale of laughter.

"They're just being funny," the woman explained. "We aren't into telling people what to do. We have a way of life we recommend, but we don't force people to do anything. We accept that everyone has questions, and we don't pretend we have all the answers."

Zara nodded, smiling politely. But afterward, when the Methodists had gone, she and her family had discussed it, wondering why anyone would go along with the Methodist way of life unless they were afraid of the consequences of doing forbidden things. Who wanted a religion that did not provide all the answers? The minister was such a nice lady, with a gentle, comforting way, and they could see why people would follow her. But it was perplexing that the leader did not really lead.

Zara told her family she wanted to learn more about the oddities of the different Christian denominations. "We better try to understand it, so we don't make mistakes. I mean, they'll probably have similar groups in New Jersey."

"We're going home, Zara, not to New Jersey," Abdelatif had remarked pointedly.

Zara was no longer sure she wanted to return to Darfur. She kept her thoughts to herself, although she suspected Safia and Sumah shared her reservations about returning to mud huts, and an absence of electricity, schools, computers, and running water.

When Sumah's time to give birth had approached, the Methodists came back with baby clothes, toys, and more useful household objects, all of which delighted Sumah. The minister took the time to answer Zara's questions and asked several of her own about their asylum status, none of which Zara understood. She had given Sumah her phone number, in case she needed help when she felt the baby coming. Her family expressed their gratitude for the kind offer of help, trying to explain that African women were used to giving birth in challenging circumstances.

There had been plenty of warning because Sumah had been through six previous pregnancies. Safia and Zara walked her to the local hospital, a mile away, thinking nothing of it because most African women would expect to walk for hours to find so much as an aspirin. Two hours later, after Yusuf's birth, they had sat around Sumah's bed, marveling at the spotless, bright hospital facilities and the kindness of the nurses and doctors.

"Thank you so much for taking care of me," Sumah said to the doctor, through her daughter. "May God bless you."

The following weekend, the Methodists had arrived with baby clothes and a used crib, fit for a prince.

"Will they expect us to convert to their religion?" Abdelatif had wondered aloud, as they passed around the tea and hard cookies once more.

Safia promptly repeated her brother's question to the minister.

Their generous visitors had laughed, much to the surprise of the Darfuris. "We know you've got your own faith," the minister assured them. "You're welcome at our services, but we're not in the business of bribing people."

Zara wanted to tell the English visitors that she'd gladly go to a Methodist service, just to see what it was like, but she was afraid of provoking the wrath of God, and the fury of Sumah and Abdelatif by doing so. She admired the exterior of the old Christian buildings as she walked around Doncaster, and she longed to see inside.

Architecture was becoming a source of great interest and pleasure for Zara. She knew her grandfather had wanted her to be a doctor, but she was drawn much more to beautiful and unusual buildings. At recess she went to the school library to look at books about architecture. Until Zara discovered the Gothic cathedrals, she had believed the Chrysler Building in New York was the world's most superb edifice. Now she could see where the creator of the Chrysler Building had found some of his ideas. It was a revelation, and as she turned the pages she noticed more links from Greece, Rome, Japan, and Egypt directly to European and American architects.

Zara admired Western styles, but she kept returning to a battered old book of photographs of the world's greatest mosques that was also in the school library. Isfahan, Istanbul, Cairo, Damascus, Samarkand—their holy buildings made her soul rise up in excitement. Why had they no gorgeous mosques in Darfur? she wondered. Their mosques were squat, plain, ugly squares, just like every other modern building. Sometimes, when falling asleep was difficult, or a nightmare woke her, Zara would design a splendid mosque for her village in Darfur.

꙼ ꙼ ꙼

Leeds, a massive, sprawling city, was about twenty-five miles northwest of Doncaster. The coach journey took Zara and Abdelatif through housing projects, former industrial warehouses, and busy shopping streets. The local people, huddling at bus stops along the way, had grey teeth, Zara observed. Yet they had water coming out of taps in their homes, she reflected. In Africa they had to walk miles for water, and toothpaste was unbelievably expensive, so they used sticks. Zara had seen no one using the end of a twig to clean their teeth between meals. Evidently it was not a British custom, even though twigs could be found anywhere and were free.

They were met by Ismael and Halima, a Darfuri couple who had been in the UK for a month longer than they had. Halima was willowy and stood a good two inches taller than her portly husband. And although her face was thin, she was blessed with an amazing set of cheekbones. Meanwhile Ismael, who wore glasses, was very slightly cross-eyed. It gave him a permanently amused appearance, and Zara warmed to him immediately. Ismael explained that their ten-year-old son, Muhammad, who had picked up English quickly, was their translator in everyday matters around the city. He and Abdelatif laughed about how the kids were in charge, but Zara wasn't sure they really found it funny. She knew enough about the Darfuri male ego to see the pain in their eyes.

The group walked to the meeting, talking excitedly about people they knew back home, and how they were distantly connected by marriage. It was a typical Darfuri conversation, Zara thought; everyone was keen to establish blood links. The breeze pushed and pulled at them as they made their way. Abdelatif complained that it was cold all year round, and Ismael agreed. Zara, however, preferred the cold to the dust storms and heat back in Darfur—a view she kept to herself.

At the meeting Abdelatif and Ismael went around shaking hands, while Zara took a seat beside Halima. Zara expected the woman to launch into a list of complaints about being in Britain, like her husband, but instead she said, "In our apartment we've got a washing machine. At first I was afraid of flooding the place, but now I've got the hang of it I really love it. In fact I've never loved any possession more than I love this washing machine. Has your mother got one?"

"No, but we walk to a laundromat and use one there. My mother says it gets everything so clean."

"She's right. They should put me on the TV, in those commercials where women sing the praises of their washing powder," she laughed. "And we've got a microwave too. Fantastic! Have you got one?" She added, "I wish I'd had this stuff back home."

"There's lots of things here I wish we had in Sudan. Like schools and hospitals and public libraries."

"My son's announced he's going to study medicine," Halima grinned. Then she lowered her voice. "To be honest, and please don't take this the wrong way, but I'd actually like to stay here until my kids have been through the English school system."

Zara nodded. Her mother had admitted the same sentiment, out of earshot of Abdelatif, of course, saying she hoped little Yusuf could benefit from Western education just as Safia and Zara were.

"What about you? Are you going to be a doctor? You seem very intelligent."

Zara smiled at the compliment, "Thank you," she said and paused. "Actually, I'd like to be an architect."

It was the first time she had given voice to her dreams, or even acknowledged them to herself. She wondered what her grandfather in paradise would have to say about her bold rejection of medicine; and it made her feel somehow shameful, as if she was betraying him.

The meeting was called to order, and Abdelatif returned to her side. However, it soon emerged that the chairman was more interested in the rivalry between the various Darfur rebel factions, and who would claim what posts in a future Darfur government, than in stopping the war.

"This guy has forgotten that people are being slaughtered as we sit here," Abdelatif commented to Ismael.

"Tell him that," said Ismael. "Go on, put your hand up." Abdelatif glanced at Zara, the panic on his face evident. She nodded her encouragement, and he slowly raised his hand.

"Perhaps we could consider how we can best make our presence felt in Britain. Should we try to influence the decision makers here—the faith leaders, the government?"

"That's a point well made," agreed Ismael loudly.

Zara thought the chairman looked furious, but he smiled, explaining that it wasn't as easy as people imagined. "All that matters is what the Americans say," he declared. "We have the highest-level contacts in Washington. Britain is just a poodle."

"But for those of us who are living with the poodle, we'd like to make sure the poodle remains the faithful follower of the big dog," Ismael called out, a twinkle in his eyes.

The chairman turned away without even attempting an answer.

Abdelatif cleared his throat. "We should ask the Jewish people for help. Six million Jews were killed in World War II, and it was also genocide. And while we're at it, we should go and see the leaders of the Christian faiths. Is my family the only one that's been helped by people of sincere faith since we arrived here with nothing?"

"There are several Jewish temples here," said Ismael. "What are they called? Synagogues. If we could get British people lobbying on our behalf, the politicians might listen to them."

The chairman shrugged, as if it was all a waste of time. Another man suggested that a steering group should be formed to reach out to the faith groups, and Ismael and Abdelatif were swiftly elected as chair and deputy chair. The meeting drew to a close, and email addresses and cell phone numbers were exchanged. Zara enjoyed watching the animated faces around her, so distinctively Darfuri. Then she saw a man with glittering, lizard-like eyes approach Abdelatif. He shook his hand and pulled him away for a quiet word.

A minute later Abdelatif was at her side, more energized than she had seen him in weeks. "That guy says there's a Sudanese restaurant owner in Doncaster who's looking for some help. Below the radar, you know, off the books. He says he'd give me cash."

Elated, they returned to Ismael's home, where they spent the night. Abdelatif and Ismael stayed up until dawn, discussing their plans. Zara was interested in their conversation, but too weary to stay awake; she fell asleep on an air mattress in the spare room. She knew they had to be on the six o'clock bus back to Doncaster so she wouldn't miss school. Abdelatif slept on the bus the following morning, but Zara studied the world going past her window, ever curious and making the most of each new experience, delighted her brother had found a purpose.

CHAPTER EIGHTEEN

A sandstorm had been howling across western Darfur for the past six days, and normal activity in the refugee camp had come to a halt. The storms came every year, but they had been getting worse recently. The locals blamed global warming for the prolonged droughts and the southward creep of the Sahara.

A few enterprising souls persuaded the UN to give them plastic sheeting to drape over their huts. Still, the sand seemed to coat people as they slept, turning up in each mouthful of food.

Ahmed was grumpy because the weather made his twice daily soccer games impossible, and Mary declared that after anyone arrived or left, they must pull the tent flap closed to keep the dust out. Nevertheless Hawa spent much of the day instructing her volunteers to sweep up sand and cover their patients with sheets.

Yet, even in a sandstorm, news spread at a surprising rate. Hawa and Ahmed had heard rumors that one of the rebel groups was building up a secret arms cache within the camp. Now the stories had accumulated more credible details, and they worried about how long it would be before the security services raided them, causing more devastation.

Halfway through the morning, a rangy young man appeared at the clinic. It was only when he unwrapped his turban and scarves that Ahmed realized the visitor was one of his soccer center forwards, a tall, nimble seventeen-year-old called Murad. He beckoned Ahmed to join him by the flap.

"We're having a meeting this evening to discuss the situation in the camp." Ahmed rolled his eyes, but moved closer as Murad continued. "We have to protect ourselves because the UN isn't allowed to do it." Murad tipped his forehead toward the line of patients, their wounds oozing blood through inadequate bandages. "We're paying too high a price."

Ahmed made a face. "If you're talking about hiding guns, then you're courting disaster," he said through clenched teeth.

Murad's eyes flashed. "I'm talking about defending our people."

Ahmed groaned, weary of plots hatched by impetuous young men and anxious about the consequences. He appreciated how impotent they felt, caged up while the war raged around them. But he was also under no illusions about the overwhelming strength of the Sudanese authorities. The army and the security services were heavily armed with the latest Chinese technology, traded for Sudan's oil. In comparison, the rebels were a lightly armed, often disorganized collection of tough guys and genuine heroes. Ahmed and Hawa encountered them often enough when they delivered their wounded colleagues to the clinic in the dead of night and then whisked them away again before dawn when they might be spotted by the authorities.

"I'll come to your meeting but only to try to talk some sense into you," Ahmed responded with an air of resignation. "You're putting us in danger. Their spies probably know about it already."

Murad ignored this point, telling Ahmed he would be back later to lead him to the secret meeting place. Then he carefully wound his scarf around his neck and face before slipping through the flap.

During their lunch break at the clinic, the volunteers listened to the BBC World Service in English, with Mary providing a simultaneous translation. The only news story concerning Darfur was a proposal from President Bashir in Khartoum. He had invited the leaders of the various rebel groups' political wings to a secret location to discuss a peace plan.

Mary and Hawa returned to work, leaving Ahmed to the sports report. Twenty minutes later another young man arrived, but this time it was to summon help for a woman who had gone into labor prematurely. Her relatives were afraid of carrying her to the clinic because she was bleeding, he explained. Mary grabbed her midwife kit, calling to Hawa, "You take care of the UN visit. They'll be here any minute."

Hawa, who was taking a patient's blood pressure, felt her heart leap into her throat. A group of foreign visitors was scheduled to tour the camp, and Mary was supposed to show them around the clinic, whenever they arrived.

"They'll have a translator with them," Mary added, seeing the combination of doubt and panic on Hawa's features.

"But," the young woman began and gestured toward Ahmed at the other end of the tent with his back to them. "Shouldn't he do it?"

Mary shook her head. "You do it. You'll be fine." She paused. "Ahmed," she called, "I'm going to need your help, please." Then she smiled briefly at Hawa and ducked out of the tent, followed by Ahmed, who took Hawa's hand surreptitiously and squeezed it briefly as he went past her.

Although they were together every day, and he was her closest friend, Hawa and Ahmed had not become a couple. They lived in a traditional, conservative Muslim society, and any public display of affection was frowned on. The war had put normal life in a deep freeze; no one got married because no one could afford to, and most of the young men were dead or off fighting with the rebels.

It was unthinkable in their world that Hawa and Ahmed would even have a conversation about their feelings. No woman could initiate such an exchange, and no man would dare to unless his family could afford a dowry and an elaborate ceremony. Nevertheless, they showed each other kindness in a hundred ways each day, and as far as Hawa was concerned, she felt butterflies in her stomach each morning when she saw him arrive at the clinic.

Hawa watched Mary and Ahmed depart, wondering why the nurse so often threw her into demanding situations with no notice. On this occasion she had no time to work herself into a nervous state about the visit because a moment later she heard the sound of several four-wheel-drive vehicles pulling up outside. She straightened her headscarf and went to greet them.

The following twenty minutes went by in a blur. To Hawa's surprise she found the courage to give her guests a welcome speech and to walk them around the clinic, pointing out what facilities they could offer, and more to the point, what basic equipment and supplies they lacked. She answered questions without hesitation, amazed that she knew the answers, and as the senior UN official left she gave Hawa a thumbs-up gesture. "Good job, Hawa. Thanks."

I wish my mother could have seen me do that, she thought, going back to her work, a little smile at the edges of her mouth. *Maybe my sister did.*

Murad was waiting for Ahmed at the end of his shift. They discussed Tottenham Hotspur's recent dismal soccer performance, picking their way through the sandstorm in the dark, collecting another three young men on their way. Ahmed was surprised when Murad led them to a large UN tent usually occupied during the day by officials and bureaucrats. "There's no chance of them coming back out here this evening and finding us," Murad explained.

"You could get the UN thrown out if the army hears their facilities are being used for this," Ahmed commented, furious.

"Oh, that would be a tragedy," responded Murad, his voice dripping with sarcasm.

"The UN are the heroes here," Ahmed fumed. "They're the only thing stopping the tanks rolling in and killing every last one of us."

Murad was uninterested in Ahmed's point of view. It had become fashionable among the young men to denigrate the UN and the international charities. It was part of their macho posturing, accusing everyone else of cowardice and incompetence.

Ahmed was even more alarmed by the growing rage and intolerance among the boys, especially toward women who had survived being raped by the Janjaweed. When their clan elders told them not to beat the women, they denied they had done it, and then, when the elders persisted, the boys shrugged off their words. Two years ago, no boy would have behaved so disrespectfully. But after being cooped up in the camp, the old ways were being eroded by gang culture based on the bravado of the young leaders, not the calm wisdom of the hereditary sheikhs. Ahmed had overheard several clan leaders wondering out loud how their young men could possibly return to life in the village after rampaging around the camps, tasting the temptations of the towns.

Ahmed found more than fifty young men and boys waiting in the tent that was dimly lit by lanterns and buffeted by the howling wind. A few tribal elders had turned up, clearly curious to find out what was happening beneath their noses. "Word of this'll get back to the security people in town—you can be sure we have snakes among us," one sheikh warned. "It'll give Khartoum the excuse they've been waiting for," he lamented, his voice breaking. "Who gave you children the authority to do this?"

Several of Murad's friends fired back, "You're the ones playing into their hands by being so limp." "We're fed up with being pushed around and murdered." "When you were put to the test, you ran away like women."

Their disrespectful comments brought cheers, prompting one of Rashid's uncles to get to his feet, visibly quivering as he turned to survey the crowd. "This talk of stockpiling weapons is ludicrous. You stupid boys don't understand you're playing with fire. Leave this to the ones who know what they're doing."

"So you can make a profit on the deal?" someone called, provoking laughter.

Rashid's uncle looked astonished, his jaw hanging open as he measured the boys' defiance. "How dare you talk to me like that!"

"Look where it's got us leaving it up to you," a young man jeered.

"I'm the son of a sheikh," Rashid's uncle howled, his voice like the cry of a wounded antelope. He looked stunned, as if every law he had taken for granted had just been proved wrong, as if gravity no longer existed. A stream of insults followed him as he made his stumbling, inelegant exit from the tent.

Ahmed considered trying to talk some sense into the boys, but they were in no mood to confront the reality of their relative weakness in the face of the regime's military and security apparatus. Anyway, he was just a soccer star to them, not a gang leader. Shortly after, he also left the meeting.

Perhaps the boys need to blow off steam by gathering together and talking tough, he reflected, deep in thought as he picked his way home through the sandstorm. Maybe common sense might prevail, once they had vented their rage. He also wondered if the rebels would seriously rely on impetuous boys to represent them within the camp.

Two days later, when the sandstorm subsided, Mary arrived at the clinic bearing grim news. As she washed her hands, she told them that the air force had attacked the secret gathering of rebels. "You remember there was supposed to be a meeting between the regime and the rebels?" she asked. Hawa and Ahmed nodded, bracing themselves for bad news. "Well, the rebels sent their big men, and yesterday afternoon Khartoum bombed them, and dozens of them are dead."

"So the whole thing was a trick?" asked Hawa, astonished.

"What will the foreigners say?" exclaimed Ahmed, the veins at his temples popping. "They're the ones who want these peace talks."

Mary shrugged, buttoning her white smock. "President Bashir's spokesman says the rebels' military representatives are terrorists who are trying to overthrow him, so he's got the right to take defensive action."

"And?" prompted Ahmed, holding out his hands. "Surely the world won't stand by and allow this to happen?"

"The diplomats haven't got the stomach for a fight with the regime." She paused and straightened her headscarf, her expression weary. "The foreigners don't want to annoy the regime in case they jeopardize the chance of peace talks."

Ahmed sank onto an empty cot, his hands hanging loosely between his knees. "I don't understand why the world powers don't just stop selling arms to the regime. Or they could enforce a no-fly zone over Darfur—it's really not so complicated. And they could help the African Union monitors protect us. Why won't someone do something?"

"Well, someone *is* doing something," Mary shot back, her eyebrow arched. "There're rumors Sheikh Uthman had an urgent meeting with some of Abdallah's rebels late last night in El Geneina."

"Oh no," moaned Ahmed. "I had a feeling Rashid's people wouldn't like this challenge to their power."

"What's going to happen?" asked Hawa, looking from Ahmed to Mary. Neither of them replied or caught her eye, and her spirits sank, trying to imagine the possible repercussions.

"Back to work," said Mary, using the familiar but artificially cheerful voice she adopted to divert them from their preoccupations. "Prin-

cess Hawa, you're going to remove a bullet this morning. They're bringing in a little girl who has one lodged in her thigh. Ahmed, you hold the
child down. And find a clean twig for her to bite on."

That night, Ahmed was awakened by the noise of boots outside
his hut. Two sets of hands reached in and pulled him out by the collar
of his robe.

"Don't make a noise or we'll break your neck," one of his
captors hissed.

Disorientated and confused, Ahmed was dragged toward the
back exit of the camp, farthest from the road to El Geneina. When
they reached the field where they held their soccer games, Ahmed saw
thirty or so familiar faces. His fellow soccer players were sitting on the
ground with their hands on their heads, guarded by militiamen with rifles. His captor shoved hard, causing Ahmed to stumble forward. "Put
your hands up, like the others, and shut up." They strode off on their
next errand.

Ahmed wanted to ask the boy next to him what was happening,
but from the expression of stark terror on the boy's face it was clear
no one knew. The men guarding them were Darfuris in trousers and
t-shirts; and although they wore turbans, they weren't even bothering to
cover their faces to disguise their identities.

Every few minutes another boy was delivered to the group at the
soccer field. It was too dark to be sure, but Ahmed thought he recognized many of the boys who had attended the young troublemakers'
meeting two nights before. When he craned his neck he found Murad
sitting a few yards away, hands trembling as they rested on his head.
The guards hissed at them to get to their feet and assemble into a long
line. The boys did as they were told, and they were led away in silence.

☱ ☱ ☱

The following morning the camp was gripped by the news: Abdallah's
rebels had taken fifty-four boys in the night. Hawa worked throughout
the morning in a numb state of terror, as acquaintances stopped by to offer

their theories about what had happened to the boys. Hawa said nothing, hoping that she would wake from the nightmare soon, praying Ahmed would walk into the tent any moment now, as if nothing had happened.

Mary went to see the UN officials during her lunch break, hoping they might have news from their various sources. When she reappeared, her expression was tense and her eyes were unusually sunken. She headed straight for Hawa, drawing her outside, away from the patients.

"They've been sold," she began without preamble.

"What?" Hawa whimpered, hit by a wave of dizziness.

"One of the sheikhs did the deal, so the story goes. The rebels needed more recruits, and the sheikhs wanted to get rid of the camp troublemakers, so they sold them."

"But Ahmed wasn't making trouble," Hawa protested, her eyes misting over. "Who did this," she asked, her voice not much more than a whisper. "Was it Uthman?"

"That's the rumor," Mary said, pulling Hawa toward her and stroking the back of her head. "Oh, you poor girl."

"He'll die," she cried into Mary's shoulder. "I know they'll kill him. They'll put him at the front and make him fight the Janjaweed."

Mary held her close. "No they won't. Half these rebels never engage the enemy in battle, you know. They ride around in their jeeps looking tough, but they don't actually encounter the army or the Janjaweed."

"I can't go on," Hawa cried, her voice hoarse. "I can't stand it."

"Don't say that," said Mary firmly, pulling away and holding her at arms' length. "You must take care of yourself for when he comes back. He'll need you."

Hawa shrugged. "I sometimes wonder if he sees my dead sister, the one he loved, when he looks at me."

Mary peered into her eyes, her brows knitted. "You have a low opinion of him if you think he's still obsessed with someone who's dead. Did he tell you that?"

Hawa shook her head, squeezing her eyes closed, as if she was trying to block out the conversation.

"Take it from me, Princess—he's only interested in you. Why do you think he spends so much time with you? Do you think he taught a dead girl to read and write?"

Hawa covered her eyes. "I don't know."

"I do," Mary said fiercely. "Don't ever tell him you think he only cares about your sister because it'll break his heart."

Hawa stared at her feet for a moment, trying to calm her pounding heart.

"You have to be here for him when he comes home," Mary continued. Then she hesitated. "You know, it's so much easier for us Christians to show we love each other. I feel sorry for the people here, so strangled by these customs."

Hawa struggled to swallow the lump in her throat. "My mother brought me up to value my honor, not my happiness. If she were alive, she would consider me worthless because I didn't die fighting off the soldiers. It's okay for men to survive being attacked, but not women."

"But that's not how Ahmed thinks. You *are* worthy of him," Mary said, the irritation gone from her voice. "I hope you understand that. You've made yourself worthy. Ahmed's very proud of you. We all are, and you should be proud of yourself."

Hawa's tears stopped. "That's because of you," she sniffed. "You remember when you told me to stop wasting air?" She laughed, drying her cheeks with the edge of her scarf.

"I did, didn't I?" Mary smiled. "You're my greatest success." She squeezed the girl's shoulder. "Back to work, I guess."

Hawa nodded, and she didn't mention Ahmed's fate again that day, although she thought of nothing else. Later as Hawa was returning to her hut, she spotted Rashid in the distance, heading home from his regular soccer game, a game Ahmed should have been enjoying. A wave of fury swelled up inside her and she started running toward him.

"So, your granddaddy sold all the brave boys and left the cowards behind," she called, once she caught up with him.

"What?"

"The goat boy's pretending he's too stupid to know his grandfather's a slave merchant."

Rashid stopped dead in his tracks. "Go away!"

"Are you proud of your family?" she yelled, astonishing the people nearby who had never seen a mere girl heaping abuse on a sheikh's grandson. "How can you live with yourself, you coward?" she screeched.

"Your grandfather's sold our boys, and you wander around like a five-year-old, not a care in the world."

Rashid, aware of the gathering crowd, tried to slip away, but Hawa dogged his every step, shouting at him. "Aren't you embarrassed to show your face here, you coward?"

He swung around, grabbed her by the shoulder, and slapped her in the face. "Leave me alone!" he bellowed, pushing her away from him. She fell in the dirt.

Rashid continued his journey home, walking twice as quickly as normal, in case any one else dared to challenge him. He had doubted there would be any more shows of defiance after last night's purge of the "restive elements," as his grandfather had described them. But he had not counted on Hawa's hysterical outburst. Even as he tried to forget the hatred on her face, he kept hearing her yell "coward," and he walked faster, as if he might escape the word.

Hawa was helped to her feet by two women. The side of her face was painful, yet she was beyond tears. She felt strangely at peace, even euphoric. She had seen the fear on Rashid's face, even as he hit her, and she suddenly understood how profoundly he could be hurt by her words.

"I'll destroy that coward," she assured the startled women before turning in the direction of her hut. As she walked, Hawa held herself upright, despite her smarting cheek. *I'll never stop reminding him he's a coward,* she thought, relishing the prospect.

At six thirty the following morning, a khaki-colored armored vehicle from the National Security and Intelligence Services drew up before a bright blue door in a quiet street in Omdurman, a suburb of Khartoum. Three men in khaki uniforms clambered out of the back and stood in a semi-circle behind their commanding officer, a short, flabby man in dark glasses. He hammered on the door and glanced up and down the street, registering the fear on the neighbors' faces. Those who poked

their heads out of windows or doors to investigate the arrival of the unfamiliar vehicle soon withdrew, keen on invisibility.

A middle-aged man wearing a long white robe opened the door.
His eyes flashed in terror and his mouth opened slightly as if he was
gulping in air.

"Do you have a brother called Ismael living in England?" the officer asked.

The man nodded, and the commanding officer took a step back as
his men forced their way through the doorway. The owner of the home
was knocked down as two of the men dragged him out of the path of
their commander. They shoved him and he sprawled on the cement floor
of the modest sitting room. They pinned him down with a boot on each
shoulder while the third man closed the window shutters, switching on
the overhead light.

A woman and two toddlers appeared in the doorway, eyes flicking
between the visitors and the man on the floor. The children grabbed fist-
fuls of their mother's robe, while she tried unsuccessfully to shoo them
back into the kitchen.

The officer flashed a toothy grin. "Peace be upon you." He folded
his sunglasses into his breast pocket.

She returned the greeting automatically, but in not much more
than a whisper.

"So, you're a long way from home," the officer sniffed in a nasal
tone, bouncing his baton in the palm of his hand.

The man on the floor stared up at the officer, his eyes wide.

"And your brother's even farther from Darfur, in the north of England. Leeds, I gather, hasn't even got a decent soccer team. Now why
would you choose to live in the north of England if you weren't going to
be in Liverpool or Manchester?"

The officer pulled a handkerchief from his pocket, honking his
nose. "My allergies are terrible at the moment." He took his time refold-
ing his handkerchief, slipping it back into his pants pocket. "So, what
are we to do about this brother of yours in Leeds? He's been telling lies
about his country. That's not the act of a patriot, is it? Why's he telling
these lies?"

The man on the floor watched the officer without blinking.

"You don't appear to have any explanation for your brother's treachery," he continued. Then he looked at the man's wife. "Perhaps you'd be kind enough to pass on a message to your brother-in-law."

The commanding officer pointed his baton at the boy lurking behind her. The third man, not engaged in holding the children's father down, pulled the boy into the center of the room. His mother reached out to hold her son back, but the man shoved her out of his way, and she bounced against the wall with a dull thud.

The officer glanced around, noticing a side table at one end of the sofa. He stooped awkwardly and dragged it into the center. "Spread his hand on it," he instructed the soldier. The boy tried to wriggle free but he was no match for the man, who grabbed his hand and held it palm down on the surface of the table.

"No," said the boy's father. "Don't do this."

The officer offered an expression of mock surprise. "Ah, you speak Arabic? I wondered if perhaps you didn't understand my questions."

His wife stepped forward. "If you have to hurt someone then let it be me," she said. "Please don't touch the boy. He's only four years old."

"Perhaps your brother-in-law should have thought of that before he started spreading disgraceful lies." He sniffed, twitching his nose.

"I beg you," the woman whimpered. "Please leave my boy alone."

The commanding officer nodded at the man, who shifted his grip up to the child's elbow, forcing the tiny hand flat on the side table.

The officer raised the baton above his head and brought it down swiftly. In the second before the child screamed, everyone heard his bones crack. After another nod, the soldier released the boy's arm, and stood aside as Mrs. Ismael rushed to her son.

"Get him out of here," the officer shouted above the child's shrieking. Then he glanced down at the father, who was weeping. "I'm still not sure you've understood. You monkeys are so stupid, you need to be told things several times before it penetrates your thick skulls."

The officer nodded at the third man who withdrew his baton and began beating the helpless man on the floor. His commander stood back, preferring not to get his uniform covered in blood. He took a seat and blew his nose, rubbing his eyes and sniffing every few seconds.

The boy in the kitchen was screaming, and the other toddler, running back and forth along the corridor between the sitting room and the kitchen, cried at the top of her lungs. The decibels produced by the Darfuri family were headache-inducing, and the officer wished he could have plugged his ears without seeming weak before his men. Yet, he was unconcerned that a neighbor might call the police about the noise; people knew to keep their noses out of other folks' business. And the police were there to instill fear, not to protect civilians or recover stolen bicycles.

When the man on the floor finally stopped breathing, the third man carefully wiped the blood off his baton, using a decorative shawl spread on the sofa. His colleagues used corners of the shawl to mop the specks off his face and shirt front. Watching them, their commanding officer was moved by the pride his men took in their appearance, and the care they showed each other.

When they left the house they didn't bother to close the front door behind them.

CHAPTER NINETEEN

Three teenage boys sidled up and slid onto the bench opposite Zara at her table in the school library. From their light brown complexion and their sharp features, she knew they weren't white English, but they weren't from anywhere near Sudan either.

"Hi, I'm Tariq," said the one sporting a wispy attempt at facial hair. Zara looked back at her book, hoping he and his pals might take the hint and go away. Abdelatif had warned her not to make friends with British boys. Not that she had any interest in these pimply specimens with their gelled hair and inelegant posture.

Despite her silence, Tariq leaned toward her conversationally, "So are you from Somalia?"

"Do you speak Arabic?" she asked in Arabic. Tariq looked blank. "I'm from Darfur, in Sudan," she continued in English.

"Where?"

"East Africa."

Tariq's eyes flashed. "That's where Somalia is."

"Darfur's hundreds of miles from Somalia."

She watched as the words penetrated Tariq's brain. "But you're a Muslim, right?" he asked, indicating her headscarf.

She nodded.

"So am I," he said proudly.

"Where's your family from?"

169

"Pakistan."

"But you don't speak Arabic? So you can't read the Koran in the original?" Zara remarked, enjoying the irritation her questions provoked, hoping the boys would leave her alone to study.

"Me and my mates are going to join the jihad in Somalia," he sniffed defiantly.

Zara frowned. "Who will you fight?"

"The ones who are trying to overthrow the Islamic government. It's like Iraq, in case you didn't know," Tariq grinned.

"Somalia doesn't have a government," Zara commented. "That's what the BBC says."

"Western propaganda," sneered Tariq. "All Muslim men should go to the aid of the Islamic Courts movement in Somalia."

Zara's eyes widened. "*You're* going to be a soldier?" She tried not to laugh in his face, with its pathetic attempt at a beard.

"Me and my mates. We're going to a training camp and then to Somalia where we'll kick the Great Satan out and make it safe for a proper Islamic state."

"So what's it like in Somalia?" asked the boy sitting on Tariq's right, his eyes bright with excitement.

Zara shrugged.

"But you're from East Africa, right? So what's that like?"

Zara kept her voice just above a whisper, hoping the boys would take the hint and follow her example. "Very hot in the day and cold at night. You must walk miles for water. Food is scarce, and there's no electricity, or running water, or inside toilets."

"You're joking!" exclaimed Tariq's friend, sitting back as if someone had taken a swing at him.

"They'll find food for us," Tariq proclaimed. "They treat the soldiers like kings, they do, in Somalia."

"What's the nightlife like there?" asked Tariq's other friend with a leer.

Zara put her head to one side, and offered them a thoughtful look. "No electricity, like I said, so people go to sleep early. Candles and paraffin for lanterns is expensive. And we get up at four thirty or five, whenever the sun rises."

"What?"

"Not even telly or DVDs?"

Zara struggled not to laugh. "Do you think there's Blockbuster Video in Somalia?"

The boys looked appalled.

"No hamburger, no fried chicken, no computer games, no electric sockets for IPods." She paused. "But we go to pray many times each day."

"Sod that," commented Tariq's startled friend. "I'm not going to bloody Somalia if it's like that."

Tariq gave her a lingering, steely look of hatred. "My Dad says you lot should bugger off home to Africa because you're making things worse for us here."

"Thanks for the Islamic solidarity," she commented, looking back at her book.

"You should piss off back to Africa," Tariq added, before loping away with his friends in tow.

☙ ☙ ☙

The following morning at breakfast, Abdelatif looked exhausted.

"You got in late," his mother commented.

"I have to clean up the place when it closes."

Zara's brother had just taken a job working for a Sudanese exile in Doncaster called Salim who had a pizza restaurant. Abdelatif refused to talk about what his work entailed, which Zara took as a bad sign. She guessed he was doing what a Darfuri man would call "women's work." However, Salim had said he would pay cash, unofficially, so the British immigration authorities would not know. And he had advised his new employee to find somewhere else to live, so the immigration people wouldn't know where to find him, if they eventually refused his family refugee status. But when Abdelatif had mentioned the idea, his mother had dismissed it with a confidence she would never have expressed back in Sudan. To Sumah, their apartment was a luxurious palace, and she refused to leave unless she had to.

"Is it really safe for you to be walking around at that time of night?" Sumah asked Abdelatif her brows knitted with concern.

He focused on spooning sugar into his tea. "Don't worry, Mom."

"How often will you be working that late?" she persisted, rocking the baby on her knee.

"Look, we need the money," he said. "And it's not like I'll be doing it forever," he added.

A brief look passed between the women, none of whom relished returning to the privations of village life. After a moment's uncomfortable silence, Yusuf gurgled.

"So, why doesn't this Salim sell our kind of food?" asked Safia, changing the subject.

Abdelatif swallowed a spoon of his Sudanese porridge—he hadn't made the switch to toast and marmalade like the women in his family, who loved it. "Believe it or not, the word Sudan doesn't conjure up the same pleasant images as Italy. How many people go to Sudan for their vacation?" Abdelatif's laugh was bleak. Then he pointed his chin at her breakfast. "You're not a very good example of sticking with our heritage, are you?"

Safia rolled her eyes. "I like to try new things," she shrugged.

"Anyway," Abdelatif continued, refilling his mug from the teapot, "the English can't get enough pizza. So that's what Salim gives them. Very cheap, by the slice, all day long. More melted cheese and tomato paste than you'd believe possible. I don't know how they digest it."

"No wonder they're so fat," Safia smirked.

Adbelatif sighed. "They all look the same to me, the English."

"And they complain quite a lot," Sumah commented, gazing at Yusuf. "You know, that well-baby clinic they sent me to was fantastic. They're going to give him inoculations against more diseases than I knew existed. It's really a wonderful service, this health system. But you should listen to the English whining about it in the waiting room."

"How do you know they're whining?" Abdelatif asked, grinning, thinking he had outwitted his mother, whom he knew did not understand English.

Sumah tilted her head toward Safia. "My translator told me."

Abdelatif nodded. "They're much happier when they're eating pizza, actually," he laughed. "Anyway, I bet everyone at the clinic admired this young man," Abelatif commented, tickling the infant. When Sumah beamed with pride, it occurred to Zara that their mother looked younger and happier than she had in years.

At that moment, Abdelatif's cell phone warbled, and he went to the window, looking out over the rain-soaked streets below. The women ate in respectful silence, certain his phone call would be from one of the British Council of Darfuri Refugees members. Ever since the meeting in Leeds, Zara had noticed the change in her brother. He was now an important node in a network of Darfuris across Britain.

"Good news," Abdelatif announced, returning to the table. "The people in the office of the Chief Rabbi in London say they'll sign an open letter to the Prime Minister. We've already got signatures from the Archbishop of Canterbury and the Roman Catholic Cardinal too."

"What about the top Methodist?" asked Zara.

Abdelatif rolled his eyes. "I'll make sure we get her or him too. And the Buddhists also, if that makes you happy."

"This letter," Safia said, rapping the table with her knuckle, as if she were bringing a meeting to order. "You send it to Tony Blair and then what happens?"

"We release it to the media," he paused for a sip of tea. "And we're contacting all the churches and synagogues, urging them to mention Darfur during their sermons."

"What about the mosques?" asked Safia, her eyebrows arching once more.

Abdelatif shrugged. "That's more difficult."

"Why do the Arab leaders defend the butchers in Khartoum?" asked Safia. "They are not all Islamists—they don't force people to obey Sharia law in their countries, do they? I mean, they aren't all stoning people to death and chopping off hands, like the Saudis? And in most Arab nations they have judges and courts rather than some illiterate bunch of mullahs passing judgment on everyone," she said with distaste.

"Yes, but Arab leaders talk about Islamic solidarity when it suits them. And they wouldn't be the first people to use religion as a way of stirring up hatred, or deflecting attention from their own misdeeds." He drained his mug of tea. "You two should be heading off to school. And I've got some calls to make," he added, heading for his bedroom.

"I hope he's not going to work himself to death," Sumah said, loud enough for him to hear. "As soon as we get our legal status, he can go to school and learn a proper trade."

"Like plumbing," Safia added, for Zara's benefit. "Yesterday, at the well-baby clinic, everyone was saying it's impossible to get a plumber round here. And the pay's good too."

Zara nodded, but she suspected her brother would sooner return to Darfur. *I want to go to New Jersey*, she told herself as she got her books ready for school. *I know that's what Grandfather would want. I just have to get there. But how?* she wondered, following Safia down the ninety-two stinking steps.

Ӿ   Ӿ   Ӿ

Later the same day, on her way back from school, Zara came across their neighbor, Mrs. Edwards, outside the supermarket. The old lady had not noticed Zara because she was absorbed in a battle with her shopping bags. One of the plastic hand straps had broken and Mrs. Edwards was struggling to keep the contents from spilling out on the ground.

"I can help you please, Mrs. Edwards," Zara said with a timid smile.

Her neighbor looked startled and drew away from her.

"Please. I don't steal. I'll help carry this home, okay?"

Mrs. Edwards hesitated and then she nodded warily. "Thank you."

A moment later they were walking slowly, side by side, back to the tower block. Zara forced herself to slow to her neighbor's arthritic pace. "How are you?" asked Zara.

Again Mrs. Edwards looked startled. "No one your age asks that anymore. My hip's hurting, actually, and this damp weather is pretty rough on my joints. I expect it's a bit of a shock for you, too."

"I'm not complaining because here I'm safe," Zara responded, using one of the phrases she had memorized for use with locals.

"I imagine so," Mrs. Edwards said thoughtfully. "I must say, it's a lovely change having such quiet people living next door. You're not like those drug addicts who were there before. What terrible noise they made, day and night!"

When they reached the lobby, the elevator was broken, so Zara took the other shopping bag gently but firmly, saying, "It's not good with a bad hip."

"Thank you. Well, it serves me right for being so ancient. Ha!"

"You're not ancient. Chartres Cathedral, that's ancient," Zara said seriously, slowly climbing the ninety-two steps.

"Have you been there?" asked the old lady, incredulous.

"Just in library books. Have you been there?" Zara asked, automatically mimicking Mrs. Edwards' phrasing and intonation.

"Actually, I have. I went there on my honeymoon, donkeys' years ago. My husband, my late husband I should say since he's been dead nearly twelve years, he took me to Paris when we were married, and then we had day trips on the railway to Chartres and Reims and Versailles."

"Was it marvelous?"

Mrs. Edwards stopped and turned to look at the girl, laughing, "Oh, it was marvelous."

Zara noticed the woman's face was suddenly transformed. Instead of the scowling, suspicious old woman, there were sparkling, kind eyes. When Mrs. Edwards smiled, she revealed cheekbones good enough to impress even an African.

"No one in our street did things like that back then," she continued as they carefully negotiated the litter-strewn stairs. "This was back in the late 1950s, you know, and people went to the seaside on their honeymoon. But we thought we'd do something unforgettable, so we got the ferry to France. By Jove, it was fantastic. And the food? Out of this world."

"And the churches and castles?" asked Zara, as they trudged upward like pack mules on a mountain path.

"They were wonderful, too. D'you know, I still have the guides we bought in each one we visited. Would you like to see them?"

"Yes, please. Very much," Zara said eagerly.

"Then come in and have a cup of tea. Oh. What's your name? I didn't ask."

"I'm Zara."

"What a lovely name. And where are you from, dear?"

"I'm from Darfur in Sudan, where there's a war."

"Darfur? Oh. How terrible! My granddaughter was telling me about that. It's shocking."

"Your granddaughter?"

"She's studying international relations at university in London. She's very clever."

As Mrs. Edwards fumbled for her front door key, Zara put down the bags, saying, "I'll just tell my mother I'm in here, okay?"

"Of course, dear. Just pop in. I'll leave it open."

Five minutes later, Zara was leafing through a yellowing black-and-white booklet about Chartres Cathedral. They drank several cups of tea while Mrs. Edwards told her about her honeymoon, and how her husband George was very clever and knew every detail about the kings of France and the historical background of the buildings they had visited.

"Where is your family now?" asked Zara. She had noticed framed photographs of children propped up on side tables around the sitting room.

"Swindon and Peterborough," Mrs. Edwards answered. "That's in the south," she added. "They had to move there to find work. And like I say, Sarah's at university in London. Kings College." She hesitated. "Zara almost sounds like Sarah doesn't it? Isn't that funny?"

Zara smiled as Mrs. Edwards continued. "Next time I talk to her, I'll ask her about Darfur. Of course, she's very busy, and a girl her age doesn't want to be bothered with her old grandmother, does she?"

"Maybe I'll meet her when she visits you?"

"Well, I usually go down there, to Swindon, at Christmas. You know . . ." her words trailed off and the light left her eyes. "But I'll phone her tonight and tell her about you. She's very concerned about the human rights situation, I know. She's always going to demonstrations about Burma and China and all that."

"I wish I could speak better English to talk to you," Zara ventured.

"You speak better English than some of the local English people here," Mrs. Edwards laughed. "And I bet you're doing better at school than some of the kids in this housing project. Dear Lord."

"I study all the time," Zara admitted. In fact she made top of her class, as did Safia, who was two years ahead of her.

"How about your family?" asked her neighbor. "Is that your mother living with you next door?"

"Sumah is her name, and my baby brother Yusuf, and cousin Safia, and older brother Abdelatif."

"Give her my congratulations on the baby. Is she okay, your mother?"

"Fine, thank you."

"That's a nice family."

Zara nodded, suddenly subdued. "Everyone else is dead," she explained, her voice flat.

"Oh no. I'm so sorry . . . do you mean your father?"

"Father, grandfather, grandmother, other brothers and sisters, cousins . . ."

Mrs. Edwards peered into her empty tea cup. "You poor little thing." She looked up at Zara. "You're so grown up, but I suppose you've seen more than a life's worth of troubles, haven't you. You're like the Blitz generation here, the ones who survived the war—World War II," she added quickly.

"Six million dead Jews," Zara recited automatically. "The battle against fascism."

Mrs. Edwards sat back, impressed. "Goodness, you are bright." Then she hesitated, as if she was choosing the right words. "I must say, you're very brave, coming to a strange country."

Zara smiled. "My grandfather told me I must be strong and study hard. Then he was killed. He was a very intelligent man, very modern. He sent me to school in Darfur, and not many girls go to school there."

"He must have been a very smart fellow," Mrs. Edwards commented. "I'm sure he'd be very proud of you, dear."

Suddenly Zara felt the tears pricking in her eyes. She looked down to hide her face. As Mrs. Edwards passed Zara a piece of paper towel, she said, "I cry about my husband all the time," she said. "We can't always be strong, can we? It wouldn't be human."

Zara took a deep breath, trying to bring her emotions under control.

"Now that I know I've got an art lover next door, we better get together to talk about churches and castles and paintings, hadn't we?

That'll be lovely for me to have a friend here." She hesitated. "There aren't many people around this neighborhood who care about the finer things in life. It's a shame really. They don't know what they're missing."

Zara sniffed the last of her tears away.

"There's a nice lady dentist on the third floor," Mrs. Edwards resumed. "Marja. Polish, I think, very charming and educated. I wish I saw her more often, but she works the most unbelievable hours. But other than that, well, some of the people in this block leave a lot to be desired. I wonder where it all went wrong. Mrs. Thatcher, I suppose. Rampant greed and the end of civility. 'There's no such thing as society,' Thatcher told us. And she got her wish." The old woman shook her head. "You come and see me soon, please," she added as Zara left. "Take care, dear."

The following morning at breakfast, Abdelatif arrived late at the table, barely acknowledging the others. Sumah peered at him across her toast and marmalade, but decided against giving him another lecture on his working conditions. Instead, the women continued their discussion of Zara's visit to Mrs. Edwards. "Her family's left her alone in this place, and she has to go to the other end of the country to see them," Safia paraphrased for Abdelatif's benefit. "She's a very nice person, too. It's not like she's an old grump you'd want to avoid."

"It must be hard," Sumah commented. "Coping by herself."

"The people here really are odd, aren't they?" sniffed Safia. "The kids at school hardly seem to talk to their parents, and they never have meals together. They have their own television, so they sit in their rooms, alone, watching their favorite program."

The women exchanged mystified expressions.

"You really are exhausted, aren't you?" Sumah asked the silent Abdelatif. "Can't you work fewer hours? You're killing yourself."

"It's not that," he said flatly. "Don't bother me about it again, okay?" he said. Then he rubbed a hand over his cheeks, as if willing himself to wake up. "Sorry, Mom. Look, I got a phone call yesterday afternoon, from Ismael."

The women stared at him, aware he was on the phone to Ismael several times a day. They wondered what had happened to make a single phone call so significant. "What's wrong?" asked Sumah, concerned by the doom in his voice.

"He has a brother in Omdurman, you remember? Well, the security people came to see him about our activities and how we're supposedly spreading lies about the regime."

Zara wondered how the authorities in Khartoum knew about it, and then she understood. She often heard her brother warning that the regime had spies in England, but she hadn't really understood what it meant. A chill ran down her spine as she contemplated the consequences of the security services tracking the activities of the Sudanese Diaspora. Every comment Abdelatif and his friends made at their meetings, every letter to the editor they wrote, each interview they gave, would be reported back to the heart and soul of the regime, its security and intelligence apparatus.

"They smashed his brother's little boy's fingers. It'll be a miracle if he can ever hold anything," Abdelatif reported quietly, his eyes on his coffee mug.

Sumah held a hand to her mouth and closed her eyes.

"And they killed Ismael's brother."

His mother moaned and uttered a prayer. Zara and Safia sat rigid at the table, too stunned to move.

"So, it seems we've got to be careful, even here," Abdelatif concluded mournfully. Then he glanced at his watch. "Time you were getting ready for school."

The girls left the table and headed for their room in silence.

CHAPTER TWENTY

Rāshid found it hard to get an audience with his grandfather. The young man loitered outside the tent, hoping he would be called inside to speak to the sheikh in between the old man's morning meetings. He became increasingly impatient as other supplicants were summoned in before him.

Rashid was well aware of his grandfather's traditional duties, but he also knew Sheikh Uthman lacked the patience to tolerate windbags unburdening their parochial grievances. Therefore it was far more likely his grandfather's visitors were business connections, accessing the sheikh's influence with the authorities without being seen to cooperate with their oppressors.

Eventually, when his grandfather broke for lunch, Rashid's uncle summoned him. "Don't waste his time," he warned him. "He's had a tiring morning."

Uthman was reclining on a pile of cushions. His eyes were closed, and he was listening to the soccer results on the BBC World Service.

To his dismay, Rashid found that his courage evaporated as he stood uncertainly before the sheikh. "Grandfather," he began, his voice hardly rising above a whisper. He cleared his throat, "Grandfather, I need to speak to you, please."

The sheikh stirred, opening his eyes. He blinked, squinting as he focused on Rashid. For a few seconds the old man seemed confused, as if unable to imagine why the boy was standing before him. Rashid's spirits sank as he wondered if the old man was trying to place a familiar face.

"What do you want?" he asked the boy at length.

Rashid took a deep breath. "Everyone's saying you sold the boys to the rebels."

Uthman yawned, rubbing his face as if he were washing without water. He began to pull himself upright on the cushions, and then thought better of it and eased himself back again. Once more his eyes closed and he grimaced. "Everyone?" he asked in a mocking tone.

"The people in this camp. They're saying you accepted money from Abdallah's people in exchange for the boys they took."

"Why are you wasting my time with this?"

Rashid faltered. After a moment he said, "I'm here to tell you that I'm joining the rebels because it is the only honorable thing to do. Everyone's saying I'm a coward, allowing my grandfather to sell the other boys so I can remain here, playing soccer."

"I didn't know you were that good," Uthman commented blandly. "Would they miss you from the team?"

A prickling current of rage sizzled through Rashid's veins. "It's the duty of our family to lead our people into battle, and it's the duty of the men here to protect our families. So, I'm going to do my duty."

For a moment the sheikh lay still, his hands clasped across his round belly. Rashid wondered if he had drifted off to sleep or was simply concentrating on the soccer scores. Then Uthman sighed wearily, wiping a hand across his mouth. "It sounds to me as if you're practicing to become a politician with your stirring little speech—and your stupidity."

When Rashid started to protest, Uthman cut him off with a dismissive wave of his hand. "You're not a war hero. And no one in my family's going to lay down their lives in this ridiculous skirmish."

"You said we're fighting for our identity as Darfuris," Rashid responded, his fists clenched. "You said it to the rebel leaders last week. I heard you!"

"And I'm a very generous supporter," the sheikh said without missing a beat. "In effect, I pay so my own flesh and blood doesn't get involved. And it's a fight we'll never win, by the way. Within a generation no one will speak our tribal languages. Everyone will be using Arabic, and we'll all be competing to prove our Arab lineage. That's the story of Sudan since the Arabs arrived here twelve centuries ago. And only sentimental fools think they can cling to our noble tribal ways you're so proud of in the face of globalization and all the rest of it." He yawned again. "Now run along and leave me alone."

Rashid swallowed a surge of bile in his throat. "So why did you tell us those stories when we were little, about how brave our men are, the bravest in Africa, and how we killed lions with only simple knives, and how we inherited a thousand years of courage?"

The old man flapped a limp hand in Rashid's direction, closing his eyes. "I'm trying to listen to the radio."

"But I have to face the boys in this camp."

"Get used to it," Uthman laughed. "It comes with our position. Someone will always be jealous of us."

"I'm talking about our honor, Grandfather."

"Leave me to my one pleasure, child."

"I'm going to join the rebels, just to prove we're not all cowards and scoundrels in this family."

Uthman snapped off the radio and sat up abruptly, a look of fury on his face. "What did you say?"

Rashid's first instinct was to retreat in the face of the sheikh's scowl, but he willed himself to stand his ground, even though his knees felt like jelly.

"You foolish goat boy," the sheikh started. "Who gave you the right to criticize me? I see you enjoy the fruits of my work every night as you sit here filling your stomach. So evidently I'm not such a scoundrel that you can't benefit from my lamb and bread, while the rest of them go hungry."

"I'm just saying . . ."

"Get out of here and don't come back until you apologize."

Rashid stared at his grandfather, unable to move.

"Get out!" Uthman roared.

Rashid stumbled, groping for the tent flap, his heart pounding against the wall of his chest. Then he heard a click and the announcer continued his breathless analysis of the latest Chelsea game.

Rashid wandered aimlessly through the camp, his pride stinging. He had been treated like a tiresome child having a tantrum, not a young man who was offended by the family's soiled reputation. Yet again he had not been taken seriously.

He ambled slowly around the perimeter, picking his way through piles of litter, past a couple of starving donkeys. *Had he been hoping his grandfather would talk him out of joining the rebels? he asked himself. Did he expect a show of concern or affection? Did he imagine his grandfather would finally take notice of him if he threatened to sacrifice himself?*

Rashid stopped in his tracks, bleakly taking in a bedraggled line of stunned, dust-covered arrivals, clinging to a few pathetic possessions, waiting patiently to register with the authorities.

What kind of place is this for me to linger? he demanded silently. *Not even my flesh and blood believes I have any purpose here.*

He changed direction abruptly, walking toward to the hut where he knew he would find Abdallah's representative.

The following morning two UN helicopters arrived at the airfield outside El Geneina. Instead of the usual delivery of UN personnel, or much-needed pharmaceutical shipments, the helicopters brought a delegation of politicians, journalists, and soldiers from a Western nation. The local people who observed their arrival were unclear where the white people came from; their presence was extraordinary enough in itself. The soldiers accompanying them were carrying machine guns but they were also wearing blue helmets, meaning they were UN peacekeepers, assigned to protect the white men, the locals learned later.

The visitors tottered down the helicopter steps, blinking and glancing around them in the dazzling sunlight. One or two seemed startled when they noticed the burned out wrecks of planes and helicopters that had crash landed some time ago. There was nowhere to put the scrap metal, and no one to do the cleaning up, so the aircraft had been dragged off the strip of grass used as a runway and had been left to disintegrate into the earth, a grim reminder of the fate of less fortunate travellers.

Waiting for the visitors were three officials from the UN's refugee agency based in El Geneina. They had brought seven white four-wheel-drive Land Cruisers to the airstrip with them, and the politicians, soldiers, and journalists piled into the vehicles. Less than a minute after they had landed, they were speeding away from the airstrip.

Their first stop was the headquarters of the African Union observer mission, near the airfield. After a forty-minute meeting, the politicians stood within the African Union compound, beside armored personnel carriers and gave interviews to the television crews they had brought with them. They spoke about the "security situation" in Darfur. Then the politicians and soldiers waited while the journalists packed up their gear, and everyone got back in the vehicles.

Next they drove to the camp, pulling up outside the tents occupied by the administrators of the UN High Commission for Refugees. Once more they received a briefing, and when they emerged fifty-five minutes later, they gave interviews about the "humanitarian challenge" in Darfur. Then they returned to the tents for lunch with their UN hosts. The soldiers stood guard outside.

Finally, the visitors were driven two hundred yards through the camp to Sheikh Uthman's tent, where a group of community leaders had been assembled to meet them. The UN had brought in a stack of plastic chairs and everyone sat in a circle. Several chairs were shuffled into a second row, however, so that the television crew could set up their equipment. The UN peacekeeping soldiers stood outside the tent, keeping an eye on the gang of children that had gathered to stare at their white skin and bulky uniforms and guns.

The visitors, speaking through interpreters, explained that they had come on a fact-finding tour, and that they wanted to hear the concerns of the people in the camp. Each politician took five minutes or so, giving a speech and being filmed, and then the UN official asked the local men for their contributions. There was silence, and the camp inhabitants looked at their feet.

One of the visitors grinned and asked, "How's the UN doing here?" The UN staff and their visitors laughed lightly, nervously.

Finally Sheikh Uthman spoke, "We're very grateful our highly esteemed guests have come to see our living conditions and to hear about the suffering of our people. We've all lost so much—our sons, our livestock, our homes, and our heritage. But we're very appreciative of the job the UN is doing."

"Why do you think the war is happening?" asked one visitor. "Are they trying to make you convert to Islam?"

There was an embarrassed clearing of throats and a hurried exchange in the local language. "They're Muslims already," offered the UN official mildly, keeping any hint of contempt from his voice. "It's in the south of Sudan that they're Christian."

"So, why'd the war start?" asked another visitor.

The Darfuris waited for the sheikh to speak, but he said nothing. Some took this as a signal that they too should be quiet. However, one independent-minded old hothead with a sharp, crooked nose raised his voice.

"They're paying the Janjaweed to force us off our land. They can't stand anyone who disagrees with their political system."

Uthman interjected with a smile. "We used to live peacefully," he offered. "But global warming came along and now there isn't enough farming and grazing land. So what we need here is aid and development."

Undeterred by the sheikh's emollient tone, the crooked-nosed hothead plowed on, prompting some to look away, appalled by his disregard for traditional etiquette. "We need weapons so we can defend ourselves, and we need soldiers who can take the guns away from the Janjaweed."

The visitors looked dismayed when the hothead's words were translated. None of them had any response ready, and they looked helplessly at the briefing papers on their knees.

"You must tell the regime to stop bombing our villages," another local man volunteered, evidently emboldened by the hothead.

"We need a political solution," the hothead resumed. "They keep saying this is a humanitarian disaster, but it's part of the Islamist regime's master plan to drive us out of Sudan. This government is hand in hand with Bin Laden, so it's in your interest to defeat them, too."

Again the visitors didn't know what to say. One of them wrote down the hothead's words. Another sipped at his bottle of water.

Uthman offered the visitors a benign smile. "We hope to rebuild Darfur when this is over, and we'll need to institute a program of peace-building and reconciliation here, and we'd like your support to make it a success," added the sheikh, holding out his hands, palms up. "Capacity-building, income-generating projects."

The visitors nodded vigorously, relieved to be on solid ground once more, using the development industry jargon they were comfortable with. The meeting adjourned shortly afterward, and the politicians conducted another series of interviews outside the tent, using the rows of refugees' huts as a backdrop.

Altogether the visitors spent less than three hours in Darfur. However, they returned to their country and thereafter spoke with great authority about the "situation in the region." They accepted praise for their courage in visiting a "war zone," and added another area of foreign policy expertise to their resumes.

The visit was the subject of much discussion in the camp for days to come, particularly when there was an item about it on both Voice of America and the BBC World Service news bulletins. During their tea break at the clinic, the staff and volunteers listened to a phone-in program, during which several contributors took issue with the amount of security given to the visitors, compared to the total absence of protection for the refugees.

"It reminds me of Rwanda," one listener said indignantly. "The peacekeepers there had orders to shoot the dogs to stop them eating the bodies and spreading disease. But not to stop the genocide by shooting the killers manning the barricades who were wielding machetes."

When the phone-in was over, Mary turned to Hawa. "What did you think of that?"

"Well, at least the visitors bothered to come and see Darfur for themselves, even if it was just for a few hours," she added uncertainly. "If they hadn't made the effort, there wouldn't have been a single news item about Darfur this week."

Mary nodded. "That's why the regime stops the journalists getting in here on their own."

"So, let's hope lots more of these white politicians come here to get their picture taken." Hawa shot her a sad smile, still too battered by concern for Ahmed's safety to be free of the constant nagging worry weighing on her shoulders. "Anyway, I'm on firewood patrol today," she said, getting slowly to her feet. "See you later."

Mary gave Hawa a look that she knew meant 'be careful.' She nodded in response.

Ψ Ψ Ψ

Hawa was the first to hear the drumming of the horses' hooves. She stopped dead in her tracks and held up a hand, signalling the other women to be quiet. They listened to the sounds of the bush around them, standing as still as statues, hardly daring to breath.

Their children had been left in the camp, and each woman was wearing dun-colored robes, hoping she might blend into their surroundings. All fourteen women remained motionless, their arms aching from supporting their bundle of twigs and branches. Sweat ran in little tickling rivers down their faces and necks. Flies attacked their eyes and nostrils, but they dared not even swat them away for fear of attracting the attention of the men who stalked them whenever they ventured out.

Every rustling leaf or snapping branch sent a seismic shock down Hawa's spine. She strained her ears, imagining herself like an antelope, trying to guess from which direction the lion would spring. Unlike animals of prey, the Janjaweed did not have to approach downwind: they had horses and open-top vehicles with mounted machine guns, known as "technicals" at their disposal. The women had only their legs.

Just then Hawa heard a horse snort, and three Janjaweed crashed through the trees. She dropped her firewood and started running, but a hand grabbed at the robe billowing behind her. He dragged her along behind his horse for several yards and then stopped. Although she was stunned, she struggled to stand upright. However, the man dismounted quickly, sliding out of the saddle, shoving her back to the ground.

A scarf was wound around his head, revealing only eyes and nose. He held a machine gun trained on her stomach with one hand. He dropped to his knees, straddling her, and with his free hand he ripped off her robe. Without thinking, Hawa put up her hands and tried to pull the clothes back over her body. He sat back on his haunches, grasped his machine gun with both hands, and brought the butt of the grip smashing into her face. She jerked back to the ground, her head on fire with the pain in her nose.

"Lie still, you filthy black dog," he yelled at her in Arabic.

She felt dizzy and passed out briefly, but a moment later she was dragged back to consciousness by a knife-like pain between her legs. The Janjaweed had discarded his gun and was lying on top of her, ramming inside her. After six thrusts he groaned and withdrew roughly. Then he spat on her and got to his knees, leaving a slimy string of semen dripping onto her.

She rolled over and turned away, expecting a spray of bullets to pummel into her body at any moment. She quickly prayed that one day God might reunite her with Ahmed. She hoped that in the meantime Ahmed would have a long healthy life, protected from the enemy's bullets. She prayed that in heaven he wouldn't know she'd been raped again. And if they both survived the war, she hoped Ahmed would forgive her for what had just happened to her.

Instead of the rattle of the ammunition belt she heard the Janjaweed rearranging his clothing and walking away. She lay still for a moment, throbbing with pain, legs trembling.

Nearby a vehicle whined, brakes squealed, doors opened and closed. Men spoke in a language she didn't understand, but with a formal speech pattern, like an officer issuing orders. *If they were Janjaweed, she thought, they'd be speaking Arabic, and they wouldn't sound like a professional army. Maybe they can help us.*

Hawa groped around for her robe, forcing herself to her feet and into her clothes. She winced with every move she made, struggling to breathe through her crushed nostrils. Using her sleeve she wiped the blood from her eyes, heading for the idling vehicle. Behind her several familiar voices were crying, begging for pity. *The best way I can help them is by finding help.*

When Hawa reached the edge of the bush she found a Land Cruiser bearing the African Union logo on its door. Two soldiers listened to the radio, comfortably cool in their air-conditioned bubble. They stared at her when she rushed toward them. She called out, and when they did not open the door she slapped her bloody hand on the side window, leaving a brownish red smear on their clean glass.

"Janjaweed!" she cried, pointing back into the bush. "Kill women! Now! Help!" she tried again, using the few English words she knew.

Hawa watched the two men converse inside the vehicle. Impatient and terrified of what was being done to her friends, she pointed at the bush and said, "Now, Janjaweed!"

The driver started the engine and drove off.

Hawa stared after their dusty trail, too stunned to move. When the noise of their engine had faded, she heard the moans of the women once more. Someone screamed, followed by coarse male laughter and Arabic insults; the Janjaweed were still at work. Then, abruptly, the sound of hooves and shouting grew near once more, and she ran for her life. *This is it. They've come to finish me off.* She headed for a thick outcrop of thorny bushes thirty yards away. She plunged into the scrub crawling toward the middle, her flesh speared by a hundred tiny needles. Then she lay on her side, struggling for breath, praying the Janjaweed would not find her again.

$$ \text{Ħ} \quad \text{Ħ} \quad \text{Ħ} $$

It was an hour or so before sunset when Hawa heard the last of the Janjaweed's horses canter away. When she found the other members of the firewood collection group, she counted six able to walk back, two who could not get to their feet, and two were dead. They waited while a third died, holding her hand and praying that God would take her quickly to bring her suffering to an end. It was agreed between them that they had seen three girls carried away by the Janjaweed. Inevitably, the ones to be taken were the youngest. The women built a fire for the two who were too badly injured to move, leaving them as many items of clothing as they could to keep them warm overnight.

They arrived back at the camp after dark, grateful there were few people around to witness their return. Hawa led the battered, bloody group straight to the clinic tent. She barely looked up as she entered, hoping to avoid Mary's inevitable expression of horror. Hawa ordered her companions to wash themselves as best they could in the yard behind the tent, standing over the buckets of water, and then to lie on the cots, awaiting attention.

To her relief Mary did not make a fuss. Every week they treated groups of women who had been raped while out gathering firewood, so it was not as if their appearance at the clinic tonight was a novelty. Without a word passing between them, Hawa fetched the rags, hypodermics, and sewing needles she required, and she and Mary worked their way methodically through each woman in turn. They also dosed them with aspirin to help dull the pain. Then finally, when it was after midnight, Hawa sank onto a cot and allowed Mary to tend to her.

The nurse worked in silence, setting Hawa's broken nose, disinfecting her wounds. Hawa lay with her eyes squeezed shut, wondering what Ahmed would say, wondering if Ahmed had also been wounded, or killed. How long would it be before bad news about him reached her, if he had been injured or if he were dead? Would anyone bother to tell her? Or would she learn of his fate in snatches of gossip?

Finally, Mary said, "It's better if you talk about it."

Hawa nodded, surprised to find she wanted to talk to Mary, keen to stop thinking about Ahmed's uncertain fate.

"The African Union monitors were there," she began. "They knew what was happening, but they drove away."

Mary's eyes met hers. "They were there at the same time as the Janjaweed?" she asked, her voice rising.

Hawa explained what had happened, then paused, taking a deep breath. "How could they do that?"

Mary set her jaw, and the muscles in her cheeks flexed. "They'd say their mission is to report on incidents. They don't have a mandate to intervene or to protect civilians. And they don't have weapons. They just write reports. That's why the Khartoum regime agreed to let them come here in the first place."

"What'll they 'report' about—the girls who were taken away as slaves, or the three who died today?"

Mary sucked in her lips for a moment. "Unconfirmed reports of an attack on women by unidentified militia men."

Hawa blinked away the tears stinging her eyes. "How can these men live with themselves?"

"The monitors? They never asked to come to Darfur and it's not their war."

"But they're African, these soldiers. They're as black as we are."

"So?" Mary asked. "They haven't been given the authority to intervene, so they are just trying to save their own skin."

"Then why bother?" Hawa grumbled.

"Do you really want to talk about this, now?" Mary asked her patient.

Hawa gestured at her swollen nose. "Better than thinking about this, and the other," she added, referring obliquely to the wound between her legs.

"Okay," Mary conceded, winding up a roll of gauze bandage. "The international community won't put pressure on Sudan for a variety of reasons, such as business links with the regime. But, instead of admitting they want to build oil terminals here, they say they want to give Khartoum a chance to hold peace talks with the rebels. Everyone involved knows no rebel with a brain would trust the regime, and their promises are worth nothing. But the foreign nations don't want to hear that because it's inconvenient. And another reason Khartoum is getting away with this is because they've convinced the Americans that they're on their side in the war on terror. The bottom line is the white nations don't want to send their own sons to die here."

"I understand about the business reasons for being friends with Khartoum, but this war on terror is a mystery to me," Hawa said, exasperated. "I thought the Americans hated Muslims."

"They're against the Muslims who are friends with Al-Qaeda."

Hawa frowned. "But on the radio it said that Bin Laden lived in Khartoum for five years. He's an Islamist, and he's best friends with the regime."

Mary tried to suppress a smile, and Hawa's eyes narrowed.

"What is it?" she demanded.

"It's just that you've come a long way, since the first time you were lying in my tent," Mary commented fondly. "Here you are, discussing current affairs and international politics, while anyone else would be crying in pain."

Hawa frowned. "I've done enough crying to last me a lifetime," she remarked. "And I've been eaten away by hatred and anger, and that didn't help either."

Mary nodded. "I'm . . . well, it isn't only Ahmed who's proud of you."

Hawa's eyebrows arched, and she smiled, despite the discomfort involved. "You're my teacher, but you're very bossy too, so I just do what you tell me to," she joked.

"Anyway," Mary resumed, clearly embarrassed. "Bin Laden. After the attacks on America, Khartoum decided to dump him because it wasn't too clever to be an enemy of the USA. So now the regime's giving the Americans information about their former friend, Bin Laden."

"What kind of information?"

"Rather stale information, I suppose, since they haven't seen him since 1995."

"Oh." After a moment Hawa added, "I still don't understand it, I'm afraid."

Mary stroked Hawa's fretful forehead. "No one does. My father told me it's the first sign of wisdom, you know—challenging the nonsense other people accept without question. Now, try to get some sleep, okay?"

Hawa nodded, relieved she didn't have to stumble through the dark to her cold little hut.

"I'll see you in the morning, but no work for you tomorrow, not until you've had a chance to mend. Stay in bed and rest," Mary said, patting her hand. She started to get up and then she paused. "I'll be a little late tomorrow because I've got to do something in El Geneina first," Mary concluded, squeezing her hand.

Hawa tried to find a position on the cot that did not hurt, lying on her side with a rolled-up rag wedged between her knees. She wondered if it would take her hours to go to sleep, if she would lie awake, reliving the attack. But the next thing she knew it was morning, and one of her day shift volunteers had just set a mug of tea down beside her.

The pain returned when she pulled herself upright, but Hawa felt strangely triumphant. *I survived,* she thought. *I made it and I'm here and I survived. They're not going to destroy me that easily.*

Mary wore her usual inscrutable expression when she arrived a couple of hours later. She bustled about the tent, issuing directives and pointing out the imperfections in the volunteers' efforts at changing dressings. Hawa did as she was told, napping throughout the day. At one point, when she was awake and lying quietly, Mary sat on the edge of her cot, her expression grave.

"I made a phone call to headquarters on the satellite phone."

Hawa's eyes widened. "To Holland?"

"Yes." Mary hesitated. "The people at headquarters are collecting information about the incidence of rape here, and they want as much evidence as possible. Statistics, dates, names, and facts." Mary picked at her cuticles for a moment. "The humanitarian workers here stay silent because we're afraid we'll be expelled. But we can't go on like this, doing their lying for them, not telling the truth to the outside world."

Hawa knew that the word "them" took in several aspects of the regime—the security chiefs who would withdraw permission for charities to drive along certain roads, stopping their staff and supplies getting to the camp. Or the regional governors who just as unpredictably suspended the overseas workers' permits and internal travel documents, which meant staff couldn't go from their compounds in El Geneina to the clinics just a mile down the road.

Hawa smiled, hoping to lift Mary's spirits. "I'm glad you talked to them."

"I better get back to work," responded the nurse with characteristic gruffness.

☩ ☩ ☩

That night, as Mary walked back to her home in El Geneina, a military vehicle pulled up beside her. It was dark, and Mary had been picking her way along the familiar road by the light of the moon. When the vehicle came to a halt, she strained to see who was on the other side of the window. She assumed she was about to be subjected to the usual time-wasting security check on her identification papers. *Anything to make life more tiresome,* she thought. *Anything to inconvenience the wretched aid workers at the camp.* "Idiots," she muttered under her breath in English, digging around in her backpack for her papers.

But before she could hand them through the window, a soldier appeared out of the darkness, ripping her backpack out of her hands. The door swung open and a pair of hands hauled her into the backseat where a blank-faced soldier trained his pistol on her.

"Where are you taking me?" she roared, flopping backwards as they accelerated.

A snigger came from the front passenger seat, and a man in an officer's uniform turned around, craning his neck. "You're the Christian nurse, aren't you? The one from the south?"

Mary gave him a stony glare.

"You shouldn't be here, in Darfur, or in Sudan, for that matter," he said in a superior, lecturing tone. When Mary failed to respond he continued, "And if you had a decent husband, he wouldn't let you work. Only prostitutes work outside the home—teachers, nurses, doctors—you're all disgusting whores."

Mary took in his smug expression, aware she represented everything the Islamist regime hated—she was a black African, she was a Christian, and she was a professional woman.

"Why do you people despise women so much?" she asked him at length. "What are you so frightened of?"

The officer's self-satisfied smile faded, and there was a flash of fury in his eyes. He turned away from her and stared ahead through the windscreen into the night.

Mary sank back in the seat, rocking with the rhythm of the vehicle over the rutted road, heading to the security services headquarters, she assumed. *There would be hours of interrogation or worse*, she guessed. *Perhaps death.* But instead of terror she felt relief, and a strangely peaceful feeling settled on her. She had expected this moment for so long, ever since she had come to Darfur. Thinking about it, she saw her whole life had been leading her to this, from the time she had sat at her father's knee, listening to him explain his simple humanitarian values, absorbing his pride in being who he was. "God created all people equal," he had said, "We are all the children of Abraham."

Yes, Father, she thought, looking at the profile of the officer in the passenger seat. *But some of us are better at demonstrating our brotherhood than others.*

ꙮ ꙮ ꙮ

Early the following morning her backpack was found on the stretch of road where she had been walking. It bore the logo of the Dutch charity for which she worked, and an African Union patrol dropped it off at the clinic. Hawa recognized it immediately, although it was empty. Mary always carried it. *No!* Hawa screamed silently, hugging the battered backpack to her chest. *No! I cannot lose Mary too.*

Mary's body was found the following day, in a ditch on the other side of El Geneina. Her husband identified her by her wedding band. Otherwise it would have been hard to tell, such was the damage to her face.

Several days later, the Dutch charity released its report on rape in Darfur. It was widely covered in the international media, although interest in its conclusions lasted only a few hours before something else took its place.

The president of Sudan denounced the report, saying it was a work of fiction, written by imperialists and Zionists plotting against Muslims. The authors proved they knew nothing about Sudan, he sneered: "It is not in the Sudanese culture or the people of Darfur to rape," Bashir explained. "It doesn't exist. We don't have it." The women who had given their so-called testimony were obviously relatives of rebels, or prostitutes, inventing terrible lies.

Hawa heard a human rights activist on the radio, saying rape had become a weapon of war. It was an integral part of genocide because it destroyed the very fabric of a traditional society such as Darfur. During the same broadcast, a scholar from Saudi Arabia phoned in with a different interpretation. He said that when women in a Muslim society claim they have been raped, it means they wanted it, and it is their fault. Women tempt men into bad behavior, he explained. It just proved that the Saudi way was the correct way, and women needed to be considered as only half human; they were just irrational bundles of lust and emotions.

Hawa felt her heart pounding in anger. *How could people who prided themselves on being such pious and pure Muslims say such terrible things?* she wondered. *Does this mean I'm no longer a good Muslim, because I reject what the mullahs say about the inferiority of women? How can my God be merciful if He really thinks half of humanity is worth so little?*

As she worked, Hawa found her thoughts wandering back to the religious rules she had been taught as a child. She was told no one must ever question any aspect of their religion, and to have doubts was unforgivably evil. *Was her faith supposed to make her feel miserable?* she wondered. Mary had told her that Muslim women in other countries had careers and ran businesses and became politicians. *Why were things so different in Sudan, when Muslims all over the world were worshipping the same God?* Puzzled and unsettled, Hawa did her best to focus on her work and not to think about Mary's death.

In due course, headquarters in Holland sent a message to Hawa, explaining it would be several weeks before Mary's replacement arrived. In the meantime, they believed she would manage perfectly adequately. Hawa surprised herself by accepting both their decision and their confidence in her. She knew she could do the job. She could read and speak Arabic, she understood which medicines were needed and how to treat various wounds and infections. When she wasn't working at the clinic, she studied Mary's books. In truth, she deliberately kept herself busy, to avoid thinking about Mary's last moments. In the same manner, she tried not to speculate about Ahmed's safety.

During the day, Hawa retreated to the numbness of survival mode, striving to close down each cell capable of feeling pain. But when she lay in bed, often on a mat at the back of the clinic tent, her thoughts wandered. She wanted God to pass messages on to Mary, but she wasn't sure if it was blasphemous to treat God in such a manner. *Please tell her how much I miss her,* she thought. *Please tell her how grateful I am that she saved me. I hope she knew what a difference she made to me.* Then she wondered if God was still listening to her, or if she had offended Him with her relentless, nagging questions.

The replacement from headquarters didn't arrive for another six months. The authorities, retaliating for the rape report, refused to grant entry visas to the troublesome Dutch charity, threatening to expel the entire staff, including the locals like Hawa. Shipments became even less reliable, sometimes stopping for weeks. Hawa persuaded various UN agencies and aid groups to give her supplies, in exchange for translating and training their new staff to be "culturally sensitive" to traditional Darfuri ways.

Two years ago, it would have been beyond Hawa to have a conversation with a UN bureaucrat; now she approached them regularly, striking bargains, sharing information, briefing their visitors on local conditions. Back when Ahmed had begun teaching her to read and write, she would never have believed she would soon be fluent enough to understand the BBC's Arabic Service news reports. Nor did she think that she would also be teaching others how to be nursing assistants.

Sometimes, at the end of the day, when she took a moment to enjoy a cup of tea in peace, she wondered what had happened to the frightened little girl who Mama Mounah had rescued. She often prayed for Mounah, not daring to speculate on what had become of her village. But she wished the spirited old lady could see her now. She told herself that perhaps Mounah *could* see her, and was helping her make it through each day, sitting on her shoulder, as Mary had explained it. *Thank you, Mounah. Thank you, Mary.*

Finally, a young female doctor from Australia arrived and promptly became so ill she was sent to Nairobi to recover. A month later she was on a plane back to Sydney, too unwell to stay in Africa. Headquarters asked if Hawa could carry on running the clinic, and she assured them she was managing fine. She didn't mention that she was heavily pregnant. She knew the bosses in Holland wouldn't know what to do with that information. And being Westerners, they might not understand that Hawa would be able to manage once the baby arrived, since coping was what African women did.

꒕   ꒕   ꒕

Shortly after volunteering to become a rebel soldier, Rashid realized he had been nurturing rather romantic notions of what a freedom fighter's life entailed. He had imagined months of intensive training in secret camps, instilling discipline and an iron code of honor and brotherhood.

He assumed he would reach a peak of physical perfection after gruel-ling exercise and tests of his stamina, including learning almost superhu-man self-denial. There would be lectures about their struggle against the regime, and about the history and culture of Darfur.

In fact, he was given little training, beyond how to shoot various weapons. Within two weeks he was part of a regular patrol. Most of the time, his unit roared around in a "technical" that had recently been sto-len from a Western charity called Save The Children. Rashid's first job had been to scrape the logo off the doors.

Rashid had been aware all along that there were "good" rebels and "bad" rebels in Darfur; it was dawning on him that the group he was with were a little short on valor. But he kept despair at bay by assuring himself that they were bound to engage in battle shortly. *It's just a ques-tion of picking the right moment. Suicidal gestures don't help anyone. I'll get my chance to serve my people. My time will come.*

Wherever they went, Rashid and the others stood or sat in the open back portion of the vehicle, giving hard stares to the civilians they passed. He had learned nothing about military discipline, but he soon picked up the importance of wearing dark glasses to disguise his expres-sion from anyone who dared to look at him. For the first time in his life, he wore Western trousers, shirts, and boots, supplemented by scarves wrapped around his head and neck—standard rebel dress code—be-cause traditional robes were considered impractical. He watched the other militiamen swagger, intimidate, and strut. It came down to chan-nelling feelings of contempt for noncombatants, he discovered. He was now part of a special breed, and because they told themselves they were defending their homeland, they were entitled to take what they needed to succeed.

His commanding officer was a twenty-one-year-old previously called Omar, who had renamed himself T-Bone in the manner of an American rapper. He was consumed by an interest in running shoes, also gleaned from rap culture. Consequently he had picked up an im-pressive knowledge of various types and makes of sporting goods, none of which had ever been available in Sudan.

On Rashid's third day on patrol, T-Bone flew into a rage when he heard that several other units had "acquired" Thuraya satellite phones.

He swore and sulked like a toddler. Then, as they were helping them-selves to some flat bread and boiled eggs in a village where the local people were sympathetic, they learned that a German medical charity would soon be arriving on a scheduled visit. The sheikh of the village, apparently dismayed that the rebel unit was stripping his people of their food supply, as well as making their village a target, suggested they might move on and ask the German aid workers for supplies.

The unit dug in half a mile from the village, and sure enough the Germans arrived two days later. They came in a convoy of five shining new white Land Cruisers, weighed down with pharmaceuticals, dress-ings, food, and water, all essential to a rebel army on the move.

But T-Bone was more excited by their Thuraya and the top-of-the-line Nike shoes worn by the German doctor in charge of the expe-dition. One of the Germans, a woman, made a terrific fuss, and had to be slapped around, but the foreigners soon quietened down, handing over the keys to the vehicles. T-Bone allowed the German men to keep the underwear they were standing in. He left the female doctors fully dressed because he disapproved of women wearing trousers. He had no use for their garments.

T-Bone distributed the keys, grinning as he handed one set to Rashid. "Time for you to learn how to drive, I guess," he smirked.

の の の

The atmosphere in the El Geneina camp crackled with gossip. People sat or stood in groups, discussing the Voice of America news bulletin — the UN Security Council had voted to send a fully-fledged peacekeep-ing mission to Darfur to supplement the current force of African Union monitors. They said that by January 2007 there would be 26,000 troops, a mixture of United Nations and African Union, protecting civilians.

Camp dwellers assured each other that God had rescued them, and it was only a matter of time until Khartoum left them in peace to gov-ern themselves. Then the displaced people could return to their fields to plant their crops.

In the excitement, they hardly noticed the latest bedraggled group of survivors arrive, shuffling with leaden footsteps. They stumbled about in the fading light, finding a spot to build their huts. The old man leading them nodded politely to a younger man who was going to be his new neighbor. They exchanged a few words about the region from which the new arrivals had escaped, and how many in their village had been killed. The younger man was only half listening because he had heard it so many times now from other new arrivals. However, something the elder said caught his attention, and he asked him to repeat himself. Then he gave him a drink of water and led him to Hawa's clinic, knowing the educated people should hear the old man's news.

Hawa gave him more water, urging him to take his time and catch his breath.

"But I have to tell you about this, even if it kills me," the man rasped. "It's the Arabs from Chad. They arrived in our village after the Janjaweed finished with us, even while we were still burying our dead."

"From Chad?" Hawa asked, her brow furrowing. So far the flow of refugees had been from east to west, from Darfur into neighboring Chad, where people had naïvely hoped they might escape the violence.

"They moved right into our houses and told us to go. They said they had been invited to come here to populate our villages. They showed us their new Sudanese identity cards."

"Who's invited them?" asked Hawa, fighting off the wave of fear creeping through her veins like ice.

"The regime, they said. They're going from village to village in Chad, promising the people nice homes, good farm land, plenty of livestock."

Hawa gazed through the open tent flap into the gathering darkness, hardly able to breathe. The people in Chad were Arab. That was why Khartoum was inviting them to replace the black African tribes of Darfur. It was ethnic cleansing in reverse. They were creating their racially pure Arab nation.

Hawa promised the old man she would see the UN officials immediately. Following Mary's death, she made sure the officials understood she wished to remain anonymous, yet she felt it was her duty to pass on information that might prompt the UN to challenge the regime.

"I just want to go back to my land," the elder said, clearly bewildered by the turn of events that had landed him at the El Geneina camp. He thanked her several times and stumbled out into the gathering dusk.

Hawa set out for the UN tent, walking slowly across the camp, minding where she stepped, careful to avoid bumping her swollen belly into obstacles. Although she had promised the elder that his information would reach the highest levels, she knew it might never get to the people with power who needed to hear it. But she had wanted to give the old man hope that someone might care, holding out some prospect of justice.

It's never a waste of time, reminding the world what's happening here, she thought. *That's what Mary told me. It's always worth a try.*

CHAPTER TWENTY-ONE

Zara studied her brother's troubled features across the breakfast table. Abdelatif had been working at the pizza parlor for almost a year, and although he still came in late each night, it had been a long time since he had looked so exhausted.

At the end of his first week's employment his boss had cheated him out of his overtime pay. When Abdelatif had complained, the owner had told him to take it or leave it; he was an illegal immigrant with no right to employment. Since then Abdelatif had come to an understanding with his boss. He spent several hours a day at the pizza parlor on the phone, dealing with British Council of Darfuri Refugees business. His boss dare not complain for fear of appearing bad before the Sudanese community in exile.

"What's wrong, Abdelatif?" Zara asked.

"They deported Ismael," he began, his eyes rooted on the untouched porridge before him.

Zara felt a surge of panic. Her mother's hand, halfway to spooning food into the toddler's mouth, hung in midair. "When?" asked Sumah, incredulous.

"Ismael's wife Halima called me yesterday morning," Abdelatif continued, his voice leaden. "The immigration people had just picked him up, she said. They were planning to put him on the overnight flight to Khartoum." He paused, absentmindedly running his fingers up and down the shaft of the sugar spoon. "I spent most of yesterday on the phone to lawyers and journalists, but the immigration authorities weren't interested in the details about human rights abuses in Sudan. As far as they're concerned, Ismael failed to get refugee status. So he's out."

"And his wife and kids?" asked Sumah.

"They came in separately, after Ismael, so they didn't process their paperwork together," he explained. "But they may come for them at any moment."

"I didn't realize he'd exhausted the appeal process," said Zara uncertainly. "Did you?"

"Ismael isn't the type to burden others with his problems. He always brushed off my questions about his legal situation." He hesitated. "Halima was in a terrible state."

"God help her," murmured Sumah, giving the toddler a hug.

"We really must go to America," Zara said suddenly. "We should start applying for American visas."

Sumah noticed the look of pain on Abdelatif's face. "Leave him alone, Zara. It's time you went to school," she said firmly.

As the girls walked though the housing project five minutes later, Safia said, "I don't know why you think America will be different from here. They have problems too—all those young, unmarried girls having babies, all those drugs. And the violence and pornography!"

"At least they welcome refugees fleeing persecution and tyranny," Zara shot back. "How long before they come for Ismael's wife? How long before they come for us?"

Safia shrugged, unwilling to dwell on Zara's point. "The longer I'm here, the less I understand some aspects of Western life."

Zara gave a halfhearted laugh.

"The kids in my class are obsessed with the most horrible computer games," Safia continued. "They think they're so cool and tough because they play games where they're chopping people into pieces. They're brave warriors when they're sitting in the safety of their bedrooms, staring at their computer screens." She paused. "Such terrible images, and they seem absolutely unaffected when they see film reports of real carnage, or when you try to tell them about what's happening at home. They have no idea what it's like to actually be chased by someone with a gun."

Zara walked on in silence, preferring not to recall her own journey across Darfur to Chad.

"The goats in Sudan have healthier family structures," Safia continued.

"But what about our friends in New Jersey?" asked Zara. "My grandfather once told me that Martin and his family had a special meal together at the end of every week and celebrated a religious ceremony."

Safia nodded. "That's because they're Jewish and they value being different. They keep a hold on their identity, and their faith tells them there's something bigger than they are as individuals. Just like ours does."

Zara was quiet as they crossed the road. "So, you seem happy to stay here; in England I mean, not in Doncaster."

"Look, there's something you should know," Safia said abruptly, ignoring Zara's observation. "My teachers want me to sit the exams this year."

"Really?" Zara gasped. "That's fantastic."

"It'll only be fantastic if I pass them, but if I do okay then I'll go to university in London in September."

Zara glanced away, afraid her fear would show. She was delighted for her friend, but she was also afraid of losing her.

"They've got a great course in international relations and human rights at the London School of Economics," Safia continued. "Then I could study law after that."

Zara nodded. They had discussed Safia's plans to become a human rights lawyer, to help others like themselves. Zara had guessed from the first day they had met on their walk across the savannah that Safia was very smart. Safia never talked about her former life, but it was clear she had come from a distinguished family and had benefited from years of formal education. Even when she had been dropped into a totally different culture, learning in a foreign language, Safia had been top of her class within three months.

"Well, I hope some of your brains rub off on me," Zara commented. "You know, it's really helped me, studying with you, living with you, practicing English together. It's forced me to keep up." She smiled. "It's a little like training beside a superb athlete."

Safia threw her head back and laughed. "But that's exactly how I've felt about you. I'd never have had the self-discipline to keep my nose to the grindstone if I wasn't always trying to keep up with you."

Zara gazed at her, wide-eyed with surprise. Then she laughed. "Anyway, I'm really pleased for you about the exams." She considered saying she didn't want to be separated, to lose Safia's friendship, but she knew it would impose an unfair burden on her friend. "You'll keep in touch, won't you?"

"That's why they invented the Internet," Safia replied with a grin.

ṃ ṃ ṃ

The baggage hall at Khartoum airport was notable for two reasons — the conveyor belt had long ceased functioning and a family of cats had taken up residence there. They marched importantly among the cases as the men in uniforms placed bags on tables, sifting through the contents, searching for banned publications.

Ismael was not given the option of collecting his luggage when he reached Khartoum. His wife had thrown a few things into a case before he was hustled away from their home in Leeds, and as far as he knew, the case had made the journey with him, to Heathrow and then to Sudan. However, the moment he reached the tarmac, and the blanket of dark heat enveloped him, he was taken firmly by both elbows and steered away from the rest of the disembarking passengers, bypassing the cats and the baggage.

The uniformed men said nothing as they led him to a four-wheel drive vehicle, pushing him into the backseat. Within moments they were on their way into the city, along roads empty of other vehicles. Ismael peered into the darkness, at the silhouettes of squat minarets and the occasional darkened stores. He suspected they were driving him to one of numerous anonymous safe houses around the capital where they tortured human rights activists and others who questioned the regime's right to imprison an entire nation against its will. Now that he was looking into the abyss, he felt strangely at peace with the choices he had made. The moment he had feared for months had arrived, and bearing in mind the regime's track record, there was only one possible outcome. There was nothing he could do about it but maintain his dignity as best he could, and pray.

He cleared his throat and leaned forward so the commanding officer sitting in the front passenger seat could hear him.

"You know, one day you'll all be indicted before the International Criminal Court in Holland."

The commanding officer craned his neck and stared at his prisoner, clearly astonished.

"I promise you, my brother," Ismael continued, "The British and the Americans and the French will make sure you're held accountable for what you've done to all the innocent people who've been through your hands."

The commanding officer raised his eyebrows.

"They're watching you—the ICC is," Ismael continued, buoyed up by a wave of confidence. "Even idiots like you—they know your names and what you do. They've got dozens of lawyers and investigators compiling files on you. And one day when I'm just a pile of dust; one day, I promise you, you'll pay the price."

☧ ☧ ☧

The official cause of death was heart failure. Five days after her husband was deported from Leeds, Halima received a phone call from Sudan. It was from her sister-in-law in Omdurman, giving her the bad news. They had already collected Ismael's body, and according to the custom, they had buried him immediately. Neither woman mentioned the possibility that Halima might have traveled to Khartoum for the ceremony or to bid her husband farewell. Apart from the more prosaic considerations, such as the expense, they both knew it was a fair bet that Halima would meet a similar fate if she ever set foot on Sudanese soil.

At the next meeting of the Darfuri refugee activists in Leeds, the men held a wake and made speeches in honor of Ismael. Abdelatif stumbled through his tribute, too choked up to lift his eyes from his handwritten text. He spent the rest of the ceremony staring bleakly ahead, his emotions bordering on despair. Ever since they had been given the news from Khartoum, he kept imagining what his colleague had been through before he died. *A small piece of me has also died,* he reflected silently.

On the bus back to Doncaster, Abdelatif sat behind two men discussing a popular television program that billed itself as a "reality" show. He had encountered it while flicking through the channels, searching for something to soothe the persistent turmoil in his head. But rather than amusing or distracting him, he found the program pointless. *These people have no idea what reality is,* he thought.

As Abdelatif listened to the men on the bus, he wanted to ask them, *If you want reality, why don't you go and work in a refugee camp in a war zone? Or maybe you leave that to the little Irish nuns and American doctors who have no reason to risk their lives in a Muslim country like Sudan. God bless the real united nations of volunteers,* he thought, *the nameless heroes who risk their lives to defend us — who believe that it's possible for people of different cultures and religions to live together in harmony.*

Then he realized with a jolt that the simple dream he had just silently articulated was exactly the dream his grandfather, Sheikh Muhammad, had shared with his children and grandchildren. It brought a smile to his face. *I must remember to tell Zara that,* he thought.

CHAPTER TWENTY-TWO

On the day Hawa gave birth, she held her newborn son in her arms, blocking out the activity around her in the clinic. She tried not to recall the nephew she had pulled from the fire and carried across the savannah, or the regime's plans to kill as many male Darfuris as they could. *Just to spite them I'll make sure my boy survives and becomes a great leader.*

Gazing into his scrunched-up baby features, she told herself, *Giving birth to a child is the most hopeful thing a person can do.* She had decided to call her son Ahmed. When she looked at him, she believed she saw her friend's eyes and mouth, refusing to accept the paternity of an ignorant, ugly Janjaweed boy, bleary-eyed with hatred and rage.

When Hawa realized she was pregnant, she had known she had a choice: to reject the child because it was the result of violence and shame, or to accept the baby as a living embodiment of love and hope. It reflected her own dilemma: to be angry for the rest of her life, or to get her strength from turning the page.

Everywhere there were women pregnant as a consequence of being raped, but no one discussed it. Giving voice to their feelings would have meant admitting they had been raped, thus inviting social exclusion and contempt. There was also no acknowledgment that many newborn infants had been left to the side to die, rejected. Everyone preferred not to mention it. *Hypocrisy and denial are the foundations of our world here,* she thought.

The traditional view still prevailed, despite the overwhelming evidence that the women who went to collect firewood did not enjoy being attacked and tortured, humiliated and defiled with sticks, branded like cattle. At first, those who survived were shunned and ignored, as if they did not exist. Pretending these women were invisible might have been an option in the first two years of the war, but now their numbers had grown significantly, and they were impossible to overlook.

In the weeks following Ahmed's birth, Hawa noticed the overt hostility toward women who gave birth following rape. Old men and boys hissed at them; women snubbed them, refusing to make eye contact, pulling their scarves up. Previously, Hawa had merely observed the reaction of the camp inhabitants to Janjaweed babies. Now that she had little Ahmed, she was on the receiving end of the harsh treatment, although the arbiters of these high moral standards withheld their censure while she was wiping up their vomit and feces in the clinic.

During her working hours, Ahmed stayed with the mother of another Janjaweed infant. Hawa paid the woman to care for her baby. She earned enough from her job to leave him with the bright young woman whom she knew well and trusted to keep her baby safe and fed.

Matters came to a head one afternoon when a rumor reached the clinic that there had been a mass beating somewhere in the camp. The staff and volunteers assumed the Sudanese security services were to blame. Whenever they patrolled, they picked on anyone who did not scuttle obediently out of their way. Hawa warned the staff and volunteers to prepare for an influx of wounded people.

When the first bloody, battered victims limped in, holding rags to their wounds, she saw that they were all women and infants. As she cleaned and sutured their cuts, Hawa coaxed the women to tell her their story. It soon emerged that their injuries were not due to heavy-handed Sudanese policing.

"I was alone, outside my hut, caring for my baby, when these three young men came along. They were carrying sticks, and they insulted me for defiling the honor of our tribe, and then they accused me of consorting with the Janjaweed. They were so angry, and they started beating me, and they wouldn't stop until I was bleeding from my forehead and nose."

"I could see it in their eyes—I knew I was in danger. I wrapped myself around my baby to protect him, so they beat me on my back and legs. Then they moved on. They walked past my neighbor, but then I saw them beating the only other woman in my condition in our row of huts."

Another woman added, "I was cooking beside my hut when the young men walked up, saying hello to the people who live next door, and suddenly they started beating me with their sticks. They told me I was an unclean whore and I should have died rather than brought dishonor on our people. They were no more than boys."

A pattern emerged from Hawa's informal interviews—the young men seemed to know exactly where they were going, as if they had planned it beforehand. They did not hit people randomly, but when they found the "unclean" women, they attacked them in a frenzy of hate. Several babies had suffered broken limbs and deep cuts.

No one reported the incidents to the authorities because it was assumed that no action would be taken against the men; women simply had no power or status. For centuries they had obeyed their men and been beaten for any perceived infraction. Listening to the tearful, terrified women, it was clear no one had come to their aid, and Hawa suspected more than a few inhabitants approved of this variety of vigilante justice. Only those who had endured being raped might feel sympathy, and they wisely kept their opinions to themselves.

That evening, Hawa sat at one end of the clinic, keeping watch over the wounded mothers and babies, trying to ease their pain with aspirin and compassion. She felt powerless to remove the stain of shame and rejection that had provoked the attacks in the first place.

This is how they will destroy us, she reflected bleakly. *We are resilient people so we can withstand drought and floods, hunger and disease. We adapt and cope and improvise. But they've found a way to tear us to shreds. By raping every woman and girl they can, they remove our foundations. Men will turn on women, boys will despise girls. The traditions that have helped us endure war and pestilence over the centuries will be like a house made of reeds in a gale.*

Hawa had been raised to follow her society's rules without question. Yet, sometime ago she had crossed an invisible line. In the part of her brain that Mary had nurtured, the ability to think rationally, Hawa understood that her people must adapt to the new reality or else their culture and identity would die.

We will eat ourselves alive in this camp, she thought. The women with Janjaweed offspring had nowhere to go; the restless young men were caged up and bored, turning their anger on the most vulnerable—the women with babies. Khartoum was succeeding in its aim. In the first wave of genocide they killed the men who might resist them, and in their second genocide they destroyed Darfur's society.

Only we can save ourselves, she thought, gazing into the terrified eyes of a woman with a bulging, oozing dressing tied around her head. Then a happier image came to mind: Mama Mounah and the circle of her female friends who came to help Hawa as soon as she arrived in their village. Mounah had formed a community based on mutual support, independent of men. Perhaps the way forward was for the rejected women in the camp to create their own world within the bubble of hatred surrounding them.

For Hawa, this realization was like a light illuminating the darkness. When she went home that night, collecting Ahmed on the way, she lay awake for hours, considering her plan, exploring the barriers she might find in her way. *Mama Mounah's example will give me the strength I need,* she promised herself, finally drifting off to sleep, at peace with her decision.

The following morning at the clinic, she approached one of the women who had been beaten the previous day. The young woman seemed intelligent and quick on the uptake, so Hawa sat down beside her and explained her idea.

"They want us to be invisible," she began. "They expect us to hide, alone and ashamed, so they can forget we exist. But why should our babies be blamed for what happened? Why should they suffer?"

"They're born to misery. It's their fate," the woman mumbled.

"No, I don't think we should accept fate anymore," Hawa retorted, her voice rising. "We've endured the same torment, so we should work together in a group, a women's group, where we help each other, rather than hiding, hoping no one'll notice us or our children."

"I don't understand. What would such a group do?" asked the young woman.

"We have no one to help us, so we must help ourselves and each other," Hawa explained, her enthusiasm growing, her eyes sparkling. "We should take turns caring for each other's babies, freeing up several women to stand in line for water or find a job in the town, like cleaning someone's home, for instance."

The young woman stared at Hawa, startled, "You mean we create our own family?"

Hawa smiled, stroking the woman's hand. "That's a good way of putting it—a family."

The young woman pulled herself into a sitting position, "And together we're stronger?"

"They'll treat us like outcasts," commented a woman in the next cot.

"They already do," another responded. "We have nothing to lose. The people in this camp are two-faced."

"We should stand up to them."

"We have to stand up for each other," Hawa reminded her gently. "We mustn't be consumed by hatred, but we must direct our energy to helping each other. We owe it to our children."

"What do we do next?"

Hawa surveyed the battered but eager faces around her. "Spread the word to the others like us. Then we'll get together and decide what practical help we need in our daily lives. And we'll form a network so we need never feel alone or afraid."

One of the older women shrank back in her cot, clearly dubious. "They'll beat us again when they find out."

"Not if we keep going. Anyway, women are stronger than men—we all know that."

"I think you've talked yourself into another job, Hawa," said the young woman Hawa had first approached.

"What do you mean?"

"You've just become our leader."

☙ ☙ ☙

From the minute Rashid joined the rebels it was clear that his commanding officer treated him differently. T-Bone was aware of, and impressed by, Rashid's family connections. No one cared that the young man had nobly volunteered to serve, rather than being press-ganged or sold to the rebels. But it mattered a great deal that Sheikh Uthman sent boxes of medicines and food rations their way on a regular basis. Rashid had no illusions that the supplies represented a gesture of forgiveness from grandfather to grandson; The old man simply wished to keep in favor with the rebels.

Nevertheless, it took weeks before the soldiers in his unit trusted Rashid sufficiently to include him in their in-jokes and horseplay. Even then, he felt they were holding back, as if they knew he was important to their commander, aware that he was kept out of harm's way when they put themselves in danger. No one belittled him or mentioned his protected status, but Rashid could tell that they were wary of him.

Shortly after Rashid joined the unit, T-Bone gave him a truck, a driver, and three men, sending him on a nighttime trip back to the camp outside El Geneina, collecting medical supplies and food. His grandfather was as distant as ever, failing to acknowledge that his grandson was doing something brave and important. However, the old man gave generously of the humanitarian aid that he had "come across." And on this occasion, the sheikh sent Rashid away with something extra—his satellite phone number, with instructions to call in two days time.

When Rashid placed the call in due course, his grandfather came to the point immediately, "Tell your commander there's going to be a convoy of some interest, and it'll pass near you today." Uthman gave Rashid the approximate time and route, disconnecting without further comment. T-Bone offered him a broad grin when Rashid passed on the information.

"He's an extremely well-connected man, your grandfather," his commander remarked with uncharacteristic reverence. "May God bless him for his service to the movement," he murmured, as if they were discussing a martyr. "Gather the guys together, Rashid. I've got to make a phone call."

When he reappeared, T-Bone briefed his unit, explaining that they would be intercepting a convoy shortly. "This one's bigger than usual, so we're coordinating with Jibril's platoon. We meet them at two o'clock to go over the plans. So be ready to leave here in an hour." He allocated duties and then retreated to his tent to listen to the soccer commentary from Cameroon.

When they arrived at the rendezvous, Rashid was alarmed to see Ahmed in the back of Jibril's vehicle. The two had not met since the "recruitment night," as T-Bone described the abduction of the camp boys. The moment he felt Ahmed's eyes on him, Rashid was uncomfortable and anxious, trying to pretend he hadn't noticed him. He was, as ever, riled by Ahmed's annoyingly superior attitude. Somehow, without even opening his mouth, he could make Rashid feel cheap and inadequate.

The two groups of boys climbed down from their vehicles, gathering around T-Bone. Rashid steeled himself to betray no emotion before his soccer hero adversary, slipping on his sunglasses to hide his eyes. He ordered himself to relax. He was a hero now, not a privileged goat boy. He was standing alongside the big men, an honorable warrior, exactly like the childhood stories about his tribe's glorious traditions. He puffed his chest out, forcing himself to meet Ahmed's frank, cold stare.

T-Bone ran them through the plan of attack, and then they loitered in groups, waiting for the satellite phone call from the vehicle up ahead, standing by to report when the convoy came into view. The young men chatted, trying on each other's dark glasses, but T-Bone stopped them playing music or making much noise.

Rashid, avoiding Ahmed, joined a group standing as far away from him as possible. Undeterred, Ahmed headed directly for Rashid, his gaze like a laser beam.

"How can you live with yourself?" Ahmed began, his voice so loud that conversations nearby stopped abruptly. Rashid fought the impulse to shrink back as Ahmed continued haranguing him, "You're nothing but a slave trader."

In an instant T-Bone was at Rashid's side. "What's the problem, guys?" he said.

A smile flickered across Ahmed's face as he registered Rashid's fear. "We're talking about buying and selling people like they're nothing more than bags of beans."

Rashid kept his eyes on the horizon, as if he wasn't part of the conversation.

T-Bone shrugged. "That's the way of the world," he said. "Nothing you can do about it because there'll always be someone making a profit out of it. We might as well exploit it."

Ahmed snorted, "That's very high-minded of you. It fits in neatly with your noble actions as a defender of your people."

"What's that supposed to mean?" T-Bone snarled, keeping his voice not much louder than a whisper. The young men nearby had noticed their argument, and they stood in embarrassed silence, not even daring to exchange glances.

"Most of the time we hide in the mountains, while the Janjaweed rampage through our villages," Ahmed continued, raising his voice. "We attack aid convoys and steal their stuff like we're criminals. Tell me what's so honorable about that? Pretty soon the rest of the world will think all the Darfur rebels are no better than thieves. We're making it harder for the units out there who are actually trying to fight the regime."

T-Bone shook his head. "You may be a soccer star but you've got a big mouth, and T-Bone says you should shut it, okay?"

Ahmed threw the commander a withering look. "These humanitarians we're stealing from will stop bothering to come here if we keep hijacking their trucks. And if they pull out, then there'll be nothing for people to eat. No medicine, no water tanks, nothing. And once they're gone, there'll be no witnesses, and Khartoum will really get down to business then."

T-Bone laughed. "Of course they'll keep coming here." He threw Ahmed a pitying look. "Don't you get it? Their governments want them here because it gives them an excuse not to stand up to the regime or enforce their precious UN resolutions. They can't do anything that might endanger the lives of their own humanitarian aid workers, can they?"

Ahmed frowned, "That's very cynical. You're forgetting how much these aid workers are risking by being here."

T-Bone shrugged his comments away. "Their governments just want to feel good about themselves, handing out milk powder to the starving refugees. It's all a game. They feed us until the regime gets around to killing us."

Ahmed gritted his teeth. "You talk like everything is just for show."

T-Bone flashed him a wide, menacing grin. "Now you're finally catching on, soccer boy."

"We're losing credibility with our own people."

T-Bone clicked his tongue, annoyed by Ahmed's insubordination. "Our own people?" He sneered, his voice rising. "No one cares what the little village guy thinks, and they never will. Life is all about the big man with the power, not the little man in his flip-flops, hiding in his hut, hoping no one notices him, always trying to stay away from trouble."

T-Bone paused, mopping the perspiration from his brow. His audience looked apprehensive, uncertain which way their leader's notorious temper would go.

"Oh, of course, I'd forgotten you're a soccer hero so you know everything about military strategy!" he exclaimed, swiveling his head around. "Everyone, meet the soccer hero general!"

The young militiamen laughed, just as they always laughed at T-Bone's jokes. As ever, they watched his lips carefully, hoping for a signal or a warning that their mercurial leader was about to be witty, and then they raced each other to be the first to join in.

"Keep the noise down!" a deep baritone voice bellowed.

They turned to find a tall, beefy man glaring at them. His arms were as wide as a man's thighs, hanging at a forty-five-degree angle from his vast torso. He glanced at Ahmed and then at T-Bone, his ebony face distorted and bloated by fat.

"Are you bothering my Beckham?"

T-Bone raised his eyebrows, all innocence. "Who's Beckham?"

With the slightest nod of his massive head, Jibril indicated Ahmed. "Leave him alone."

T-Bone tried to make light of it, offering a grin. "Beckham, huh?"

"One day, when this is finished, we'll sell him to a big international team—Man U, Liverpool, Real Madrid, AC Milan," he recited.

T-Bone remained silent, evidently unwilling to clash with Jibril, but reluctant to back down before his men. His dignity was saved by the satellite phone call from the vehicle keeping watch up ahead.

The rebels piled into the technicals, weapons at the ready, and roared off to intercept the humanitarian convoy of seven vehicles.

Their Kalashnikovs were for show because they knew the aid workers would have no protection and would put up no resistance. Hundreds of charity staff innocently and trustingly wandered across the wilderness of Darfur, often without even a satellite phone. The African Union monitors were vastly over-stretched, without enough gas or water to leave their camps. Even if there was fuel, the AU mandate was to observe and write reports, not to accompany convoys, nor to intervene to stop banditry.

Within a matter of seconds, the rebel units had swarmed around the charity's vehicles, bringing them to a halt. Everyone knew the routine by now: the rebels leapt down from their technicals, ready to play their choreographed part. The aid workers looked terrified, leaving their vehicles without much of a fuss.

However, on this occasion a white man in a Real Madrid soccer shirt, who appeared to be the leader, started arguing with the rebels. He went red in the face and yelled, but since no one understood a word he said, the soldiers jabbed him with the barrels of their rifles. His local driver tried to calm him down but the white man was too angry to listen.

T-Bone told his men to line up the aid workers at the side of the road. Nevertheless the convoy leader in the Real Madrid shirt kept complaining, his staccato voice like a machine gun.

"This man is really getting on my nerves," commented Jibril.

Without hesitation, Jibril's deputy took the initiative and smashed the man in the teeth with his rifle butt.

Rashid was shaken by the ferocity and swiftness of the attack, but excited by it too. Evidently Jibril was surrounded by men who wanted him to be happy, without waiting for him to issue direct orders. He was shocked by what he had just seen, but it stirred something inside of him, like a flame being lit.

As the Real Madrid man slumped to the ground, one of the white women began screaming, while her colleague pulled off her headscarf, holding it to his wound.

Rashid watched as a second white man stepped forward, his jaw jutting. Then he froze, as if he was weighing the wisdom of shouting at the rebels. Whereas his shoulders had been taut and twitching a moment before, Rashid noticed he suddenly slumped, like a dummy cut down from a tree, his arms hanging uselessly at his sides.

T-Bone caught Rashid's eye, and it was evident he had also noticed the fight draining out of the aid worker. "Good thing he changed his mind about that."

Rashid grinned.

Then T-Bone ordered his soldiers to go through the white people's pockets. The screaming woman shuffled back, shrieking like a wounded donkey, unwilling to let them touch her or take her possessions. Rashid moved closer, intending to hold her still so the others could search her. Her lip curled in disgust as she made eye contact with him, and then she spat.

The spittle landed on Rashid's neck, dribbling beneath his tank top. He felt his heart stop beating for a moment, the spit running down his chest. Then something inside his head clicked, like a radio being switched on, and a flood of ear-piercing white noise gushing out, deafening him, making it impossible for him to think clearly.

Rashid slapped her so hard she reeled backwards losing her balance, crashing to the ground. Before he could think he was on top of her, ripping off her blouse. Several soldiers gathered around, cheering him on, and three of his colleagues knelt down to hold her still while he tore at her flimsy trousers. He glanced up, acknowledging their chanting approval, and then slapped the woman again. But when he looked up once more, instead of seeing his colleagues' grins, he only saw Ahmed glaring down at him. In an instant, his head cleared of the raging fury that was gripping him. His arousal vanished, and he got to his feet, pulling up his zip.

"That's enough to teach her a lesson," he told the other soldiers with a halfhearted laugh.

But as he walked swiftly away another boy took his place, lowering his trousers.

"No," Ahmed said, pulling at the boy's arm. "You do that, and we're as bad as they are."

It was clear that "they" were the Janjaweed and the regime because the boy's half-crazed leer faded. He hitched up his trousers, scowling.

Ahmed looked down at the white woman. Her eyes were like watery slits, puffed up from Rashid's punches. She drew herself into a ball, trying to cover her breasts with her arms. Ahmed peeled off his Manchester United shirt and handed it to her. She snatched it and put it on, trembling as she tried to pull it over her head. Then her white colleague helped the woman to her feet and out of their way.

"Maybe we should tidy up?" T-Bone asked Jibril. "It's not a good idea to leave any witnesses, after what just happened, I mean."

"No," said Ahmed clearly, stepping forward, inserting himself in T-Bone's space. "You kill them, and you make sure we lose any sympathy from the rest of the world. They'll be able to say, "Those Sudanese are all as bad as each other. Let's leave them to get on with it."

T-Bone sighed and slid his dark glasses up the bridge of his nose.

Jibril seemed to be giving the matter due consideration. "Beckham's right," he said after a moment. "Let's take the trucks and get out of here." He paused. "Better make an anonymous call to the peacekeepers, too. Tell them to come and fetch these guys."

Rashid stood to one side of T-Bone's technical, wondering if he had lost all credibility in the eyes of his unit. They would probably never include him in their horseplay. He would always be the sheikh's grandson, useful for his family connections.

Then he caught sight of Ahmed, walking slowly toward him, preoccupied and unhappy. For a moment it crossed his mind that his adversary might be about to congratulate him for doing the right thing. His heart leapt slightly and he was embarrassed by how vulnerable he felt. He hated himself for craving Ahmed's approval, just as all his life he had yearned to impress his grandfather.

As he drew near, Ahmed narrowed his eyes, calling out something Rashid couldn't hear. He hesitated, knowing he should ignore Ahmed and get into the technical. But he walked toward him, like a child, eager to hear what he had to say, even if it was hurtful and critical. He loathed himself for being so pitiful and weak, but still he went to Ahmed.

"What?" he asked Ahmed, trying to sound tough.

"They're doctors."

"What?"

"I went through the stuff in their trucks," Ahmed continued. "They are from Spain and they're doctors. They were coming to heal our people."

Rashid felt his knees wobble, and it took all his willpower not to snivel and hang his head. A terrible pain wrapped around his skull, and he prayed he wasn't about to wilt on the spot. Overcome with shame, he turned away, his motions jerky and uncoordinated, to scuttle back to the technical.

CHAPTER TWENTY-THREE

Zara was skipping school for a good reason. Abdelatif was now the chair of the British Council of Darfuri Refugees, and he wanted her to accompany him to London to a meeting with the British government. Although his English had improved, Zara knew he lacked the confidence to put his points across in such intimidating circumstances. He seemed to suspect that everyone he encountered judged him because of his poor English and shabby clothes. Whereas Zara had learned how to smile her way out of awkward situations or misunderstandings, he became defensive.

Zara felt a surge of excitement as their red double-decker bus chugged through the London traffic. Emerging into Parliament Square, her heart missed a beat as she caught sight of Big Ben and the vast neo-Gothic legislature building beside it.

When they stepped down from the bus, she glanced at her brother. He was struggling to hide his fear whereas she was excited to be standing where history had unfolded. For a moment she thanked God she was a woman: it was much easier not to have to worry about male dignity. Admitting she didn't know all the answers was not a crushing blow to her ego. Since arriving in Britain, she had realized how much people enjoyed sharing their knowledge, even if it was just handing out advice about which type of bread to buy or which street to take.

The previous week a human rights campaigner named Sandrine Truscott had left a message in English on her brother's cell phone, encouraging him to attend so the government officials could hear "an authentic voice of Darfur."

Zara had returned the call on Abdelatif's behalf and had learned that there would be several other humanitarian and human rights groups at the meeting.

"But none of us are from Darfur," Sandrine had explained. "We haven't survived a Janjaweed attack or lost our families because of the Sudanese army."

"How will I recognize you, please?" Zara had asked, wondering how she would explain that most white people looked similar to her.

"I've got blonde hair, I'm twenty-three years old, and I'll be wearing a silver Ethiopian necklace."

Zara was so startled that a twenty-three-year-old would be the director of a human rights group that she almost forgot to describe herself, until prompted by Sandrine. "I'm black and five feet seven inches tall and I'm seventeen years old. And Abdelatif is twenty-one years old and five feet ten inches tall."

Before they said goodbye, Sandrine explained how visitors to Parliament pass through various security checks. "Ask the police on duty which way to go." Sandrine paused. "The police here are generally helpful, not like where you come from."

Zara followed her instructions and they were soon in line, waiting to be x-rayed. Abdelatif kept his eyes straight ahead, stiff and suspicious. Soon they were climbing flights of elaborately carved stone stairs, beneath ancient ceilings painted blue with a sprinkling of gold stars. The corridors were lined with alabaster statues of mustachioed statesmen, the gilded heraldic shields of families who once ruled the land, and leather-bound books on shelves reaching from the floor to the ceiling. Officials dressed in black stockings, shiny buckled shoes, and frock coats, like characters from a historical drama, nodded respectfully and offered them directions.

Through open doors, Zara caught glimpses of the River Thames, and she would have liked to linger, but Abdelatif urged her to quicken her pace. Even the doorknobs and carpets were neo-Gothic, Zara noticed. She wanted to take in the ornate designs, but Abdelatif reminded her they must be on time for the meeting.

They were directed to a committee room at the far end of a long, grand corridor, lined with books and dingy paintings of historical scenes. A tall, slender, beautiful young white woman approached. "Are you Zara?"

"Sandrine?"

They smiled and shook hands.

"And this is Gillian Lusk from *Africa Confidential*," said Sandrine introducing them. "Let's sit together," Sandrine suggested, her blue eyes sparkling.

A moment later, Zara found herself sitting beside a window overlooking the Thames. Without craning her neck, she could watch as double-decker buses trundled across Westminster Bridge and boats plowed up and down the river.

"Welcome everyone," began the meeting chairman. "We're pleased to have the minister with us, and I'm going to start by asking him to say a few words about the situation in Darfur."

A thin man with a gaunt, narrow face and round, wire-rimmed glasses read from a sheet of paper without looking up at his audience. He remained seated and spoke very quickly, as if he would have preferred to be elsewhere.

"It's been quiet in Darfur for several months now. We're engaging all parties in bilateral talks, and of course we were instrumental in establishing a hybrid African Union and UN peacekeeping force through the UN Security Council."

The minister reeled off a series of statistics listing how much humanitarian aid Britain, America, and the European Union were sending to Darfur. Zara did her best to translate the most important points in a whisper. Abdelatif studied the ground between his feet, frowning.

The minister spoke for less than five minutes, and the moment he finished, Sandrine's hand shot up. Zara stared at her, amazed by her bravery. She had looked as timid as Zara felt, but her pretty face wore an irritated, determined expression.

"How can the minister say Darfur's been quiet when we have reports from several different sources in Darfur confirming that the Sudanese air force continues to bomb villages, often in planes painted in the UN's colors to confuse villagers?" Sandrine then named five villages and the dates on which they were bombed.

"We have no information about that," the minister commented, pointing to the next questioner. Zara watched as Sandrine's eyebrows knit in consternation. She started to speak, but there was to be no comeback to the minister's answer.

Gillian, sitting beside Sandrine, was called next. "Could the minister please comment on reports that the Sudanese government is being allowed the power of veto over which nations will be sending troops to Darfur to make up the new peacekeeping force?"

"Now look," answered the minister, a pained expression on his face. "We need to get peacekeepers in place as soon as possible. We have more than two million people depending on food aid, and our priority is to guarantee humanitarian access to the refugee camps."

Gillian started to respond, but the politician simply switched his attention to his next questioner, as if she had ceased to exist. Zara watched as Sandrine and Gillian shared a heavenward roll of their eyes. She turned to her brother, translating the exchange for him. He closed his eyes and shook his head mournfully.

"Say something," she urged him. "It's important this man hears the truth."

He pondered her words and then nodded. When Zara was called, she explained she was translating for her brother who was the head of the Darfuri community in the north of England. The room went silent as people strained to hear.

"Sir," Abdelatif began, "All of us knew bullies when we were children. The regime running Sudan is made up of bullies. Right now you're giving in to the bullies. Before long, the international community will regret this. The only way to handle bullies is to stand up to them, united. Then they crumble because bullies are cowards."

As Zara translated, the politician kept his eyes rooted on the sheet of paper before him.

"The international community has the moral authority of several UN Security Council resolutions behind it," Abdelatif continued. "By giving in to Khartoum's demands, you signal your weakness. The regime will take advantage of this, and they'll push their luck, again and again, and they'll win."

A few heads nodded, but others looked uncomfortable as he continued, "I can assure the respected minister that my people would rather have a lasting political solution, and do without the humanitarian aid for a while. Please, do not pretend you are helping us when you are doing deals with Khartoum."

The politician ignored his comments, but Sandrine caught Abdelatif's eye, nodded and gave him the thumbs up sign. Gillian flashed Abdelatif a grin. "He didn't like that," she whispered. "Well done. He'll remember what you said."

As the meeting broke up, Abdelatif gestured at Gillian. "Zara, ask this lady why the minister answers none of our questions. Why are we here?"

Gillian laughed sadly. "So the government can say it consulted its stakeholders."

Sandrine had been standing to one side, her cell phone pressed to her ear. She rejoined the conversation. "Zara, what time's your coach back up north? I've just been talking to Al Jazeera, the Arabic channel, and they want to interview Abdelatif. Now."

Abdelatif's lips parted as Zara translated. He looked at Gillian, and saw that she was nodding enthusiastically. The next hour was one of the most extraordinary Abdelatif and Zara had ever lived. One moment, it seemed, Abdelatif had been cleaning the floor in a pizza parlor in Doncaster, and the next an Arabic-speaking technician was threading a clip-on microphone up underneath his shirt, pinning it beneath his Adam's apple, asking him to say a few words for "level."

Abdelatif perched on a sofa in what looked like a sitting room abandoned in the middle of a TV studio. Fierce white lights dazzled him, and a man sat at a right angle to him, speaking Arabic into his microphone, hardly acknowledging his guest. Somewhere beyond the lights Zara, Gillian, and Sandrine were watching him.

"Welcome to the show," the interviewer started, extending a hand. "We're feeding in live, and we're doing it in Arabic. I hope you're okay with that."

Abdelatif nodded. "Where's this being broadcast?" he asked.

"All over the world, if the other guy ever gets here. He's cutting it fine." He glanced at his watch.

"What other guy?" asked Abdelatif, feeling almost paralyzed by terror.

"The Sudanese ambassador. You're debating him live."

At that moment, a small, neat man in an expensive suit was escorted into the studio by two bulky wrestler types with wires curling out of their ears. The ambassador sat beside Abdelatif, offering him a perfunctory nod.

"Coming to you in five," said the cameraman, "Four, three, two . . ."

The interviewer gazed into the camera, welcomed his viewers, and introduced his guests. He turned to Abdelatif. "What did you tell the British government today?"

For a second, time ground to a halt, and Abdelatif gulped. Then suddenly he found the right words.

"Khartoum has proved time and again that it will not honor its international commitments," he concluded.

The ambassador sighed wearily. "This gentleman is simply a stooge of the Zionists who wish to conquer Sudan so the Americans can steal our oil."

Abdelatif realized the diplomat was not going to debate his points, so he played the same game. "Most of my family was murdered by your soldiers on the orders of your government, as part of your master plan to ethnically cleanse the people of Darfur."

"All your funding comes from Israel," the ambassador plowed on. "It is part of a grand imperialist plot against the long-suffering Muslim people because the Americans wish to destroy us."

Abdelatif held out his hands, mystified. "What kind of Muslim sends soldiers to rape our women. You betray the most fundamental elements of our faith."

"This is all propaganda and lies," the ambassador retorted smoothly, but without an ounce of passion. "First Palestine, then Afghanistan and Iraq, and now they're closing in on Sudan because we won't do what the Americans demand."

"You expelled Bin Laden precisely because Washington told you to," Abdelatif shot back. "So please don't pretend you're standing up to Washington on behalf of the world's oppressed."

Not a flicker of emotion registered on the ambassador's smooth brow. "What do you want done," the interviewer asked Abdelatif.

The ambassador glanced at his watch as Abdelatif recited the measures already approved by the UN Security Council, but never implemented. "And there must be a travel ban against the leading members of this corrupt regime," he concluded.

The ambassador looked horrified. "That's outrageous," he exclaimed, his lower lip trembling.

"You don't care about murdering Muslim children, but you're upset at the prospect of being denied your shopping trips to Paris," Abdelatif remarked, triumphantly. "That defines what your regime is all about."

"Thank you both," said the interviewer.

As Abdelatif emerged from the studio, stunned and shaking, his new friends pumped his hand and showered compliments on him. Zara noticed that for the first time in months, perhaps years, he stood up straight, confident and comfortable in his own skin.

Gillian and Sandrine accompanied them back to their bus, firing questions at him, through Zara. They had ideas for using Abdelatif more effectively to rally opinion within Britain, the European Union, and the Muslim world, they told him. By the time he and Zara climbed onto the coach and waved goodbye, Abdelatif felt as if he had been in a remarkable dream where everything, miraculously, went right. "They have so many plans," he remarked to Zara as the coach pulled out into the traffic. "Do you think we'll hear from them again?"

Zara laughed. "Tomorrow, I'll bet you. You've really started something."

Finally Abdelatif allowed himself a broad, triumphant smile. "That felt good," he conceded.

He was awakened the following morning at 6:40 by a call from a radio station in Cairo. "Sandrine said to phone," the journalist began in Arabic. "Can you do an interview down the line for us?"

"When?" asked Abdelatif groggily.

"Er, now."

He paused, thinking of the people waking in their squalid refugee camps, terrified by what another day might bring. "Fine," he answered, pulling himself upright in bed.

Two hours later, it was the Arabic service of the BBC World Service, the greatest prize of the bunch. "Can you get to the BBC regional studio in Doncaster, and we'll do you live into our bulletin?"

"Of course," he replied calmly, even though his palms were perspiring.

Within a week, Abdelatif was doing two or three phone interviews a day, contributing to Arabic language radio stations around the world, and penning articles for the Arabic press.

"He's articulate and passionate and authentic," Sandrine told Zara, to whom she spoke regularly. "There's been a vacuum, a need for a genuine Darfuri voice, a fluent representative who can see the big picture and give a proper political analysis."

"It's great," commented Zara. "He's beginning to enjoy living here," she admitted. "Not that there's anything wrong with being in Britain, of course," she added.

"It's okay. I'm sure he misses home, but what about you?"

Zara felt as if she was betraying her country by admitting that she was happy in England. "I really like going to school, and I'd like to go to university, too," she conceded.

"Of course," Sandrine responded, as if it were obvious. "What do you want to study?"

"Architecture," she said, afraid it sounded absurd for a girl from a mud hut in the savannah to be dreaming of creating great buildings.

"Great," said Sandrine.

Zara grinned from ear to ear.

However, her good humor did not last long. The following morning a letter arrived informing Zara's family that their status as asylum seekers was being "considered." They were invited to go through a "re-documentation" process, and an interview with Home Office immigration officials.

"This is what happened to Ismael," said Abdelatif with a gloomy shake of his weary head. "This is the beginning of the end."

彝   彝   彝

Zara volunteered to accompany her brother to see the UK Borders Agency officials, knowing he lacked the language skills to survive one-on-one. The letter had assured him a translator would be available, but other Darfuris had warned there was often no one present to help. At best they might be offered someone speaking a very different version of Arabic, almost impossible to understand. Added to that, Abdelatif knew several families who had been tricked into signing voluntary return forms, agreeing to be deported.

Both brother and sister were immediately wary when they were shown into the interview room. The officials who greeted them were a bearded man and a woman in glasses, both local English people, sitting behind a table piled high with manila case files. However, to one side was a black man with unfortunate skin and a weedy mustache whom they instantly recognized as Sudanese. The female official introduced the Sudanese as Sadiq, explaining he would be translating. He flashed them a shark-like smile.

"Please start by explaining where you're from and why you think you qualify for asylum in Britain," prompted the bearded white man.

Sadiq translated the sentence and then added, "And if you tell them lies about what's happening in Darfur, your family at home will be very sorry."

Zara felt as if she had been pinned back in the seats of a car that was suddenly accelerating.

"This man is from the Sudanese embassy in London, isn't he?" she asked the woman, who looked surprised that Zara could speak English.

"What's wrong with that?"

"His government is ethnically cleansing our people."

The woman laughed as if Zara was being melodramatic. "You're all from Sudan, that's right, isn't it?"

"We're from Darfur, and that man works for the regime in Khartoum."

"Yes," she conceded, "and he's here to help us find out why you don't want to go back there and to help us assess the validity of your claim."

"Does he work for the Sudanese embassy?" asked Zara again.

"I believe so, yes," said the female official, clearly impatient to get on with the interview.

"In that case he's a representative of the regime that is committed to expelling everyone who disagrees with them. Their agents control everything: the law, who gets a place at college, or a job."

"Oh, please," she exclaimed, not bothering to hide her irritation. "Sadiq is here to help us process your claim. It's all quite normal, I assure you."

"He just threatened us when he translated your words."

"That's absolute nonsense," Sadiq chipped in. "They're using lies to avoid answering your questions, I'm afraid."

"Calm down, everyone," said the male official. "The Sudanese embassy is helping us assess the validity of asylum claims. Now, it seems to me that since Sadiq isn't from Darfur, there should be no problem having him present."

"But he's a representative of the Khartoum regime. It's a totalitarian government, like the Taliban were in Afghanistan," Zara said, her voice rising.

Sadiq shook his head, offering the Home Office bureaucrats an apologetic shrug. "Obviously this isn't true. There's no danger awaiting these people back in Sudan. If you send them to Khartoum, they'll be fine. The truth is, they're economic migrants. They know they can make lots of money in England. They're pretending to be refugees. I'm sorry."

Zara felt as if her head were about to explode. "Please," she continued, "do you know about what is happening in Darfur?"

The female official nodded. "There's thousands of people in refugee camps, and we can see why you'd want to escape from that. It's a humanitarian disaster, but that doesn't apply in Khartoum, does it?"

"The people are in the camps because the Islamist regime in Khartoum is forcing all the citizens of Sudan to obey their rules," Zara persisted. "Extreme Sharia law, no democracy, and no impartial legal system," she added, hoping the British official would understand. "The Islamists have a plan to spread this violence all across Africa and even Europe."

Sadiq shook his head. "There's a civil war between the tribes in Darfur who are farmers, and some nomadic tribes, who are arguing about access to land and water. But they're all intermarried, and really, this has been going on for centuries."

Zara was on the verge of tears. "The nomads are being paid by the regime. I think you know about this?" she asked, looking hopefully at the officials.

They leafed through their files, shrugging. "I'm not blaming you for trying to find work here," commented the bearded official mildly. "But that's different from seeking asylum from persecution."

The female official screwed up her eyes, studying their file.

Meanwhile Sadiq planted his steady gaze on Abdelatif. "What tribe do you claim to be from?" he asked in Arabic.

Abdelatif responded in the local language, to prove his origins were authentic.

Sadiq turned to the officials and shook his head slightly. "He can hardly speak a word of it. I doubt they're who they say they are." He hesitated and pursed his lips. "I'm sorry. It's embarrassing for my country that these people come here and exploit the kindness and generosity of the British people."

Zara translated Sadiq's words for her brother, who duly unleashed a volley of Arabic at the Sudanese.

"It's pathetic," Sadiq continued in English. "The number of these people we see who can't even speak the language of the tribe they claim to come from."

Zara translated quickly.

"I can bring you people from the Darfuri community here who'll swear who I am and where I'm from. I can provide signed letters from these people," Abdelatif fired back through Zara.

The bearded official tapped his pen on Abdelatif's file. "But we can't recognize just anyone as being an authority on the tribes and languages of Darfur. That's where Sadiq can help us verify people's claims. We have special criteria to establish ethnicity, you see."

"But he is not an impartial judge," Abdelatif responded through Zara.

The male Home Office official sighed. "Round and round we go."

"Do you have any papers proving where you're from?" asked his female colleague.

"Everything was destroyed when we were attacked."

"So you can't provide any documentary evidence to back up your story?"

"It's the same for other refugees, yes?" asked Zara, but the officials looked back at their notes, without comment.

Finally, the bearded man cleared his throat and began speaking in a lifeless monotone. "We're turning down your application for asylum status on the basis that you cannot provide any evidence that returning you to Khartoum would endanger you whatsoever. If you aren't satisfied that we've taken all appropriate steps to verify the circumstances of your claim, then there's an appeals process. Thank you." He glanced up at them, smiling thinly, and closed their file.

A moment later, Zara and Abdelatif were out on the street in the rain, too stunned to speak. They walked, side by side to the bus stop, shoulders hunched against the cold wind. Zara felt raindrops clinging to her eyelashes, but to brush them away would mean taking her hand from her pocket and exposing it to the chill. They stood by the bus stop, watching their breath form clouds in the air, a sight that never ceased to amaze Zara.

"I hope you agree we've got to start finding a way to get to New Jersey," Zara suggested. "*If* we can get there."

Abdelatif looked defeated. "I suppose so."

That afternoon, Zara screwed up her courage and called Rachael in New Jersey. Zara had written to her shortly after they arrived in Doncaster, and they had communicated thereafter by email, to which Zara had access at the school library. Transatlantic phone calls were expensive but there was a new urgency to their situation. If their appeal failed, the British government would deport them swiftly, keen to be seen to be expelling illegal immigrants.

Though Rachael Bennett was used to being contacted by Darfuris, thanks to her involvement in the Save Darfur campaign, she hadn't been expecting to hear from England. Zara apologized for bothering her and tried to summarize their situation coherently.

"Okay, well, the group I chair here has been helping quite a few Darfuris get residency," Rachael began. "And it turns out you can make an application as a refugee while you're still in England. As far as I can see, you and your family qualify because you're in danger of serious threat, such as persecution, if you return to your homeland."

"That's right."

"I think you can fairly say that you've had actual experience of persecution on the grounds of your race, right?"

"Right."

"Fine, then that's where you start. I'll send you the website link to the U.S. Citizen and Immigration Service, and you can download the forms and make the application at the nearest U.S. Consulate in Britain."

"Okay," said Zara, her mind frazzled by all she had to absorb.

"And I'm going to start collecting some donations to pay for the airfare. I guess that's needed, right?"

"I'm very sorry," Zara began.

"So, how many of you will there be?"

"There's my mother, my brother Abdelatif, and my baby brother, Yusuf, and me. That's four."

"What about your cousin? What's her name?"

"Safia's staying in England. She's passed the exams to go to the London School of Economics."

"Well, we can find room here for the rest of you," Rachael continued.

"You're a very good person to help us like this," Zara told her. "We'll find work and our own place to live just as soon as we can."

"Actually, you're going to school, young lady."

"I can work after school and weekends, too," Zara promised.

"I admire your spirit," Rachael laughed. "You'll be a good example to my kids."

Zara promised to fill out the application immediately, thanking her again before they said goodbye.

Grandfather, she said to herself, smiling broadly, *we're really going to America. Maybe.*

CHAPTER TWENTY-FOUR

It was just after lunch, when the sun was at its most brutal, and sensible people were resting in the shade. Hawa was completing a written assessment of the previous six months, reporting to her employers in the Netherlands. She heard a vehicle draw up and stop outside the clinic, and she was relieved to put the document to one side. But even so, she was wary. Once it had been the tradition of her people to welcome strangers. The war had changed all that. Civilians were at the mercy of men with guns and bandits who had absolute power if they chose to use it.

The tent flap opened and two white men in military uniforms entered. The older one, with more flecks of grey than black in his hair, had a makeshift bandage wrapped around a wound on his arm, and he hopped in on one foot, leaning on the younger man.

Hawa rushed forward, pointing at an empty cot in the men's section. To her amazement, the injured man greeted her wearily but politely in Arabic. His younger friend eased him onto the cot, carefully lifting his leg. His trousers had been shredded by shrapnel, and he was bleeding from several places.

Hawa issued a series of instructions to her volunteers, and set to work cutting away the fabric to assess the extent of his wounds. The younger soldier stood to one side, looking hot and extremely worried.

237

Hawa glanced at him. "Please tie a tourniquet around his arm, above the wound."

He stared at her, holding out his hands feebly and shrugging.

"He doesn't speak Arabic," explained the injured man, wincing as she peeled away fabric that had stuck to his wounds with congealed blood. He took a deep breath, repeating Hawa's instructions in English. His hovering colleague nodded, doing as he was told.

"Now, please ask him to help bring me some hot water," she said.

The younger soldier returned shortly carrying a pan of steaming water. Hawa methodically cleaned the leg and arm wounds.

"Don't watch," she instructed as she tweezered fragments of shell casing from the leg wounds. "I'm sorry I can't give you painkillers, but the only kind we have here would stop your blood from clotting."

Both men averted their eyes as Hawa disinfected the wounds with alcohol and began sewing them closed. Beads of perspiration dappled the injured man's forehead, and he jerked each time the needle pierced his skin.

"We've run out of those staple things, I'm afraid," she explained conversationally, hoping to keep her patient from passing out. "I'm expecting some antibiotics tomorrow, though, so we can treat any infection you might have picked up," she added cheerfully. "You know, we find it's a good idea to try to take people's minds off the pain, so please tell me why you speak Arabic. You look like an American."

"It's that obvious?"

"You sound like the announcer on Voice of America."

The patient closed his eyes, laughing softly. "I'm with CivPol," he explained, using the acronym for the units of overseas civilian police officers stationed in Darfur. CivPol was attached to the recently arrived UN African Union Mission in Darfur, the peacekeepers known to everyone as UNAMID.

He shuddered as she closed a wound. "And I speak a little Arabic because I was stationed in Lebanon."

"You speak it better than the president of Sudan," she remarked, making him laugh again.

"Oh, him," he grunted, as the needle pierced his skin once more. "He's not my best friend right now."

Confused, Hawa glanced up. Then seeing the light in his eyes, she realized her patient was trying to make light of his predicament.

"Really?" she asked playfully. "Have you had a fight? Did he beat you at basketball?"

"You could say that, yeah. Some friends of his threw a few of their shells at us this morning." He nodded at his wounds. "In theory we're supposed to be working alongside the Sudanese armed forces . . ." His words trailed off.

Hawa looked up at him and saw his eyelids fluttering, as if he were about to faint.

"What happened?" she asked, hoping to keep him conscious.

"We were on patrol with the UNAMID guys, investigating a report about an attack on a village just west of here. Jeff and I," he added, motioning toward his increasingly pale friend who was watching Hawa's needlework, horrified. "But suddenly we ran into a Janjaweed ambush," he continued, squeezing his eyes shut. "And as we were beating a hasty retreat, we got incoming shells from the Sudanese armed forces, although they'd never admit it was them."

He paused, opening his eyes once more, looking into Hawa's face. "I should explain why we're here, by the way. We don't have any medical supplies, and we don't have a clinic to go to, if you can believe it. We hardly have enough food or gas, either."

Hawa peered at him, astonished. "Was it like this in Lebanon, when you were serving there?"

"It was a lot better than this in Lebanon."

For a moment, she studied his eyes, fascinated by their delicate shade of blue. *The same color made some white people look cruel,* she thought, *but this man seemed gentle and kind. Maybe it was because he was older, and his manner was relaxed, despite the wounds. He didn't seem to be trying to prove anything.*

"What's your name?" she asked, surprised by her forwardness.

"Bill."

"My name's Hawa," she smiled, her eyes darting away from his. "And I'm only patching you up in a very basic manner, so your friend here should really try to get you on a plane to Nairobi, where they can give you better treatment."

"Believe me, I'm grateful for your help." He turned his head to his fellow policeman and passed on Hawa's remarks in English. "Go talk to them at the UN tent, please. They'll know what's going on."

"It's his first posting overseas," Bill explained as his colleague stepped out into the glaring sunshine. "He didn't realize how hard the regime would make it for us to do our job."

Hawa dabbed at the perspiration on his high, suntanned forehead. "I promise you, you *are* making a difference. We wouldn't be alive without the CivPol and the UNAMID. If they didn't know you were around, they would have bombed this camp months ago."

"That's what they said in Bosnia, too."

"You were there also?" she asked. "Was it like this?"

Bill sighed. "The Serbs got their thrills killing boys and raping girls, just like your government's soldiers do."

Hawa searched his eyes, feeling a chill run up her spine. She took a deep breath to steady her racing heart. "So it was the same as here," she said, turning her attention back to his arm. She wondered if he had guessed that she too had been a victim. She shook her head quickly. "Tell me more, please." *Now I'm the one needing to take my mind off the pain.*

"It's okay, Hawa. I don't think I'm going into shock. So you don't have to keep me talking."

"I like listening to you and your perfect Arabic," she added with a grin. "How long did you live in Lebanon?"

"Four years," he smiled. "I even married a local woman, a lawyer from Beirut."

"So, that's why your Arabic's so good." She gave him a shy look. "Do you have children?"

"A grown-up son from my first marriage. He's still speaking to me, so it can't have been that bad. How about you?"

She gathered up the bloody pieces of rag lying around the cot, avoiding his eyes. "I have a beautiful baby son, named Ahmed."

"Congratulations."

"Bill? Are you okay?" Jeff asked, approaching tentatively, as if his colleague might be dead. Seeing him, Hawa retreated to dispose of the rags and pieces of shrapnel.

"I'm feeling much better. Surprisingly good."

"I've got bad news, I'm afraid. Very bad news," Jeff reported, rolling his eyes.

"What's up?" asked Bill, still apparently calm.

"Brace yourself," said Jeff, sinking onto the cot alongside him.

"I've never been more braced in my life."

"The next plane is in six days."

"Okay."

"Okay?!"

"The antibiotics arrive tomorrow, so I'll be fine so long as Hawa says I can stay here."

Jeff stared at him, bewildered.

"Why don't you return to the HQ?" Bill suggested. "Before it gets dark."

"I can't just leave you here!"

"I'm in excellent hands. I feel like I'm being taken care of by the daughter I always wished I'd had. And don't ask me to explain it, okay? Now, go."

Jeff's blinked, as if his brain had short-circuited. "I'm not happy about this."

"Go, while there's light," Bill urged. "And make sure you tell the UN guys which route you're taking. Did you charge the Thuraya?"

"Yes, but . . ."

"Hawa," Bill said, as she reappeared. "The plane doesn't come for six days."

Her eyebrows arched. "You mustn't ride in the jeep again until your wounds start to heal," she instructed.

"But won't you need this cot?" he asked.

She shrugged. "If there's another attack then you'll have to share, but luckily, we aren't too busy right now, so it's no trouble." She smiled. "If you stay, you can tell me all about your life, working around the world, and I'll improve my Arabic too."

Bill looked at Jeff, shrugging. "She says I can stay," he reported with a satisfied smile, as if he were looking forward to a gourmet feast. "Go."

The younger man rose slowly, unconvinced. "Good luck, chief," he called as he stepped through the tent flap into the baking afternoon air.

CHAPTER TWENTY-FIVE

Twelve miles away, in an obscure valley, Rashid and his fellow rebel soldiers had arrived at a rendezvous with Jibril's group. T-Bone was in charge of both units while Jibril was indisposed with a stomach complaint. T-Bone had been ordered to protect a nearby village where they feared there would be a Janjaweed raid any day. The Sudanese air force was bombing its way along a string of villages, missing the ones inhabited by Arabs, and destroying those where the non-Arabs lived. The local sheikh, a well-connected, opinionated trader of considerable wealth, was grumbling that his people supplied the rebels with food and shelter when asked, but got nothing in return. T-Bone's commander had decided he would send a few soldiers as a show of force for the next two or three days. Most of the sheikh's villagers had fled, but their homes, land, and grain stores remained, needing protection.

T-Bone briefed his rebel warriors on their objective: lie in wait outside the village and be ready to intercept the Janjaweed. As T-Bone spoke, none of the boys displayed any emotion, wary of appearing weak. Wearing dark glasses made it easier to appear fearless and nonchalant. However, before they piled into their vehicles T-Bone called Rashid to one side.

"I want to get a second opinion on our strategy," he began casually, as if it were no big deal. He had been conferring with Rashid often, ever since he had brought them the intelligence about the Spanish convoy, thanks to Sheikh Uthman.

"That one has such a big mouth," said T-Bone, inclining his head in Ahmed's direction. "I don't know if we can trust him. I mean, it's bad for morale to have this guy running down the movement, questioning our tactics, sounding off about stuff. What d'you think?"

Rashid pursed his lips, but before he could think of a response, T-Bone continued. "I think he should stick to kicking a soccer ball around," a note of anger crept into his voice, "instead of offering his opinions all the time. He gets on my nerves, with his moral superiority. Jibril adores him," he grunted contemptuously. "Beckham."

Rashid made no comment. He had no idea what he was supposed to say, but he suspected he was being tested.

"He can run fast, no doubt about that," T-Bone continued, "so I think I'm going to send him up ahead this time, to do some reconnaissance."

Rashid offered his commanding officer an entirely blank expression. Was T-Bone waiting for him to object, to point out that sending Ahmed ahead was akin to sacrificing him? Did Rashid's future depend on agreeing with T-Bone, or did T-Bone wish to share the blame for putting Jibril's future investment in harm's way? Rashid felt a surge of panic, calculating which answer was required of him.

"I think you should go with your instinct," he said finally.

T-Bone peered at him over the rim of his dark glasses. "Yeah," he drawled. "That's exactly right. I'm sending him up to the front."

Relieved, Rashid climbed into the front cab of the technical, between his commander and the driver, his new privileged position.

The attack was already underway when they approached the village. The Sudanese air force had made several passes, dropping their bombs, and the air was thick with smoke. Most of the huts were on fire, and they could hear the dry, sporadic cracking noise of gunfire.

T-Bone told the driver to stop immediately. They all knew that small arms fire meant the Janjaweed were sweeping through the village, and it was likely they were being supported by the Sudanese armed forces.

"They're too well equipped," he commented to Rashid. "No point in engaging them."

Rashid nodded wisely, although he had no idea what he would do if he were in charge right now. He noticed that the atmosphere in the technical had suddenly lightened the moment their commander ruled out the prospect of going into battle. Rashid felt a wave of sickness and anger as he realized just how relieved he felt, too. *What kind of warrior am I, anyway?*

"The only time to attack is when we've got the element of surprise, catching them sleeping or eating," T-Bone pointed out, as if he was conducting a strategy lesson with his pupil, Rashid. *Does this mean he considers me worth promoting?* the young man wondered.

"But not right now," T-Bone continued. "They're already hyped up, rampaging around, ready to slaughter anything in their path." He chewed his lip thoughtfully and then raised his voice so his driver could hear him. "Okay, pull back off the dirt road and into those bushes, behind those boulders."

They halted and turned off their engines. T-Bone motioned that everyone should get out of the technicals and take cover in the shade. A moment later Rashid saw him pull Ahmed to one side, instructing him to go ahead, to find out what was happening and how many men they were up against.

Rashid watched as Ahmed picked up his rifle, walking toward the sound of gunfire. Ahmed hadn't argued with T-Bone, and yet Rashid assumed the soccer star must have realized what lay in store for him up ahead. As his eyes followed him, Rashid asked himself if he possessed the courage to accept his orders as calmly and with such dignity, without begging to be spared. He stared at Ahmed's retreating back, feeling a child-like mixture of admiration and jealousy. In the next breath, he was overwhelmed by irritation, realizing that the self-righteous, perfect, admirable Ahmed had brought it on himself by speaking the truth too often. *Look what your precious truth has earned you,* he thought with a sneer.

But his disdain was short-lived, and suddenly he felt deflated. *No one in my family speaks the truth,* thought Rashid. *And no one dares tell us the truth because of the strings we pull. We have power, but no honor.* Hawa's taunting face popped into his head. *Hawa hates me because I'm too spineless to face the truth.*

"I don't blame her," he sighed. Then suddenly Rashid picked up his gun. *Maybe it's not too late,* he thought. He started to follow Ahmed. *I have to stop him.* He knew he must seize the chance to do something decent, rather than giving in to his worst instincts, as he usually did.

Rashid crouched down, keeping as low to the ground as possible, while carrying his weapon ready for action. He heard T-Bone hiss behind him, "Hey, what are you doing?" But he kept going.

As he trotted along, he told himself he would catch Ahmed and pull him back into the bushes, out of the line of sight. Then Ahmed would realize Rashid had saved his life, and finally, he would respect him.

Then, just as he quickened his pace, a spray of automatic weapon fire peppered the ground in front of him. Time seemed to slow down as he watched the sand before him dancing in tiny, startled ringlets. *It looks beautiful,* he reflected numbly.

Then it was as if he slammed forward into real time. He dropped to the ground, trembling with the most profound terror he had ever known. There was another burst of fire and he heard a thud and a groan, just ahead. Arab voices shouted out, followed by silence.

Rashid froze, straining his ears, hoping for an indication that the armed forces were withdrawing. He heard a jeep shift into gear, rolling toward his position. Then it halted, a mere twenty-five feet from his bush.

"There he is," they called out to each other in Arabic. "He's alive." "Don't finish him off. They'll want to question him."

Rashid was so scared his legs lost their feeling, and although he wanted to get up and run, he couldn't move. He lay panting like a trussed goat, listening as the soldiers crunched across the sand. Then he heard a groan. "Get up, slave boy." Silence. "Get up!" they roared. "Lazy slave," one of them muttered. "We'll have to drag him."

Their footsteps retreated, the back flap of the jeep opened and slammed shut, and the engine whined as they accelerated away.

Rashid gasped as he started breathing again. He got to his feet cautiously and looked around, still dizzy with fear. Through the thorny bushes he saw the Janjaweed and army pulling out. He was reluctant to raise his head to get a better view, so he crouched down again, retreating to where he hoped T-Bone's technicals were parked. He walked for what felt like hours, panicking that his colleagues had gone. T-Bone might have concluded that both he and Ahmed had been taken, and that he had no reason to linger in harm's way.

What will I do if the unit's gone? he wondered. *Where can I go? Did I really believe I was going to be a hero? Why didn't I just stay put and keep out of trouble?*

He hesitated, crouching down and reviewing his options. There was no point returning to the village because it had been destroyed. The sun was sinking rapidly, casting giant shadows, making it harder to trace his way through the scrub and trees without being scratched. His legs trembled as he started walking once more, praying he hadn't lost his way in the confusion.

He nearly cried out with relief when he spotted T-Bone's technical, tucked in behind a rock. He paused, struggling to bring his shaking hands under control, ashamed that he was like a column of jelly. He took several deep breaths, composing himself, standing upright, doing his best to look proud and tough.

Thwack.

The bullet felt like a bee sting, biting his shoulder. It sent up a mist of blood, like a halo. He craned his neck, studying it, no more than mildly surprised.

"Get down!" T-Bone yelled.

Rashid collapsed as a bullet whizzed past his ear, followed by another. Several pairs of hands hauled him into the technical, while T-Bone yelled at the driver, "Go faster! Turn here. Faster! Quick, down there." Rashid, sprawled over the knees of several boys, was aware of shouting but he couldn't focus on the words. Someone ripped off his shirt, pressing a piece of rag over the wound, as the technical rocked and bucked over the sandy road.

ᚗ ᚗ ᚗ

He wanted them all to be quiet, to stop pulling him, firing instructions at him, lifting him, hauling him, peering at him. Then he heard a familiar voice telling him to drink some water, and he reluctantly opened his eyes.

It was Hawa. She held the back of his head in her hand and guided his mouth toward a cup. "Try to stay awake while I get this bullet out, okay?"

"Unhhh," he grunted, too disorientated to speak.

"Hold him down," she instructed his colleagues. "And slap him if it looks like we're losing him," she added matter-of-factly.

He reared away from her as she rooted around inside his wound, but she persisted, following him across the cot, like a big cat prowling after its prey. He slipped into unconsciousness for a moment and then shot up, vomiting and retching.

"Got it!" she announced triumphantly.

The bullet tinkled as it dropped into a bowl, but the sound was drowned out by Rashid's wail of anguish.

"More hot water," she commanded. "The needle and thread. Clean bandages. Quick!"

Rashid shrank back on the cot, his eyes wide with terror, sweat pouring off him. "What are you doing?" he jabbered at her.

"First I disinfect, then I sew up the wound, and then I bandage you to stop infection," she recited.

Rashid looked around, startled, as he realized T-Bone was standing to one side, still wearing his dark glasses.

"You're going to be okay," he commented. "You'll be out of here in three days, she says."

"Hold him down again," Hawa instructed the soldiers squatting on either side of the cot.

Ψ Ψ Ψ

When Rashid awoke it was quiet, and the soldiers and T-Bone had gone. He had no idea how much time had passed, and at first he was unclear about what had happened or why he was in the clinic tent. Then he heard Hawa talking to someone and he tried to prop himself up on one elbow. The pain was like a scorching piece of metal pressed against his flesh, and he slumped back on the cot. The afternoon's events came back to him in a shameful collage of unflattering images.

A moment later Hawa was at his side, her face blank. "How do you feel now?" she asked.

He tried to speak, but his voice was no more than a squeak. Suddenly he felt the need to hold her hand, to feel her skin, to draw her close to him, just to have her arms around him, holding on to him, steadying him in all the confusion.

"Your grandfather's here," she said. "I'll make sure you have some privacy."

She slipped away before he could stop her, and Sheikh Uthman eased himself into the chair someone had fetched for him. "We'll get you on the plane to Khartoum tomorrow morning," he announced.

Rashid frowned and mouthed "Khartoum?"

"They'll patch you up properly."

"She did a good job," Rashid announced, his voice returning abruptly. "I'll be fine. It was just a flesh wound."

"What would people say if they thought I'd let my own grandson lie in this stinking tent?"

Rashid glared at him, tears welling up in his eyes. "So it's about what people will think, rather than what might be best for me?"

The sheikh yawned. "Don't be tedious." He glanced at his watch, shifting uncomfortably on the chair. "You've only yourself to blame for this." He lowered his voice. "I told you not to join them."

"And you'll never understand why I *had* to join them."

"Oh, please spare me the speeches about valor and honor and duty," he rolled his eyes. "You'll put me off my evening meal."

"Perhaps you make me feel sick, too."

Uthman's brows shot up, and Rashid detected something shifting behind his eyes. His grandfather got to his feet and walked out without another word.

"That looked like a warm and loving family encounter," Bill commented quietly to Hawa, seeing Uthman stalk out.

Hawa frowned. "Don't get involved."

"Thanks for the advice. Hey, this is pretty good, by the way," her patient commented, indicating the sorghum pancakes and goat's milk pudding Hawa had brought him. She had asked the young mother who cared for Ahmed to cook a few Darfuri dishes for her new American friend.

"I was sick of you telling me how Lebanese food is the best in the world," she smiled.

His grin quickly faded. "The strange thing about Lebanon is that last summer there was a war there, and about 1,200 people were killed, and the fighting lasted thirty-four days before the international community stepped in and stopped it. Whereas here, the war's been going on since 2003, and 300,000 are dead, and it keeps being pushed off the agenda by other world events."

"So a Lebanese life is worth more than a black African one?" asked Hawa.

"Something like that," he conceded, shifting on his cot.

Hawa encouraged her patient to drink more water, then glanced into his eyes. "You know America is our hope?"

"Yes, I know," he said. Then he sighed. "Despite all our mistakes, overthrowing governments, propping up regimes run by monsters, polluting the planet, and gobbling up its resources. We are *still* the hope of the world. And so many of the people I've met on my travels tell me they keep on looking to Uncle Sam to deliver the dream." He closed his eyes. "Free speech and democracy and tolerance," he said, his tone solemn.

"It's what freedom fighters everywhere aspire to."

"That's quite a burden," he said, his eyelids drooping.

Hawa allowed herself a couple of minutes of peace, sitting by his cot, watching him drift off to sleep.

CHAPTER TWENTY-SIX

The soldiers pulled Ahmed out of the vehicle, dragging him across a courtyard, through a doorway, and along a corridor. They pushed him into a dirty, stuffy, windowless cell, where he stumbled and collapsed onto the floor. The bullet he had taken, out in the bush, had lodged in his left hip, but Ahmed doubted it was a serious wound. It would be life-threatening only if they left the bullet in him and did nothing to staunch the bleeding. So far there was no sign they were going to provide even the simplest medical help, not even a drink of water.

The heat in the cell was stifling. They hauled him up onto a metal chair, securing his hands behind him. He sat balancing on one buttock, trying to avoid even greater pain and blood loss from the wound. After only a few minutes, perching awkwardly in the chair, his back was going into spasms. Even when the blood stopped dripping down the chair leg and pooling beneath him, the injury throbbed.

The soldiers left the room, and Ahmed closed his eyes, wondering what was about to happen. *Will they interrogate me? They'll soon realize I'm a nobody and they'll let me go. Perhaps in a couple of hours I'll be back outside in the fresh air, gulping down bottle after bottle of water. This could all be over soon,* he promised himself. *Then somehow I'll get back to the camp clinic and Hawa. One day, when this is over and we're surrounded by our grandchildren, I'll tell them about the time I was arrested and interrogated during the war. Hawa will tell the kids, 'I thought I'd never see your Grandpa again, but then it turned out okay.'*

251

Maybe this wound of mine will stop me playing professional soccer, but I can live with that, if it means getting out of here, he thought. *I'll give anything to get out of this place.*

To take his mind off the heat and the pain, he thought about how cool the dawn air used to feel as he emerged from his hut, back in the village, when he used to run. He had loved the snug sensation of slipping his feet into the perfectly fitting running shoes given to him by Khalil. After the first few paces he would have gotten into his stride, leaving the village behind, like a streak of lightning, like the wind. *They're going to realize I can't tell them anything useful, and they'll let me go soon.*

When the interrogator arrived, accompanied by two soldiers, Ahmed recognized the uniform of the National Security and Intelligence Services, or "the security." A tall man with moist lips and a long, narrow face, the officer explained in a voice without passion or intonation that he had a few simple questions, and that Ahmed was not leaving the room until he had provided the answers.

"If you try to be brave, you'll find that my questions become monotonous," he warned without the slightest hint of menace, as if he was too bored to even go through the motions of scaring his subject. "So save yourself the trouble, and answer right away. Do us all a favor, okay, so we can get home," he advised.

Then he took a seat, pulling a pad of paper and a pen toward him. "What are the names of your commanders and to whom do they report?" he read from his pad. "Do they take their orders directly from the government in Chad? Do they get all their arms from Chad, or are they also from Israel? Where do they smuggle them across the border into Sudan, and how often? When, where and how are they planning to attack Sudanese armed forces bases?"

Ahmed replied that he was a lowly soldier, recruited forcibly from the camp outside El Geneina, and that he knew nothing of value. The commander of his unit had sent him up front to do reconnaissance, knowing how risky it was because he was of so little importance to them.

The interrogator ignored his remarks and asked him the same questions again and again. Ahmed tried to explain his insignificance over and over again.

His mistake was to become facetious.

"If you asked me how Chelsea needs to restructure, or where Man U's weaknesses are, or why England can't put together a decent team, I could speculate with some authority, but you're asking me things I really don't know about," he told his interrogator.

The man with the moist lips smirked as he absorbed Ahmed's response. "A soccer fan, eh? And do you play also?" The long, thin face broke into a broad grin, as if the mouse he had been tracking for hours had just blundered directly into his trap. He looked his prisoner up and down. "I bet you're a center forward, come to think of it. Am I right?"

Ahmed glanced away, realizing he had foolishly revealed too much. The glint in the man's eyes was the giveaway, as was the spring in his step as he rose and paced across the cell to his tool kit, humming.

A second officer was instructed to pull off Ahmed's boots, and hold his foot still, while the interrogator tinkered among his knives, saws and pliers, laid out on the rickety wooden table at the edge of the room, like instruments in a rather unsanitary operating theater. A third man in uniform stood at the door, silent and averting his eyes, clearly bored.

No! Ahmed screamed inside. *I'm not brave enough to withstand this. I have to get back to Hawa. They mustn't do this to me. Are they going to kill me or just torture me to make their twisted point? Will they let me go free?*

The officer sang softly as he examined his tools. He picked up something shiny, weighed it in his hand and put it down again with a clinking sound.

If I get out of here, I'll never again be so arrogant to want to be a world famous soccer star. I'll be content to be alive, to catch Hawa's eye across the chaos of the clinic, to sit beside her at the tea break. Did she even know how many times he had scared off her potential suitors, taking whatever poor young man it was back behind the clinic and threatening to break his neck if he even looked at her?

Still, the officer stood over his instruments. *It's part of his performance,* thought Ahmed. *I suppose they get used to seeing us beaten and broken. The smell of fear coming off my body, the terror in my eyes. As I sit here, wondering if I'll get out alive, the man by the door is no doubt counting the minutes before his shift ends and he can go home to bounce his baby son on his knee.*

Finally the officer returned to the table, knife in hand. The shock, when it came, was not due to the agony. Ahmed had assumed there would be much more pain before his interrogation was over. What surprised him was that the interrogator could so easily cut away Ahmed's skin, revealing the pale white bones and tendons in his foot like the medical diagrams he had seen at the clinic. What alarmed Ahmed most was that the sight of it had not caused him to pass out. He had hoped that in such circumstances, his mind would take pity on him and plunge him into oblivion, but it seemed that he was being granted a front row seat for the dissection of his own anatomy.

Please God, he prayed, *do not deny me the merciful darkness I crave right now. Let me sink into unconsciousness until this is over. And if that means death, then I accept it as a blessed release.*

But instead of oblivion, he was aware of the smell of fried meat on his torturer's breath, presumably consumed earlier, when Ahmed had been in the back of a jeep, being brought into the headquarters.

His captors had not blindfolded him. *It could be interpreted as a bad sign*, he thought, because it showed they had no intention of letting him out alive. Alternatively, they knew their impunity was guaranteed in a one-party police state. *Please God, I want to get out of here alive.*

He invented a coughing fit to hide his screams, refusing to give the interrogator the satisfaction of knowing he was breaking him. But all that now existed was the pain he was experiencing, endless second by endless second. Even Hawa was fading. It was harder and harder to conjure up her pretty face with the slightly upturned nose. At the clinic he would watch her out of the corner of his eye, without her realizing he was admiring her. She was worth clinging to life for. The rest of it was pointless, but he held on to her shy smile and her perfect cheekbones and the light of excitement in her eyes whenever she had mastered another newspaper article or book.

If I get out of here alive we'll be together, Hawa, he thought. And even if they killed him, they would still be together in paradise, eventually. And in the meantime, he vowed to watch over her.

Without warning, the interrogator and his sidekick stopped and left the room. Ahmed strained his ears as the echo of their boots retreated along the corridor, and a door slammed shut. A moment later, the third soldier was at his side, holding the mouth of a water bottle to his lips.

"They've gone for something to eat. Now, if you take my advice, you'll swallow this pill," he said quietly. "It's a painkiller."

Ahmed gulped down the water and the pill without hesitation. The soldier let him finish the rest of the water.

"Thanks," Ahmed whispered.

"My uncle's a pharmacist, and he lets me have them," the soldier explained. "I told him what happens in here."

"He's a good man."

"He's ashamed of what's being done here. Most of us want peace, just peace, for God's sake."

"Is he going to kill me, your commanding officer?"

"I don't know. It varies."

Ahmed let out a sob, and the soldier rested his hand on Ahmed's shoulder for a while as he wept.

※ ※ ※

The following morning, T-Bone sent his deputy to the camp to check on Rashid. As soon as he entered the clinic tent, disguised by a long dark blue scarf revealing only his eyes, Hawa recognized him and knew he was here with news of Ahmed. The soldier had often brought her wounded men to patch up in the middle of the night, and he knew that Ahmed had been her close friend. Her heart missed a beat, and she fought a wave of dizziness and sheer, raw panic. So far all she had heard were sketchy rumors, but no one had any solid information. Consequently Hawa had barely slept, and she felt as if she were on the edge of a precipice.

"What's happened to Ahmed?" she asked the young militiaman, dispensing with any preamble.

"They got him."

"The Janjaweed?" she snapped.

He shook his head. "The security."

"And have you heard anything yet?" she fired back. It was all she could do to stop herself from shaking the young man by the shoulders.

"They've still got him. That's all we know, but we can't be certain of anything until they let him go, or until we find his body."

Hawa hurried away, determined not to cry before the militiaman or her patients. She ducked through the tent flap and walked aimlessly around the camp for twenty minutes or so, seeing no one in her path, hearing nothing but the pounding of her heart in her ears. *Please God, don't let this be happening to* Ahmed. *Please God, if you really are merciful then save this good man of mine.*

Finally, the trembling subsided, but her brain felt as if it was being jerked repeatedly by an electric current. Her mind switched back and forth between the leaden certainty that they had killed him already and the belief that there was still hope until she heard otherwise.

Hawa returned to the clinic at the same moment that Sheikh Uthman arrived, looking annoyed and hot. He pushed past her as if she did not exist, waddling along the line of cots to Rashid.

"You summoned me, I gather?" he snapped, lowering his bulk onto the edge of a neighboring bed.

"You remember Ahmed, the soccer player?" Rashid began equally abruptly.

Unaccustomed to his grandson's disrespectful tone, he offered a curled lip in response.

"He's one of the guys you sold," Rashid continued in a matter-of-fact tone. "Anyway, the security's got him."

Uthman held out his hands. "What's this got to do with me?"

Rashid lowered his voice, gesturing his grandfather to draw closer. "Can you use your influence to get Ahmed out?"

The sheikh groaned. "Do you really think I'd use my limited leverage for *this?* You lack judgment, to put it kindly." He paused to pick a shred of lamb from his teeth. "This isn't how one uses one's minimal influence."

"But it's important."

Uthman sighed. "You dragged me across the camp for this? I was hoping you'd finally seen sense about going to Khartoum. We can still get you on the plane before you pick up every infection under the sun in this dog's nest."

Rashid held his grandfather's eyes. "I'd like you to call in a few favors and get Ahmed back here."

"What for? What do I get out of it?"

"The satisfaction of knowing that you've finally done the right thing."

Uthman leaned forward and slapped Rashid so hard it was like hearing a branch snap. All activity in the tent stopped and there was silence, except for the sound of Rashid gasping.

The sheikh pulled himself wearily to his feet and waddled back out into the morning sun.

☖ ☖ ☖

The scheduled delivery of medicine did not arrive that day. By the evening, Hawa, already distracted and fretful, was concerned about her American patient. Bill was becoming weaker and paler by the hour. She disinfected and dressed his wounds regularly, but it was clear that he badly needed antibiotics.

"I've sent one of my volunteers to the UN tent to find out what's happened to the delivery," she explained to Bill as she perched on the edge of his cot. "There's been a delay—there often is—but just hang on, okay?"

He offered her a brave smile. "I'll pull through just fine."

"I feel ashamed that you've come thousands of miles to help us, and we can't even give you the medicine you get at home."

He shrugged. "Why do so many African women die in childbirth in the twenty-first century? Why are people dying of simple infections or from dirty water? The cures are so cheap and simple. If we can deliver Coca-Cola everywhere in the world, why can't we manage a few pills?"

She smiled. "I admire your concern for the rest of the continent while you're lying here suffering. I'll get you some more water, and you should sleep, instead of talking to me."

Bill started to say, "I like talking to you . . ." but he was interrupted by the arrival of T-Bone's deputy, his head swathed in scarves once more. He stepped into the tent looking even more apprehensive than usual. He beckoned to Hawa with an urgent gesture and stepped back outside, waiting for her to join him in the relative safety of the darkness.

With just one glance at him, she knew.

CHAPTER TWENTY-SEVEN

As Hawa hurried across the clinic toward the tent flap, she understood the worst had happened. Every cell in her body sensed the militiaman had brought her bad news. She rushed after him, each footstep taking forever, every beat of her heart banging against her rib cage.

"What's happened?" she blurted out when she joined him in the dark. "Tell me!" she whimpered.

"I'm sorry, Hawa, but they found him." He paused, overcome by emotion. "They found his body, about three miles from the security headquarters."

Hawa felt as if someone had kicked her in the stomach. She bent double, overwhelmed and feeling faint, too stunned to speak. She clawed at the side of the tent, struggling for breath, certain she was about to melt into the ground like spilled water. "No," she murmured. "No, no, no, no."

She curled into a ball and tucked her head into her arms, trying to block everything out, wondering how she could rewind time to just five minutes ago, when there had still been hope. "Please, God, no," she wailed.

"I'm sorry, Hawa," the soldier said. "Look, you should go home now. I'll tell the rest of them. Just go home."

She unfolded her limbs slowly, sniffing away her tears. "I'll go home," she agreed numbly. "I'll get my baby and go home."

He helped her to her feet and watched her stumble into the darkness.

Back in the tent, he headed for Rashid. "They found Ahmed, just before dusk. It's terrible, what they did to him." He shook his head in anguish.

Rashid stared at him, wide-eyed.

"Look, I'm leaving, but you've got to make sure Hawa's okay," the militiaman instructed him, before slipping back into the night.

At first Rashid asked himself why he was being given the responsibility of looking after Hawa. *She only wanted Ahmed,* he thought dimly. Then suddenly he saw that his role was glaringly obvious. She no longer had the prospect of Ahmed taking care of her and being with her. She was alone, and yet helping thousands of people by running the clinic; she was leading all the single mothers in the camp, as well as bringing up her infant son. If Hawa could shoulder so much, for the good of their people, then perhaps it was Rashid's duty to marry her and give her son his name.

He lay back on his cot, staring at the roof of the tent, trying to work out what he felt about her. All his life he had been told what to think and do by his family. But now he'd taken a giant step away from them. It was hard to imagine his grandfather forgiving him for his impudence so there would be no reconciliation, nor did he want there to be. Over the years, whenever he had fantasized about telling the old man what he really thought of him, he had wondered if he would soon weaken and go crawling back to his family, begging for forgiveness. But since he had spoken his mind to Uthman, he had hardly given it a second thought. He felt free, for the first time in his life.

What do I really want? he asked himself. The answer came quickly. *I want to be an honorable man who takes care of his family, a decent man who speaks the truth, and a brave soldier who fights for our right to live here.* Satisfied with his decision, he closed his eyes and drifted off to sleep.

꿔 꿔 꿔

The shipment of medicine arrived the following afternoon. Bill's temperature had risen to one hundred and two, and his wounds had puffed up. Hawa had reopened and cleaned them, and then left them open, allowing the infection to clear.

As his temperature returned to normal, Bill had tried to joke about his spectacular injuries, and how he missed her needlework, but Hawa had retreated into her shell, silent and preoccupied. When he questioned her gently, she'd explained about her friend's death. Bill had told her how sorry he was and encouraged her to take time off to be with her baby. But she had shrugged off his suggestion, explaining that keeping busy was the best treatment for misery, just as Mary had taught her. Whenever she had a moment, she sat on Bill's bed listening to his stories, although she was far more subdued than before. *It's all I can do not to scream all the time,* she thought.

The day before Bill was due to catch the flight out of El Geneina, he waited until there was no one within earshot, and asked Hawa to sit with him for a minute.

"I know you're in agony, and you probably can't bear to think of the future, but I'd like you to consider an idea I've had," he began.

She peered at him, curious, despite the leaden weight pressing down on her.

"If you ever decide you want to study medicine in the United States, my wife and I will sponsor you through university. We'll get you a student visa, and we've got a spare room in our apartment where you can stay."

She gaped at him, astonished, but he mistook her expression for one of horror, and he rushed on, "Or you could stay and study in Cairo or somewhere nearer home," he suggested.

Hawa began to weep quietly. "You're such a kind man and a good man, too," she said at length. "Thank you. Thank you for asking me," she sniffed, wiping her eyes. "But my duty is here, in this clinic, as long as I am needed."

"I thought that might be the case," he said. "But maybe after the war ends."

"You really think I can be a doctor?" she asked.

"Of course you can. And then you can serve your people even better."

"It's true," she nodded. After a moment she said, "Even after this war ends, there'll always be work for me in Darfur." She dried her tears, trying to smile. "You know, I owe much to a very great woman called Mary who worked here before. She taught me to be a human being instead of a slave."

"Mary did a good job." He pulled a piece of paper from his pocket and handed it to her. "When you're ready, here's how you can find me."

"Thank you."

"I bet Mary would be very proud of you."

"I hope so," she sniffed, offering him a small, brave grin.

卅 卅 卅

Rashid was comparatively strong and well-nourished, so his wound healed well, without complications. As soon as he could leave the clinic he went straight back to T-Bone's unit. His commanding officer was less convinced the young man was ready for action and told him to recuperate with his grandfather for a week or two.

"I'm not going back to the sheikh," Rashid informed him stoutly. "And I won't be able to help you with those things anymore either," he added, his message clear to both of them. As the meaning sank in, Rashid braced himself. He expected T-Bone to dismiss him out of hand, or to tell him he was insane.

T-Bone raised his eyebrows, looking thoughtful. "Well, in that case I guess you better borrow my tent," he said at length. "Come back when you're ready, okay? I've got plans for you."

Rashid tried not to betray his concern. "What kind of plans?"

"I need another deputy."

"Me?"

"You're surprised?"

Rashid did he best to look casual about it. He had assumed he had disgraced himself by foolishly running off after Ahmed.

"The day we attacked the Spanish convoy," T-Bone explained. "You made the right decision, and I need men like that."

Buoyed up by his promotion, Rashid headed straight to see Hawa. When he arrived at the clinic, she was finishing her dispensing round. He waited while she locked away the pill bottles, and then he approached her, trying to look blasé. "Hawa, I want to talk to you outside for a moment," he informed her.

Without a word, she turned on her heel, heading for the tent flap. Once outside she went to the shade of a tree, walking quickly, impatiently. Rashid tried not to look as if he was trotting after her, but he struggled to match her pace. He glanced around, hoping there were no eavesdroppers around. When he drew even with her he said, "I want you to know that I've forgiven you, and I'll take you as my wife, even with the baby."

Her eyebrows rose. "What have you forgiven me for, Rashid? I don't understand."

He looked annoyed. "For what happened."

"For being raped and impregnated by the Janjaweed?" she prompted, enjoying the embarrassment her forthrightness caused him. She knew it was exactly what Mary would have said.

Rashid looked away. "We won't speak of it. We'll forget it."

"I see," she said mildly. "The problem is that *I* can never forget it. Besides, I haven't forgiven you. So I'd prefer to manage by myself, with the help of the other women here who've been through what I have."

To her surprise, Rashid was silent. She expected him to shout at her or hit her, not to gaze at her, his expression calm and undisturbed. "I'm going to work here," she continued, a strident note in her voice. "I'm going to do something useful, instead of just being your servant."

His face remained impassive, and she faltered, confused by his lack of reaction. When he said nothing, she added, "Your grandfather can get you another wife easily enough. You buy and sell people all the time, but you can't buy or sell me."

Still Rashid said nothing, though she thought she saw him flinch slightly at her words. She sensed a strength in him she hadn't detected before and wondered what he was thinking. They stood for a few seconds without speaking. Feeling irritated by his continued silence, she sought to provoke him. She crouched down, gathering up a handful of sand. When she stood, the grains slipped through her fingers into the wind.

"You see this?" she asked angrily. "It may not be much to wealthy people like your family, but hundreds of generations of my family's blood have nourished this soil."

Then, recalling Mama Mounah, Hawa's anger leached away abruptly and she smiled slightly. "For a thousand years, the women of my family have given everything for this land, and when I think of their sacrifice and devotion, I realize that you and I are no more important than these grains of sand."

Rashid made no comment, but studied her face intently as she brushed away the particles sticking to the palms of her hands.

"It's when you put all the grains of sand together," she continued, "that you get a force that can't be beaten." She swept her hand toward the endless horizon. "In the end, that's all that matters—keeping our identity and our freedom."

She bent down once more and gathered another handful of sand. This time she kept it cupped in her hands as she rose.

"This is my duty, to fight for our land in the best way I can," she said as the sand gradually slipped between her fingers. "That's why I'm going to stay at the clinic, and I'll study to become a professional nurse and maybe even a doctor."

Her expression hardened. "I know it'll be a struggle, being alone with my boy. But I'd rather do that than be your illiterate servant, praying to God you don't beat me every time life disappoints you." She tilted her chin up defiantly, waiting for Rashid's angry reply.

Finally he spoke. "I know," Rashid said simply, "and I agree with you."

Hawa stared at him, astonished.

"I'm going back to the unit, to fight, in the best way I can," he added. "I'm going to fight for the same reasons you're going to be a doctor, except I'm not as smart as you, so I'll just be a soldier. And if I survive, then I'll come back when this is over, and I'll keep asking you to marry me. Maybe someday you'll say yes."

Then, although the cool look in Hawa's eyes scared him, he found the strength to do something he had never done before. He smiled at her.

CHAPTER TWENTY-EIGHT

Marja was usually up and around by five, savoring the best part of the day as the world came to life. She made the first of many cups of tea, standing at her kitchen window, hands cupped around her mug, watching the sky shingle with pink as the sun rose over Doncaster.

Marja, a thirty-one-year-old Pole, had been a dentist in England for eighteen months. She intended to stay as long as the sterling-Euro exchange rate made it worthwhile. Then she would return to Poland with her savings to build a fine house for her three-year-old baby girl, currently living with her grandmother back home in Wroclaw.

This morning Marja was distracted by the arrival of two police cars at the entrance of the public housing project in which she lived. She reached for her cell phone and called Mrs. Edwards, living in the same apartment building, two floors up. After apologizing for waking her, Marja asked, "You're got some nice Sudanese neighbors, haven't you? The ones who've been having the problems with the immigration people? Well, the cops have arrived, and there's usually only one reason they come here at this hour."

Mrs. Edwards thanked Marja and called the Rigby family who lived on her floor, on the other side of Zara. Their conversation was equally brief.

Mrs. Edwards then phoned Zara, instructing her to take her mother, Safia, and Yusuf next door to the Rigby home.

Zara, sleepy and confused, asked what was happening. "I don't know the Rigby family. I've only just said hello to them in the hall. How can I knock on their door at this time in the morning?"

"The police are here, and they've probably come for you, so don't ask questions, dear," Mrs. Edwards said firmly but pleasantly. "Mr. Rigby's expecting you. Then you and Abdelatif come round here. Quickly! And remember your passports and papers!" she added.

It took the police several minutes to identify the correct building; the project was a maze of identical ugly apartment blocks. It was not somewhere they enjoyed visiting, but they were reluctant regulars after dark, when the fights started. Some of the roughest elements in Doncaster were dumped in the project, right next to asylum seekers who were too terrified of the more feral locals to leave their apartments.

The elevator was out of order so they picked their way through the garbage in the stairwell, trudging their way to the fifth floor, handkerchiefs clamped over mouths and noses.

No one answered when they hammered on the door. They popped the lock open using a credit card. Inside, the bedclothes were still warm. They shrugged and retreated. Another day, another vanishing family of illegal immigrants, saved, no doubt, by the local inhabitants who hated the forces of law and order even more than they disliked foreigners.

Next door, Mrs. Rigby, a petite forty-year-old with black nail polish and a magnificent head of gothic raven hair, was handing around tea mugs and cookies. Although she was still in her dressing gown, she assured her guests it was no trouble to play the hostess so early in the day.

"It's been lovely having you next door. You should have seen the lot who was there before you. It was like having a rave going on seven days a week, right on the other side of a very thin wall. Anyway, we hate the cops, don't we Big Ant?" she giggled.

Big Anthony, all three hundred tattooed pounds of him, grinned lovingly in response. Their Rottweiler, Tyson, lay at his feet, chewing happily on a vast bone. Little Ant, aged seven and the size of a sumo wrestler already, was still asleep in his bedroom.

"Those cops," Big Ant grumbled. "They ought to go chase some child molesters for a change, instead of bothering decent people."

Two doors away, Mrs. Edwards was making breakfast for Abdelatif and Zara. "That was a close one," she laughed, passing the toast. "They'll probably be back same time tomorrow."

Zara and Abdelatif exchanged a worried look. "Is it too early to call our friends in London?" Zara asked her neighbor.

"No, dear, not under the circumstances," Mrs. Edwards advised. "I expect there are arrangements to be made." She spread her Marmite evenly and took a bite. After a thoughtful chew she added, "I shall miss having you here, Zara. But you've inspired me to get with the twenty-first century, you know?"

"Really?"

"Mr. Rigby's finding me a computer. You know he deals in second-hand goods? Well, I don't want to know the details, but anyway, he says he'll find me a laptop so I can stay in touch with my granddaughter." She smiled brightly. "It's time to bring myself up to her level, instead of expecting her to keep in touch the old-fashioned way, or take the train here. It's so expensive."

"This is very good news," Zara smiled encouragingly. "Now you'll be connected with the whole world, even just sitting in your apartment."

"I'll email you my address, when I'm all set up."

"Zara, please phone Sandrine," Abdelatif said in English. Then he switched languages. "I can see you're having a nice tea party here, but if the police find us they'll deport us immediately. Please. We're in serious trouble."

She registered the tension in his voice, and reached for the phone, still reluctant to bother their friend at such an early hour. Three minutes later, the call was complete. Mrs. Edwards looked at her, expectantly.

"One of Sandrine's colleagues will let us stay in her house in London for a few nights," Zara reported. "Sandrine says it'll be safer in London, while we wait for the tickets and everything. It's easier for us to disappear there."

Zara glanced at Abdelatif, and he nodded that he had understood her English. "Off the radar," he added.

"Off the radar," echoed Mrs. Edwards.

"So, we go to London now," he announced, putting a note of urgency in his voice.

"What part of London, Zara? Did she say?" asked their hostess.

"Holland Park."

Mrs. Edwards pursed her lips, her eyes twinkling. "Oh, very nice. Maybe you'll be staying with Madonna or Elton John. That's where they live, you know."

"My new friends," Zara replied, and they both laughed. Then she risked a glance at her brother, finding fear and impatience in his eyes. "I'm so sorry, but we must get ready to go," she added, her heart sinking as she registered Mrs. Edwards' disappointment. "But we'll stay in touch, and maybe you'll come to America to visit me?"

Abdelatif was already on his feet, twitching with nerves. However, once Zara showed signs of moving, he calmed down slightly, standing to one side as the women wept and hugged.

"You saved my life today, Mrs. Edwards," he said solemnly, shaking hands. "This is true," he insisted when she told him it was nothing. "You saved me and I'll never forget you. Thank you."

Mrs. Edwards was still dabbing her eyes as she closed the door.

The family rushed around their apartment, packing only essential items, most of which were for Yusuf. Zara hated leaving the school uniform she had been so proud to wear, while Sumah was most upset at being parted from the domestic appliances. "*All* women in Darfur should have these," she declared. "They make life so much easier."

"We'll have them in New Jersey, Mom," Zara assured her.

"Hurry up!" Abdelatif barked, for the tenth time that morning.

"And I wish you wouldn't take it for granted that you're going to the States," he growled at Zara, when they were alone. "None of this is going to be easy."

Once they were safely on the coach pulling out of Doncaster, Zara phoned the Methodists to explain that they had lost their appeal for asylum status. She thanked them for their help, reminding them there was an apartment full of furniture and clothes they might wish to hand on to another family.

Later in the journey, Abdelatif asked to change seats with Safia, so he could talk to Zara. His mood was still grave and agitated, and he got straight to the point. "When you talk to Rachael, tell her I'm not going to need a ticket."

Zara's eyes widened, a little seed of terror swelling inside her.

"My work is here, Zara, with our people. And when the war is over, I need to be ready to go back, as fast as possible, to make sure the bandits don't end up running the new Darfur."

"You can work for Darfur in New Jersey, the way Rachael does, with Save Darfur," she suggested halfheartedly, knowing him well enough to see he had made up his mind already.

He grimaced. "Everyone who goes to America becomes American so fast, overnight. If I go there I'll enjoy life too much, I'll forget what's happening at home, and everything'll be too easy."

Zara studied his face, wondering if he thought she would soon forget about Darfur if she made a new life in America. She was afraid to ask him, so her question remained unspoken. "And if you stay here, what about the rest of us?" she asked.

"You're going to New Jersey, Zara. You can take care of Mom and Yusuf. You don't need me. There's no point in you staying here, anyway."

No point? she wondered, *because I'm a girl and he thinks I can't do anything to help Darfur, or because I'm more interested in my academic future?* Zara chewed her lower lip, thinking she didn't feel particularly confident that she could take care of herself in a new and unfamiliar country, let alone protect Sumah and the infant. "But how will you avoid being caught?" she asked him, trying to change the subject.

"There are Darfuris in London who can give me a floor to sleep on. If I don't have to worry about you and Mom, it'll be easier for me to move around and stay one jump ahead of the immigration people." He let out a long breath, sinking back in his seat. "I'll be okay. And so will you because you've already packed several lives into your eighteen years. And you've got grandfather's brain. I wish I did . . ." His voice trailed off.

Zara stared out of the coach window at the car headlights shining on the rain-slicked surface of the highway. Everything was suddenly about to change, and it scared her. "But how long will you be here, sleeping on floors like a nomad? Who knows when you'll be able to go home?" she asked, terrified at the prospect of their family being split up.

He made a fist and punched it gently into the palm of his hand, emphasizing his words. "One thing I'm certain of is my role is here, organizing our people, speaking out each time the regime broadcasts its lies. All I need is my cell phone and a few friends."

"It's not going to be easy," Zara commented, her heart heavy.

He sighed. "I need to go home but you, Zara, you can adapt and change, you can move anywhere; you pick up languages like you're putting on a new scarf," he explained simply. He placed his hands on his knees, as if he was laying a controversy to rest. "That's it." He rose slowly, wearily, changing seats with Safia once more.

Zara waited until it was eight o'clock in the morning in New Jersey before phoning Rachael to update her on the day's events. Rachael expressed astonishment and concern, but Zara assured her it would have been much worse if their neighbors had not rescued them.

Once more, they rehearsed what Zara would tell the U.S. Citizenship and Immigration officers when they arrived at Newark airport, assuming that by possessing a return ticket, the family would make it past the officials at the London end of the journey. Rachael told Zara she would have to lie, saying they would apply for a tourist visa, through the visa waiver scheme, for their brief stay in the United States. Then once they landed at Newark, she would tell the officials she and her family were asking for asylum on the basis that they had been subject to an actual experience of persecution because of their race. When Rachael was satisfied that Zara had it word perfect, she ended their call, promising to phone as soon as she had the plane reservations.

The family climbed down from the coach several hours later, clinging to their possessions, tired and bewildered. Zara wondered if the police might be checking coaches arriving from Doncaster, and she glanced around apprehensively. She felt as frightened as she had when the police had arrived at their apartment block. Mrs. Edwards had helped her treat the event as an adventure, outwitting the bureaucrats who were trying to deport them. And Rachael made getting into the United States sound so simple.

Yet, Zara knew the plan could fall apart at any stage, especially if the police tracked them down. The consequences of failure were grave. Her family would be stuffed into holding cells, caged up in hostels, and then eventually deported to Khartoum. Somehow Rachael's tone of unflappable authority had lulled Zara into believing all would be well.

Looking around the bus terminal, Zara's pretence of self-confidence faltered. Then she heard Sandrine calling her name and felt her arms embracing her, and her spirits revived once more.

Sandrine shepherded them into a cab, and although Zara tried to ask her what would happen next, and whose house they were going to, Sandrine was completely fixated on Yusuf, with whom she played all the way to Holland Park.

"Please tell us about this lady who's going to help us now," pleaded Zara. "It's rude to just arrive like this."

"Okay," conceded Sandrine, still focusing most of her attention on the little boy. "Ursula's a real character."

"What does that mean?" Zara interrupted.

"You don't want to take everything she says seriously. She handles problems by being sarcastic rather than bursting into tears. Now, Ursula is what we call a yummy mummy. Good looking, clever, sophisticated, lives in a nice place with her husband who does something in the financial world," she added vaguely. "And when she's not being the perfect homemaker and mother, she's fighting genocide, making life hard for totalitarian dictators."

"Cool," commented Safia, impressed.

They piled out of the taxi in a quiet, leafy road, lined with some of the largest houses Zara had ever seen. The four-story facades were plastered with elaborate white decorations, like the wedding cakes she had seen in bakery windows in Doncaster, complete with classical designs that Zara recognized as Edwardian.

"A director of the human rights campaign lives here?" Abdelatif asked, astonished. The family had expected to be offered the floor in one room of an apartment, much like the one they had just left.

"I'm afraid it's only the basement," their hostess, Ursula, apologized, helping them carry their bags.

"I want to keep Yusuf," Sandrine whimpered. "Please!"

Ursula groaned. "You better watch it, or she'll kidnap your son," she advised the bewildered Sumah. "Only joking," she added quickly, registering Sumah's alarm.

Ursula gave them the basement—two luxurious bedrooms, a bathroom big enough to hold a party, and a sitting room with a sofa-bed and a satellite television—the granny flat, as their hostess described it.

While Ursula made dinner, Sandrine begged to be allowed to give Yusuf his bath. During the meal Sumah and Abdelatif talked to Ursula and Sandrine through their translators, Zara and Safia. A little after nine o'clock, Rachael phoned to announce that she had bought tickets for the flight from Gatwick airport to Newark the next day. "Last minute deal," she explained breezily. "Pretty good, eh?"

"I'm so happy," Zara responded. "And I'm scared, too."

"It'll be fine," said Rachael. "We'll see you tomorrow."

"It's strange, after all these years getting your postcards, thinking about you and your family. Thank you so much," Zara said. "My grandfather would be so grateful."

"This is exactly what Martin would want me to do," Rachael explained.

When Zara rejoined the conversation around Ursula's dining table, she noticed that Safia was studying their hostess closely, taking in the way she held her cigarette and wine glass, her grand yet casual manner, her understated contempt for the status quo, her ready smile. Safia and Ursula leaned toward each other as they chatted, as if they had already established a special rapport.

As she watched Safia, Zara realized there was so much they'd never talked about, even when they shared a bedroom in Doncaster. Zara still didn't know anything about Safia's family back in Darfur, or the life she'd lived before the war. There had never been the slightest hint Safia wished to discuss the past, so Zara had respected her desire for privacy. Some things didn't need to be put in words to be understood.

"So, you want to study the law?" Ursula asked Safia. "Are you looking for a summer job? A friend of mine is a human rights lawyer—he defends political refugees–lots of big bucks in that, I don't think," she snorted. "Anyway, why don't you have a cup of coffee with him and see if he needs some help in his chambers."

Safia thanked her and, Zara noticed, started copying the way that Ursula tossed her head and laughed, and her posh accent.

My remarkable, brilliant Safia, she reflected, watching her finely sculpted, animated features; like an ancient Nilotic supermodel from the wall of an Egyptian tomb; the angel who had rescued Zara when she was alone in the savannah. *Even if we never meet again, you will still be one of the most important people in my life until the day I die.*

By the following morning, Safia's plans had been revised. Ursula insisted that Safia stay on and live in the basement apartment in exchange for some baby-sitting while Ursula was out making the Sudanese ambassador's life miserable.

"I'd be most upset if you left," Ursula pointed out over breakfast. She joked, "What would happen to my social status? Last year you were no one in this town unless you'd been invited to a lesbian wedding or two. This year, you simply have to have someone from an African war zone staying in your granny flat."

Good, Zara thought. *Safia is in the right place. I can leave her here, certain that she'll be safe in the care of Ursula and her network.*

It was also agreed that Abdelatif would stay for a week or two, until he could find a spare room within the community of Darfuri activists, where he knew he could make himself useful, and feel more at ease.

Zara and Sumah, with Yusuf safely cradled in her arms, said their farewells to Abdelatif and Safia, while Ursula and Sandrine loaded the car. Everyone kept saying, "We'll see you again soon," although they knew the future was uncertain, to say the least.

When he hugged her one last time, Abdelatif whispered in Zara's ear, "Grandfather would be so happy if he could see you."

As they waved goodbye and the car pulled away, Zara thought her heart might break. She watched Safia and Abdelatif standing on the sidewalk outside Ursula's house, not even daring to blink in case she missed a moment. Then suddenly the car turned right, and they were gone. *We all begin the next part of our lives now—Safia, the chameleon; Abdelatif, a stranger in a strange land.* She prayed that God would take care of them, and then she prayed for the strength to get through the next part of her extraordinary journey.

There was no time to worry about the difficulties of bluffing her way onto the plane, because Sandrine and Ursula engaged her in a lively conversation about the principle of humanitarian intervention to stop war crimes and genocide versus state sovereignty, all the way to Gatwick airport. Later, she wondered if they had kept up the manic pace deliberately, knowing she was terrified of what awaited her at the airport. Although her mind was occupied throughout the journey, her icy hands trembled.

Once they arrived at the terminal, Zara hardly had a moment to process what was happening. While Ursula parked, Sandrine led them to the check-in counter and convinced the airline agent that the family was going to the United States for a vacation. She brandished Rachael's address and the return tickets like a machete, and by degrees the agent's frowns became bland acceptance. Soon Zara stood with her family at the entrance to the security zone with the boarding passes in her hand.

"Thank you so much. How can I really, *really*, thank you for what you have done for us?" Zara began, but she was crying too hard to continue.

Sandrine hugged her. "Go and become a great architect, and be an example for all Sudanese women. Promise?"

"I promise," Zara whispered, too overcome by emotion to speak.

"You're amazing," Sandrine called after Zara, as the family entered the security area.

"Go and sort out those Americans," Ursula added.

Zara laughed and waved, tears trickling down her cheeks. She picked up Yusuf, and she and Sumah joined the line at the security area.

It was only as they walked toward their gate that it dawned on Zara that they had sailed over the first hurdles in their path. It seemed incredible, and although her stomach still quivered with anxiety, she allowed herself a moment of exhilaration at the prospect of what awaited them at the end of their journey.

Sandrine had chosen seats for Sumah and Yusuf giving them space for the boy to stretch out and sleep. Zara had a seat farther back, but sitting alone during a seven-hour flight was nothing for someone who had walked across a war zone, she reflected.

Once the plane was at cruising altitude, Zara explored the in-flight entertainment system. She chose the sky map and settled back in her seat, watching the little plane begin its journey across the Atlantic toward New Jersey. There were many challenges ahead—a long legal process to negotiate before they could be confident they could stay and become Americans, and she would have to adapt to American schools and habits. There would be difficult and lonely moments, she knew.

She gazed at Europe and Africa on the right of the sky map, thinking about what she was leaving behind. She remembered her grandfather's face, and his hand drawing the alphabet in the dirt with a stick. She recalled the long walk to Chad, hiding in the dried riverbed to avoid the helicopters, trudging across the desert alone until she met Safia. She thought of the wretched man at the Chad border who had wept because his faithful donkey had died after carrying him across the desert to safety.

She traced the route of the little plane west, across the Atlantic, to where her future lay. As her eyelids drooped she conjured up her favorite image, the Chrysler Building, sparkling in the dazzling sunrays of a new dawn in New York City.

I'm really going there, she thought, astonished that her dream was on the verge of coming true. *If I work hard enough, I'll be an architect in America and I'll create a more beautiful world, with buildings that inspire people and bring them joy.*

She smiled sleepily, imagining what her years at university would be like, and the kind of buildings she would one day create, the home she would live in, the friends with whom she would share her happiness and her triumphs.

Suddenly she was aware of a familiar voice in the back of her mind. *Zara, don't ever stop being the girl who ran for her life. You're a proud survivor from Darfur, and that will always be your greatest strength.*

Yes, Grandfather, she thought, sinking back in her seat, closing her eyes.

✶ ✶ ✶

To Zara's relief, their arrival in the United States was just as Rachael Bennett had predicted. The family formally lodged their request for political asylum when they arrived at Newark airport, and were allowed temporary entry into the USA. They knew that ahead of them lay months of interviews and paperwork, but within a few hours of landing, they were hauling their meager possessions into the arrivals hall.

Zara could see that her mother was exhausted by the long flight and the uncertainty at either end of the journey; the normally good-natured Yusuf was so tired he had become irritable and more demanding than usual. As they looked around at the crowds, Sumah's panic and fear were evident.

"It's okay, Mom," Zara told her. "The worst is behind us — I promise. We're all right now."

But before her mother could respond, a petite, dark-haired woman in jeans and a green "Save Darfur" sweatshirt rushed up to them, a huge grin on her face.

Over the years Zara had rehearsed what she would say when she finally met Rachael. She wanted to convey how much her grandfather would have liked to meet her and thank her; how important Rachael's father had been to Muhammad; and how there had been times when the knowledge that she had friends in New Jersey had been the only thing keeping Zara going.

But as she felt the woman's arms around her, Zara's little speech was forgotten and she burst into tears, sobbing too much to say a thing. Rachael too was weeping and laughing at herself, wiping away her tears; then starting to weep again as she took in what was left of Muhammad's family.

It was Sumah who spoke first, grasping both of Rachael's hands in hers and fixing her with a solemn expression.

"You are best friend to us in the whole world," she said, using her limited English.

After more tears they headed for Rachael's car. Zara pulled herself together sufficiently to report that everything had gone smoothly with the immigration officials.

"I've had a little experience with this," Rachael explained as she drove them to her home, "In my voluntary work with Save Darfur we're contacted by lots of people in your situation."

As Zara translated for her mother, Sumah asked to know more about Save Darfur.

"We put pressure on elected officials and decision makers," Rachael summarized. "We try to inform people about what's happening in Sudan, but our biggest challenge is to keep Darfur on the news agenda when so many other things are going on in the world."

Rachael glanced sideways at Zara, in the passenger seat. "We also hold regular meetings. I'd like you to come with me to the next one. People would like to meet you."

The thought made Zara uncomfortable, but she nodded politely, as Sumah commented,

"How incredible that these people here in America really care about what's happening in Sudan. And they're not even Muslims! It's humbling," her mother added, wiping away her tears. "Please tell Rachael how grateful we are."

During the following week, as they settled into two small rooms in Rachael's basement, they continued to express their appreciation as best they could. Sumah took over all domestic tasks while Rachael was at work, and Zara started school immediately.

"You can pay me back by working hard and getting to college," their host had told the girl.

After two weeks, Zara, Sumah, and little Yusuf moved into an annex belonging to a generous local Save Darfur supporter, a banker who worked overseas much of the time. The woman refused to accept rent from them. "It's her contribution to the cause," Rachael had explained.

Zara had expressed profound gratitude, but she did not feel as if she was "the cause." She often thought of Abdelatif's noble commitment to the people left behind in Darfur, but Sudan felt a long way away now. Zara and her family had survived and were busy adapting to the States as fast as they could.

The guilt weighed on Zara as she considered what her older brother was enduring back in London, but she felt she should put all her energy into getting to university, then finding a job that allowed her to support her mother and Yusuf. Unconsciously or not, she had begun to shut Sudan out of her thoughts; recalling the horror was a distraction.

Within a month of starting school, Zara was astonished to find she was at the top of the class. Her teachers moved her up a grade and suggested she would soon be ready to take the SAT.

One evening shortly after they moved into their new home, Rachael dropped by, bringing them some kitchen equipment. Zara had already learned that it was not Rachael's style to beat around the bush with pointless chit-chat. "I'd like you to come to my Save Darfur meeting in the city tomorrow night," she told the girl.

Zara wanted to run from the room, to bury her head in her pillow. But instead she gave Rachael a serious look. "I've got a lot of homework," she answered.

"Well, I'd like you to come," was the firm response. "And I'm sure Abdelatif would like to know what we're doing here."

It would have been rude to refuse Rachael, so Zara went with her the following evening. More than fifty people had gathered in a community center, and they discussed a forthcoming exhibition of Darfuri children's drawings brought back to the States by one of their committee members.

Karen Freeman spent fifteen minutes telling the meeting about the International Criminal Court, saying the drawings had been shown around the world. "I'm hoping we can get thousands of people here to see them too, especially local school groups, maybe as part of their global studies classes."

After an hour and a half they broke for a buffet supper. Since Rachael was surrounded by people who wished to talk to her, Zara helped herself to some salad and found a seat at a table away from everyone else. She did not want to be drawn into conversation because it usually led to polite questions about her background.

A moment later a gaunt, thin, middle-aged looking man approached her and gestured at the seat opposite her.

"Hi," he began. "Mind if I sit down?"

She smiled and nodded.

"My name's David," he said, and Zara picked up a slight accent. He hadn't been born in America, she guessed. As she looked at him she noticed his eyes were grey, and his hair was thin and colorless. Even his skin seemed as lifeless as tissue paper. *He's like a ghost.*

"I'm Zara," she replied.

"Welcome to the States. How are you settling in?" he asked. *Has he talked to Rachael about me? Did she send him to keep me company?* she wondered. She could tell David was patiently going through the social rituals while working his way toward something more important. They made polite conversation about how long he had been involved in Save Darfur.

"Actually, my name is really Daoud, but I changed it to David when I arrived in the States." He looked Zara in the eye. "I'm from Bosnia," he explained, pronouncing each word slowly and cautiously. "I was in the Omarska concentration camp."

Zara felt as if time had ground to a halt, as if the oxygen had been sucked out of her lungs. *Please God, I don't want to hear this,* she thought.

"Have you heard about Omarska?" he asked.

Across her inner eye flashed images of starving young men with sunken eyes lined up on the far side of a barbed wire fence. They wore no shirts and their ribs stood out against their pale skin. Their cheekbones were sharp from starvation. She had come across the photos when researching the Holocaust and other genocides online in England.

She nodded and glanced down at the untouched food on her plate.

"I was fifteen when the Serbs came to my town in 1994."

Zara glanced up at him, astonished that he now looked so old and worn. Then she thought, *Why wouldn't he?*

"They rounded up all the men and boys and they put us on trucks and drove us away. You can probably guess what they did to our mothers and sisters and wives," he added, his manner calm and quiet.

Zara nodded again, eyes down, terrified of making eye contact.

"The Serbs took us to an unused army base and put us in these stinking barracks with no food or heat or electricity, like we were animals. No, worse; if we'd been cattle, we might have had some value to them."

Zara looked across the room to where Rachael was sitting, evidently in the middle of an animated discussion with Karen Freeman. *This was Rachael's idea,* she thought, *sending this man over to talk to me. Why can't she leave me alone?*

"These Serbs who guarded us," David continued, "they were in uniform, but they didn't understand military discipline. They took drugs and got totally drunk, and they were famous for running away on the rare occasions they found themselves in a fair fight, when they were rampaging across Bosnia, killing civilians, doing their ethnic cleansing."

Zara put down her fork, abandoning her salad. A terrible pressure was building up in her head, and she wanted to ask David to please stop talking.

"The guards were bad enough," he continued, "but every weekend a whole bunch more of them would arrive. On Friday night they'd finish work early and drive over the mountains into Bosnia and come to the concentration camp. They weren't soldiers. They were teachers and accountants and truck drivers, these guys, but they got their kicks by pretending they were military heroes saving their race in their spare time. On Sunday night they'd go home to Serbia with their cars packed with microwave ovens and video recorders, even washing machines, all this stuff they'd stolen from the houses of Bosnians who'd been ethnically cleansed."

He knows all this is familiar to me, Zara thought. *He's manipulating me.*

"Anyway," David continued after a sip of his soda, "these Serbs, when they got to Omarska they'd entertain themselves by inventing ways to humiliate us. I suppose it made them feel like real men, tough guys. They'd start drinking and then the games would begin."

Zara tried to close her ears. She wanted to scream at him, *just let me get on with my life!* But still he talked, with his quiet, perfectly modulated, grammatically correct English, with his thin, elegant hands fluttering over his plate.

"I saw them force young men to perform oral sex on their own fathers, or else they said they'd shoot them," he explained, his voice sorrowful rather than angry. "When they were drunk they'd use power saws to behead my friends."

Zara closed her eyes, trying to rid herself of the image.

"And you probably wonder how I can speak of this, but here's the thing, Zara. Until I joined Save Darfur, I never used to talk about it, not even to my American wife. Then one day Rachael asked me to go with her to a meeting with a politician. We wanted to get his support for Save Darfur's campaign, but he seemed to think Darfur was a famine or a natural disaster. Rachael tried to explain to him that genocide is different because it's a disaster deliberately created by humans, and it happens when people dehumanize their neighbors to such an extent that they can kill them.

"Well, I could see this politician just didn't get it, and he was saying there were humanitarian emergencies all over the world. And suddenly I realized I had to tell him what genocide really means; what happened to me and my family, and what I saw in Omarska. All the horror that had been inside me, lurking in a dark corner, it all came out. And when I'd finished, the politician started to cry. This man finally understood genocide because I'd made it personal to him.

"And our good friend, Doctor Bennett," he inclined his head in Rachael's direction, "she told me I must go from college to college, to churches and synagogues and town meetings, telling people my story. And I said, no Rachael, you don't understand. I came here to forget about all that. I have an American wife and kids now, and I never want to think about this again. And Rachael said I didn't have an option. She told me I'd been saved for a reason, and it was my obligation, my role, to keep telling my story."

David paused and sipped his soda, still studying Zara's expression. "So now I'm a professional Bosnian, you see? A professional genocide survivor. And the point is, I don't want to do this, going to universities and meeting senators, telling them the intimate details of my life, but it's not a choice; it's what I *have* to do." He hesitated. "You know why I told you this?"

Zara nodded.

"Good."

"But I want to have a normal life. I want to be an American college student," she protested. What she left unsaid was, *"Haven't I been through enough already?"*

"Oh, Zara." He gave her a sad smile. "Who are you kidding? You'll never have a normal life. You can't run away from who you are."

"What about all the other people who survived?" she asked, anger flashing in her eyes. "Why can't they do this 'professional Sudanese' performance you're suggesting I do?"

"Not all of them have your brains, and they don't speak English, and they're not here in New York, and they don't have access to the most powerful people in the world."

Zara peered at him, confused.

"Save Darfur wants to take you to meet important politicians in Washington. They want you to explain your story because you're authentic and articulate. And then they want you to visit universities, talking to students. They want to offer you to the media for interviews. Listen, if you were a television producer, would you put a white middle-aged guy from New Jersey on screen, or an attractive, articulate young woman from Darfur?"

Zara sighed and stared at her hands, folded in her lap.

"I know what they're asking you to do. I know better than anyone here." David peered into her face. "But I'm finally at peace with myself. I've stopped pretending I can sit at home watching ball games."

Zara sat up straight and took a deep breath. She shook her head in surrender. "Okay, you can tell Rachael you've succeeded."

David grinned. "She'll be very happy."

Zara gave him a wry look. "I feel like I've been surrounded by the men with feathers in their hair, you know, the guys on horses in those Western movies," she laughed.

Three weeks later Zara went to Washington with the national officers of the Save Darfur campaign. "We'd like you to give evidence to the Senate Committee on Foreign Relations," they had said, explaining its function and powers, and the effect their proceedings had on the administration's policy on Sudan.

Zara spent the journey rehearsing what she should say, jotting down facts and figures on a yellow legal pad. By the time she arrived at the Capitol she was so terrified she could barely put one foot in front of the other. *This is not really happening to me,* she thought.

Well-meaning people kept stressing how grateful they were she'd agreed to come because the hearings were incredibly important. An unthinkable number of people would be watching her on television. "You'll do a great job," they smiled. *Didn't they know how frightened she was?*

When she took her seat before the microphone in the committee room she avoided looking at the senators or the cameras. Her eyes remained rooted on her notepad. As she was introduced she looked at her notes for the hundredth time—the mortality rates, the percentages of villages destroyed, the numbers of survivors in refugee camps, and estimates of how many had never made it to the camps.

But when the committee chair urged her to begin her statement, Zara's mind went blank. She looked down at the legal pad and then pushed it away.

"I'd like to start by telling you about one day when I was fourteen years old, when I was running to hide from a helicopter gunship sent by the Sudanese armed forces to kill people like me; that day I was running for my life."

She hesitated and looked at the panel of politicians studying her, following her words.

"No," she corrected herself, feeling flustered. "I'm sorry. I think perhaps it would be better if I begin by telling you about an American hero called Martin Bennett. He was a brave man from your country who changed the life of my grandfather. And this man and his daughter Rachael, they're the reason why I am here today," she began. "An American family saved me. This family, they are America at its best."

She paused and swallowed the lump in her throat. Then she looked from one politician to the next. "And I am here today to ask you, the lawmakers of America, to please help save the other families like mine that are still in Darfur."

AFTERWORD

This story began in the summer of 1966, in the backyard of our modest family home in Toronto, Canada. I was six years old, playing happily in the sandbox with our long-suffering cat, when one of my mother's friends detached herself from the tea party going on inside the house and came out to see me. She picked me up in her arms and twirled me around, but instead of giggling with delight I was distracted by a series of numbers tattooed on her skin just above her wrist.

Later, when the guests had gone and my mother was clearing up the cups and saucers, I asked her why Mrs. Zlotnik had numbers on her arm. My mother was never one to turn down the chance to impart knowledge with a baseball bat rather than a gentle nudge. She sat me down and with the help of some books about World War II, she told me about the Holocaust. She explained how Mrs. Zlotnik's family in Poland had been rounded up by the Nazis and put on cattle cars to be transported to death camps. She showed me photographs of the gas ovens into which the Nazis' victims were herded, alongside pictures of heaps of starved corpses. Then she explained that only Mrs. Zlotnik, who had been about my age in 1945, had survived.

I was very angry and puzzled that human beings could do such monstrous things for no rational reason. For weeks after, I mulled it over and whenever a question popped into my head, I quizzed my mother relentlessly about the Nazis' motivation. I was desperate to find an explanation or some assurance that the Holocaust would not be repeated.

"Were the Nazis very stupid people?" I asked her.

She shook her head. "German soldiers would spend all day killing Jews and then go home to listen to Beethoven and read Goethe. In fact, the Germans were one of the most educated nations in the world."

"Were they terribly poor? Were they driven to do it because they were starving?"

My mother shook her head.

"Did it happen without warning?"

"No. Hitler wrote a book about it years before, and he mentioned his hatred for the Jews in every speech he made."

"So, were the Germans brainwashed? Did Hitler cast a spell on them?"

"They were taught to obey orders," she conceded, "but many of them volunteered to participate in the killing."

This did not satisfy me. I knew there had to be an explanation, and it started me on a lifelong journey to try to understand genocide and those who participate in it.

Until the Bosnian war began in the early 1990s, I thought genocide was purely a matter for history books and grainy black-and-white documentary film footage. But suddenly I found that a group of Europeans were being massacred (ethnically cleansed) because of their religious identity. The shelling of Sarajevo was on the news each night, but the rest of the world did nothing to stop the Serbs.

We watched, incredulous, as a brave journalist named Penny Marshall uncovered a series of concentration camps run by the Serbs and brought out film of starving men and boys standing behind barbed wire fences. The images were hauntingly like those from Belsen and Auschwitz, yet the international community appeased the architects of the genocide, regarding them as their partners in the search for peace.

I joined with a group of Jews, Muslims, and Christians in London, where I had lived since getting my degree from the London School of Economics, to send humanitarian aid to the survivors who were in refugee camps in neighboring Slovenia. We continued to help the same families long after the war ended as they tried to return to what was left of their country and their homes. Ours was a small gesture, but it enabled me to sleep at night.

In April 1994, as the Bosnian war ground on, there was another less-televised genocide happening in Rwanda, a tiny, green, mountainous country in the heart of Africa. I recall thinking at the time that Africa was fittingly called the heart of darkness, a desperate, hopeless place where natural disasters, disease, and starvation claimed millions of lives in the normal course of events. The scale of Africa's horrors was too much for me, so I focused on Bosnia. In the back of my mind I thought that perhaps war and genocide in Africa was not so different from all the other misfortunes on a Biblical scale that they faced—famine, drought, and other "natural" scourges. Besides, families in Bosnia used microwave ovens and video recorders. They were more recognizably "human" to me. There was nothing I could do about the undifferentiated horror of Africa, whereas there were practical, although admittedly small, steps I could take to help the Bosnians.

Several years later, in April 2004, I went to a meeting at the Imperial War Museum in London that coincided with the tenth anniversary of the Rwandan genocide. Linda Melvern, the world expert on Rwanda, explained how the Western powers knew what was going to happen in Rwanda years in advance, and yet had either done nothing, or, in the case of the French, had actively and deliberately trained and armed those who masterminded the genocide. Once again I felt like the furious six-year-old, unable to understand why so many people needlessly died.

After Linda spoke, a man in the audience rose to make a comment. He said he was from Darfur, an obscure area in western Sudan. "We've got terrible trouble in Darfur," he began haltingly. He looked unsure of himself and his English was poor. Several people muttered, irritated that an interloper was trivializing events in Rwanda by comparing it to some tribal skirmish in Sudan. How dare this man deviate from the theme of the meeting.

"What is happening to my people is not on the scale of Rwanda," he said apologetically. "But it soon could be if you don't help us."

As he sat down, a shiver ran down my spine, and I felt obliged to do something this time. The first step was to find out what was truly happening there. A few weeks later, I went to hear Jemera Rone from Human Rights Watch talk about what was unfolding in Darfur. She had just returned from a fact-finding trip, and she described a systematic campaign of wholesale ethnic cleansing sponsored by the extremist Islamist Sudanese junta. The man from Darfur had been right—his country was quickly going the way of Rwanda, and the time for action was *now*. Then, I got my chance. A friend, Lord David Alton, asked me to accompany him to Rwanda. Some years earlier, David had founded Jubilee Action, a charity for vulnerable children. He wanted me to tag along as a scribe, to write a few articles about how Rwanda was recovering from genocide ten years on. "And I thought we might nip into Darfur, since we'll be in the neighborhood," he added.

"Great," I said glibly.

As our plane descended into Khartoum airport, the screen above our heads informed us that it was 96 degrees outside. Since it was eleven o'clock at night, I assumed the thermometer was broken. It wasn't, and it never got cooler.

We were met by a group of courageous local Christians who were risking their lives to help us. They warned us we were being tailed from the airport to our hotel by Sudanese intelligence. On every street corner, we were flagged down by soldiers with guns. They demanded to see our identity cards, which they held upside down as they scrutinized them.

"There's a rumor about a coup," explained our hosts. "There are always rumors. It gives the regime an excuse to have curfews and to crack down on any freedom of movement. In a police state, they prefer a mood of hysteria."

At five o'clock the following morning, we returned to the airport, and using a smattering of tourist Arabic I had picked up on a trip to Syria, David and I bluffed our way onto the plane for El Geneina in western Darfur. For three hours, we flew west, first crossing the Nile, and then over hundreds of miles of extinct volcanoes and parched desert. Welcoming us at El Geneina airport were the rusting hulks of Sudanese air force planes and helicopters that had crash landed over the years. No one had bothered to clean up the wreckage.

Our hosts, a medical emergency assistance charity, were nervous about our presence because we lacked the necessary permission for internal travel. Had we applied to visit Darfur, we would certainly have been forbidden entry. Every good dictator knows you should do your killing away from the prying eyes of journalists or outside witnesses. Our hosts explained that each day the charity's work was impeded by Sudanese government officials who randomly invented new restrictions, or suddenly required obscure documents before they would allow access to the refugee camps.

The charity workers took us directly to a camp, and by eight thirty in the morning we were taking down the testimony of survivors. David met the men, while I interviewed dozens of women. Sitting in the shade of a tree, I recorded their personal histories in my notebook one at a time, writing at top speed, perspiration dampening the pages, thinking my hand would cramp into a spasm.

The world knew little about events in Darfur in 2004, and there had been no journalists or film crews at the camp. Our conversation, through a translator, was the women's first opportunity to tell outsiders what was happening to their people.

Darfuri society is traditional and conservative, and people do not unburden the traumatic personal details of their lives in the manner of American talk shows. In common with many people in Africa, the Darfuris still have a defined private space and a great sense of dignity. I was a stranger, and it took time for the Darfuri women to feel safe enough to admit what had happened to them. At first they used euphemisms for rape, such as "molested" or "beaten." As we talked, they revealed more about their experiences at the hands of the Sudanese army soldiers who had raped and branded them like slaves. By the time I left, my exotic whiteness had been forgotten, and they were giving me horrific and detailed descriptions of the torture and humiliation handed out routinely to women in Darfur by their own government.

The women told me about how the Sudanese air force had bombed their villages. The aerial raids were followed by attacks by uniformed Sudanese soldiers in official jeeps often supported by the Janjaweed militia on horseback or camel. Very soon a pattern emerged—the village was attacked, the men and boys were killed, children were thrown onto fires, bodies were stuffed into wells to pollute the water supply, houses were set on fire, and women and girls were systematically raped and beaten.

After the men raped the women, they branded them with white-hot pokers, telling them they were diluting their inferior African blood with their superior Arab blood. They told them that the first genocide was when they killed the men and boys and the second genocide would be when HIV/AIDs killed the women and girls. I kept writing, as the women told me this, but I was dumbfounded; exactly the same sentiment had been expressed by the Serbs raping Bosnian Muslim women, and by the soldiers in Rwanda. For the first time I fully understood that rape is a weapon of war and an important aspect of genocide.

At night in El Geneina, back in the relative safety of the medical charity's gated and guarded compound, I gazed up at the most spectacular sky I had ever seen. The nearest streetlights were two or three hours flying time away. As I studied the stars, I was humbled and frightened by what the women had requested: You must be our voice, they had said. No one comes to Darfur; no one asks us what has happened to us. It is up to you to speak for us.

I explained that I would make a most imperfect messenger because I am not an African, I am not a Muslim, and I have never endured the fear and terror and abuse suffered by the women I met. But they took what little I had to offer, and made me promise I would do my best to let their voices be heard.

The Sudanese security forces in El Geneina soon caught up with us, and we were bundled onto the next plane to Khartoum. Once back in the capital, we met diplomatic staff at the British embassy. They did not understand why we were making such a fuss about Darfur. They had worked hard to get the Sudanese regime to sign a peace agreement with the southern Sudanese rebels, and the last thing they wanted was a sideshow in a region no one cared about.

Pushed by the Bush administration, the military junta in Khartoum had been forced to halt its twenty-year campaign of genocide aimed at ridding Sudan of black Africans and Christians in the south. By arming and paying Arab tribes to do their dirty work, the military junta had killed an estimated two million people in the south, giving the junta access to vast oil deposits that they were keen to develop with the help of the ever-obliging Chinese and Russians.

When we arrived back in London, David Alton and I addressed a packed meeting in the British parliament and began lobbying decision makers for action to prevent the genocide in Darfur. David asked parliamentary questions, tabled motions, and made speeches. We both wrote articles for newspapers and gave media interviews. I also went to universities and schools, talking about what I had seen, and I soon had a band of brilliant and motivated volunteers who were as angry about the genocide as I was. We formed an organization called Waging Peace as a vehicle to inform the public and to put pressure on decision makers.

We began by asking a simple question: Why hasn't anything been done to stop the killing in Darfur? There is no one big answer, but in our journey to raise awareness about the genocide, we have uncovered several facts that explain why the killing continues.

We found that international diplomats deliberately treat Darfur as a humanitarian disaster requiring blankets and food parcels, rather than a political conflict requiring a political solution. Officials in several countries suggest to journalists that the Darfur rebels were just as responsible for the murder and mayhem as the Sudanese government, encouraging the public to think that both sides were bad.

Representatives of the so-called international community also stir up fear that any intervening peacekeeping force consisting of white soldiers will be met by resistance from Osama Bin Laden's friends. In fact the opposite is the case; Darfuris we interviewed specifically asked the international community to send white soldiers for a variety of reasons:

They are better disciplined and they won't rape us.

They are rich so they won't be bribed by the Sudanese to look the other way.

They'll find it so hot and unpleasant here that they'll get the job done so they can go home.

Despite the evidence to the contrary, the international community's envoys also choose to believe Khartoum's promises, thereby ignoring the legacy of twenty years of frustrating negotiations with the junta. The track record shows that Sudan's leaders are skilled at tying up negotiations for years, and for signing on to peace agreements that are immediately broken.

The UN Security Council passed a series of excellent resolutions outlining measures to be taken against the masterminds of the genocide in Khartoum. *Almost none of the resolutions have ever been implemented.* Why? Because Sudan is faithfully supported by its friends—the Russians and Chinese. Both countries supply Khartoum with arms, and China buys 80 percent of Sudan's oil. China and Russia also have their own reasons for defending a country's right to do whatever it wishes to its own civilians within its own borders.

Sadly, almost no African country has protested to Khartoum about the fate of its black African population, either in the south or in Darfur.

One possible explanation is that some of Africa's leaders do not relish the possibility that their turn will come to have the spotlight turned on their undemocratic or corrupt ways.

Moreover, the Darfuris are the wrong kind of black Africans — they are poor. And they are the wrong kind of Muslims — black, and not of Arab origin. With few exceptions, African leaders prefer to cozy up to the increasingly oil-rich regime in Khartoum. There is also a long and sorry track record of Gulf Arabs buying off and manipulating African rulers and others who should know better. Their objective is to call on their votes whenever the United Nations considers censuring Israel.

In addition, the military junta running Sudan routinely exploits the U.S. intervention in Iraq, stirring up the Muslim and Arab world by casting itself as another victim of the neo-colonialist, anti-Islamic crusade, and American oil-greedy imperialism. The U.S. government was not as close to the Sudanese regime as some other international players, and President Clinton is still hated for authorizing the bombing of a Khartoum factory correctly suspected of making chemical weapons in 1998.

Finally, our thirst for intelligence in the war on terror means the fundamentalist, totalitarian dictators in Khartoum are our new partners in the clash of civilizations. For all the speeches condemning Field Marshall Bashir's genocidal policies, the Sudanese president knows that no genuine action will be taken to stop him killing his own people. Bashir is, belatedly, "on our side" in the war on terror. We pretend to be serious about getting tough with Sudan, and Sudan pretends to be outraged by our words.

Khartoum has played a masterful game, spinning its sketchy and stale intelligence about Al-Qaeda for much more than it is worth. The former head of Sudanese intelligence, Salah Gosh, one of the masterminds behind the genocide in Darfur, was a regular and honored guest in the UK and at CIA headquarters in Langley, Virginia. Consequently, Khartoum is not unduly concerned by lofty UN resolutions. They understand that some things matter more than 300,000 dead Darfuris.

Despite this depressing list of reasons why nothing has happened to stop the genocide in Darfur, the outlook is not hopeless. Nor are the solutions difficult. There is a way forward that involves neither putting U.S. soldiers in harm's way, nor spending billions of dollars. The answer, put simply, is to enforce the existing UN resolutions against the regime in Khartoum. All the necessary levers already exist and they have already been approved by the UN Security Council. What is required is the political will to enforce these existing resolutions.

There is another reason to keep pressure on the Khartoum regime: following a referendum in January 2011, the people of South Sudan voted overwhelmingly to form their own country. The new South Sudan has 80 percent of the former nation's oil reserves, and Sudan watchers fear the totalitarian government in Khartoum, the capital of the new North Sudan, will not let go without a fight. They are already paying and arming groups of mainly Arab nomads to attack the mainly black and Christian groups who live along the border area where the oil is.

In all the excitement about the creation of a new South Sudan, the people of Darfur must not be forgotten. The Khartoum regime is still bombing and killing civilians in Darfur with impunity. The violence continues there in a media vacuum. Now more than ever it is vital to enforce the UN resolutions, stopping civilians from being bombed and bringing justice to the long-suffering people of Darfur.

The "Things You Can Do to Help" section of this book tells you more about what can be done by the organizations that are already in place and by individuals who, like me, are outraged at genocide and want to do something to put a stop to its perpetrators.

It is never a waste of time to put pressure on our decision makers about their inaction on Sudan. My Waging Peace team in London, England, recently struck a victory for common sense and humanitarianism, following several years of advocating for the rights of Sudanese refugees in the United Kingdom. The British government has been deporting non-Arab Sudanese political refugees back to Sudan because so-called illegal immigrants are unpopular with some voters. This has caused misery and fear among the Sudanese Diaspora, terrified of what awaits them at the other end of their journey. Deportees are often handcuffed and forced onto planes in tears, knowing they are regarded as enemies of the Sudanese regime to which they are being delivered. They face the prospect of arrest, torture, and death at the hands of the Sudanese National Security and Intelligence Services in Khartoum. We know that several deportees were met from their plane by "the security" and vanished, until their mutilated bodies were discovered, dumped in the dead of night, days or weeks later. Other deportees, including an eighteen-year-old young man faced with the prospect of being returned to Khartoum, have chosen suicide, rather than being tortured to death.

When we drew all this to the attention of UK officials, they demanded proof that deportees had been killed, saying there was no war in Khartoum and therefore Sudanese should have no fear about being sent there. The officials willfully ignored the fact that the genocide being waged against the people of Darfur and southern Sudan was being organized from the capital by the Sudanese regime. Only when we tracked down the deportees' death certificates did the UK authorities finally relent. Thanks to our relentless pressure, in October 2009 the British government finally granted refugee status to non-Arab Sudanese in the UK. One of the reasons we keep advocating for Sudan is that I have never managed to forget the women I left behind in Darfur. They had never heard about the Holocaust or Bosnia, and they do not have the luxury of fretting over man's inability to learn from our past mistakes. The women who told me their stories were not at liberty to climb onto an airplane and escape as I was. Since my trip to Darfur, I have gone to sleep every night in a soft, warm, dry bed, with my stomach full, without injuries or diseases making me unwell, knowing I am safe. I have learned that many of the women I interviewed are no longer alive because their camp has been attacked many times by the Sudanese. Their death makes it doubly important that their voice be heard and not forgotten, and that we act to protect them.

One Darfuri woman in a refugee camp said to me, "It's very kind of you to send the food and blankets, but this is Africa, and we're used to being hungry and coping with very little. What we'd like you to do is please take the guns away from the people who are killing us."

Unfortunately, after the murder of 300,000 people, we have yet to act.

Rebecca Tinsley
California
January 2011

THINGS YOU CAN DO TO HELP

There *are* things you can do that will make a difference. This section contains a list of simple but effective ways for individuals to take action and concludes with links for additional resources and information about Sudan.

A. SPEAK UP

The first and most important thing you can do is put pressure on your elected officials to stop the killing in Sudan. Make your voice heard — write, call, or email the president, your senator, and your congressperson. If enough people speak up, the situation can't continue to be ignored.

Reflecting on the Rwanda genocide the late Senator Paul Simon said,

> *If every member of the House and Senate had received 100 letters from people back home saying we have to do something about Rwanda, when the crisis was first developing, then I think the response would have been different.*

WRITE, PHONE, OR EMAIL THE PRESIDENT:

President Barack H. Obama
The White House
1600 Pennsylvania Avenue NW Washington, DC 20500
www.whitehouse.gov/contact/
Comments: 202-456-1111
Switchboard: 202-456-1414

FAX: 202-456-2461
TTY/TDD: 202-456-6213

Please find a sample letter or script you can use at the bottom of this page.

YOUR SENATOR:

(Name of senator)
United States Senate
Washington, DC 20510
www.senate.gov/general/contact_information/senators_cfm.cfm

YOUR CONGRESSIONAL REPRESENTATIVE:

(Name of representative)
U.S. House of Representatives
111th Congress, 2nd Session
Washington, DC 20515
Phone: 202-224-3121
TTY: 202-225-1904
https://writerep.house.gov/writerep/welcome.shtml

THE UNITED NATIONS:

You can contact Ban Ki-moon, the UN Secretary-General at this e-mail address: inquiries@un.org and ask him to publicly condemn the actions of all parties involved in the conflict.

Here is a sample letter or script you can use to contact elected officials and representatives:

"Dear (Name):

I am concerned that the violence and suffering continues in Sudan. I urge you to put pressure on the United Nations Security Council to enforce its resolutions on Sudan, calling for:

- A no-fly zone to stop the Sudanese air force from bombing its civilians;

- An arms embargo on Sudan; and

- Financial sanctions targeted against the architects of the genocide.

In addition, the United States must apply pressure on the Sudanese regime to keep its promises to abide by its obligations under international law."

Sign Your Name

If you wish to write in more detail about specific policies you will find information at the end of this chapter.

B. DON'T INVEST IN COMPANIES THAT SUPPORT THE SUDANESE REGIME

Many pension funds and insurance companies hold the stock of businesses operating in the oil sector in Sudan. The regime uses 80 percent of its oil revenue to buy weapons. Phone your broker to make sure you are not investing in Sudan. If you have a public or union pension fund, find out if the fund managers have dumped their investments in firms operating in Sudan. For more information go to www.savedarfur.org.

C. LET OTHER PEOPLE KNOW WHAT'S GOING ON IN SUDAN

1. Write to your local paper or television station asking them to increase their news coverage in Sudan to raise public awareness.
2. Write a letter to the editor. Make it short and direct. Here's a sample:

   "Since 2003 a genocide has been waged against the people of Darfur in Sudan, Africa. The Sudanese regime is forcibly trying to impose an extreme form of Islam on people who have made it clear they prefer democracy and free speech. The result is an estimated 300,000 dead civilians, and three million refugees.

The international community often pledges that it will never allow another Holocaust or Rwandan genocide. Yet, Darfur has been largely ignored. The Sudanese regime is desperate for the benefits that come from being friends with the United States, but it must first stop killing its own citizens. Americans should be proud of sending humanitarian aid to Darfur, but a lasting political solution is needed guaranteeing the rights and security of the Darfuris. There will be no peace without justice. Now is the moment for the United States to offer the Sudanese regime both the carrots and sticks of diplomacy. The Darfuris have waited long enough for our support."

3. Exhibit the children's drawings. We have exhibited the Darfur children's drawings mentioned in this book and displayed them on our website http://www.article1.org/index.php?option=com_content&view=article&id=150&Itemid=32 and around the world. If you know of a museum, university, faith group, or institution interested in hosting an exhibition of the drawings, please contact TinsleyRC@aol.com. Experts on the Holocaust and Bosnia have remarked on the similarity between these Darfur images and those of children involved in those earlier genocides. Not surprisingly, the Darfur pictures are sometimes exhibited side by side with Holocaust drawings.

4. Invite a speaker to speak to your group or to a gathering of friends and neighbors in your home. We speak to groups in the United States, Canada, and Europe about what is happening in Sudan, and about genocide generally. If you are involved in a civic society group, faith group, college society, or another institution, please let us know if you would like a speaker and a slide show about Sudan and Rwanda. Contact TinsleyRC@aol.com.

5. Tell your friends about Sudan and give them this book.

6. Familiarize yourself with the area. Many people don't really know where Sudan is. Look at a map of Africa to see where this story takes place. Knowing which countries border Sudan will give you a better idea of the forces at work there. The war has already spilled over into neighboring countries like Uganda and Chad with devastating results.

7. Keep up to date with events in Sudan by going to http://www.WagingPeace.info.

D. CONTRIBUTE

PRACTICAL HELP

If you live in the United States and want to give practical help to survivors of genocide in Africa we suggest you support the specific programs in Rwanda and Uganda at Jubilee Campaign www.jubileecampaign.org. This U.S.-based humanitarian group helps courageous communities rebuild their lives in the wake of genocide and conflict. Please visit their website to see the simple but effective ways you can give a helping hand to brave, resilient people who are already helping themselves against incredible odds. Donations are tax-deductible.

If you live in the UK and want to help Darfuri refugees, please visit www.Article1.org to make a donation. All gifts are tax-deductible. Please also visit the Article 1 website to see the drawings by Darfuri children mentioned in this book.
http://www.article1.org/index.php?option=com_content&view=article&id=150&Itemid=32

E. LEARN MORE ABOUT WHAT THE US GOVERNMENT CAN DO

Here are specific policies that can be implemented or simply enforced:

1. Enforce the UN's proposed no-fly zone over Darfur to prevent the Sudanese government from bombing its own civilians. Just over the border in Chad there are French

air force bases from which the zone could be monitored by NATO. We are told that satellites can read license plates from space—why can't they spot the Sudanese air force when it is on its way to bomb civilians? A no-fly zone would work as follows: Each time a Sudanese plane or helicopter attacked a village, NATO would confirm it belonged to the Sudanese air force (to avoid mistakenly targeting planes carrying humanitarian aid) and would destroy them once they were back at their airfield or base.

2. Freeze the financial assets of the masterminds of the genocide. The men who run the Khartoum regime enjoy a lavish lifestyle compared to the vast majority of their citizens. They take a personal cut from oil revenues and stash the money away in offshore bank accounts. If we have entire intelligence operations devoted to tracking down the funds of terrorists and narco-criminals, why not apply the same forensic analysis to those responsible for genocide? The UN has already authorized an array of asset freezes but they have yet to be activated and enforced.

3. Enforce a travel ban on leading members of the military junta and their officials. Whenever it is suggested to a Sudanese ambassador or general that he might miss out on his shopping trips to Paris, he becomes furious. Being accused of genocide does not concern them, but they are deeply offended by the prospect of being denied their trips to Hermes and Chanel.

4. Close down the international accounts of the web of businesses owned by the Sudanese state and military personnel. The junta's members have generous stakes in a complicated network of businesses. We should be following the money if we wish to squeeze the architects of the genocide.

5. Most important, the international community, with the United States in the lead, must demand a comprehensive peace plan for all of Sudan, not just the Darfur region. There will never be peace for the long-suffering Sudanese unless every region is guaranteed the democratic rights and self-determination we take for granted.

SOURCES FOR MORE INFORMATION ON SUDAN

www.WagingPeace.info
www.hrw.org
www.savedarfur.org
www.genocideintervention.net
www.darfurdivestment.org
www.helpsudaninternational.org
www.ushmm.org
www.crisisgroup.org